A MOTHER TO MAKE A FAMILY

BY

EMILY FORBES

THE NURSE'S BABY SECRET

BY

JANICE LYNN

Emily Forbes is an award-winning author of Medical Romances for Mills & Boon. She has written over 25 books and has twice been a finalist in the Australian Romantic Book of the Year Award, which she won in 2013 for her novel *Sydney Harbour Hospital: Bella's Wishlist*. You can get in touch with Emily at emilyforbes@internode.on.net, or visit her website at emily-forbesauthor.com.

Janice Lynn has a Master's in Nursing from Vanderbilt University, and works as a nurse practitioner in a family practice. She lives in the southern United States with her husband, their four children, their Jack Russell—appropriately named Trouble—and a lot of unnamed dust bunnies that have moved in since she started her writing career. To find out more about Janice and her writing visit janicelynn.com.

A MOTHER TO MAKE A FAMILY

BY
EMILY FORBES

Published in Great Britain 2017
By Mills & Boon, an imprint of HarperCollins*Publishers*
1 London Bridge Street, London, SE1 9GF

ISBN: 978-0-263-92640-8

Our policy is to use papers that are natural, renewable and recyclable products and made from wood grown in sustainable forests. The logging and manufacturing processes conform to the legal environmental regulations of the country of origin.

Printed and bound in Spain
by CPI, Barcelona

Dear Reader,

I'm so pleased to finally give you Rose's story—the third in my Tempted & Tamed miniseries. Many of you wrote to me after reading the first two books, asking me to write Rose's story. It was always my intention to do that, although it has taken a little longer than I planned! But I think it's worked out well. Rose had plenty of obstacles to overcome, and she needed some time before she was ready to fall in love. I also needed time to find her the perfect man, and I hope I have done that with Mitch.

Rose is the youngest of the three Anderson sisters—Scarlett, Ruby and Rose—and the last one to find her happily-ever-after. If you missed the first two books you can read about Scarlett and Ruby in *A Doctor by Day...* and *Tamed by the Renegade*.

If you have a chance to read all three books I'd love to know if you've enjoyed them—and did you have a favourite? Drop me a line at emilyforbes@internode.on.net.

Until then,

Happy reading,

Emily

For everyone who asked me for Rose's story;
thank you for your patience
and I really hope you enjoy this,
Emily

Books by Emily Forbes

Mills & Boon Medical Romance

The Christmas Swap

Waking Up to Dr Gorgeous

The Hollywood Hills Clinic

Falling for the Single Dad

Tempted & Tamed!

A Doctor by Day…
Tamed by the Renegade

His Little Christmas Miracle
A Love Against All Odds

Visit the Author Profile page
at millsandboon.co.uk for more titles.

**Praise for
Emily Forbes**

'Have your tissues ready because you are gonna need them…it's that good! Prepare to be hooked on Medical Romance and Emily Forbes!'

—*Goodreads* on
A Love Against All Odds

CHAPTER ONE

A SCREAM SPLIT the air, cleaving through the thick muggy silence that suffocated the land.

Mitch recognised the sound and it sent a shiver of fear down his spine.

The hairs on the back of his neck rose up and the wrench fell from his hand as he sprinted from the shed.

He was halfway to the horse yards before the scream ended and the silence that followed stabbed at his heart. He'd never known silence to be so terrifying. It was ominous. After thirty-nine years he knew trouble when he heard it.

The sound of his boots as they slapped the dirt echoed across the ground and the pounding of his feet imitated the pounding of his heart, which had lodged somewhere in his throat. He listened for more noise, another sound, anything, as he ran. Anything would be better than the oppressive silence.

Time stood still. Red dust flew from under his boots but it might as well have been quicksand. The horse yards weren't getting any closer.

He rounded the corner of the staff quarters and almost collided with his six-year-old son.

'Dad, Dad, come quick! It's Lila.' Jed grabbed Mitch's hand but Mitch didn't slow his pace and his hand pulled out of his son's grasp. He still didn't stop. He'd make better time alone. He kept running, knowing Jed would follow.

He had to get to Lila. He had to get to his daughter.

He skidded into the horse yards and felt Jed come to a stop beside him. He scanned the enclosures, searching for his two other children.

Charlie was standing still. He was holding Ruff, their Australian terrier, in his arms. The little dog was squirming and wriggling, desperate to get down. Ruff wasn't supposed to be anywhere near the horse yards but Mitch didn't have time to think about that now.

His daughter lay flat on her back on the hard, red ground. Her face was ashen and she lay as still as a corpse, her eyes open. His heart was lodged firmly in his throat now and he fought to breathe. The air was thick and muggy, choking him as he tried to force it into his lungs. He'd already lost one daughter. He couldn't lose Lila too. His children were all he had left.

And then he saw her chest move. Rising and falling as she breathed.

She was alive.

The lump in his throat dislodged and he sucked in a breath.

Ginny was kneeling over her and Mitch crouched in the dirt beside her.

'Lila!'

He wanted to gather her into his arms, to pick her up and carry her away, but he didn't dare move her. He knew it wasn't safe.

His daughter's lips were parted, her eyes huge and dark in her pale face. They brimmed with tears and her bottom lip wobbled.

'It hurts.'

Mitch could hear the catch in her voice and it was almost more than he could bear. 'Where?'

'My back.'

Shit.

'You haven't moved her, have you?' he asked Ginny. He hadn't acknowledged the governess until now. He'd been far too intent on Lila.

'No.' Ginny shook her head. 'She landed like this.'

The ground was as hard as concrete. They'd had no rain in this distant corner of Queensland for three years, even the river was dry. The station was relying on water from the artesian basin for the cattle, there was nothing spare to soften the ground or water the gardens. Who knew what injuries Lila might have sustained? What damage had been done?

Mitch slipped his fingers into Lila's palm. 'Can you squeeze my hand?'

He relaxed ever so slightly as he felt the reassuring squeeze.

'Don't move your legs,' he told her, 'but see if you can wriggle your toes.'

Lila was wearing elastic-sided riding boots. He couldn't see if she was moving her toes but she winced.

'Could you do it?' he asked.

'Yes. But it hurt.'

That was a good sign, Mitch thought. Not that he wanted his daughter to be in pain but pain was often absent in serious spinal injuries. 'I know, sweetie, you're being very brave.'

Tears spilled from Lila's lashes onto her cheeks.

Mitch wiped the tears from her face. 'It'll be all right, Lila.'

He turned and spoke to Ginny. 'What happened?' It didn't really matter what had happened, what mattered was getting some help, but he had to know. He had to make some sense of the situation.

'Ruff got loose. He spooked Fudge and she threw Lila off,' Ginny explained. 'I'm sorry. It all happened so quickly, there was nothing I could do.'

Ginny sounded upset but Mitch didn't doubt her recounting of the incident.

He glanced over to where his stockman was standing with Lila's horse's reins firmly in his hands. Both Jimmy and the horse were standing quietly against the railing of the yard. Jimmy was keeping the horse as far away from Charlie and the dog as he could without going out of sight. Mitch knew that Jimmy would have calmed the horse and then stayed in the vicinity in case Mitch needed him. Seeing Jimmy settled his nerves to some degree. Despite his physical disability Jimmy was the best horse handler Mitch had ever seen and he knew that something must have happened that had been out of his control. Fudge had a placid temperament normally but for some reason she hated the little dog with a passion and Ruff reciprocated her feelings and delighted in nipping at her rear hooves. Jimmy never would have let the little dog within cooee of the horse.

But Mitch didn't have time to think about the dog or the horse and he didn't have time for recriminations either. Ginny had been the governess on the station for the past twelve months; she was responsible and level-headed, she'd grown up on cattle stations and knew her way around horses. Mitch knew she had the best interests of his children at heart—that was why he'd hired her. Ginny was close to tears and Mitch needed her to stay composed—he needed her to look after the boys. Neither Ginny nor Jimmy would have made a deliberate error. It sounded like an accident and he wasn't looking for anyone to blame. He knew from past experience that it made no difference to the outcome. What was done was done, and his priority now was Lila.

Thankfully she'd been wearing her helmet. Thank goodness she'd had some protection. He didn't remove it. He couldn't risk the movement. Not until her injuries had been assessed. He knew what to do but she needed more attention than he was able to give her and somehow, when the situation was personal, it became harder to remain objective. He didn't want to do the wrong thing. And that was the trouble—he didn't trust his own judgement any more. Lila needed medical attention, but they were in Outback Queensland, hundreds of kilometres and a five-hour drive from the nearest hospital.

'Go to the house,' he instructed Ginny. 'Call the flying doctor on the satellite phone and bring it back to me along with the medical chest.'

She stood up and Mitch noticed that her knees were shaking, her hands too, and her face was ashen. Everyone was on edge. 'Take the dog,' he called after her as she hurried away. Ginny came back and took Ruff from Charlie's arms. 'And make sure he's tied up.'

He turned back to his daughter. 'Do you know what day it is, Lila?' he asked.

'Wednesday,' she replied, and Mitch breathed a sigh of relief.

'Do you know what happened?'

'I came off Fudge.'

As far as assessments for concussion went it was as basic as they came but hearing the correct responses was a positive sign. Her eyes were open, she wasn't confused and she could move independently even if it hurt. Fourteen points out of a possible fifteen on the Glasgow coma scale, Mitch thought automatically, although that was only part of the story.

He sat in the dirt and held Lila's hand as he waited for Ginny to return. Waiting was the hardest thing. He was useless until he had the medical chest and even that wouldn't be enough. He was pretty certain that Lila had sustained fractures and there was the risk that she had also suffered internal injuries but he didn't want to start an assessment. He didn't want to be the one to cause her pain. He'd wait for the medical chest, at least then he'd be able to check her blood pressure and get a bit of an indication as to what they were dealing with but he was convinced she would have to be evacuated. They needed the flying doctor.

He kept talking. Soft, nothing words, just sounds really, letting her know he was there, that he wasn't going to leave her.

Her eyes fluttered closed and he fought back another wave of panic while he reminded himself that she didn't seem concussed. She seemed alert enough, even if she was in pain.

'Is she going to be okay, Dad?'

Jed stood beside him and Mitch noticed that he had his arm wrapped around his little brother, comforting him. Mitch should be doing that but he found himself stretched to the limit, as had been the case so often in the past two years. There just wasn't enough of him to go around.

'She'll be fine,' he replied. He had no other answer. He didn't want to lie but he had to believe she would be okay. He had to believe his own words.

'You can fix her, can't you, Dad?'

'I'm going to need some help, Jed, but the flying doctor will be here soon. Why don't you and Charlie go down to the kitchen for smoko?'

He hadn't heard the bell but it must be nearly time for morning tea. The station staff would all converge on the kitchen and a drink and a piece of cake would keep the boys occupied.

Ginny returned on one of the quad bikes. She had the medical chest strapped to the back of the bike and a blanket thrown over her lap. She carried the medical chest over and put it down beside Mitch before draping the blanket over Lila. Mitch hadn't thought of the blanket, the temperature was nudging thirty-four degrees Celsius, but if Lila went into shock he might need it.

'The plane is on its way and the base is holding for you,' Ginny said as she handed him the satellite phone.

Mitch knew that depending on where the plane was coming from it could take an hour to reach them. He took the phone as he instructed Ginny to get his head stockman and pilot to prepare the runway for the plane.

He spoke to the doctor at the Broken Hill base and relayed the information he had while he opened the medical chest and found the few things he needed. He checked her blood pressure, kept her warm and gave her some pain relief and then he waited.

And waited.

Time stood still as his daughter lay in the dirt, in pain.

Lila looked so like her mother that Mitch's heart ached every time he looked at her. Dark hair, dark eyes. All three of the children had his dark eyes but the boys were much more like him. They had the same white blond hair he'd had as a child. His hair had darkened with age and had even gone a little grey with stress.

He'd been trying his best not to let his feelings show over the past two years. He didn't want the children to grow up sensing his pain. His loss. It was their loss too but he knew they felt it differently. They were so young, so much more resilient than he felt, but he'd vowed to do his best by them.

He'd become very good at disguising his feelings, an

expert at pretending everything was okay. But he didn't know if he had the strength to get through another tragedy. Hopefully it wouldn't come to that, but if it did he'd have to find the reserves somewhere. The children were all he had and he was all they had.

He knew he had to keep his composure, had to stay calm, and he was grateful that no one else had been injured. He'd seen more than his fair share of injuries, and even a couple of fatalities, from accidents with horses. But being around horses was a way of life on the station and Mitch knew it was important that the children were familiar with them. Of course, he'd always insisted that they wear helmets when they were riding and fortunately that was a rule they'd never broken. Lila's accident could have been much worse; it wasn't as bad as it got but it was close.

In the distance he heard the sound of an engine. The familiar whine of the flying doctor plane. It was coming from the west and he looked at the sky, searching for a flash of silver and white. There. The plane was silhouetted against the endless, clear blue sky. He watched as it dropped lower, heading for the dirt landing strip behind the outbuildings, and waited again for the doc.

Darren, the head stockman, pulled up in a dusty four-wheel-drive and the doc and the flight nurse piled out. He recognised Doc Burton. Mitch reckoned he'd worked with all of the doctors over the years. He nodded in acknowledgement and then relayed what he knew of the events, what he'd given Lila for pain relief, and her medical history and then he stepped aside to let them examine his daughter. He wasn't one of them any more, he was just Lila's father.

Lila was alert and talking as they checked her pupils, got her to move her fingers and toes and gradually worked their way up her limbs. She seemed to be able to move her upper limbs reasonably comfortably but her legs were a different story. Doc Burton gently palpated Lila's neck before removing her helmet. He moved to her abdomen as the nurse retested her blood pressure.

Lila cried out in pain as the doc pressed on her pelvis and Mitch had to restrain himself from leaping in and stopping the examination right there. He couldn't stand to see Lila in more pain.

'Temp thirty-six point two degrees, pulse one hundred, respirations twenty-two, BP ninety on sixty, oxygen ninety-eight percent.' The flight nurse relayed Lila's vital statistics.

'Can you run five hundred millilitres of normal saline and draw up five milligrams of morphine? I want to give her a shot before we move her.' The doc finished speaking to the nurse before turning to Mitch.

'I agree with you,' he said, 'there's no apparent head injury and her spine seems okay but it looks like she has a fractured pelvis so we'll need to take her with us to the base.' Back to Broken Hill, to the hospital. 'I don't think she has major internal injuries, her observations are quite reasonable, which suggests that there's no excessive internal bleeding but I won't really know until we get her to Broken Hill for scans. She may need to go to Adelaide but you know the drill.'

The doc took the syringe from the nurse and injected the morphine into Lila's abdomen. 'This will sting a little, Lila, but it will work fast to take the pain away,' he told her.

Mitch knew the drill all too well. Doc Burton would take away the pain and then he'd take Lila. Mitch had known that would be the case. He'd known her injuries were too severe to be treated out here. He'd known she would need to go to hospital and he would follow. He hadn't set foot in a hospital for two years but that was all about to change. He'd known the day would come when he'd have to face up to the past and that day was now. He would have to cope, for Lila's sake.

He picked up Lila's hand, holding it, not sure whether he was comforting her or himself.

'All right, we need to get her in the plane.' Doc Burton looked at Mitch and Mitch knew his face would be pale under his tan. 'You're coming?'

Mitch nodded as the doc and the flight nurse wrapped a brace around Lila's pelvis and rolled her onto a spinal board. He'd managed to avoid the hospital for two years but deep down he'd wondered what it would take to get him back there. Now he knew. This was it.

Mitch looked at the length of the stretcher and then at the four-by-four utility parked nearby. The ground was dry, hard and corrugated, he didn't want to drive Lila over it to the airstrip.

'Can we carry her back to the plane?' he suggested. 'Three of us should manage it easy.'

Jimmy had taken the horse back to the stables, leaving just the three men and the flight nurse. Mitch put himself at the foot of the stretcher where he could keep an eye on his daughter. Doc Burton and Darren took one side each at the head and the flight nurse loaded the equipment back into the four-by-four and drove it back to the airstrip. The boys came running from the kitchen as the procession headed to the runway. Charlie tagged at Jed's heels, doing his best to keep up with his older brother.

Ginny fell into step beside Mitch. 'You're going with her.' Her words weren't a question. He nodded and Ginny took the boys' hands as they reached the airstrip, keeping them under control, one on each side of her. Thank goodness he had Ginny to help out. But not for much longer. Ginny was leaving soon, heading off to travel the world with her boyfriend. Mitch needed to do something about finding a replacement but that was a problem for another day. He had enough to worry about for the time being.

Once Lila was loaded onto the plane Mitch bent and kissed the tops of his sons' heads. 'Ginny will look after you,' he said. 'I'll be back as soon as I can.'

'Lila too?' Charlie asked. He adored his sister and followed her around constantly. The boys would be lost without Lila. So would he. He couldn't imagine losing all the women in his family.

'Lila too,' Mitch replied, hoping he could keep his promise.

Shirley, the cook, had appeared from the kitchen and she pressed a paper bag into his hands. He knew the bag would contain food and although he couldn't imagine that he'd feel like eating he took the bag anyway, he knew it was her way of coping. He climbed into the plane, choosing a seat from where he could keep watch.

Lila was drowsy now, the pain relief was working, and as the engines started up her eyelids fluttered and closed.

Through the window Mitch watched the station fall away as the pilot lifted the plane into the air. Red dirt, chestnut cattle, the dry, stony creek, grey-green trees and the silver, corrugated-tin roofs of the buildings that glinted in the sunlight. He looked down onto Jed and Charlie as they stood at the edge of the runway and watched him leave.

He could see it all laid out before him, his entire life, and he wondered when it would get back to normal. Would it ever?

The past two years had been the most difficult of his life. How many more traumatic events could they be expected to endure?

The last time he had been in the flying doctor plane on his way to Broken Hill he'd been with his wife and unborn child.

He turned away from the window, his gaze seeking Lila. He was determined to come back with his daughter. He couldn't bear the thought of returning alone again.

CHAPTER TWO

ROSE'S RIGHT FOOT ACHED, complaining about being crammed into uncomfortable shoes. She should have worn socks, she thought, something that would cushion her misshapen foot from the unforgiving canvas of her sneakers, but socks had looked ugly so she'd gone without and now she was paying the price for her vanity.

She had to wear closed-toe shoes for work but she wished she could wear ballet flats, something prettier than canvas sneakers. Work dress rules allowed ballet flats but she couldn't wear them any more. They wouldn't stay on.

Rose undid the laces and slipped her shoe off. She hated these shoes, hated the fact that she couldn't wear anything pretty any more. She hadn't minded these shoes on occasion before, but *having* to wear them, or something similar, every day had certainly taken the gloss off. She was sick of the sight of them. And the feel.

Once upon a time appearances had been so important to her but she was having to adjust her thinking on that. She was having to adjust her thinking on a lot of things.

Gone were the days of wearing her towering, strappy, glamorous shoes. She was prepared to admit that by the end of an evening out she had always been glad to remove them, they hadn't necessarily been made for comfort but they had been pretty. Now she had traded impractical, pretty and uncomfortable shoes for practical, *ugly* and uncomfortable. If she had to sacrifice comfort she wished she could at least look pretty.

Winter would be better, she thought. She could get a pair of flat boots. She'd tried wearing ankle boots but even in the air-conditioned hospital rooms her foot had got too hot and it had swelled up and ached even more.

She rubbed her foot on the back of her left calf, trying to get her circulation going. She knew she was supposed to be desensitising her foot by rubbing it regularly with different textures but she hated even looking at it let alone touching it. How ridiculous that toes that didn't exist any more could give her so much trouble.

She knew that her toes had had to be amputated. She knew there hadn't been a choice but that didn't mean she had to like it.

And now she knew all about phantom limb pain. Thank goodness she wasn't missing an entire limb; she could only imagine how painful that would be.

She needed to remember to be grateful. Her psychologist had told her to keep a list of all the things she was grateful for and to recall it when she was feeling maudlin. She started to run through the list in her head as she continued to rub her foot.

She was alive. That was a big one. A good one to start the list.

From the outside she looked the same but Rose knew that looks could be deceptive. She was different on the inside and underneath, but she didn't have to show those parts of her to anyone. She could keep that hidden, which was exactly what she intended to do.

Two—she had finished her degree and was now a qualified teacher. But that was as far as she got running through her 'grateful' list before the door into the office she shared with two other teachers opened and her manager walked in. Rose quickly tucked her right foot under her desk, hiding it from view, and slid it into her sneaker.

Jayne was a tall woman, her grey hair closely cropped to her head, her frame athletic, a little masculine. She was hard muscle from all the running she did and there was nothing left to soften the edges. Rose hadn't known her long but she seemed to be constantly on the go, always training for a running event, a half-marathon or marathon. That was something else Rose wasn't able to do—run. She'd never imagined that losing three small toes would make such an impact. Her doctors had told her she would be able to run again but she wasn't sure about that yet.

'Rose, do you have time to see one more patient before you finish for the weekend?' Jayne asked.

Rose closed the browser on her laptop as she replied. 'Sure.' Despite the fact it was Friday night she had nothing she needed to rush home for. That wasn't unusual; her social life had taken a battering—spending months in hospital tended to do that—and her confidence had also suffered. She hadn't dated for two years and she wasn't sure she was ready for that to change. She had nothing in her life except for work, her mother, her sisters and her niece. But that was okay. That was enough to handle at the moment.

'The patient's name is Lila Reynolds, she's eight years old. Her parents haven't requested educational support but the social worker is advocating for it. She says Lila is very withdrawn. She's from Outback Queensland and doesn't have any family support here in Adelaide.'

Rose remembered being eight years old. That was the year her father had died. The year she had gone from being his little princess and thinking the world was perfect to realising that it wasn't and that just because you wished something was so didn't make it real. It was one of life's lessons that she was relearning again at the age of twenty-three.

'No one?' she asked.

Jayne shook her head. 'The social worker has been leaving messages for her parents but is yet to speak to them. There's no file yet.'

Rose knew the files were often not much help anyway. The file the education system, and therefore the teaching staff, had access to was different from the case notes that the hospital staff—doctors, nurses, social workers, physios and the like—wrote in. The teachers weren't privy to all the private and sometimes confidential information about their young pupils but were given just the basic facts. Age, gender, and medical diagnosis were shared but only so that the teachers were aware of any impediments that would affect their learning. They were often given just enough information to put the children into the system but not enough to be useful—Rose could remember one of the other teachers telling her that when she'd first started this job.

'The social worker thinks it might be helpful to have one of us spend some time with Lila unofficially while she continues trying to speak to the parents,' Jayne said. 'She thought that if you had time you might have more luck with getting her to talk.'

In the six months since Rose had started working at the Royal Children's Hospital she knew she had garnered a reputation as someone who had a good rapport with the more reserved children. She'd always felt a connection with the quieter kids. She could empathise with their emotional scars and now, from more recent experience, with their physical scars as well.

'And if that doesn't work,' Jayne continued, 'then the

consensus is that if you can give her something to occupy her time then she might at least get some benefit from that.'

'I'll see what I can do,' Rose replied. 'What are her injuries?'

'She was thrown from a horse and sustained pelvic fractures. She was transferred from Broken Hill to Adelaide and underwent surgery a week ago. Her pelvis was pinned but she is able to get out of bed and can now move around with the aid of a walking frame.'

'Okay.'

Rose stood as Jayne left the office. She reached up and ran her fingers along the spines of her selection of books that she'd stored on the shelves. Since starting this job she'd added to her collection of children's books and she chose a few now that she thought might be of interest to an eight-year-old. If Lila didn't want to talk perhaps Rose could read to her. If Lila had been rushed to Adelaide for emergency surgery she probably hadn't brought much with her. Reading might help to pass the time and also might prompt a conversation. It had worked in the past.

Rose tucked the well-worn volumes under her arm. She loved shopping in markets and second-hand stores, something her sister Ruby had fostered in her, but while Ruby had always bought clothes, Rose had spent her time searching through the old books. Scarlett, her eldest sister, had started reading to her after her dad had died. Escaping into a book had helped her to get over her grief but it had also fed her imagination. She liked drama, tales of princesses, weddings, romance and young love. She wished the real world was more like her literary world. She didn't choose to read stories about war or crime or misery. She chose books where the characters got to live happily ever after.

She tugged on the back of her right sneaker, pulling it up over her heel to secure the shoe. God, she hated these shoes. If anything, her foot was even more uncomfortable now than before. She had thought these shoes would be okay but by the end of the day her feet ached and in reality these shoes probably didn't have enough support. She didn't think she was on her feet a lot but the hospital was big and there was a fair bit of walking just to get from the main entrance to the wards and to the classrooms. Which was good for her fitness but not so good for her feet.

The familiar smell of the hospital ward assailed her as she stepped out of the elevator by the orthopaedic wards. She didn't spend a lot of time on the wards, most of her time was spent in the classrooms, but the distinctive smell of the hospital was hard to ignore and hard to forget. She thought it was lodged in her subconscious, a lingering and not altogether pleasant after-effect of her time spent in ICU and the transplant ward.

She checked in with the charge nurse before heading into the four-bed ward to find Lila. Only two beds were occupied. It was mid-afternoon and Rose knew the ward had probably been full this morning but paediatric patients got discharged quickly and regularly, especially in the orthopaedic wards. There was a high turnover when patients could be sent home to be cared for by their parents.

Rose suspected that Lila would be in hospital for some time. It would be difficult to discharge her home to Outback Queensland if she needed rehabilitation for her injuries. Rose had learnt a lot in the past six months about a whole host of medical conditions. In fact, she'd learnt a lot in the eighteen months prior to that too but that had all been to do with her own experience.

A girl of about five years of age was in a bed to Rose's left and on the opposite side of the room, next to the window lay a girl who looked more likely to be Lila. Rose scanned the patient names above each bed just to be sure before she crossed the room.

'Lila?' she asked as she stopped beside the bed. She was a dark-haired, solemn-eyed little girl. Her skin was tanned and appeared healthy and brown against the white hospital sheets. She was thin but apart from that she looked too healthy for a hospital ward.

The little girl nodded.

'My name is Rose. I've brought you some books to pass the time. Do you like to read?'

Lila shook her head.

'Oh.' Rose put the books on the bedside cupboard but she refused to be deterred.

'What *do* you like to do?'

'Ride my horse.' There was no elaboration but at least she was talking.

'What about when it's raining?'

'It never rains.'

'Never?'

Her question was answered with another silent shake of her head.

'Oka-a-a-y…' Rose drew out the word as she thought about what to ask next. 'What about if it's too *hot* to go outside?'

'Then I like to draw.'

'What do you draw?' Rose asked as she looked around, expecting to see some drawings taped to the walls, but the walls were bare. 'Have you got any drawings?'

Lila nodded.

'Would you show me?' Rose asked.

Lila pulled a piece of paper from the bedside drawer and held it up. 'It's not very good 'cos I don't have any pencils.'

The paper was lined, Rose recognised it from the hospital case notes, but on it Lila had drawn a fabulous picture of a horse.

'Is this your horse?' Rose asked.

Lila nodded.

'What's her name?'

'Fudge.'

'That's an interesting name.'

'She's the same colour as caramel fudge,' Lila explained, 'but it's hard to tell 'cos the nurses could only find a lead pencil.'

'Well, I think she's beautiful.'

Rose noticed that Lila's voice became a little more animated when she was talking about her horse. Maybe that was the secret to getting her to engage. But wasn't that the same with all children? You just needed to find something that they were interested in. Rose knew that if you did that it was often hard to stop them from sharing.

'Does she smell like caramel?'

'That's silly.' Lila couldn't hide her smile. 'Horses don't smell like caramel.'

'Well, what does she smell like?'

'She smells like a horse.' Lila giggled and her dark eyes sparkled, losing their serious intensity. She looked like an eight-year-old girl now and Rose had a moment of self-satisfaction that she'd been able to make this little girl laugh. That she had been able to make a connection, however small, gave her a sense of achievement. This was what she loved about teaching, establishing a connection with the children.

Lila's giggles continued and Rose knew she was intrigued, but before she could say anything further she became aware of someone on the periphery of her vision. Someone else waiting and watching as she listened to Lila's laughter. She looked up to find a man standing in the doorway of the ward.

Possibly the most gorgeous man she had ever seen.

Tall, dark and handsome.

Her heart skipped a beat as she wondered who he was. A doctor she hadn't met yet? An orthopaedic surgeon? She was certain she'd never seen him before—his was not a face she would forget.

Rose ran her eyes over him. He would be a shade over six feet tall with a slim build but his shoulders and chest were broad, his arms were strong and muscular and his legs were long. He was casually dressed in jeans and a navy T-shirt, not the normal doctor-on-staff outfit—no white surgical coat, no tell-tale stethoscope—but Rose noted these things almost subconsciously as her gaze remained locked on his face. His very handsome face. It was tanned and he had a full head of thick, brown hair, cut short, with dark brown eyes to match. His jaw was triangular, darkened by a shadow of stubble, and he had a slight smile on his lips.

She bent her knees and her thighs tensed, ready to push her out of her chair, ready to cross the room and introduce herself to a handsome stranger. It was a reflex response, a reaction completely outside her conscious control, but before she could actually complete the movement the rest of her brain woke up and she realised what she was doing. She relaxed back into her seat, barely managing to rescue herself from complete embarrassment, and took some comfort in the thought that he hadn't noticed that she'd been about to stand as his attention was focussed on Lila.

The drive to go to him had been strong and the attraction she felt was primal, carnal and, while the result might have been pure embarrassment, it pleased her that she could still experience these feelings. That she still had the desire. The want and the need.

She couldn't remember the last time she'd felt such an immediate attraction to a man. She hadn't been remotely interested in men or relationships for the past two years yet somehow, with just one look, she knew she would change her mind for this man.

Who was he?

She checked for a hospital ID lanyard hanging around his neck but there was nothing. If he wasn't a doctor, who was he? Should he even be in the hospital?

He stepped into the room and crossed the floor, and Rose held her breath.

She was vaguely aware that Lila's giggles had stopped and out of the corner of her eye she saw Lila turn her head as she noticed the man's movements.

'Daddy!'

This was Lila's father?

He reached his daughter's bed and bent over, kissing her on the forehead. 'Hello, princess.'

Princess. Rose's father used to call her that. But she forgot all about her father as this man straightened up and looked at her.

Her breath caught in her throat, stuck behind a lump that had lodged there.

Now that father and daughter were side by side Rose noticed that they had the same eyes. Dark and serious. His chocolate eyes were intense, probing and forceful and she felt as if he could see right into her soul.

Mitch straightened up and looked again at the woman who sat by his daughter's bed. He'd noticed her as soon as he'd stepped into the room. He'd heard his daughter giggling, a sound he didn't hear enough of, but he'd been distracted by the woman sitting beside Lila's bed. She was not the type to go unnoticed.

He thought he'd imagined her at first. She didn't look real. Her face was round and serene, perfectly symmetrical. Her green eyes were enormous and iridescent. Her mouth was wide and her nose small. She looked like a woman from a Renaissance painting. Maybe that Botticelli one, the one of the young Madonna with the baby Jesus and the two angels. The light from the window bounced off her golden hair, making it shine like spun silk and making him forget that he hated hospitals, making him forget that he wished he and Lila were a thousand miles away. She was absolutely beautiful, but he had no idea who she was or why she was by his daughter's bedside.

She was watching him now, staring, silent, frozen like a deer in a spotlight. There was something fawn-like about her. Innocent. Young. Maybe it was her huge, luminous eyes.

Who was she?

She wasn't a nurse. She had a hospital ID badge hanging around her neck but she wasn't wearing a uniform and unless things had changed considerably since his last foray into a hospital he was pretty certain nurses didn't have time to sit idly at patients' bedsides. Unless the patient was critically ill, which he knew Lila wasn't.

A feeling akin to dread flooded through him as it occurred to him who she might be. 'Are you from social work?' he asked. The social worker had left several messages for him on the station answering machine but by the time he got in at the end of the day it was well past office hours and too late to call back. He knew he could have returned to the house during the day to make a call but he'd been nervous. Worried about what the social worker might want. Worried she might want to talk about what had happened two years ago. That she might want to talk about

Cara. He had refused counselling before and had no qualms about doing it again. They didn't need it. They were all fine.

'I meant to call you back,' he fibbed.

She was frowning. A little crease had appeared between her green eyes, marring the perfect smoothness of her brow.

'I'm not a social worker,' she replied.

Mitch relaxed; expelling the breath of air he hadn't even been aware of holding.

'I'm Rose,' she continued. 'I'm just here to keep Lila company.' She stood up. Her hair fell past her shoulders and she lifted her hands and gathered it all, twisting it into a long rope and bringing it forward to fall over one shoulder.

Now it was his turn to stare. Her movements were fluid and effortless. She'd obviously done this a thousand times before but to Mitch it was one of the sexiest things he'd ever seen and he was transfixed.

'But now that you're here, I'll get going,' she said, and before he could find another word to say she had stepped past Lila's bed and was on her way out of the ward.

He couldn't stop himself from watching her go and his eyes followed her out of the room.

She was slim but under her dark trousers he could see the two, full, round globes of her buttocks. They bewitched him as she stepped out of the room. She wore a soft white top that floated around her torso and reinforced his first impression of her as a golden angel.

Or maybe a golden rose.

Rose who? he wondered. She had left without a decent explanation of who she was and why she was there.

She was young and pretty and her name was Rose. That didn't seem like enough information. He wanted more. But just thinking about her made him feel old. He couldn't remember ever feeling young. He felt like he'd always been old. He knew he'd only felt that way since he'd lost his wife but he struggled to remember how he'd felt before. So now it felt as if he'd been born old.

His life was defined by before Cara died and after Cara died. But the more time that passed the harder it was to remember the before. He was so busy running the station and trying to figure out how to be a single father that he never seemed to have time to stop and sit and remember her. He was asleep before his head hit the pillow at night and up at dawn and he didn't stop all day.

If he had time to stop he might realise he was lonely but this was not something he noticed on a day-to-day basis. He had got used to life on the station and the absence of his regular weekly trips into Broken Hill and he only noticed his loneliness when he visited the city. At the cattle station, despite its isolation, he was surrounded by people who knew him; some of the staff had worked for him for close to ten years. But in the city no one knew him and he knew no one. He could go all day without talking to a soul. Despite the fact that there were hundreds of people around him in the city he was alone with too much time on his hands.

He didn't enjoy the city but he was going to have to keep returning until he could take Lila home. Maybe he should make an effort to make some connections with people. Talk to people, to complete strangers. In the country he wouldn't hesitate but city people were different. He'd been one of them once but now he just felt disconnected. They seemed busier, more caught up in their own lives, existing close together but without any meaningful interaction. He was so used to sharing his day, his life, with his workforce. At least until dinner was finished but after that he put his children to bed and was now in the habit of spending his nights doing the bookwork before going to bed alone. It was becoming a sad existence. A self-perpetuating cycle.

His mind drifted back to Rose. Thinking about her was a pleasant distraction from the dozens of other things that had been occupying his mind of late. It had been a long time since a pretty woman had caught his eye. It wasn't as if he met a lot of new women in Outback Australia and he'd just about given up noticing. He was tired and jaded, so it was a pleasant change to notice a pretty woman and he almost felt human again. But he knew he didn't have time for anything more than an appreciative glance. His days were busy, too busy for romance.

And despite the pleasure that seeing a beautiful woman had given him, he couldn't imagine ever falling in love again. It wasn't worth the risk. He would have to recover as best he could and move on. Alone.

Next time he came to the city he would bring the boys with him, he decided. They wanted to see Lila, they were missing her, and now that she was on the road to recovery he knew she would like to see her little brothers too. He'd bring the boys and they would provide him with company. Then he wouldn't need to think about young, blonde, Botticelli angels called Rose. He wouldn't have time to wonder if he'd see her again.

CHAPTER THREE

'IS SHE ASLEEP?' Rose asked as her sister walked into the kitchen.

Scarlett had been settling her daughter, Holly, for her afternoon nap while Rose had chopped what felt like a mountain of cabbage and carrot to make coleslaw. But she'd been glad to have a job to do. She was hoping it would keep her mind busy so she would have no time to think about gorgeous men with kind faces and daughters in hospital. Lila's father had unsettled her. Her reaction to him had her on edge but she found if she kept herself occupied she could almost manage to push him to the back of her mind. Wielding a sharp knife was making sure she stayed focussed on the task at hand. She scraped the vegetables into a bowl and started tossing them together to make the salad.

'Yes,' Scarlett replied, 'but she was fighting sleep every step of the way. I think she has too much of her father in her—she knows there's a party going on and she doesn't want to miss out!'

Rose smiled. Her brother-in-law did like a party. He'd grown up in a big family; he was the youngest of six siblings so there had always been plenty of people in the house and even now he liked to surround himself with family and friends. There was no special reason for today's gathering but Jake never needed a reason. He loved a crowd and didn't mind being the centre of attention. He'd worked as a stripper to put himself through medical school and Rose had heard he'd been very good at it. She had no doubt he'd loved every minute of it. Scarlett, by comparison, was happy behind the scenes. She only needed the attention of one person, her husband.

Like Jake, the old Rose had loved a party too. She'd enjoyed attention and she knew she got more than her fair share, but now that attention made her uncomfortable. Now it only made her more aware of everything that had happened to her. Aware of the contrast between the pretty Rose of her youth and the new Rose. She felt much, much older than her twenty-three years. She'd been through a lot in the past two years and had come out the other side a lot less positive about the future. She knew now that some things were out of her control and just because *she* had a plan it didn't mean that *life* had the same one for her.

Things were different now.

Rose had been avoiding parties but Scarlett had refused to listen to any of her excuses. The only reason Rose had agreed to come to this barbecue was because Scarlett had threatened to withhold time spent with Holly if she didn't attend. It was emotional blackmail—Scarlett knew Rose couldn't bear to think of being separated from her niece. Holly was one of the few highlights in her life. One of the things that Rose had fought so hard for. She adored Holly and Holly adored her.

Having a family of her own was all Rose wanted. It had been all she'd wanted since she was eight years old. Her dreams had been so different from those of her two elder sisters yet now they were both married and Scarlett had a daughter. Scarlett and Ruby were living Rose's dream and Rose couldn't help feeling a pang of jealousy when she thought about it. Scarlett had professed that she was never going to have kids, she'd always intended to focus on her career, yet look at her now, Rose thought: a qualified anaesthetist and mother to the most adorable little girl.

Ruby, the middle of the three Anderson sisters, was a different kettle of fish altogether. She was nomadic, nothing remotely like Rose, who was the epitome of a homebody. Marrying Noah was the first ordinary thing Ruby had ever done, but even then she'd gone for the unusual. Not too many people were married to professional race car drivers. Ruby had always had a point of difference, whether it was her dress sense, her living arrangements or her boyfriends; no one could ever accuse her of being ordinary, whereas Rose longed for an ordinary life—a husband who adored her, perfect children and her own happily ever after.

She wanted to re-create that perfect world she used to live in. The world she'd inhabited until the age of eight. She wanted to fall in love and have her own family. She believed in true love and part of her still hoped it would happen for her. She still imagined her white knight would come and sweep her off her feet. He would give her the world and would be so blinded by love that he wouldn't notice all her flaws.

The Anderson sisters had grown up with their own labels. Scarlett was the clever one, the career girl; Ruby was the fun one, the slightly wild and offbeat sister; Rose, not overly ambitious, had been content to be the pretty one. Until recently.

She used to be so confident, used to be able to walk into a room and know that men would look at her. She knew she was pretty and her blonde hair and big green eyes lent her an air of innocence that men couldn't resist. But Rose didn't feel pretty any more. She was scarred, emotionally and physically, but she hated the idea of anyone else knowing it.

She was also scared. Scared that no one would want her now.

Scarlett kept telling her to give herself time. To get back out into the world without expectations. To relax, have fun and see what happened. Her psychologist was telling her the same thing—give yourself time—but Rose wasn't convinced that time was the great healer that everyone professed it to be.

It had been almost two years since her last relationship had ended and she didn't feel any closer to being ready for another one. Not when she knew she would have to open herself up.

She was scared and scarred and she didn't believe that was a combination conducive to finding love.

Scarlett held out a tray of burgers and shashliks to Rose. 'Would you take these out to Jake for me, please?'

Rose could see her brother-in-law at the barbecue, talking to one of his friends.

'I know what you're doing,' she said.

'What?' Scarlett replied, all wide-eyed and innocent.

'You want me to talk to Rico.'

'He's a nice guy.'

'I'm not saying he's not, but—'

'You're not ready.' Scarlett finished the sentence for Rose with her usual retort but that hadn't been what she was about to say. 'I'm worried about you, Rose. You need to get out there. You'd have fun with Rico. It doesn't necessarily have to be anything more than platonic fun but at least you'd be out and about. Working and spending time with Holly isn't enough. You're twenty-three, have some fun.'

Rose couldn't mount a good argument so she reached out and took the tray of barbecue meat, resigned to the fact that she would have to let Scarlett win this round. Scarlett won most rounds. She was the bossy older sister. Rose knew she did it out of love and so she gave in. It was easier that way. 'All right,' she sighed, 'I'll go and talk to him.'

She was aware of Scarlett watching her through the kitchen window as she stepped outside. She knew her big sister was worried about her. Scarlett had always mothered her. They had all suffered when Rose's father had died suddenly and their mother just hadn't coped with the aftermath. Scarlett, at the relatively young age of sixteen, had taken it upon herself to be the champion for her two younger sisters and that instinct had never quite left her, even though her sisters were now both adults.

Rose looked around, taking in Scarlett's house, small but filled with love, her gorgeous husband, and a garden overflowing with their friends. Despite the fact that Scarlett was eight years older than Rose, Rose couldn't deny that she wanted what Scarlett had. A career, a husband who adored her, and a baby. Actually, she would settle for two out of three; unlike Scarlett, she wasn't that interested in a career. She enjoyed teaching but it was a job rather than her calling, and she didn't have the same burning ambition about it that Scarlett had about her career as an anaesthetist.

And Rose knew exactly why Scarlett was pushing her to get outside and mingle. She had never made a secret of the fact that she dreamt of marriage and babies, certainly not to her sisters, but she wasn't sure that she was in the right frame of mind to mix and mingle today. Although she couldn't complain about the talent on offer. Jake's friends were lovely, a good mix of polite, gentle, charming and good-looking; many of them, including Rico, were professional men who were also former colleagues of Jake's from the strip club, The Coop. They took pride in their appearance without, for the most part, any vanity, and Rose was happy to appreciate the efforts they went to in order to stay fit and in good shape. But she wasn't sure that getting involved with one of her brother-in-law's mates was a good idea. What if things didn't work out? Wouldn't that be awkward?

Scarlett had insisted that Rico was a genuinely nice guy who treated women with respect. Rose knew she could do worse than go out on a date with him.

Not that he'd asked her yet, she chided herself as she crossed the paving and headed for the barbecue. She was thinking of excuses unnecessarily. Why would he be interested in her? Just because Scarlett had put the idea in her head it didn't mean that Rico was entertaining the same notion.

'Could I have your number?'

Rose had been chatting to Jake and Rico for several minutes when Rico asked the question. She was glad he'd waited until Jake had taken a tray of cooked hamburgers inside to Scarlett. She didn't think she had the heart to turn him down in front of his mate but she couldn't give him what he wanted. He was handsome in a swarthy, dark, Mediterranean way, he had a great body, hours in the gym having toned it to perfection, and he seemed genuinely nice, but there was no spark. Rose wondered if she'd ever feel that spark again. Rico was just the type of man she normally fancied, tall, dark, good looking, a few years older than her but she wasn't interested. She hadn't been interested in a long time.

Not quite true, she thought as she remembered a man with chocolate brown eyes, a triangular jaw and an easy smile. She might make an exception for a man like him. But that was just a silly fantasy about a complete stranger. She didn't even know his name.

'I'm sorry,' she said, 'I'm not dating at the moment.'

She knew she had to figure out how she was going to

fulfil her dream of having a family when she didn't feel ready for a relationship. She still dreamt of finding love but in reality she was scared. She knew she couldn't wait for ever, she didn't *want* to wait for ever, but she was afraid to take that first step back into the dating game. She knew that first step would lead to others, which would lead to her having to share parts of herself, and that was the part she wasn't ready for.

Rico looked as if he might be getting ready to plead his case and Rose tried to remember how she used to turn invitations down without appearing rude. 'Why don't you give me your number?' she added. 'And if I change my mind, I'll call you.'

'Sure.'

'Great,' she replied, pleased he wasn't going to argue with her. 'I'll just grab my phone.'

She ducked inside and rummaged through her handbag. Her phone was lying in the bottom of the bag under a tin of coloured pencils she'd bought for Lila. She pulled the pencils out with the phone. She'd get Rico's number and then she would go and see Lila. She'd had enough of the party. She knew it would only be more of the same. Talking to Jake's friends, getting asked for her number. She made her excuses to Scarlett, promising to call back later, hoping that Jake's friends would have left by then and she could play with Holly without interruption.

But right now there was somewhere else she'd rather be. Someone else she'd rather talk to.

He was there.

He was sitting beside Lila's bed, his long legs stretched out in front of him, feet crossed at the ankles, watching as his daughter scrolled through what appeared to be photos on his phone.

She couldn't deny she'd been hoping to see him but now she was ridiculously nervous. What had she expected? That she could just feast her eyes on him from a distance, hiding in the shadows without being seen herself?

That was exactly what she'd hoped. She hadn't thought about the reality of seeing him. Of talking to him. She wasn't ready to make scintillating conversation. She had nothing to say. She was completely out of practice.

But she couldn't stand in the doorway for ever. She crossed the room and the movement caught his eye. He lifted his head and his chocolate eyes followed her progress. He stood up as she got closer and Rose put another tick in the box that would be beside his name if only she knew what it was. He had manners. She adored men with manners. Having someone who would open a door for her or pull out her chair at dinner and seat her first, not because he thought she was incapable, just because it was a nice thing to do, always made her go weak at the knees. She always thought it gave a little glimpse about what he would be like as a husband or a lover. A mark of consideration and kindness. A man with manners would treat a girl properly.

'I didn't mean to interrupt,' she said. 'I just brought some drawing things for Lila.'

He smiled at her and Rose's knees wobbled as the ground tilted a little under her feet. She'd liked his smile yesterday when he'd looked at his daughter but that was nothing compared to having him smile at her. His face brightened and his brown eyes warmed and darkened like melted chocolate as he looked straight at her. 'You're not interrupting, Rose.'

A rush of happiness flooded through her and she could feel a faint blush stealing over her pale cheeks. He'd remembered her name!

She stopped next to Lila's bed before realising she should have continued to the opposite side. She was standing far too close to him. Her head barely reached his shoulders. If she turned her head towards him, all she could see was the powerful breadth of his chest; if she looked down she got an eyeful of a narrow waist and long, lean legs; if she breathed in she could smell him. He smelt clean and fresh as if he'd not long been out of the shower, and his scent overrode the antiseptic smell of the hospital.

Her heart was racing, making her hands shake. She wasn't sure why but he really unsettled her and she was unbelievably nervous. As she reached forward to pass the pencils and sketch pad to Lila the tin slid from her hands. The lid popped off as the tin hit the floor and pencils spilled around their feet.

His reaction time was faster than hers. He crouched down and gathered the pencils up as she stood there, trying to work out what had just happened. His head was level with her knees and she could look down onto the top of his head. His hair was cut short but it was thick and she had a sudden urge to reach out and thread her fingers through it. Instead, she curled them into a fist at her side.

He stood and handed her the pencils but the touch of his fingers sent a jolt of awareness through her that was so strong she almost dropped them a second time.

Maybe it had been a mistake, coming here. She was well and truly disconcerted and had lost all trace of coherent thought.

'I can't stay,' she said as she finally managed to put the pencils and sketch book on the end of Lila's bed. 'These are for you,' she said before she bolted for the door as fast as her disfigured feet would allow.

He followed her from the ward. She didn't turn around but she could feel him behind her. Her whole body was tense, her nerves taut, fighting against her as she tried to walk away.

'Wait!'

Her steps slowed of their own accord as he called to her and then he was beside her, his hand on her elbow, sending her heart crazy. She turned to face him.

'Thank you for getting those pencils for Lila. Can I reimburse you?'

She was looking into a pair of eyes that were so dark she could see her own reflection. Her eyes were wide, startled, and she knew that he had caused that look as his touch had sent her body wild.

He was waiting for her answer. She shook her head. 'No, I wanted to do it. I thought it would help to keep her occupied.'

'I meant to bring her things with me, she asked me to, but with all the other hundred things I had to organise to get away I forgot. Her brothers have been acting up, they're missing Lila and are upset with me for leaving them behind, and with all their carry-on I got completely distracted and forgot to pack Lila's things.' He paused to take a breath and gave her a half-smile along with a slight shrug of his shoulders. 'But you don't want to hear about all of that.'

Oh, but she did. She wanted to know everything.

'If you won't let me reimburse you, can I at least buy you a coffee?'

She gathered her hair in her hand and twisted it, bringing it forward to hang over her shoulder. She toyed with the ends, something she always did when she felt out of her depth. Keeping her hands busy helped to calm her down and it worked again now, giving her just enough breathing space to be able to reply. 'I don't even know your name.' As if it mattered. She already knew what her answer would be.

'It's Mitch. Mitch Reynolds.'

Mitch. It was perfect. The Reynolds part she had assumed but the rest of his name suited him perfectly. It was strong, straightforward and honest. He had an honest face and an honest name. He seemed like the type of man who could be trusted. He would call a spade a spade.

He put out his hand but Rose hesitated. She'd been thinking about him all night but even so her reaction to him today had surprised her. She was almost afraid to touch him again, afraid of what she would feel, afraid her body would betray her and he would be able to read on her face all the conflicting emotions that were coursing through her. Part of her wanted to see if she experienced the same sensation again but she knew she had to prepare herself first. If she was flustered she didn't want him to see. She needed to appear in control.

Almost against her better judgement she put her hand in his. His fingers closed around hers, his grip strong but not threatening, and Rose had the strangest sensation of familiarity, that her body already knew his touch. It certainly responded to it as though she'd had some knowledge, some experience, of him before.

'So now that we're no longer strangers, will you let me buy you a coffee? I wanted to talk to you about Lila.'

He had sounded so guilty about forgetting Lila's things; he'd sounded like he had the weight of the world on his shoulders and Rose couldn't deny she was desperate to know more. This could be her chance to find out.

She nodded, not trusting herself to speak. She didn't want him to guess how he affected her and she suspected her voice would be high and quavering. That was not the way to appear in control.

'The social worker stopped by the ward after you left yesterday,' Mitch said as he placed the cafeteria tray on the table and handed her a coffee. 'Did you have anything to do with that?'

Rose knew that the social worker had been trying to contact Lila's parents but she'd had nothing to do with the visit. She shook her head. 'No. I imagine she'd left instructions with the nurses to call her when you got here.' She took a bite of the doughnut that Mitch had insisted on buying for her and asked, 'Who came to see you?'

'Annabel.'

'What did she want?'

'She wanted to find out about Lila. Something about hospital policy for children who have no family support. Lila has family support, but I can't be in two places at once.'

Mitch didn't wear a wedding ring. She already knew that. She'd checked. She'd also done a little investigating yesterday after she'd left Lila's bedside and discovered that there didn't appear to be a Mrs Reynolds. Was that why Mitch needed to be in two places at once?

But surely Lila had a mother? She must have one. Rose wondered where she was. Wild horses wouldn't have kept her away from her own child if they'd been hospitalised and she thought it odd that she hadn't come to town, even if she wasn't part of Mitch's life any more.

If she wanted to know the answers, she would have to ask the questions. 'What about Lila's mother? Where is she?'

'My wife died, there's only me.'

'Oh.' That wasn't the answer she'd been expecting. Surely that was the sort of information that should have been passed on to her? But before she could say anything further, Mitch kept talking.

'So, if you're not part of the social work team, what is it that you do here?'

Obviously his wife, his dead wife, was not a topic that was up for discussion.

'I'm a teacher,' Rose replied, going with the subject change.

'A teacher?' Mitch queried. 'The social worker mentioned educational support… Are you what she was talking about?'

Rose smiled. His phrasing wasn't quite the way she would have put it. 'Yes, but not just me. We have a school here.'

'In the hospital?'

She nodded. 'Children who will have long hospital stays or frequent admissions, thereby missing school, can attend classes in the hospital. It stops them from getting too far behind and also keeps them socialising. We have a lot of kids, like Lila, from the country, and being away from family can be quite isolating. I imagine Annabel thinks Lila would benefit from attending classes.' Rose knew that was the case but she got the impression that Mitch wouldn't want to know the staff had been discussing him. She suspected he would want to feel like the idea and the decision to enrol Lila in the hospital school was his. 'I teach middle primary mainly.'

'So you would teach Lila?'

Rose nodded.

'How does it work? School of the air I'm familiar with, but that's about it for schools out our way.'

'We have several teachers on staff covering everything from kindergarten through to high school and we have several classrooms. If children can make it to the classrooms they attend there but we can also teach them in their beds.'

'And Lila can join in?'

'Yes. Any child who is going to be in hospital for longer than a couple of days or is admitted frequently can be enrolled and we work closely with their regular school to make sure what they are learning is relevant.'

'Why is this the first I'm hearing about this?'

Rose smiled. 'I would guess Annabel has been trying to tell you, and if you'd called her back you would know.'

'Touché,' he said, before taking another sip of his coffee. 'Lila would probably enjoy being in a classroom and having other kids her age around instead of just her younger brothers. How do I organise this?'

'You'll have to email Annabel and she can put a request in on your behalf,' Rose explained.

Mitch pulled out his phone, asked for Annabel's email address, and sent an email off straight away. He copied Rose in to the email and her phone beeped as the email hit her inbox. She glanced at her screen. Mitch's signature on the bottom of the email included the contact details for the station.

Emu Downs.

It sounded so romantic. 'Emu Downs. That's a beautiful name.'

Mitch smiled and Rose's heart soared. It was crazy how she reacted to his simple gestures. She'd spent months telling herself she wasn't ready for a relationship yet this man, virtually a complete stranger, was able to make her body spring to life.

'You're imagining huge mobs of emus running across the land, aren't you?' Mitch's question interrupted her fantasy.

Emus? She hadn't been imagining anything of the sort! But she couldn't tell him the truth—that she was feeling such a strong pull of attraction that she was amazed he hadn't noticed. She couldn't tell him the truth so she fibbed. 'I was. Are there lots?'

'Not any more. The dingoes and the drought have wiped a lot of them out.'

'It's a cattle station, is that right?'

Mitch nodded.

'Has it always been in your family?'

'It belongs to my wife's family.'

The dead wife. That brought her back down to earth with a thump. This man with the gorgeous eyes and kind smile had children and a dead wife. He ran a cattle station out back of nowhere and he'd told her he had a lot on his plate. Hooking up with a random girl was probably not high on his agenda.

But Rose couldn't shake the feeling that fate had brought him to her. That they were supposed to meet, that there was *something* between them and that he was going to be important to her in some way.

Or maybe she was going to be important to him. He looked a little distracted, lost in his memories, and Rose instinctively wanted to help. She had a tendency to feel other people's pain. Perhaps because she'd suffered a major loss, the death of her father, at a young age, it had fine-tuned her empathy but she definitely felt as though she was the one who could help him. But how?

She wanted to reach her hand across the table and take his. Offer him comfort. But even she was able to realise how strange that would seem.

Before she had a chance to embarrass herself Mitch pushed back his chair and stood up. 'I'd better get back to Lila. Thanks for your company.'

He looked at her with his dark brown eyes and Rose knew he was seeing her now, he wasn't caught up in the past any more, and she thought he was going to say more but he simply came around to her side of the table and held her chair for her, waiting to pull it out as she stood. It seemed their coffee date was over.

'I'll speak to Annabel on Monday,' Rose said, 'and get Lila into classes.' If she was teaching Lila she would possibly have an excuse, a reason, to keep in touch with Mitch. And for now that would have to do. And for now that gave her hope.

CHAPTER FOUR

ROSE HAD BEEN at the hospital bright and early on Monday. She'd quietly hoped that it might give her a chance to see Mitch but soon found he'd returned to the station the night before. She did, however, manage to get everything sorted for Lila to attend school and she would be joining in for the afternoon session today.

Rose had five other children in the class, all of whom had been in hospital for some time, and she introduced them to Lila.

'Okay, everyone, we have a new student joining us today. This is Lila, she lives in the Outback on a cattle station and normally does School of the Air so once Lila has settled in perhaps we'll find out more about her school and how different it is from the schools you go to. Lila, this is Skye, Elise, Tuan, Alistair and Jade.'

Skye and Elise suffered from cystic fibrosis and were regular inpatients who had become good friends. Tuan was in hospital being treated for leukaemia, Alistair was a post-op surgical patient and Jade had a gastro-intestinal disorder that required regular admissions but today they were simply Rose's students. Attending school gave them a chance to forget about their illnesses. What was wrong with them ceased to matter as they focussed on the tasks that Rose set for them and Rose loved helping them to feel like normal kids.

'This afternoon we are going to make posters,' Rose told the children. She had planned a simple project for them to start working on today. She hadn't yet spoken to Lila's School of the Air teacher to see what she was doing in class but this project would get all the children interacting and let Lila settle in. Lila had nodded to the other children when Rose had introduced her but hadn't said a word. Rose knew Lila didn't say much on the ward but she was hoping she might be inclined to chat to her peers. Maybe she just needed time. 'I want you each to choose your favourite zoo animal and we are going to research it. There are some facts I need you to include and then you can decorate your poster however you choose.'

She knew Lila would enjoy illustrating her poster and hoped that would help her to feel comfortable. Once she had a chance to settle in, perhaps then she'd start talking. 'I want to know why the animal is in the zoo. Is it for educational reasons or is the animal under threat of extinction or for some other reason? Where does the animal come from? Are there any left in the wild? What is its habitat, diet and predators and you can include any other interesting or unusual facts or characteristics.'

Rose wrote the required information on the whiteboard and handed out laptops and brightly coloured poster paper and there was much animated discussion as the children tried to decide on their favourite animal.

'Rose?' Alistair stuck his hand in the air. 'Lila wants to do her project on horses but they're not a zoo animal.'

'Actually, there are types of horses that are found in zoos,' Rose replied. 'Why do you want to do horses, Lila?'

'They're my favourite animal.'

'What about a zebra?' Jade suggested.

'No.' Lila's tone was definite and Rose thought she looked close to tears. She needed to find out what was wrong. She didn't want Lila's first day going pear-shaped.

'Okay, once you've chosen your animal you can start looking up the information.' The children all knew how to use the internet, better than Rose did, and she knew that would keep them busy for several minutes while she had a chat with Lila.

She pulled a chair out and sat beside Lila. 'Horses aren't really a zoo animal. You'll find it hard to give me the information I'm after if you choose horses.'

'But I'm worried about Fudge. I want to do a project on her in case I have to give her away.' Once again, Fudge seemed to be Lila's preferred topic of conversation.

'Why would you have to give her away?' Rose asked.

'Because of what happened.'

'But it was an accident. It wasn't Fudge's fault.'

'No, it was my fault.'

Rose remembered being eight years old and feeling like every bad thing that happened was a direct result of things she did. The sense that cause and effect were all controlled by your actions. When her dad had died she could remember thinking that if only she'd eaten all her peas or picked up her toys when he'd asked her to that he wouldn't have died. She doubted very much that the accident had been Lila's fault but she wasn't going to discount her fears. 'How was it your fault?'

'I should have checked that Ruff was tied up properly.'

'Who's Ruff?'

'He's our dog. He's not supposed to go near the stables. He barks and nips at the horses' heels and scares them. The boys tied him up but I should have checked. Sometimes the boys don't put his collar on tight enough and he slips his head out.'

Rose did her best to allay Lila's fears. 'I will speak to your dad and ask how Fudge is, make sure everything is okay. In the meantime, why don't you look up Mongolian horses?' She wrote down the name so Lila could spell it. 'They are special horses and some of them live in zoos. You might like to do your project on them. They aren't that different to Fudge.'

Rose called Mitch at lunchtime but only managed to reach an answering-machine. While it was good to hear his voice, even if it was only a recording, she really needed to speak with him. She left a message and her phone number and asked him to call her back. Lila was beginning to open up to her and she wanted to make sure she followed through with her promise to speak to Mitch. She didn't want to disappoint Lila, she didn't want to give her a reason not to trust her and to keep her thoughts to herself. Rose knew that Lila still wasn't talking much to the nursing staff, remaining a quiet, self-contained child, and Rose wanted her to feel that she would listen if she spoke.

It took three days for her call to be returned, by which time she had left three more messages. She'd planned on setting Mitch straight, explaining that his daughter needed to be one of his priorities and asking why it had taken him so long to call her back, but he cut off her argument before she'd had a chance to get started.

'Rose, I'm sorry it's taken me so long to get back to you. I've been away from the house. I had to repair some of the windmills and check stock.' He seemed to expect her wrath and that took the wind out of her sails.

'I left the first message three days ago!'

'I know but the windmills aren't outside the back door. The station is the size of Trinidad and Tobago, it takes a while to check them all and longer if I need to do repairs.'

Even his voice was enough to make her pulse skyrocket. She closed her eyes as she listened to him speak, letting the deep notes of his voice caress her soul.

His explanation made sense.

'Trinidad and Tobago?'

'That's about as big as Kangaroo Island.'

'Wow, I hadn't realised.'

'There's no reason why you should. But tell me why you rang. Is everything okay with Lila?'

'She's fine,' Rose reassured him, remembering the purpose of all the calls she'd made. 'She's doing well, enjoying the classes, but she is concerned about her horse.'

'Fudge? Why?'

'She's worried you might get rid of her horse because of the accident.'

'What? Of course not. Would you please reassure her that Fudge is fine. Tell her Jimmy is taking good care of her and she'll be waiting for Lila when she comes home.'

'Sure.'

'Thank you. I should be around the homestead now for the next few days at least, so will you call me if there's anything else? I promise to get back to you as soon as I can but it will usually be late at night. It's the only chance I get to sit in the office and take care of the bookwork and any messages. I realise it's out of hours for you, will that be a problem?'

It wouldn't make any difference to her. He was calling on her mobile but chances were she'd be home anyway. She was tired at the end of the day. Being at work was taking more physical effort than she had anticipated. She knew she would gradually get stronger and that her endurance would improve and she wasn't going to admit defeat, but at the end of the day she was more than happy to come home and put her feet up. Mitch could call at any time. She doubted he'd be interrupting anything important and she was more than happy to talk to him.

'You have my mobile number, you can call anytime.'

Mitch leant back in his office chair, stretched his arms over his head, and tilted his head from side to side, easing the tension in his shoulder muscles. He'd had a busy few days and today had been no exception. He'd spent the day repairing fences. It was tough, physical work even with all the modern machinery and he was looking forward to a long, hot shower, but first he wanted to call Rose before it got too much later.

He had taken Rose at her word and had been calling every few days on the pretext of checking on Lila but really that was just an excuse. He was worried about Lila but he realised he couldn't be in two places at once. He couldn't be away from the station indefinitely; even though his stocks were low he needed to oversee the cattle he did still have to make sure they were being properly looked after. He knew Lila was in good hands but her hospitalisation gave him a reason to pick up the phone and talk to Rose.

He wanted company. Female company. He spent his days in the company of men but in the days of old he'd been able to finish his day with a nightcap on the veranda with his wife, talking about their kids, the station, their future. Until that had all ended. He missed those days.

There was a shortage of women on the station and he noticed their absence. Ginny brought the tally to three, along with Shirley, the station cook, who was in her early sixties, and the station mechanic's wife. There was the occasional jillaroo on staff but they tended to come and go with the seasons.

He missed Cara but talking to Rose filled that gap. It gave him a sense of being connected to something bigger than him, bigger than the station. He missed the connection to another person.

He was lonely but there wasn't anyone who was going to replace Cara. He couldn't imagine ever falling in love again, it wasn't worth the risk. But all the same he didn't want to spend the rest of his life alone. He wanted company and for now Rose was giving him that company, even if it was only over a telephone line.

'How was your day?' Rose asked, after she had given him an update on Lila. This was what he missed, among other things, having someone to share the simple things, the everyday things with. Someone who knew his moods, could tell if he'd had a good day or a bad one just by the tone of his voice or the set of his shoulders. 'Did you get the fences fixed?'

He closed his eyes as he imagined her sitting down, talking to him. He pictured her in the outfit she'd been wearing on the day she'd brought the pencils to Lila. She'd looked gorgeous. She'd been wearing a loose top in a pale pink that had swung around her body and had left his imagination to fill in the gaps about what was hidden underneath, but she had paired the top with cut-off denim shorts that had shown off her amazing legs and hadn't required him to use any imagination at all. Her blonde hair had been loose and had cascaded in shiny waves over her bare shoulders. He could see her now, one hand holding the phone, the other playing with the ends of her blonde hair. Her hair had looked silken and soft and his fingers had itched to touch it and feel it for himself.

'I did,' he replied. He'd spoken to her two days ago, explaining that he might be out of reach for a day or two as he had to check some fences that had come down. Rose didn't need to know his whereabouts—the medical staff were the ones who might need to get in contact with him—

it had just given him an excuse to call her. As it was, he had spent a day and a half mending fences before leaving a couple of his station hands to finish off the job tomorrow. He'd wanted to come back to the homestead, wanted to pick up the phone and talk to Rose, wanted to hear her voice. 'A camel train had been through.'

'Why is there a train line through one of your fences?'

Mitch laughed. He knew Rose enjoyed getting an insight into station life and he was used to the fascination that city folk had regarding Outback life, but he normally found it a difficult thing to describe. Somehow it was different with Rose. She asked questions that prompted him to recall different events and her easy laughter made him strive to recount the amusing aspects of his day. He wanted to amuse her. He loved hearing her laugh. Her laughter brightened his day and no matter what sort of day he'd had he always felt better once he'd spoken to her. 'Not an actual train full of camels.' He chuckled. 'I meant a herd of camels.'

'Oh.' Rose joined in with his laughter. 'I thought a group of camels was called a caravan.'

'I think there are a few different collective nouns and all of them would be far nicer than what I was calling them today; my fences were completely flattened.'

'Well, no one could ever say station life was dull.'

'No, it's far from that.' It could be lonely, he'd admit, but it wasn't dull. 'But I could do without the camels, they're terribly destructive.'

'Can you build bigger fences?'

'I have hundreds of kilometres of fencing. I can't make it *all* camel-proof, it would cost a fortune and camels are pretty stubborn. They'd rather go through something than around it and I'd need pretty strong fences to stop them. If they're thirsty, once they smell water not much will keep them out. They're pretty big and can do a lot of damage *en masse.*'

'So when you have the camels under control, will you be coming to town again?' Rose asked.

He could hear the smile in her voice but what he wanted to know was, was she asking because she wanted to see him? Dared he hope she was enjoying the phone calls as much as he was?

'Lila is missing you,' Rose added, dashing his hopes.

He had already decided to get back to Adelaide as soon as possible. He needed to see Lila but he was also keen to see Rose. This was another reason for his call tonight. He'd wanted to let her know of his impending visit, wanted to make sure she'd be around.

'I'll be there on Friday. I'm bringing the boys this time.' It had been a couple of weeks since he'd last been down to the city and the boys had been pestering him to take them on the next trip.

'Lila will be thrilled. She's told me all about her brothers. She's missing them too.'

Mitch laughed. Rose's comments and observations often made him laugh. It was a good release, and he knew he hadn't laughed often enough over the past two years. It was good to talk to someone who hadn't known Cara, someone who didn't seem to think it was wrong to want to be happy. 'I'll remind her of that next time she complains that they are bugging her.'

'How long are you staying?'

'A few days. I need to see my accountant and take care of a few other business matters.'

'What will you do with the boys while you're in meetings?'

'I'm not sure. I guess they'll just have to come with me.'

'They can come to school if that's easier.'

'In the hospital?'

'Yes.'

'Are you sure?'

'Of course. Siblings of country kids are welcome at the school, it's no problem.'

'That would be fantastic. I'll see you on Friday, then.'

Mitch hung up the phone. He was excited. Excited at the prospect of seeing her again. It had been a long time since he had looked forward to anything with as much anticipation.

Heads turned as Rose and her sisters walked into the restaurant on Tynte Street. They were a striking trio. Scarlett, Ruby and Rose didn't really look alike yet they were all beautiful. Ruby and Rose had inherited their maternal grandmother's green eyes and all three girls had their mother's long legs.

This dinner had been in Rose's diary for weeks, scheduled to coincide with Ruby's visit to Adelaide, and Rose was secretly relieved that it had been booked for Wednesday night. She didn't want any commitments for the weekend. Mitch was coming to town and she wanted to keep her diary clear. Just in case.

They were shown to their table where the fourth member of their party was already seated. Candice stood up to greet her girlfriends, kissing each of them on the cheek. She was almost like their fourth sister. Like Ruby, she was a nurse and she had worked with both Scarlett and Ruby and had also grown up with Scarlett's husband, Jake.

'Drinks?' Scarlett asked the girls before the waitress left them to peruse the menu.

'Just water for me,' Ruby said. She didn't drink alcohol any more.

'Water is fine with me too,' Candice said.

Scarlett looked at Rose, who nodded. She wasn't a big drinker, her body and her medications made it difficult to process alcohol. She was happy to start with water and maybe she'd have a glass of wine with her meal.

'What would people like?' Scarlett asked once their drinks were sorted. 'Shall we order a selection of the shared plates? That way we can try a bit of everything, including some vegetarian options for you, Ruby.'

'That sounds fine,' Candice said, 'as long as it's nothing with soft-boiled eggs or raw fish.'

'Oh, my God!' Ruby exclaimed. 'You're pregnant?'

Candice grinned. 'Yep, ten weeks, I know it's still early but I've been dying to tell you guys.'

Rose also had to avoid those foods. She wished it was because she was pregnant too, rather than for the real reason, which was to make sure she avoided infections. Although she had recovered from the bacterial meningitis she'd contracted, it had left its mark and she had to live with the after-effects. She couldn't afford to jeopardise her health by eating high-risk foods; it was safer just to cut out certain raw or undercooked foods from her diet.

'You and Jake need to have another baby now so mine can have a playmate,' Candice was telling Scarlett.

'We're trying.' Scarlett smiled. She looked so content and serene, sometimes Rose was still amazed at the change marriage and a baby had wrought in Scarlett. She still loved her career but it was no longer the most important thing in her life.

'Ruby? What about you?'

'God, no. Our lifestyle doesn't allow for a baby.' Ruby's husband, Noah, was a professional race car driver. 'We travel the circuit for nine months of the year, can you imagine trying to do all that with a baby? I'd end up stuck at home or in a hotel room.'

'I can't imagine you stuck at home.'

'Neither can I.' Ruby laughed. 'So that means no babies for now. I'm not letting Noah have all the fun.'

'Congratulations, Candice, I'm really pleased for you.' Rose finally added her congratulations to her sisters'. She was happy for Candice but it didn't stop her from feeling a little melancholy. Everyone else was living the life she wanted.

'You'll be next, Rose.' Ever-observant Scarlett must have seen the wistful expression in Rose's eyes.

'Only because I'm the last one left.'

'Are you still leaving a trail of broken hearts in your wake?' Candice queried.

'No. I'm not dating.'

'Rico asked for her number,' Scarlett said.

'Oh, I remember him,' Ruby said. 'Has he called?'

'I didn't give it to him.'

'Why not?'

Rose shrugged. 'There was no spark.' She didn't want to waste time on someone who was unlikely to set her world on fire.

'You're not going to find your perfect man unless you get out there. Contrary to the fairy tales they're not going to arrive at your door on a white horse and carry you away to their castle.'

'I know that,' Rose protested. She didn't mind what colour the horse was. 'But do you really think love can grow if there's no initial spark of attraction?'

She wondered what colour horse Mitch rode. She couldn't help thinking of him. He'd called her often over the past two weeks and she was counting the days until he would be back in town. Only two more now. While Rico was nice, Mitch was another matter entirely. Just the sound of his voice and the tone of his laugh over the phone was enough to set her pulse racing. That was what she wanted. That was what she was waiting for. That feeling of excitement, of nervous anticipation. The sense that she couldn't wait to see him again and couldn't bare it if he didn't look at her, smile for her, touch her, kiss her. That was what she wanted in a man.

She looked each of the girls in the eye. She knew they understood what she wanted. She knew for a fact that they had all been knocked for a six the first time they'd laid eyes on their husbands.

'Noah was virtually unconscious the first time you saw him,' she said to Ruby, 'and you still knew there was something there.'

'That was my hormones.'

'Exactly. You felt it straight away. That's what I want. What if I'm out on a date with someone who I know could only ever be a friend and I miss my opportunity to meet "the one"?' She shook her head. 'I think I'll wait for the spark.'

'But what if the guy you're out with happens to be friends with the guy who will be "the one"? What if that's how you meet? You have to get back out there. You have to give yourself a chance of meeting him,' Candice said.

'Why don't you ring Rico? He knows a lot of people. Even if you don't think he's right for you, he has got lots of really nice friends,' Scarlett suggested.

'I don't think so.'

'Well, would you at least promise us that you'll consider going on a date with the next man who asks you out?'

Rose thought about Ruby's suggestion. If she wanted what her sisters and Candice had found, her own happily ever after, she would have to start living and stop hiding behind excuses. She'd been given a second chance at leading a normal life and she needed to start making the most of those opportunities. She needed to be open to the possibility of finding love. She was certain Rico wasn't the one but that didn't mean there wasn't someone out there who would love her even if she wasn't perfect any more, and when the time came, when that man appeared, she needed to be ready. It was time to start opening herself up. It was time to be brave.

'Okay, I'll consider it,' she said, and as she agreed to Ruby's request Mitch's face popped into her mind. Would he be the next person to ask her out? She crossed her fingers under the table. Could she be that lucky?

Despite arriving in Adelaide late the previous night, Mitch and the boys had been up for hours. It was force of habit to rise at dawn with the early morning chorus of birds and even in the city Mitch could hear the birds before the traffic noise started. He was at the hospital in time for the morning ward round as he wanted to chat to Lila's doctor in person and was relieved to hear her recovery was on track. He took the boys to breakfast while they waited for lessons to start.

Classes started at nine and Mitch was at the classroom door ten minutes later. He didn't want to appear too eager, too desperate but he also didn't want to wait any longer to see Rose.

She was leaning over one of the desks, talking to a student, her dark trousers stretched across her hips, and all Mitch could see was the round globes of her perfectly shaped bottom. His reaction was immediate but not altogether unexpected. He'd been thinking of her constantly for the past few days, eager to see her. She straightened up and turned when she heard the door close and Mitch stepped behind Jed, looking for some cover to hide his visceral response. It wasn't unpleasant but it was inappropriate for a classroom.

She smiled at him and crossed the room. She was glowing, she looked sunny and bright and suddenly Mitch's day seemed full of possibilities.

Rose squatted down to introduce herself to his sons. Her manner was natural, calm and relaxed and he could see the boys lapping up her attention. He knew exactly how they felt.

She took them each by a hand and walked with them over to Lila while Mitch stood by the classroom door, waiting like an expectant suitor standing in line for a chance to talk to her.

The boys were used to spending time amusing themselves; at home, they spent more time with their governess and the station cook than they did with Mitch and they didn't bat an eyelid at being left in Rose's care. They were used to having different people being responsible for them and they didn't seem to mind, but Mitch still felt a twinge of guilt that they were so independent at such a young age.

If Cara was still alive, would it be any different? The station staff were like one big family so Mitch suspected it might have been the same. Everyone would have looked out for the children regardless.

Rose used the couple of minutes that it took to get the boys sorted to get her racing heart under control. It was crazy that someone she barely knew could make her feel this way. Excited, nervous, tongue-tied. She'd been expecting him but that still didn't mean she was prepared.

She took a deep breath—inhale for four, exhale for eight—just like she'd been taught in hospital to calm herself down whenever things were getting on top of her. She took a second, deep breath as she walked back to Mitch, exhaling and trying to relax her muscles as she took in the sight of him waiting by the door.

He was wearing trousers and a long-sleeved buttoned shirt in a chambray blue that highlighted his tan. Once again he had riding boots on his feet. The leather looked well worn but it had been recently polished and Rose suspected that this might be as formal as his wardrobe got.

'Thank you for organising this. It will make the day so much easier,' he said with a smile, and Rose's heart immediately kicked up a gear, threatening to accelerate away, as her tongue tied itself in knots.

Something about him made her jittery, but in a good way. She couldn't put her finger on it, it was just a feeling. She felt alive, super alert, aware of every little thing and she didn't really want to get that feeling under control. She was enjoying it but she didn't want to appear skittish. She didn't want him to think she was young and ditzy.

Her tongue felt too large for her mouth as she tried to formulate a sensible reply. 'It was no trouble. I hope the boys enjoy it. I know going to school is probably not top of their favourite things to do in the city but hopefully the novelty of today, and the fact they get to spend time with Lila, will make up for it.'

'Trust me, it's far better for them than sitting in my accountant's office. Better for me too. I thought I might take them to the beach for a swim and dinner tonight. If you're not busy, would you like to join us? Let me buy you dinner to say thank you.'

Even though she'd been hoping he might ask her out she'd managed to downplay her dreams, knowing it was unlikely to happen. She knew from their late-night phone conversations that he was a single dad with a lot on his plate—Lila, the boys, the station—but that hadn't stopped her from wishing for an invitation and she couldn't believe her wish had come true.

Despite only having had one real face-to-face conversation Rose felt as though she knew him well and it didn't seem odd that he'd invited her, a relative stranger. It seemed perfectly normal and because she'd been waiting, hoping for this invitation she wasn't about to turn it down.

'That sounds lovely. I'd like that.'

CHAPTER FIVE

MITCH AND THE boys met Rose in front of the hospital at the end of her day. The boys were dressed in swimming shorts and Mitch had changed out of his trousers and button-down shirt into a T-shirt and shorts. He had a backpack slung over one shoulder but Rose wasn't paying much attention to that. She was distracted by a pair of very nice legs. Tanned and muscular, long and lean. He looked good in shorts.

Charlie was bouncing up and down on the spot, eager to get to the beach.

'Are you ready?' Mitch asked. 'I thought we'd take the tram, is that okay?'

'Of course.' The tram was something different and would take them directly from the city to the suburb of Glenelg, which had a beautiful beach and plenty of restaurants.

'The boys love the beach, that's one thing we don't have at home.'

Rose smiled. She could understand the attraction. The beach used to be a magical place for her too. She still found the salt air, the waves and the sunshine therapeutic, even if she tended to stay out of the water these days. She fell into step and they walked through the parklands towards the city.

The sun was low in the sky but there was still plenty of daylight left and the autumn air was warm. Mitch bought ice creams as they got off the tram and they ate them as they walked to the beach.

They found a spot not far from the jetty and Mitch pulled a towel from his backpack and spread it on the sand. The boys tore their shirts off, threw their shoes in a pile and ran straight into the water.

'Are you coming in?' Mitch asked as he stripped off his T-shirt. Rose's breath caught in her throat. Again.

He was seriously ripped. He looked lean when he was dressed, and he was, but undressed she could see that every muscle was exquisitely defined. She couldn't see one ounce of fat but she could see the perfect definition of his deltoids, biceps and abdominals. Riding around looking after his cattle must be good exercise. He was in unbelievable shape.

'I...' She couldn't think of what to say. She couldn't think at all when he was standing semi-naked in front of her. He looked incredible. This was far better than anything her imagination had conjured up, and she'd been imagining plenty. She was in serious trouble. 'I—I don't have bathers,' she stammered as she tried to stop ogling a man who had no reason whatsoever to be interested in her.

'Just roll up your trousers, the water is beautiful. You can at least get your toes wet.'

No way! Rose baulked. That wasn't going to happen. That would mean taking her shoes off. She shook her head. 'I'm fine here,' she said as she flopped down onto the towel. 'I have to finish my ice cream.'

'Okay. You know where we are.'

She nodded and squinted into the westerly afternoon sun as she watched Mitch walk down to the sea. He took Charlie's hands and helped him to jump over the small waves as Jed duck-dived under them. The sound of laughter carried to Rose on the light breeze. It was a glorious afternoon and she was more than happy to soak up the sunshine and relax.

She finished her ice cream and stood up and walked to the water's edge. The sea was sparklingly clear and she longed to take her shoes off and feel the ocean but it wasn't going to happen, not with crystal-clear water, there was absolutely nowhere to hide and she wasn't prepared to risk it. She walked to the jetty and back instead, the setting sun hot on her shoulders.

She sat on the sand. Scooping it up, she let it trickle through her fingers. She wanted to feel it under her feet. She could keep an eye on Mitch and the boys from where she sat. She'd have time to get her shoes back on before they could reach her. There was no one else nearby so she slipped off her shoes and wriggled her feet into the warm sand, making sure her toes were hidden. She sat and watched Mitch. He was standing deeper in the water now with his back to her. The sun silhouetted him against the blue sky, highlighting his broad shoulders, narrow waist and long legs. The boys were taking it in turns to stand on Mitch's hands and let him lift them out of the water before he launched them into the sea off his makeshift diving board. From a distance Rose could imagine his muscles flexing and relaxing as he picked up the boys. She could remember her father doing the same with her when she was little.

She heard Mitch calling to Jed. 'Last turn, then I'm hopping out.'

She brushed the sand off her feet, using Mitch's towel to quickly wipe the sand from between her toes and over her scars. Her feet were warm and the sand stuck to her skin, she wasn't going to get it all off in time. Her heart was racing. She'd have to put her shoes on, sandy feet and all. A few grains of sand in her shoes was preferable to exposing her feet to the scrutiny of others. She shoved her right foot into her shoe and tied the laces just as the boys ran up the beach towards her.

'Can we make a castle and a moat?'

Mitch had followed behind them and he replied, 'Sure,' as he pulled another towel from the backpack and started to dry himself off.

Rose wanted to look elsewhere but found it impossible. Even as she pulled her left shoe on her eyes were drawn to him. He was standing next to her and she looked up as he towelled his hair dry. The towel covered his face and she took the opportunity to check him out. His shoulders were broad, his arms muscular, his chest and abdominals perfectly sculpted. There was a dark 'V' angling down from his neck where his skin was more darkly tanned but that stark contrast just served to highlight his chest, which, while olive toned, obviously hadn't had the same sun exposure. The water droplets on his skin glistened in the sun before they were swiftly mopped up.

He dropped the towel on the sand and sat beside her. His knees were bent and he leant forward, resting his forearms on his kneecaps as he watched the boys constructing their moat. Jed had commandeered a bucket and spade from Mitch's bag and had sent Charlie running backwards and forwards to the sea as they tried to fill the moat but the water seeped into the dry sand faster than Charlie could bring it back.

Mitch turned his head to look at her. 'The boys said they had fun in the classroom today.'

She smiled. 'I think the beach might trump that, though.'

'Possibly,' he said as he shrugged his gorgeous shoulders. 'You can't win them all, I suppose. It must be an interesting job, though. Do you enjoy it?'

'I love it but it's pretty new still, I've only been working there for a few months.'

'Is it a long-term proposition?'

'I'm not sure.' It was actually only a relief position as she was covering another teacher's maternity leave, but there was no need to go into detail about that. She wasn't sure what she would do when the contract ended but she hoped she might get offered another one. She had no great aspirations to do anything else. She didn't want to travel the world like Ruby neither did she have massive career goals like Scarlett. She enjoyed being a teacher but one of the biggest attractions for her was that it was something that she could continue to do once she was married with a family of her own. That was her ultimate goal. Even with the dramas of the past two years, her dreams for the future hadn't changed. She hadn't suddenly developed a desire to see the world or climb mountains or save the planet—her illness had just intensified her desire for a family of her own, but she was reluctant to share that with Mitch.

Rose wasn't quite meeting his eyes any more and Mitch knew there was something she wasn't telling him. He shouldn't be able to tell, he barely knew her, but she was twisting her hair in her fingers again and already he knew that was a sign that she was uncomfortable.

She let her hair fall over her shoulder and the wind picked it up, blowing it across her face. She brushed it aside and looked out to sea. The wind had strengthened. Mitch saw grains of sand swirling along the beach.

'There's a storm coming,' Rose said.

Mitch looked out across the gulf. Clouds had gathered to the west and he could see ghostly fingers stretching from the clouds to the sea, the tell-tale streaks of rain. The water was getting rougher too, there were whitecaps further out in the gulf, dancing on top of the waves as they spread towards the beach, moving closer with the wind.

'We need to get off the beach in case it's an electrical storm,' Rose added.

'Let's go and get something to eat,' Mitch suggested. The boys had given up trying to fill the moat and instead were busy constructing extra towers for the castle. He didn't think they'd object to moving if food was being offered. He started gathering towels and buckets and spades. 'Fish and chips, burgers or pizza?' he asked as the boys looked up.

'Pizza!'

They collected their things but the storm was faster than they were and by the time they were crossing the grassy strip between the beach and the shops the rain was pelting down, hammering on the tin roofs of the buildings and pouring down the street.

Charlie froze as the wind and rain buffeted him from behind.

'Come on, Charlie, it's only water.'

His lip quivered. Mitch wrapped an arm around his waist and lifted him onto his hip, hurrying to get out of the weather. The backpack slipped off his shoulder and Rose reached out and grabbed it, taking it from him, lightening the load.

'Is he okay?' she mouthed at him over Charlie's head.

'He hasn't seen rain before.'

'Seriously?'

'It hasn't rained on the station for three years,' he said as he stepped under the protection of the shop verandas. 'The last time it rained he was just a baby.' There were other things Charlie was too young to remember as well and Mitch still wasn't sure if that was a blessing or a curse.

He stopped under the shelter but didn't put Charlie down. 'It's okay, buddy, we're safe here. A bit wet, though.'

They were all drenched. It wasn't such a big deal for him and the boys as they were still in their bathers but

Rose was a different story. She had raindrops caught on her eyelashes and her hair was soaking wet but somehow she still managed to look beautiful. Her shirt clung to her skin, outlining every curve. Mitch wasn't sure where to look so he turned his gaze to the street, looking for somewhere to eat. Somewhere to escape to.

'Let's find somewhere to dry off,' he said as he continued to walk down Jetty Road. He took refuge in the first pizza bar he found. The boys needed feeding and he needed to take a breath.

'I'm just going to duck to the ladies' room. I need to dry off and there should be a hand dryer in there.'

That sounded like a good idea to Mitch. The sooner Rose's clothes were dry the sooner he'd be able to concentrate again.

By the time she returned he'd got the boys settled at a table. Rose had dried off a little. Her shirt wasn't clinging to her any more, which was a bit of a shame in his opinion, but at least he could now focus on the menu. It was pretty simple, pizzas and some pasta dishes, but he knew he would have had trouble deciphering even that much with Rose sitting across from him looking like a contestant in a wet T-shirt competition.

'What would you like to eat?' he asked, handing her a menu.

'What are you having?'

'Meat lovers for the boys, we've got to keep the cattle farmers in business, and seafood for me. You're welcome to share either of those.'

'I think I'll have a Margherita,' she replied, without even glancing at the options.

'Are you vegetarian?' he asked. He was disappointed to think she might be; vegetarians were not a good fit for him.

He tried to tell himself that he wondered about everyone and their carnivorous habits but he knew that wasn't true.

Rose shook her head. 'No, I just feel like a Margherita,' she said as the waitress put a jug of water and four glasses on their table. Once he'd placed their order she picked up the thread of their earlier conversation. 'How do you manage on the station for three years without rain?'

'There's a creek—a river, really—running through the property, but it's dry now. Luckily we also have artesian bores but I'm having to decrease stock and if we don't get rain soon we'll be in real trouble.'

'You said the station is about the size of Kangaroo Island. How big is that exactly?'

'One million acres.'

'Wow!'

'Have you ever been to the Outback?'

'No.' Rose shook her head. 'I haven't travelled much at all but I have been to Queensland's Sunshine Coast to visit my sister.'

'That's pretty,' he told her, 'but nothing remotely like our part of Queensland. We have wide open spaces and enormous blue skies. You can see for ever.' People always mentioned the wide open space but, for Mitch, it was the sky that he missed when he was away from home. 'You get the same colour sky down here but for some reason you can't see as far. I think it's the haze of the city. We get a lot of dust but when it settles the air is clear and clean. When people imagine the Outback they think of the colour red, and it is red, redder than you can picture, but there are plenty of other colours too. Blue and green, grey and white. The pink breasts of the galahs. The yellow of the sulphur-crested cockatoos. Purple and orange sunsets. Bright green tree frogs.'

'It sounds beautiful,' Rose sighed.

'It is.' As difficult as it could be at times, Mitch couldn't imagine leaving. There were a number of reasons keeping him there but one was the fact that he did love it. There really was no place like it.

Mitch looked sad. From her seat Rose could see out to the street, looking east towards the hills. The sun came out and she could see a rainbow form in the moisture that still blanketed the hills.

'Charlie, come with me, there's something I want you to see.' She stood up and held out her hand for Charlie; she was counting on the fact that Mitch would come too and she would be able to distract him from his sombre thoughts.

Charlie hopped up from his seat and took her hand. The sky over the ocean was clear again, the rain clouds having moved east, and there was a bright rainbow over the hills. Rose turned Charlie so he faced east. If he'd never seen rain, she was certain he would never have seen a rainbow and this one was fabulous. It was strong and crisp and she could clearly see six of the colours, and imagined she could also just make out a narrow band of indigo.

She pointed to the sky. Charlie's mouth dropped open and he turned to Mitch who, as Rose had hoped, had followed them outside.

'Dad, Dad, look, it's a rainbow.'

'Isn't it beautiful?' Rose said. Charlie's expression was priceless, a combination of surprise, delight and enchantment, and Rose turned around, unable to resist seeing Mitch's reaction to his son's glee.

'Yes, it is,' he replied.

Rose had expected him to be looking at Charlie or the rainbow but he was staring at her. She felt herself blush under his gaze.

It had been a long time since he'd seen anything so beautiful, Mitch thought as Rose looked at him. The sun shone on her face, making her glow, turning her golden and reminding him of the day he'd first met her.

She was twisting her hair around her fingers and he realised he was staring, making her uncomfortable. She broke eye contact, turning back to the hills and squatting down beside his son. 'Tell me what colours you can see, Charlie.'

All Mitch could see were two blonde heads together. Any stranger watching this scene would have mistaken Rose and Charlie for mother and son. He felt a pang of loneliness; Charlie barely remembered his mother.

Mitch missed Cara but more than that he missed having company. He thought the children were doing okay; they couldn't miss what they didn't remember, right? But deep down he knew that something was lacking in their lives. Female attention. They all missed it, him included, even if they weren't knowingly aware of it. It was an innate, unconscious need that lived within all of them.

But he was thinking about more than what was missing from *their* lives. He was thinking about what was missing from *his* life. More specifically, he was thinking about sex. He'd been thinking about sex a lot lately, ever since he'd met Rose. It was something he enjoyed but he'd got used to it not being a regular part of his life. Since meeting Rose he couldn't seem to *stop* thinking about it.

He felt Jed's hand seek his. His son tugged on his fingers, seeking attention and providing some distraction from some untimely thoughts. 'Can we look for the pot of gold?' he asked.

'The end of the rainbow is a long way away, Jed,' Mitch replied as he noticed the waitress bringing pizzas to the table, 'and your dinner is ready. It's time to eat.' Time to concentrate on a different simple and basic need. Food was as basic and simple as sex but he couldn't afford to be thinking about sex. He had children to look after.

The boys tucked into their pizza with gusto. The fresh sea air, the water and the exercise had made them ravenous.

Rose took small, deliberate bites and talked while they ate. 'When do you think you might be able to take Lila home?'

'I'm not sure. We're a long way from any rehabilitation services so that is going to affect her discharge. It would be a completely different story if we lived in the city.'

'How far are you?'

'It's a five-hour drive, one way, to the nearest hospital and physio, which makes it difficult. We're used to those distances, everything is far away, but it will mean an overnight stay every time Lila needs an appointment so realistically she won't be discharged until she doesn't need intensive physio. Even our next-door neighbours are three hours away.'

'That makes it tricky to borrow a cup of sugar.' Rose smiled.

Mitch laughed. 'We've become experts at ordering supplies. The truck only comes once a month although that's one benefit of the drought, the trucks can get through.'

'It sounds very isolated—don't you get lonely?'

He did get lonely but he wasn't about to admit it. 'It's not as isolated as you might imagine. There are about fifteen people living on the station with me, not counting my kids.'

'Fifteen! Why so many?'

'We have to be reasonably self-sufficient so there's the children's governess, the cook, a mechanic and his wife, and a pilot as well as the station hands. So there's plenty of company and there's always something happening somewhere nearby if we get cabin fever.'

'By nearby you mean several hours' drive away?'

He nodded. 'Mostly. But we're used to that.'

'How long have you lived there?' Rose asked as she picked up another slice of pizza.

'Almost ten years. We moved there after my wife's brother died. He was killed in a car accident and Cara's mum was diagnosed with breast cancer around the same time so they moved to Brisbane for treatment and there was no one else to run the station. We had to move. Cara's mum died just before Lila was born.'

'And your father-in-law? Where is he now?'

Mitch didn't mind talking about the circumstances that had led to him living on the station. The boys weren't paying any attention to their conversation, they were far too engrossed in their pizza and talking about people they had never met, or barely remembered, wasn't going to bother them. 'Also gone. He had a heart attack about eighteen months ago but I think he really died of a broken heart. After he lost Cara his entire family was gone, other than the grandchildren, and I think he just gave up. I'd asked him to come back to the station but he'd said he couldn't face it. Too many memories.'

'That's been a tough few years for you.'

Mitch preferred not to think about it. He preferred to keep busy, which didn't leave time to dwell on the past. But seeing it from an outsider's point of view it did sound stressful. No wonder everyone kept wanting him to have counselling. But talking about the basic, straightforward facts was one thing, talking about his feelings was another matter entirely. He was doing fine, the kids were fine, everything was okay. Loneliness wasn't a disease.

'What about *your* family, where are they?' Rose continued when he didn't reply to her earlier comment.

'Scattered,' he replied as he picked up the last piece of his pizza, surprising himself. He'd barely noticed that he'd been eating. 'We grew up in Mt Isa. Dad was an engineer on the mine, my siblings and I all went to boarding school and now we're spread everywhere. My parents retired to Townsville, I have one sister in Perth and another in Singapore. The station might technically be the halfway point but it's not easy to get to so we don't catch up all that often.'

The boys had demolished their pizza but were now both yawning. Charlie looked as if he was about to fall asleep at the table. Mitch was enjoying himself, and he couldn't remember when he'd last felt so relaxed. Rose was easy company, a breath of fresh air, but if he didn't get the boys home soon the evening was likely to go downhill very quickly.

He paid the bill and hailed a taxi to take them back to the city. By the time they were dropped at their short-stay apartment both boys had fallen asleep. Rose offered to carry Charlie inside and Mitch picked up Jed. He put them to bed and offered Rose a cup of tea. Anything to prolong the evening.

'Do you have any hot chocolate?' Rose asked.

He could see goose-bumps on her arms, and she was obviously feeling the cold. It was then that he noticed that her shoes were still wet from the earlier downpour.

'Sure,' he replied, looking at her feet. 'Why don't you take your shoes off? I'll stuff them with some newspaper to dry them out.'

'No, it's fine. It can wait till I get home.' Her feet were cold and uncomfortable and she couldn't wait to get her shoes off but there was no way she was going to do that in front of Mitch.

'Are you sure?'

'Positive.' She drank her hot chocolate as quickly as possible and made her excuses. 'I should get going,' she said as she stood up from the small kitchen table. She wasn't in any hurry to say goodnight but she needed to get out of her shoes. 'I'll call a taxi.'

'Can you drive a manual?' Mitch asked.

'Yes.'

'Why don't you take my car?'

'No.' Rose shook her head. 'I can't do that. You might need it.'

'The hospital is only around the corner. There's no other reason I would need it. If I could I would drive you but I can't leave the boys on their own. It will make me feel better if you take it.'

Mitch had stood up too. He was standing very close to her. If she reached out a hand she'd be able to touch him. She lifted her chin and looked up at him. He was watching her with his dark eyes and for one crazy moment she wondered if he was about to kiss her…

But he didn't reach for her, he reached to his left and picked up his car keys.

'Bring it back to me in the morning on your way to work,' he said as he handed her the keys. 'That way I know I get to see you again.'

Rose floated home. Okay, so he hadn't kissed her but he wanted to see her again! That was almost as good.

'The kettle's just boiled, have you got time for a cup of tea?' Mitch asked when she arrived back at the apartment the following morning.

'That sounds lovely, thank you,' she said as she took the same chair she'd had last night. 'White and one.'

'The weather bureau is forecasting more rain for tomorrow,' Mitch said as he put her tea on the table. 'I'm thinking of taking the boys to an indoor trampolining venue. They love trampolines, but I won't let them have one at home. They're way too dangerous.'

'And horses and motorbikes aren't?' Rose asked. She knew Mitch allowed the children to ride horses and motorbikes and she couldn't see what the difference was. Horse-riding was obviously dangerous, it had put Lila in hospital.

'Growing up on a station they're going to be exposed to motorbikes, cars and horses so they need to understand the risks and learn how to manage them. Trampolines are a different story. More children end up in hospital from trampoline accidents than from horse-riding and motorbike accidents.'

'And you don't think that's because more children have trampolines, so statistically it's going to happen more often?'

'Fair point,' he conceded, 'but it doesn't mean I want to invite an accident. But I wanted to invite you to come with us.'

Rose thought it sounded like fun but she already had plans. 'I have to look after my niece tomorrow. Scarlett is working and her husband is on nights so he'll come home and sleep for the morning while I look after Holly.'

'We'll go after lunch, then,' he declared. 'We can spend the morning with Lila and I'll book a time for the afternoon. How does that sound?'

'Perfect,' she said.

Mitch checked them all in at the front counter and handed them each a pair of socks with rubber soles.

'What are these for?' Rose asked.

'Trampolining socks,' he said. 'A safety requirement. Apparently they stop you from slipping on the mats.'

Once again, Mitch had chosen an activity that involved her taking her shoes off. First the beach, then getting her shoes wet in the storm. How many more times could she avoid the situation? She held the socks in her hand as she tried to figure out a way around this latest dilemma.

She went to the toilets and changed her socks. It might

seem like odd behaviour but she couldn't think of any other way around it if she didn't want to expose her feet. She checked to make sure her feet looked relatively normal in the rubber-soled socks; if her missing toes were obvious she would have to make excuses not to jump, but the socks were black, the same colour as the trampolines and, she hoped, with the constant movement no one would notice her misshapen foot. She put her shoes back on, only removing them again to store them in a locker when it was their turn on the trampolines.

The boys launched themselves from the viewing platform at one end of the massive trampolines onto adjacent mats. Rose hesitated, not quite sure of the approach etiquette for those past their teenage years. Mitch jumped down onto a third mat and held out his hand to her.

Rose took it, prepared this time for the shock of awareness that bolted through her.

The boys were happily doing flips on their trampolines, calling out constantly for Mitch to watch them. Rose bounced a little more sedately but despite her cautious technique she fell over several times. Her balance was appalling—trampolining was obviously not a sport for someone who was missing a few toes.

'I don't think I'll be trying out for the Olympics any time soon,' she joked after a few minutes of unsuccessful bouncing. 'I think I might have a rest.'

Mitch helped her off the mat and they moved back to the viewing platform from where they could watch the boys, who were now trying to bounce and throw basketballs through a hoop. Watching the boys was more fun than trying to master the art of trampolining for herself.

'I'm going to grab a bottle of water—can I get you one?' Rose asked.

She stopped at her locker and quickly changed her socks

after buying the water. She didn't intend to jump again and she knew she would feel more comfortable once she had her shoes back on. She hooked her handbag over her shoulder and went to lean on the railing next to Mitch.

'Are you okay?' he asked when she returned.

Rose frowned. 'Why do you ask?'

'Your balance was a bit off.'

'I'm just clumsy.'

'You're not dizzy? You don't have a headache or earache?'

'No, I'm perfectly fine,' she replied, hoping he wouldn't catch her out in a little white lie.

'Are you sure? Because a few other things have caught my attention…'

Rose's heart beat a rapid tattoo in her chest. Oh, God, was this when he was going to tell her he'd noticed her foot? Was he going to ask her what had happened? She swallowed nervously and asked, 'Like what?'

'You drink a lot of water and go to the bathroom often and my sixth sense says it's more than clumsiness.'

Sixth sense? What was he talking about?

She let her gaze wander around the venue as she debated whether she should ask him to explain. Was that inviting questions that she wouldn't want to answer? Did she want to open that door?

She didn't think so but before she could make a firm decision her attention was diverted by another jumper making a very ungainly landing. She heard her own sharp intake of breath as she waited for him to get to his feet.

Mitch looked sideways at her as she gasped.

'What?' he asked.

She pointed to the trampoline at the far end of the cavernous building. 'That man! He just flipped backwards and landed on his head and now he's not moving.'

The man lay face down and motionless on the trampoline and everyone else around also appeared frozen to the spot. Rose was aware of a collective holding of breath as they waited to see what would happen next. Someone had to do something.

Another young man on the adjacent trampoline stepped across and knelt beside him. He looked as though he was going to try to turn him over.

'Stop!'

Rose almost jumped out of her skin as Mitch bellowed beside her and she was aware that Jed and Charlie had stopped jumping and turned to look up at the sound of their father's voice, obviously thinking they had done something wrong.

Mitch broke into a run. 'Don't move him!' he yelled as he sprinted along the viewing catwalk and headed for the stairs.

Rose saw the young man hesitate and look up to where Mitch was racing along above him. Everyone in the entire centre had stopped in their tracks, paralysed by the urgency in Mitch's voice.

Rose wasn't sure what she should do. Should she supervise the boys or follow Mitch? She glanced at the boys. They would be okay for a few minutes, they'd be better off continuing to shoot hoops. 'It's okay, boys,' she called down to them, 'keep playing.' Then she took off after Mitch. Not at a run, she couldn't manage that, but she followed as fast as she was able.

By the time she reached floor level Mitch was already on the trampoline with the injured jumper.

'What's his name?' he was asking.

'Jason.'

He put his hand very gently on Jason's shoulder. 'Jason, can you hear me?' he asked.

There was no response.

Mitch moved his hand around to Jason's neck and rested his fingers over his carotid artery before carefully sliding his fingers under his nose.

'Call an ambulance,' Mitch said to no one in particular.

The staff seemed hesitant and unsure. Rose had her phone in her bag. She pulled it out and punched in the numbers, it would be faster for her to call 000 and then Mitch could talk to the dispatch centre. She didn't know how but he seemed to know what he was doing.

'Do you have a neck brace?' he asked a staff member as she waited for the call to connect. She was put through to the ambulance service and gave the address details and passed the phone to Mitch. 'They want to talk to you,' she said. 'Can you do that or do you want me to relay messages?'

Mitch reached for the phone. 'He's unconscious but breathing,' he said. 'Possible spinal injury. It's a priority two.'

There was a pause while the dispatcher was talking.

'I'm a doctor,' Mitch responded.

Rose blinked and listened for more. Had he just said he was a doctor?

'Yes, I'll stay on the line,' he said.

'What are you doing?' she couldn't help but ask as Mitch continued to kneel by the unconscious man. What was going on?

Mitch looked across at her. She was standing on the floor and from where he knelt on the trampoline their eyes were level. His eyes were dark and unfathomable and Rose wasn't sure that he was even seeing her properly. He certainly didn't answer her question.

'Can you get the boys and get them changed?' he said. 'Wait in the car for me, the keys are in the locker.'

Rose knew he wanted his children out of the way when the ambulance arrived. Her questions could wait.

She had to wait longer than she wanted; she didn't get to ask anything further until they were back at Mitch's apartment. He'd told her Jason had regained consciousness. He was still worried about a spinal injury but the ambulance had left the venue without sirens and flashing lights so hopefully it wouldn't be as bad as he'd first anticipated. He'd told her all that but he hadn't mentioned the thing she really wanted to know about.

'Are you going to tell me about the rest of it?' she asked. 'What happened back there? You're a *doctor*?'

'I *was* a doctor,' he replied.

Was, he'd said, not *am*. 'How do you stop being a doctor?'

'It's a long story.'

Rose saw a flash of something in his dark brown eyes. Was it pain, sorrow or regret? She wasn't sure but she wondered what the story was.

She opened her mouth to ask the question but he cut her off before she could speak. 'Let's just say it's not compatible with station life. But…' he shrugged '…it doesn't mean I've forgotten everything I learnt. That's why I was asking if you were all right before Jason's accident. I noticed your balance was a bit off and I was worried.'

The sixth sense he'd mentioned. Only it wasn't a sixth sense, it was seven years of medical school and who knew how many years of practising medicine. Rose couldn't believe what she was hearing.

'So, are you okay? Any headaches? Dizziness?' he asked again.

Rose shook her head. After the afternoon they'd had he was still going to quiz her on her health?

'I don't have a headache. I'm not dizzy or nauseous. There's nothing sinister going on. I'm fine now.'

'Now?'

Rose nodded. Knowing he was a doctor changed things a little—it would be less awkward explaining it to him. 'I only have one functioning kidney,' she told him, 'and it isn't mine.'

Mitch frowned and then she saw him do the maths. 'You had a kidney transplant?'

She nodded again.

'When?'

'Eighteen months ago. I contracted bacterial meningitis two years ago. I was in a coma for nine days but while I survived my kidneys didn't fare so well.'

Her transplant wasn't a secret. She was happy to talk about it. She'd discussed it often enough with her counsellor and with children in the hospital and she felt comfortable talking to Mitch. Their late-night conversations had given them a connection and he was easy to talk to. She didn't mind *talking* about her transplant, she was only reluctant for people to see her toes. Her abdominal scars didn't bother her, they were nothing out of the ordinary, but her disfigured toes were another story.

'So now I have three kidneys. My two useless ones and a new one. So, yes, I do drink a lot of water and when I go to the bathroom sometimes it's to take my immunosuppressant medication. I don't want to take tablets in front of the children.'

Mitch was nodding. Rose knew that most of what she'd told him made sense. It didn't explain her crappy balance but that was a story for another day.

'Your donor? Was it someone in your family?'

'No. My mum and Ruby weren't a match and Scarlett

was pregnant at the time and unlikely to be compatible if the others weren't.'

'Why do you say that?'

'We're half-sisters. Same mother but different fathers.'

'What about your father's side of the family?'

'My dad died when I was eight. There is no one else.'

Mitch had limited experience with transplant medicine. He'd been a country doctor and specialised medicine like transplant surgery was always dealt with in the city. He knew some of the theory but was less familiar with the practical side of things, though he knew enough to know that exposure to infection posed a serious risk. 'Surely a hospital is the last place you should be working, given the risk of infection?' The doctor in him, the doctor he tried so hard to forget, couldn't resist asking the question. And, as long as they continued to talk about her, the topic of his past could stay buried, which was just how he liked it.

'I had to be extra careful in the first twelve months after surgery not to get sick. I still need to be careful but it's been eighteen months now. I'm not allowed to work with children who have recently had live vaccines like polio or measles, mumps and rubella, but if the children are infectious they're not allowed into the classroom at all anyway. There are plenty of other patients who can't afford to get an infection—our cystic fibrosis patients, our chemotherapy patients—it's not just me. So it's actually a better environment for me, it's far more controlled than it would be working in a normal primary school where children will turn up after having vaccinations or when they have a cold. And working in the hospital is less tiring.' She smiled. 'There's no yard duty, no early mornings, no late-night parent interviews or concerts, no excursions. It's pretty easy.'

To someone who hadn't spent fifteen years learning how to read body language, learning to listen for the unspoken worry or to pick up on the seemingly innocuous sign, Rose would seem quite relaxed. As if she'd dealt with her situation, come to terms with it and moved on, but he still sensed that something wasn't quite right. It might not be major but he would bet money there was still something bothering her. This time he wasn't relying on his sixth sense to tell him—Rose was playing with her hair. She was uncomfortable about something.

He was intrigued enough to dig deeper but recognised that it really wasn't any of his business. He didn't need to ask questions. He didn't need to research transplant medicine. His days of practising medicine were finished. And Rose wasn't his patient.

He should forget about it. Forget about her. But he knew that was going to be difficult.

He wished he could remain an impartial spectator but he knew that was impossible. Just like today he had found it difficult to stand by and do nothing. No matter how often he told himself he wasn't a doctor any more, his training couldn't be obliterated entirely and he knew there was more to Rose's story. His sixth sense was working overtime.

He knew he should forget about her, he didn't need to know what was wrong, but he hadn't been able to stop thinking about her. He couldn't get her out of his head and now, more than ever, he knew he would continue to think about her, for all sorts of reasons. The timing wasn't right and neither were the logistics. He was only in Adelaide temporarily and had two young children in tow plus another in hospital. And he was leaving town again tomorrow. He'd be back once more to collect Lila when she was discharged and that was it. It was hardly the right time or place to develop a fascination with a woman and definitely not the time or place to get involved with her.

But that didn't stop him wishing things were different. It

had been years since anyone had captured his attention like Rose had and that was proving difficult to ignore. Perhaps his period of mourning was actually over. He hated being alone on the station, and right now he'd give anything for a chance to have a night, even a few hours, alone with Rose.

But there was no point starting something he couldn't finish.

His timing sucked.

CHAPTER SIX

THIS WAS IT.

This was the end.

Lila would be discharged on Monday, which meant Mitch would have no reason to return to Adelaide. Rose wouldn't see him any more. She'd missed her chance.

Not that he'd really given her a chance.

Should she have pushed him? The old Rose wouldn't have hesitated. But the old Rose had been full of confidence. The old Rose had never been rejected. The new Rose wasn't brave enough to make the first move. She was too scared of what would happen next. Too afraid now of physical intimacy. It was too much of a risk for just one night. She wasn't brave enough.

She wasn't ready. But she knew she was going to regret it.

Time had dragged when Mitch was back on the station. The frequent phone calls were no longer enough. She wanted to see him smile. She wanted to touch him.

The past two weeks since he'd headed north again had seemed like an eternity and she had no idea how she was going to survive once he was gone for good.

She hadn't been able to stop thinking about him. Her libido had well and truly come alive again but it was too late.

Maybe she should have taken a chance, she thought as

she pulled to a stop in front of the apartment complex where Mitch and the boys were staying again.

What was the worst that could happen? If he rejected her she could live with that. Maybe. At least if she did get rebuffed she wasn't likely to bump into him in the street and be forced to live out her humiliation all over again. Maybe it was a case of now or never. Maybe it was time for her to move forward. Maybe if she got the opportunity she should take it and see what happened.

Maybe she should be brave.

Mitch had asked if she could do him a favour and look after the boys for a couple of hours while he attended some meetings. She'd agreed without hesitation, not even bothering to find out what the meetings were. It didn't matter. All that mattered was having another chance to see him again.

'Hi,' he greeted her with a kiss on the cheek and Rose bit back her disappointment. Was that all their relationship was ever going to be now? A platonic kiss on the cheek? Had she really missed her chance to experience him? 'Thanks so much for doing this,' he said as he stepped back to let her into the apartment.

'It's a pleasure,' she said as the boys came running out of their bedroom to greet her. Charlie had his arms in the air, imploring her to pick him up, and she was happy to oblige. She lifted him onto her hip and hugged him tight, loving the way his little soft body felt in her arms. She blinked back tears. What was the matter with her?

She knew what it was. Unresolved desire. Her hormones were driving her crazy.

'I thought I'd take the boys down to the River Torrens, we might go for a boat ride on *Popeye,* depending on how long you'll be,' she said.

'I'll be a couple of hours. I hope that's okay? I have appointments to interview new governesses. In all the drama with Lila and all the backwards and forwards to town I'd completely forgotten that Ginny is about to go off backpacking around Europe. She advertised for a replacement from up our way but there hasn't been anyone suitable so she's set up some interviews down here. I'll call you as soon as I'm done and meet you in town.'

Rose gathered the boys and the backpack Mitch had filled for her with spare clothes, drink bottles and snacks.

She enjoyed spending time with Mitch's boys. It was almost as good as spending time with him but even so she was more than happy to see his smiling face when he arrived at the river bank.

'How did the interviews go?' she asked, as she handed him a packet of biscuits in exchange for a hot chocolate he had brought for her.

'Not great,' he sighed as he sat on the bench beside her. 'I had hoped that *one* of the three might have been okay. I'd hoped I'd be able to introduce them to the kids and then offer them the position and have it all sorted by the time we leave on Monday, but I'm back to square one.'

'What was wrong with them?'

Mitch chewed his biscuit and watched the boys throw bread to the ducks while he deliberated over his answer. 'I know one wouldn't cope with being stuck out in the middle of nowhere, she was far too high maintenance *and* a vegetarian. Can you imagine, on a cattle station? Some days we have red meat with every meal.'

'Maybe she was just trying to make a good impression.'

Mitch laughed. 'Well, that wasn't the way to go about it. The second one was a German tourist; she's studying to be a teacher but her visa means she can only work in a job for three months before having to move. I don't want to go through this all again in a couple of months' time.'

'Why did you even interview her?'

'I'm desperate. Ginny leaves in two weeks.'

'And the third one?'

'She was an older lady who was very old school. My kids are young and busy and they need to have fun still. I realise they need schooling but there are sports camps, rodeos, swimming in the creek when we have water, and I just can't see Mrs Abbott doing any of that.'

'And there was no one from up your way?'

Mitch shook his head. 'No. It's really difficult at this time of year. Governesses have been in their positions for less than a term, it's too soon for them to decide they don't fit with the family and want to move on and I can't manage without anyone. It's not just the schooling, it wouldn't matter if they missed a few weeks of that, but I'm going to need someone who can drive Lila to town for her appointments and rehab. Those trips will need overnight stays; I can't keep leaving the station and I can't always take the boys. Our staff numbers are low, I've had to let a lot of casual staff go because of the drought, and I really don't have the spare manpower. I'm already stretched thin.'

'Do you think I could do it?' Rose couldn't resist offering to help. She'd been mulling over the idea ever since Mitch had told her what was happening that morning. In her mind she'd come up with the perfect solution. Mitch needed help, help she was qualified to offer, and she wouldn't have to say goodbye. To him or the kids. She'd grown attached to Lila and the boys and she didn't want anyone else taking what she already pictured as her place.

'You?'

She nodded. 'It's what I'm trained to do.' Her voice was eager as she tried to convince Mitch that her idea made sense. 'If I can manage a classroom of nine-year-olds I think I can manage your three.' She couldn't physically manage a classroom of nine-year-olds, which was one of the reasons why the low-key hospital teaching job suited her, but she didn't share that information. 'I could come out there. Just for a few months,' she added, as she didn't want to seem too pushy. 'It would give you some breathing space, some time to find someone else. I'm qualified. I'm not a vegetarian. I can help with Lila and the kids already know me.'

'But you have a job.'

'I'm actually only on contract covering someone's maternity leave. She's due back at work next term and I've applied for another contract but that will depend on whether or not there's work. I won't be letting anyone down,' she insisted. 'I could do this.'

Please, say yes, she thought.

'Do you realise what it would be like? It's not a Monday to Friday job. There're not too many places to go when you knock off for the day. Actually, there's nowhere to go. We're five hours from the nearest town. You'll spend days and days on the station surrounded by the same people, eating together, socialising together, and even if you're not with the children they'll never be far away. You don't get to go home to your own space.'

It didn't sound very different to her life now. She didn't go out much any more; she'd probably have more company on the station than she had in the city. She didn't need the bright city lights. What she needed was room to breathe. Space. And Mitch would be there. She thought the station would be perfect.

'It's nothing like you might imagine, Rose,' Mitch continued. 'I don't know what you've seen on television but the reality is very different from the movies. There's a reason that movies depicting the end of the world or a desolate future civilisation are shot out my way. We haven't had rain for three years, it's a huge red dust bowl. It's stinking hot and the flies will drive you crazy.'

'But yet you're still there.' Rose smiled. 'There have to be some redeeming features.'

There were plenty of redeeming features but Mitch wasn't sure a city girl would see them in quite the same light. Lord knew, there'd been plenty of times in the past two years when he would have happily chucked it all in, redeeming features or not, but he'd kept going.

'It's my home. It's my kids' home.'

The station belonged to his children; they would inherit it, and he was just the custodian, but he owed it to them to keep it going. There were plenty of times when he could have happily given it away—it wouldn't fetch much if he tried to sell it, not in the current market—but it wasn't in his nature to give up and he did love it. He could cope with the stress caused by Mother Nature, he was used to the stress of life on a cattle station and that was preferable to the stress of moving to town.

Besides, what would he do then? The Outback got under your skin, into your blood, and he couldn't really imagine leaving for ever, but a break every now and then would be nice. Just to have the opportunity to get away, to recharge his batteries. Perhaps if he had someone to share his life with he wouldn't feel so pressured. Having someone else to help shoulder the burden would make a difference. But that wasn't a governess's role.

But Rose didn't need to know all that. The Outback was no place for her.

'What about your health? We're out in the middle of nowhere.'

'I'm perfectly stable. As long as I have my medication there's no problem. You're so isolated I imagine there's less chance of me picking up an infection out there than in town. But if you don't want me there, just tell me.'

But he *did* want her there. That was the problem. He could imagine sitting down at the end of the day and sharing a drink with her on the veranda. She was easy company and gorgeous, and therein lay the problem. He was attracted to her but he didn't want to risk bringing her out to the station. But that begged the question of *why* he felt like that. What was at stake?

He knew he was worried he might do something he'd regret. He might find temptation too strong. It wasn't that he intended to stay celibate for the rest of his life—he hadn't considered himself celibate at all—but he was planning on staying single and he didn't think Rose was the type of girl he should fool around with. She was only twenty-three, still young, just out of teacher's college, just a girl really compared to him. He was thirty-nine, jaded and weary. It would be completely inappropriate.

'All I'm asking you to do is think about it,' Rose said. 'Think about what other options you've got and get back to me.'

'Okay,' he agreed. Would it really be so terrible just to consider her offer? He knew he'd like to have her company but he wasn't sure if offering her the job was the sensible thing to do. In fact, he was pretty certain it wasn't at all sensible. But for purely selfish reasons he would consider it.

He'd agreed to think about it! Rose crossed her fingers in her lap. She was counting on the fact he didn't have any other options. They both knew that. She had decided it was time to be brave, and this was her being brave.

Plus, she thought it sounded so romantic, living on a remote cattle station. She could imagine herself in riding boots and a stockman's hat. Not actually on a horse as she didn't know how to ride, but she liked the outfit. She'd plant a vegetable garden with the children and teach them about the wide world. Not that she'd travelled far.

Was she crazy, trying to convince Mitch to hire her? He was right, she didn't know the first thing about living in a remote place.

But she did know about children. And whatever else she didn't know, she'd learn.

'The boys are asleep,' Rose said as she returned to the living room after reading them a bedtime story.

He'd invited her to stay for dinner. It was just a takeaway but this was likely to be the last night he'd have the pleasure of her company. Once he took Lila home that would be it. Unless he offered Rose the job she wanted. But that wasn't going to happen. That would be madness.

He handed her the small glass of wine that was still half-full.

She hitched her dress up above her knees as she tucked one leg under her and sat on the couch beside him. The apartment was small and sparsely furnished, and there wasn't really anywhere else to sit but tonight Mitch was very aware of how close she was. He hadn't seen her in a dress before. It was made out of stretchy cotton, nothing fancy, but it hugged her slight curves and showed off her smooth, toned legs.

She sipped her wine and leant forward, placing it on the coffee table. He could feel her body heat, smell her perfume. She smelt like roses.

Her dress pulled tight across her chest as she leant forward, drawing his eyes to her breasts. They were small and pert, perfectly shaped, and her nipples were erect, jutting against the soft cotton of her dress.

He felt his body respond. He shifted slightly in his seat

as his erection started to grow, pushing against the fabric of his shorts.

They'd shared a bottle of wine tonight but Rose was still on her first glass. Maybe his inhibitions had been dampened by the alcohol. That might not have been his smartest idea but he hadn't really expected Rose to accept his offer of wine as she normally refused alcohol.

Was she aware of him too? Had the half-glass of wine she'd drunk relaxed her?

She was close enough to touch and he was thinking about doing just that, thinking about how she would feel, when he felt her hand on his thigh. Her hand was warm and small and her last two fingers were below the hem of his shorts so he could feel the heat on his skin.

She was still leaning towards him. His senses were overloaded. The smell of her rose-scented perfume, the touch of her hand on his leg, the sight of her lips, pink and full. He couldn't keep his eyes off them and he wondered how she would taste. Her lips were moving and that was when he realised she was speaking to him. She was saying something and it took all of his concentration to listen and understand what she was saying.

'There's something I need to do. Just in case you leave on Monday without me.'

She was closer still. There were only centimetres separating them and suddenly the distance was nothing at all.

She was kissing him. Her lips were pressed against his, slightly parted, and they were warm and soft, softer than he'd imagined.

She tasted of strawberries.

That was unexpected.

Everything was unexpected but not unpleasant.

Mitch could feel his body responding. His reaction was

immediate and while it was completely understandable it was also completely out of his control.

He hadn't been a monk since Cara had died but it had been months since he'd been with a woman. It wasn't easy on the station. He didn't get a lot of time or opportunity and here was Rose presenting him with opportunity. He wasn't about to argue.

But he had his own idea of how this was going to go.

He took control, deepening the kiss. His tongue parted her lips and her mouth opened under his.

He wrapped his left hand around her hips, pulling her closer. He slid his right hand behind her neck, through the silken strands of her hair as he held her to him. Ever since he'd first laid eyes on her he'd wanted to feel her hair around his fingers but all that was forgotten now. There was so much more to feel. So much more to experience.

He moved his left hand and ran it underneath the hem of her dress, pushing it higher as his hand spanned the inside of her thigh.

Rose moaned and spread her knees, twisting so that now she sat astride his lap. He could feel his erection pressing into her, nestled in the junction of her thighs. His heart rate was rapid, working hard to pump the blood through his arteries. His groin throbbed, engorged and swollen.

Her fingers were at his throat, running down to where his collarbones met and then further, teasing open the top button of his shirt and then the next. Her palms were spread flat on his chest. Two matching circles of heat, one resting over his frantically beating heart.

His hand was under her dress and he pressed his fingers over the soft mound between her thighs. Rose moaned and pushed towards him as he cupped her. His fingers pushed aside the fabric of her underwear and slid inside her. She was warm and wet and Mitch wanted to take her right then and there. He wanted to tear her underwear off and bury himself inside her. He could imagine how it would feel to be deep inside her, to have her long, smooth legs wrapped around his waist as he thrust into her.

His thumb circled her clitoris as she arched her back.

He pushed her dress higher and felt the smooth skin of her back under his palm. He traced her rib cage and his fingers spanned her side. He moved his hand further until he could cup her breast and then ran his thumb over her nipple and felt it peak through the fabric of her bra. He pushed the cup aside and took her breast into his mouth. His tongue rolled over her nipple, sucking it and pulling it gently as she moaned and ground herself against his hand.

Her clitoris was swollen, a tight little nub under his fingers, as she spread her legs further, encouraging him deeper inside her.

'Oh, God, Mitch, I don't think I can wait.'

He wanted to bury himself inside her but he had no protection. There would be time for him later. He wanted to give her this. He lifted his head from her breast. 'I want you to come now.'

He watched her give in to the pleasure.

Her eyelids were heavy over her green eyes. Her lips were parted and her tongue darted out between her lips as she panted. She took a deep breath and he saw her breasts rise and fall as she writhed in his lap.

Her eyelids closed as she took another deep breath. This one she held and he could tell she'd forgotten to breathe out. All her energy, all her focus, was centred on pleasure.

He knew she was close now and his fingers worked a bit faster.

He watched her as she came. She cried out and he felt her shudder. Felt her muscles tense around his fingers and felt her relax once she was spent. She came to rest, her weight on his chest and in his lap. She felt good. Warm and slick against his skin. He could have stayed like that for a long time but he had other plans for her.

'Sorry, I couldn't stop,' she said, her voice muffled against his chest.

'Don't apologise. The night's not over yet.'

He wrapped his arms around her and was about to lift her up and carry her to his room when he heard a second voice.

'Daddy?'

Rose pulled back as if someone had yanked her away from him and slid off his lap. Her luminous green eyes were wide, her pupils dilated. He wasn't sure whether that was due to fright or desire. Probably a bit of both now.

Mitch looked to his right, half expecting to see Charlie standing in the doorway, but he was nowhere to be seen.

'I'm thirsty.'

Mitch breathed a sigh of relief. Charlie was still in his bed, calling out from his room.

What had he been thinking, seducing Rose while his children slept in the next room?

He hadn't been thinking. His mind had been completely consumed by Rose and he'd forgotten about his children.

Rose tugged her dress down to restore her modesty, although it was a little too late for that. She could feel her face growing hot as a blush spread over her cheeks. Thank goodness Charlie hadn't got out of bed. She would have been mortified if he'd surprised them on the couch.

Mitch was looking to his right, his thoughts clearly on his kids.

She sensed he was feeling uncomfortable. Awkward. Probably a little bit guilty. All the same feelings she was experiencing.

'I'd better go,' she said.

She knew his children were his first priority, despite what had just happened between them.

She was actually a little bit relieved that Charlie had woken up. The kiss had escalated much faster than she'd anticipated and if they hadn't been interrupted she knew she would have found herself in a predicament—wanting to make love to Mitch but not wanting to get naked. She'd need to work through that. It might be that she and Mitch would never get another chance but all the same it was a problem that needed a solution. Maybe not tonight, and maybe not with Mitch, but at some point in the future it was a bridge she'd have to cross.

'Will you still think about giving me the job?' she asked as he stood up.

'Was that what the kiss was about? The job?'

'No! I didn't kiss you to make you see my point of view. I kissed you because I wanted to. Because I was afraid that if I didn't I might miss my chance.' Rose was pleased she'd been brave enough to take the chance. The kiss had been everything she'd hoped for and even if she didn't get what she wanted in the end, even if she didn't get to go back to the station with him, at least she knew what it was like to kiss him. 'I didn't really expect it to end like that, not that I'm complaining, but now we both know we want more I really think you should give me a chance. I think you should take me home with you.'

'I can't.'

Mitch walked over to the kitchen sink and washed his hands before getting a cup and filling it with water for Charlie. There was no discussion. Just an abrupt two words.

Rose followed him. She had plucked up her courage once tonight, desperate to make the most of what might have been her only chance, but now she couldn't let it go. 'I'm not asking for forever. Just a few months. You can ignore the chemistry between us if you like but I don't have a permanent job and you need a governess. This could be good for both of us. Won't you think about it some more?'

'I didn't say I won't, I said I can't. I can't keep you safe. I live in the middle of the country, in the middle of nowhere. If something goes wrong we are hundreds of miles and several hours from even basic medical care.'

'But you're a doctor. Surely that counts for something?'

'I'm not a doctor any more. I don't want that responsibility. There's enough resting on my shoulders without willingly taking on more risk.'

She'd been desperate for an opportunity to ask him more about his past, about why he'd given medicine away, but she got the distinct impression that the topic was off limits.

'But I'm perfectly fine,' she argued. 'Surely you can see that.' When he didn't answer she added, 'What if I get medical clearance from my own doctor? Then I'm not your responsibility any more.'

'You'd still be my responsibility, everyone on the station is.'

'But I haven't even had a cold for almost a year. Scarlett can back me up, she's a doctor too. Why don't I arrange a meeting for you? I give you permission to discuss my health with her, but if she has no reservations will you at least agree to think about it? I'll speak to Scarlett and see if we can meet her tomorrow. Please?'

Mitch nodded and prepared himself to say goodbye. He would go with her to speak to Scarlett but he knew he was only agreeing so that he didn't feel like a complete heel. He couldn't just say goodbye and return to the station. Not after what had just transpired between them. That would be the equivalent of promising to call and not ringing. If he didn't acquiesce to her request he'd feel he'd taken advantage of her. So, to assuage his guilt, he agreed.

* * *

The guilt was still with him as he pulled up in front of Scarlett's house the next morning.

Guilt over what had happened and over where. He still couldn't believe he'd forgotten about his children sleeping in the next room. If Charlie hadn't woken up he would have carried Rose to his bed and made love to her. He hadn't planned it but neither of them had looked remotely capable of putting a stop to proceedings and he knew he hadn't wanted to.

He hadn't been celibate since Cara had died but none of them had elicited the reaction that Rose did. With the others he would have been able to stop.

He could walk away from them; in fact, he'd done just that. Slept with them once and once only. But something told him that once with Rose wouldn't be enough. Perhaps it was fortunate that Charlie had interrupted them. Perhaps it was for the best. He wasn't going to take Rose back to the station. He'd meant it when he'd said he didn't want the responsibility. He wasn't taking her with him and he didn't want to make it any harder to walk away. Which brought him back to the reason he was here. Guilt. He felt like he'd taken advantage of Rose, although rationally he knew that wasn't really the case.

Scarlett greeted them at the door. Rose had told him that her brother-in-law Jake would be at work. That was good, one less person to deal with.

Scarlett was not what he'd been expecting. He knew they were half-sisters but he'd still just envisaged a slightly older version of Rose, but Scarlett was dark where Rose was fair and she was shorter and much curvier than her younger sister. The far bigger surprise was her two-year-old daughter who was perched on her hip.

He'd forgotten about Holly.

He hoped he managed to hide his apprehension as Scarlett welcomed them into her home.

Holly was a month or two older than his own daughter would have been and that was much too close for comfort. Holly was dark haired like her mother and like he always imagined his daughter would have been. Dark like Lila. The familiar ache was back in his heart. He hadn't been aware of it much lately, he'd learnt to compartmentalise his pain and he usually managed to avoid babies. It wasn't difficult on the station, but there was no way to avoid Holly.

But luckily Holly wasn't interested in him. Her eyes went straight to Jed and Charlie, who followed in his shadow. Potential playmates.

Scarlett led them out to a small back garden. There was a sandpit in one corner and the boys were more than happy to play there with Holly. Mitch was free to ignore her but, no matter how much he wanted to, he found his eyes drawn to the sand pit. That could have been Jed and Charlie with their own little sister.

Scarlett offered him and Rose a drink. While she went to make tea Mitch turned his chair, adjusting it so he couldn't easily see the children. It was too difficult to watch.

When Scarlett returned, Rose took her mug and went to sit with the children, leaving Scarlett and Mitch free to talk.

'Rose told me she's applied for a governess position on your station?'

Scarlett's tone seemed to imply she thought he might be encouraging the whole idea. 'Yes…' He drew the word out, not quite sure what she wanted to hear from him.

'She also mentioned you weren't keen on the idea?'

'That's right.'

'But she seems to think that you're being a bit cautious and wants me to plead her case.'

'So she said.'

'Rose said you're worried about her health.'

Mitch nodded.

'She also told me you're a qualified doctor?'

Mitch nodded again.

'So you would know the risks.'

'I do. And that's exactly the problem. I realise from Rose's point of view the worst that would happen would be that she would contract an infection. She figures there would be no great emergency, that we'd call the flying doctor and get her some antibiotics or evacuate her. But the flying doctor can't always get through.'

'Surely they would get to you in a time. She's right, it's hardly likely to be an emergency. Rose also told me you have a pilot and a plane. Would it be so difficult to evacuate her yourself?'

'Assuming there are no other unforeseen problems or natural disasters, no, it wouldn't, but our airstrip has been out of action from flooding at times.'

'Are you expecting rain? Rose told me it hasn't rained for three years.'

Mitch shook his head. 'No,' he admitted. 'The rains generally come in summer. We'll probably have to wait another year. I know there's probably only a low risk associated with Rose being out there but a low risk is still too high in my opinion. I don't want to be responsible for her. I don't want to have to worry about keeping her safe.'

Despite telling himself Rose's transplant was none of his business, he hadn't been able to stop himself from doing some research and getting up to speed on the implications of her surgery. He still had an inquisitive medical brain even if he didn't want to practise medicine, and he could tell that Scarlett couldn't quite understand why he was protesting so much. She was right, the risk really was small enough to be managed. Unless something unforeseen happened.

And he couldn't risk that. 'I *know* things can go wrong when you least expect them to and, out there, any mistake is magnified. I've been through it before.' He paused and took a breath. 'My wife died on that station.'

'I'm so sorry. Rose didn't tell me.'

Mitch shook his head. 'Rose doesn't know the details.' He picked up his drink. He wasn't thirsty but it gave him time to think about how much to tell her. 'My wife was pregnant. I lost her and the baby. There was nothing I could do.' He lifted a hand, rubbing it over his face in an attempt to wipe the memory away. 'I'm worried that if Rose falls ill we might actually be too far from medical help. There's only so much I can do on my own.'

She understood. He could see it in her eyes.

'I didn't think you'd be advocating for this move anyway,' he said. Rose had mentioned Scarlett's protective tendencies. He couldn't imagine she would think Rose was making a wise decision. Rose wasn't a seasoned traveller or particularly adventurous. Moving to the middle of nowhere with a stranger wouldn't be the kind of thing her family would expect of her. It sounded more like something their other sister, Ruby, would do.

'I'm not,' Scarlett replied. 'But it wasn't because of Rose's health. I have other concerns.'

'Such as?'

'Her heart, not her health.'

'Meaning?'

'I don't want her to get hurt. I think she's looking at life on a station, and at you, through rose-coloured glasses. That saying is perfectly suited to her, it could have been written about her. I don't know how she manages to but she still believes in happy endings, despite everything that has happened to her. Her father died when she was young, then she got so sick. She still believes in true love. She thinks that will solve the world's problems. And her own. But I don't think she's likely to find true love in the middle of the Outback. She needs to stay in the city, not because of her health but because she needs to get out and about, she needs to meet people, to get on with her life. I don't mean to sound rude, but do you really think that living on a station in the middle of nowhere with a widower and his three kids is the best environment for her? Unless there's something going on between the two of you that I don't know about?' She raised an eyebrow and looked at him.

Thank goodness he didn't get embarrassed easily, Mitch thought. He knew his tanned, olive skin would hide any tell-tale signs of embarrassment. If Rose hadn't found it necessary to tell her sister what had transpired last night, he certainly wasn't going to. But despite his discomfiture he found Scarlett amusing. She called a spade a spade and so did he but he didn't like being questioned or told what to do and the more Scarlett tried to push him away from Rose the more he found himself thinking of all the reasons why he should take her home with him.

'So, how did that go?' Rose asked as they drove away.

'Better than I expected.'

'Meaning she agrees with you.'

'Not exactly. But she did help me to clarify a few things.'

'Like what?'

'Like why you would be perfect for the job.'

'Really?'

Mitch nodded, knowing he wasn't thinking with his head or his heart but with other parts of his anatomy. Yet, even knowing that, he was unable to stop himself from offering her the position. He knew that once he took Lila home from hospital there would be no reason to see Rose any more and he couldn't imagine saying goodbye. Not after last night.

But it was more than that. She'd been a breath of fresh air, she'd been something to look forward to, and he hadn't felt that in a long time. He knew he shouldn't be mixing business and pleasure and he should *definitely* not be entertaining thoughts of sleeping with the governess, but he couldn't imagine letting her go.

There were two very good reasons why he should offer her the job and only one reason why he shouldn't. Rose was right. He needed someone to help with the children and he enjoyed her company. He could have his cake and eat it too. And maybe Rose was also right about the station being a less risky environment in terms of exposure to bugs. There was a chance she'd be less exposed to common viruses being away from large populations of people. He knew he was talking himself into it because it was what he wanted but did that make it wrong? If it was what they both wanted, then surely that made it okay.

'I need help with the children and I've seen how good you are with them. You've even got Lila talking again. The job is yours if you want it.'

CHAPTER SEVEN

'THERE SHE IS.'

The pilot's voice came through Rose's headset and, as he banked the small plane to the right, Rose caught her first glimpse of Emu Downs.

She'd been looking out the window intermittently ever since Steve had taken off from Broken Hill but the landscape had been a fairly uniform shade of dusty ochre with the occasional dry river bed and some scrubby green-grey vegetation. Now she could pick out some small buildings, their silver corrugated tin roofs glinting in the sunlight. There were more buildings than she'd expected, a dozen at least, giving the impression of a small village and one long roof had 'EMU DOWNS' painted on it in large black letters.

Rose had seen one mob of emus running across the sand as the plane had travelled north-east, the birds' shadows stretching across the red dirt larger than they were. The sight had made her smile. Mitch might have said that the emu numbers were depleted but Rose was happy to have seen some. It made it feel real.

Her heart was in her mouth as the pilot banked. She was almost there and Mitch would be waiting.

As the plane dropped lower in the sky she could see movement. Dust rose from the tyres of moving vehicles and swirled around smaller, dark brown shapes that morphed into cattle.

This was it. She'd arrived.

The ground disappeared beneath the plane and Rose's teeth snapped together in her jaw as the wheels bumped on the dirt runway. Steve turned the plane in a tight circle and Rose watched as the wingtip passed over the thin wire strands of a fence before they straightened up and taxied to a halt next to a four-wheel drive.

Through the small windows of the plane she could see Mitch and the children waiting by the vehicle. The children were waving and Rose waved back but she was looking at Mitch. It had only been three weeks since she'd seen him but she'd almost forgotten how handsome he was.

She caught her breath. She'd been imagining this arrival for days and she could scarcely believe she was finally here.

Steve reached across her lap and unlocked the small door beside her. Rose unclipped her seat belt and clambered out. Eager to get to Mitch.

'Welcome to Emu Downs.' He was standing behind the children. She expected him to come forward, she wanted to step into his arms, but he stayed where he was, barricaded behind the kids, shielded from her.

He extended his hand. Such a formal greeting surprised her. She was completely taken aback. What was going on? But as she shook his hand and he smiled at her some of her reservations receded slightly. His smile was as warm and friendly as she remembered. Perhaps she couldn't expect a big display of affection in front of the children. That probably wasn't appropriate given that she was now employed as their governess. Perhaps when they were alone things would be different.

She smiled back and reminded herself to ask Mitch what the ground rules were going to be. That was probably something they should have discussed but the whole exercise had happened in such a rush and, admittedly, she hadn't thought rules were too important.

The kids gathered around her as she let go of Mitch's hand. Jed and Lila hugged her and Charlie raised his arms, requesting to be lifted up. At least the kids didn't have reservations.

'How was your trip?'

'Long,' she replied. 'You weren't kidding when you said you're in the middle of nowhere.' She'd caught a bus from Adelaide to Broken Hill and then Steve had collected her from there. Flying into Emu Downs had shaved hours off a dusty, bumpy trip but she'd still been travelling for most of the day.

Another man, about her age, with brown skin and black eyes and a friendly expression, came around from behind the four-wheel drive. She hadn't noticed him until he'd moved. She'd only had eyes for Mitch.

'Rose, this is Jimmy. Jimmy, Rose,' Mitch said as he picked up her bags and stashed them into the back of the four-wheel drive. 'You'll need to get to know Jimmy, he'll be teaching you how to ride.'

Jimmy smiled at her as he closed the cargo door and his teeth flashed white against his dark skin. He ducked his head in acknowledgement but didn't speak.

'You're just in time for afternoon smoko. Jimmy will take your bags to your accommodation and if you're up for it we'll grab a cuppa and you can meet everyone.'

Rose was exhausted but she didn't want to miss a minute of the whole experience. She would have loved a shower but she could do that later. Smoko meant everyone would be in one place and it would be easiest to meet them all now. Best to get it over and done with.

Mitch introduced her to Shirley first. 'Shirley is our cook,' he said. 'She's the most important person here.'

'You have some things in your room, your accommodation has a kitchen,' Shirley told her as she showed her where the tea and coffee were kept, 'but meals are served here and shared together. We're isolated enough without people eating their meals alone.'

Rose took a tea bag and mug from the shelf. On the table behind her was an assortment of food; a large carrot cake, fresh scones, fruit and biscuits.

'Do you have any allergies I need to know about?' Shirley asked as Rose added boiling water to her tea.

'I can't eat some raw foods but I can control that. I don't have any allergies,' she replied.

'So I take it you're okay with red meat?' Shirley was grinning and Rose smiled back.

'Definitely.'

Mitch introduced her to the rest of the staff while she devoured a scone and a piece of cake. She'd have to watch what she ate if all Shirley's cooking was this good.

'We'll finish the tour and then I'll let you get settled,' Mitch said as Rose drained the last of her tea. 'You'd probably like a shower but one word of advice, most of us will shower at the end of the day. It's so dusty out here there's not much point showering until you're almost ready for bed. Saves getting covered in dust all over again,' he said as they walked away from the kitchen and up a slight hill.

Rose knew water was scarce on the station but his comment just made her think about showering with Mitch—she could do her bit for water conservation that way. Mitch was still talking and she forced herself to concentrate on what he was telling her.

'This is the original house,' he was saying. 'When we built the new house...' he pointed to a second dwelling about twenty metres away '...we turned this into the school house but kept living quarters for the governess. It's more comfortable than the workers' accommodation. I think you'll prefer it here.'

He pushed open the front door and they stepped inside. It was built out of wood in the typical Queensland style, with a wide veranda and elevated off the ground to let the breeze through and stop it from drowning in a flood. There were four rooms off the hallway, two either side. The first two, left and right of the front door, had been kept as a bedroom and a living room but the next two had been knocked through and converted into one long room that ran the width of the house and was now the school room. Bookshelves and pin boards lined the walls and there were a couple of large tables in the centre that served as desks. Two laptop computers sat on a third table in the corner. A kitchen, laundry and bathroom were at the back of the house.

Rose wandered through the rooms. 'This is fabulous,' she said. 'The school room looks a much better set-up than I'd imagined.' She'd brought a whole suitcase on the plane with her that was packed with textbooks, novels and early readers as well as pencils and craft supplies. She hadn't known what to expect and was surprised by the number of resources that appeared to be at her disposal.

She stuck her head into her bedroom. The room was furnished with a pine dresser and wardrobe, a double bed, made up with pretty white linen, and soft sheer curtains framed the windows and French doors. She had her own space, which was perfect, and from her front veranda she could look across a rather dry and desolate flower garden to the main house and what she assumed was Mitch's veranda.

Two old armchairs sat on the wooden boards looking out across the river bed. It was dry and stony, completely devoid of water, but despite the barrenness of the land, the red dirt and the dust, it had a certain beauty. A sense of calm. She could just imagine sitting out there in the evening, chatting to Mitch about their days.

'Sorry, what was that?'

'I was going to take you around the rest of the buildings if you're not too tired. And then you can unpack and rest when I go back to work.'

'Sure.'

The children accompanied them as Mitch showed her the set-up. Along with the airstrip, the main house and the school house there was also a kitchen block, where she'd had smoko, a recreation room for the staff, staff quarters for the single workers, a couple of small houses for the married staff and multiple sheds plus the stables, veggie garden, chook pen and the cattle yards. It was like a small country town.

'This is not at all what I expected,' she said.

'Better or worse?'

'Better, I think.' The facilities were definitely better than she'd imagined but Mitch was different. He wasn't as relaxed. More stressed. Was he nervous? She couldn't imagine so but he seemed on edge. He wasn't quite meeting her eyes and a couple of times he'd stepped away if she got too close. She hated to admit it but it bothered her. She wanted to feel comfortable, she wanted *him* to feel comfortable, with his decision to have her there. But maybe she was being too sensitive, maybe it had nothing to do with her. Maybe there was something on his mind that she knew nothing about.

Time would tell. She wouldn't worry about it now. They both had some adjusting to do.

The first few days passed in a blur as Rose got used to her new surroundings and settled into station life. It was foreign, hot, dusty and dry but it had a certain beauty to it all and she remembered Mitch's description. He had summed it up perfectly. The clear air and the bright, crisp colours were like nothing she'd ever seen before. It was beautiful but what he hadn't described was the silence. It was enormous, particularly at dawn and twilight when it was only broken by the sound of the wildlife—the birds, the crickets and the frogs—and she found it surprisingly comforting.

But her absolute favourite time of day was the early morning. She loved the freshness and the breath of possibility that came with each new day and she found herself believing in good things again. There was no room for melancholy thoughts in her head, she was surrounded by too much beauty.

The job was demanding but exciting and her days were busy but not difficult. The role of a governess was new to her and she was having to learn fast, but she was coping. She had to get up to speed with the School of the Air, what was expected of her and what stages the children were at but that was the easy part. That was the teaching part. It was the rest of the governess's role that was challenging. Her teaching degree couldn't have prepared her for all the other associated duties that seemed to be part of her job description, including taking charge of Lila's rehabilitation, doing the laundry and getting the children ready for bed, but, like everything, once she got into a routine she felt she had more control.

She spent the morning in the classroom with the children but with just three students, and Charlie only in kindergarten, it didn't take long to get through the work assigned. Which left their afternoons free for all the extra-curricular activities that were on offer. So far they'd cooked with Shirley, been yabbying—unsuccessfully—in the few remaining waterholes and ridden the horses. Lila wasn't anywhere close to getting back on Fudge but she was quite content to spend time at the stable, grooming her. Jimmy, the young jackaroo who Rose had met at the airstrip, had started giving her riding lessons and she absolutely loved it. The exercise, along with the aching muscles, reminded her of when she could run and after just a few days she was sure she could feel an improvement in her strength and stamina. The endorphins that exercise released also helped to brighten her mood.

She fell into bed exhausted each night, as much from the fresh air as from the work. It was a good fatigue, physical rather than mental, as even though her day was long it didn't feel like work. Mitch had warned her about the long days, but she was enjoying spending time with the children and getting to know the other staff and she was almost too busy to notice that she wasn't seeing a lot of Mitch. *Almost* too busy.

She'd expected a bit more communication. A bit more of everything really—more time, more conversation, more flirting, more stolen kisses. She wasn't sure if he was ignoring her or trying to work out how she fitted into things here. Maybe he thought she didn't.

And they were never alone. There always seemed to be someone else nearby, whether by accident or design, Rose wasn't sure.

He was also leaving the children completely to her, which was not what she'd expected. After dinner he disappeared to his study. He'd told her he spent the evenings doing bookwork but somehow she'd imagined things differently and even though she could see his house from hers, they were separated by a dry and dusty flower bed and the distance it created resembled the Great Australian Bight.

From her house she could see him, late in the evening after finishing in his study, sitting alone on his veranda.

In her mind he'd looked lonely but possibly he was quite content. He certainly didn't ask for company, not hers definitely.

He didn't seem to have much down time and he certainly didn't spend it with the children. In Rose's opinion that needed to change. The staff all had their jobs to do, and hers was to help raise the children, but they needed their father. They only had one parent, and Rose knew he needed to step up but she hadn't yet worked out how to raise the subject with him. Baby steps, maybe. She needed to establish her role first but in order to do that she needed some guidance from Mitch and that was difficult when he seemed to be doing his best to keep out of her way.

The only time she could guarantee seeing him was at mealtimes. The family ate their meals with the staff, something Rose was taking a little bit of time to get used to, as it all seemed very informal. She never got time alone with Mitch but neither, it seemed, did the children.

On her fifth day he was in the kitchen building and seated for dinner before her. This was her chance. She had questions that needed answering.

She took her plate and sat at the same table. 'Hi.'

'Hello.' He smiled at her. The moment he smiled she almost forgot her concerns. His smile lit a fire inside her and had the power to make her believe that everything was okay. Although in reality she knew it wasn't. 'How are you settling in? Is there anything you need?'

Yes, some time with you.

But being so blunt probably wasn't the way to get what she wanted. 'Actually, there are a few things I need to discuss with you. Can we catch up after I get the children into bed?'

'I've got a pile of bookwork to do.'

She wasn't going to let him ignore her for ever. 'It won't

take long. It's important.' She wasn't going to let him put her off. She'd made up her mind to confront him and she intended to do just that. She didn't mind if he thought she needed to discuss the children or their schooling. That was one way to get his attention and if she was being a little sneaky she didn't care. She was getting worried and she needed to know whether he thought it had been a mistake to bring her out here. 'Why don't I come across at eight? Could you take a break then?'

'Okay.'

Rose got the children to bed and went back to her house to shower. Like everyone else on the station she'd got into the habit of showering at the end of the day to wash the dust away. She wrapped a towel around her body and walked through the house. She flicked through her clothes, looking for something to wear. She spent her days in jeans and riding boots and wanted a change, although she had to admit that as far as footwear went the boots were becoming quite comfortable as the leather softened and because everyone wore them she didn't look out of place. In riding boots her feet looked just the same as everyone else's.

The night was warm. She pulled a pair of shorts from a drawer. She would like to wear a dress as a reminder of what had happened before but she wasn't sure where she stood. Scarlett had warned her, but she hadn't been able to stop herself from getting her hopes up. So far, Mitch hadn't put a foot out of place. He'd been the complete gentleman, a model of propriety, and this wasn't an occasion to get dressed up for.

She wasn't his date; she wasn't his guest. She was his employee.

Had that one night been an aberration? Was it never going to be repeated? She really needed to know.

She looked out the side window, which looked directly at Mitch's house. She could see the light on in his study. The houses were only metres apart, separated by the narrow garden with the dry and dusty flower beds. She often wondered if the flower beds were a victim of the drought or of Mitch's wife's death. Had she been a keen gardener, had she tended to those beds or had they perished long ago from a lack of water and attention?

Sometimes Rose felt like that was going to happen to her.

She pulled her curtains closed.

She wasn't going to give up yet, she thought as she let her towel drop to the floor and stepped into her undies and shorts. She would give this some time. She wouldn't wait for ever, but she was sure he felt something for her. And there was still time. She'd only been here a week. Besides, whatever happened with Mitch she was still keen for the Outback experience. It would look good on her résumé. Perhaps they both needed time to get used to the change. Although not much seemed to have changed for Mitch. He continued doing what she suspected he always did. Ran the station. He didn't spend a lot of time with the children. It was hard, she guessed, when he never got to leave work behind. It was a twenty-four-hours-a-day commitment.

She pulled a shirt from a hanger and slipped it over her head and opened her curtains again once she was decent. From her window she could see Mitch's figure as he stepped out onto the veranda. His tall, erect posture she'd know anywhere, although who else would it be? He had a beer in his hand. She boiled the kettle and made herself a green tea and carried it across the dry and dusty garden and climbed the stairs.

Mitch stood up from the old armchair as she arrived, his manners as impeccable as ever. She took the armchair next to him. The chairs faced outwards, looking across the garden and down to the creek. Not that she could see the creek bed as the sun had well and truly set. She sat quietly, letting her eyes get accustomed to the dark. There was a sliver of moonlight but the veranda was in darkness; switching on the lights only attracted the insects.

She could hear frogs croaking and the occasional plop as they hopped across the wooden floor. She was used to seeing them pop up in unexpected places. High on the glass doors, lurking in the toilet bowls, sitting startled in the middle of the floor when she flicked the light on at night. But they were such a vibrant green and so cute that she forgave them when they frightened the life out of her.

'Can I get you a beer?' Mitch asked. His voice startled her out of her reverie.

'No, thanks, I'm fine with my tea,' she replied as she turned to look at him.

He was leaning back in the chair, his bottom at the front, his long legs stretched out across the wooden boards. He'd showered too and his thick, dark hair was still slightly damp. He was wearing clean jeans, a button-down shirt that was open at the throat and had the sleeves rolled up. His forearms were tanned, his fingernails clean. He smelt divine, and he took her breath away.

'So, what did you need to talk to me about?' he asked, getting straight down to business. Maybe they weren't going to have the comfortable conversation she'd become used to in their late-night phone calls. Did he find it easier to talk to her over the phone or was he uncomfortable with his decision to bring her to the station? She hoped he hadn't changed his mind about her being here.

'A couple of things. I'll start with Lila.' She did actually need to talk to him about Lila and she figured she might be able to soften him up before she launched into the issue that was really concerning her. 'I need to make an appointment for her to see the physio but that will mean a trip into Cunnamulla. Shirley said that's a five-hour drive, is that right?'

Mitch nodded. 'Thereabouts.'

'So I needed to check—what's the best thing to do? Which day would work best? Do I need to take the boys too and can we stay in town for the night? I don't think I want to drive back in the dark.' Rose thought she was managing well with the basics but there were so many other things about living in the Outback that she didn't understand.

'You want to go to Cunnamulla?'

'Yes. The physio clinic is there next week.'

'That would make sense. Cunnamulla have their camp draft next weekend, they'll be tying their outpatient clinics in with that, capitalising on the influx of people into town.'

'Camp draft? What is that?'

'You'd probably imagine it to be a bit like a rodeo. But it's a bit of a festival, an agricultural show and some riding competitions all rolled into one. People come into town from all over the Outback, it's a chance to socialise and shop but most will compete. There's a fair bit of prize money involved. A few of our guys will be competing and my kids usually enter some of the children's events. We could all go a couple of days early, sort out Lila's appointments and then stay for the camp draft.'

'We?'

'Of course. You have to experience at least one camp draft. But you'll have to be prepared to sleep in a tent. We'll take the camper trailer but it won't be five-star luxury.'

'That's okay.' It wasn't like she was used to five-star luxury anyway and, besides, she'd go anywhere, do anything if it meant she got to spend time with Mitch.

'All right, that's sorted. What's the other thing?'

She took a deep breath. 'I'm wondering if you're having second thoughts about me being here. I feel like you've been avoiding me.'

'I'm not avoiding you, Rose, I'm just busy. There's always something that needs my attention, a problem that needs fixing, an order that needs filling or a staff member who needs a solution.'

It sounded to her like he'd prepared his answer in advance. Was he telling the truth or making excuses?

'When you offered me the job, was that all you were offering? A job? Because I felt there was more to it.' It was unlike Rose to demand answers but she needed to know. She needed to be brave. What was the worst that could happen? Mitch could tell her he'd made a mistake. 'If you've changed your mind, just tell me.'

Mitch shook his head. 'I want you here but I haven't figured out yet where you fit in. I didn't really consider the fact that you'd be an employee. I'm not sure what to do with you.'

Rose smiled. That was good news. 'I've got a few ideas.'

'I have too, but it's difficult out here.' He smiled, but it was only a half-smile, not quite reaching his eyes. There was something bothering him.

'Is it because of Cara?'

'No. At least, not in the way I assume you're thinking. It's been almost two years. I admit I haven't been celibate since she died, although I certainly haven't been hitting the singles scene, but it's all been conducted away from the station. I'm just not sure how to do this under everyone's noses.'

'Are you worried about what they will think? It's okay to be happy. You don't need their permission.'

'No, it's not that. I'm just not sure that I want them all knowing my business. Or yours.'

'I don't care. I want to explore this thing between us.'

Rose knew she'd been given a second chance at life and she was prepared to go after what she wanted. 'I'm not going to leave you in the lurch if you tell me you've changed your mind but I'm going crazy wondering what is going on in your head. Whether or not you're even thinking about me.'

'Trust me, I'm thinking about you.'

'I need to know what you want to do. I need something to assure me that I haven't made a mistake in coming here.'

'I realise that, I get it, I just need a bit more time.'

Rose stood up. Maybe she had to take no for an answer.

But Mitch hadn't finished. He stood up too. 'I understand what you're saying but I know that once I start I won't be able to stop. You know how quickly things escalated last time. Until I figure out all the practicalities I don't think I can afford to start.'

'But I can,' Rose said. She put her tea cup on the arm of the chair and lifted herself up onto tiptoe, bringing her level with Mitch. She overbalanced—missing toes did not make it easy—and as she wobbled Mitch reached out for her. His hands were on her arms, steadying her. She wrapped her arms over his shoulders and kissed him on the lips. If he wasn't going to take the initiative, she would. If her prince charming wasn't going to come and get her, she would go to him.

He pulled her in tightly against him, holding her close as he deepened the kiss. She parted her lips, offering herself to him, and he accepted.

She felt his response, hard against her belly, as their kiss became more urgent. He still wanted her, she knew that now, and suddenly her world seemed a little better, the stars a little brighter, the moon a little larger. Maybe everything would be all right.

This was what she'd been waiting for. This was what she wanted.

But it was over almost before it began. Apparently Mitch had other ideas. She felt his hands release her before he put them back on her upper arms, forcing her back from him, breaking their contact and ending the kiss.

'Not yet,' he said as he let her go. 'I need some time and there's more you need to know. I have to head out on a muster. There are some cattle I need to collect and I'll be gone for a few days. I need you to hold the fort with the children but I promise I'll work this out.'

'Are you sure this isn't just another avoidance tactic?' Before she'd left Adelaide for the station Mitch had explained the governess's job and all it encompassed. It was far more than just a nine to three, normal school hours job. He needed help with the children on a far more constant basis. She was happy to help but not if he was making excuses.

'No, it's not. I admit it's not great timing but I have to sell off some more stock and unless we get rain soon I'll have to keep selling.'

'When are you going?'

'Tomorrow.' He reached out a hand and picked up some strands of her hair, letting them fall through his fingers. 'Can we talk about this again when I get back?'

Rose nodded. She didn't see that she had much choice. She'd signed a contract. She had a job to do and she would do it but she wished she had a personal contract as well. Maybe then she wouldn't feel quite so left out in the cold.

CHAPTER EIGHT

MITCH WAS OUT on the muster and the station seemed bigger and emptier without him. It was ridiculous to feel lonely when there were a dozen other people around but some of the gloss had worn off with his absence. Even though she hadn't spent much time with him she'd known he was there, just across the flower garden or in the sheds or the cattle yards. Now, although technically he was still on the station, he was not in sight. He was miles away and would be gone for days.

To keep busy and distract herself she planned a host of extra activities for the children. They had cooked, planted a vegetable garden, taken part in a School of the Air music lesson and each day the boys kicked the soccer ball while she helped Lila with her physiotherapy and exercises. Today she decided they'd all go to the stables after therapy. Mitch wasn't due back until tomorrow and she figured another riding lesson would help to fill in the time. She got the boys to bring Ruff into the house first. She wasn't prepared to risk another episode of Ruff versus Fudge so she shut the little dog into the wire enclosure the mechanic had made and gave him a bone to keep him occupied.

Jimmy had given Rose four lessons so far and while she couldn't imagine ever being a confident rider she was beginning to feel a little more comfortable on horseback.

At Lila's insistence, she'd been riding Fudge; Jimmy had agreed it would be good for Fudge to be exercised and she was an extremely gentle, placid horse, provided Ruff wasn't within cooee, and perfect for a beginner.

'Lemme saddle the boys' horses and then I'm gonna show you how to saddle Fudge today, Rose,' Jimmy said as she arrived at the stables.

This was the longest sentence Rose had heard Jimmy utter and she was so surprised she couldn't think of a response. Jimmy worked solely with the horses and usually had Fudge saddled in the time it took him to first see, or hear, Rose and the children making their way to the stables.

'You should know a coupla things about it, in case you ever need to adjust anything or if I'm not here.'

Rose thought it was unlikely that she would be riding if Jimmy wasn't around but she didn't know enough to argue. If Jimmy was making the suggestion she figured there must be a good reason. He wouldn't be doing it just to make conversation. Silence didn't seem to bother him; in fact, Rose imagined he rather liked it. The peace and tranquillity of working with the horses seemed to suit him.

'Sure.'

Jimmy handed her a blanket to put under the saddle. The bits and pieces were familiar to Rose but adjusting the saddle and bridle were more difficult than she'd imagined. Jimmy showed her how to tighten the saddle and then wait for Fudge to breathe out before tightening it some more. It was only as Rose watched Jimmy pull on the leather straps that she realised he was missing two fingers on his left hand. She couldn't believe she hadn't noticed before. Jimmy was never more than a foot away from her when she was riding but she realised now that he always held the reins with his right hand. She wondered what had happened. His hand looked a little disfigured; it didn't look as if it was a congenital deformity but rather the result of an accident.

'Let me do that,' she said, the words popping out of her mouth before she had time to think about what she was saying and how Jimmy might construe her words. She was worried that he might not get enough force behind his grip before she realised that he'd been saddling Fudge every time for her and she hadn't had a mishap.

'It's fine. Me hand works perfectly fine, thanks to the boss.'

'The boss?'

'Yep. He saved me hand and me life.'

'That sounds awfully dramatic. What happened?' Once again the words were out before she thought about it. She knew she would hate it if anyone asked about her foot and yet here she was subjecting Jimmy to the same curiosity she would detest. 'Sorry,' she apologised, 'you don't have to tell me.'

'It's not a secret,' Jimmy replied. 'Everyone knows. It was a careless accident. I'd gone to kill a steer for the cook for dinner and I had a gun across me lap. It was loaded and the ute hit a pothole and the gun went off. Shot meself in the hand.' Jimmy shrugged. 'Coulda been worse.'

'That sounds pretty bad,' Rose said, although Jimmy didn't seem too perturbed.

'Nah. The boss stopped the bleeding. If he hadn't been there I reckon I woulda bled to death. Somehow he managed to save two of me fingers and me thumb and that's a whole heap better than it coulda been.'

While she was riding, Rose had no room in her head to think about anything other than staying in her saddle but once her lesson was finished and she and Lila were grooming Fudge she thought about what Jimmy had said. How could he be so matter-of-fact about losing two fingers? How could she not have noticed before? And, more importantly, why had Mitch given up medicine?

She thought about this as she got the children cleaned and ready for dinner. She had a surprise organised for them. She took them to the staff kitchen to collect their meal. She'd organised with Shirley to bundle up their dinner so she could take it back to the main house. She'd decided it was time for a change.

She'd decided they needed some table manners. They ate with the staff in the staff kitchen every night. There were four large tables in the staff kitchen and people tended to sit anywhere they chose, which meant Mitch and his children very rarely sat together for dinner. Rose understood it was easier for Mitch to feed the children in the staff kitchen but she didn't believe it was good for them as a family unit. She thought they'd benefit from having a weekly family dinner, just Mitch and his children, in their own house but she wasn't sure yet how she was going to raise the subject. In the meantime she would trial it herself but she intended to make a game of it.

'Tonight we're going to eat at home,' she told the children as they collected the dishes.

'Home?' Lila queried. 'In our house?'

'Why can't we eat with everyone else?' Jed asked as Rose nodded and handed him a container of mashed potato.

'We're going to use our proper table manners. Knives and forks and serviettes.'

'Why?'

'Because it's something we all should know and practise. Besides, what if the Queen comes for dinner?'

Lila giggled and Jed laughed. 'As if the Queen would come all the way out here.'

'You know, Jed,' Shirley interrupted, 'when I was a lot

younger, about thirty years ago, the Prince of Wales came to visit a station where I worked.'

'That was in the olden days!' Jed exclaimed.

Lila was more enthralled. 'Do you think the Queen really would come?' she asked Rose, her eyes wide.

'Maybe. Shall we all dress up just in case?'

Back at the house Rose put the dinner in the oven to keep warm while they rummaged through the dress-up box.

'I want to be a princess,' Lila announced as she chose a princess dress.

'Let's get the swords and shields,' Jed told Charlie. 'We're going to be knights. We can protect the Princess.'

'That means I can be the Queen,' Rose said as she found a shiny plastic tiara and popped it on her head.

The children set the table while she dished up the dinner and they were halfway through their meal when Mitch walked through the door.

Lila jumped out of her chair and threw her arms around Mitch's waist. Rose was tempted to do the same. She was equally as pleased to see him.

'You're back early. I wasn't expecting you until tomorrow,' she said.

Even dusty and with a three-day growth he was gorgeous and her heart did a little flip in her chest, matching the somersault that her stomach was doing. She'd missed seeing his face.

'We made better time than I planned. The guys are still out with the cattle but they're not far away so I thought I'd pop home and see what I was missing. It looks like I'm missing a party.'

'We're having schnitzels,' Jed told him.

'And practising for when the Queen comes for dinner,' Lila added.

'The Queen? I wonder what she would say if we served her schnitzels.'

'Rose is the Queen tonight,' Lila said. 'She likes schnitzels.'

'Yes, I am the Queen of Austria,' Rose said in an extremely bad accent.

'Did you say Australia?' Mitch laughed.

'No, Austria.' She smiled. 'Schnitzels originated in Austria, but I don't think theirs were made with beef.'

'Dad, did you know it snows in Austria?' Lila asked. 'We've been learning about it. And there's a song about schnitzels.'

Rose stood up to fetch another plate from the cupboard. 'Are you going to join us for dinner?'

'Daddy, you can be the King,' Charlie said.

'I don't think I'm dressed properly, and I need a shower first,' he said. He was looking at her intently and Rose had a fleeting, ridiculous notion that he'd come back for her and was almost surprised to find the children there with her. Had he made a decision? He'd told her he would. Dared she hope he was going to choose her?

Rose let him go. They could hardly have that conversation now, not in front of the children.

By the time Mitch returned the children had finished eating and were getting restless. They weren't used to sitting at the table unless there was food in front of them.

Jed pushed his chair back and stood up.

'Not so fast, Jed. You need to ask to be excused from the table.'

He looked at her in bewilderment.

'You put your knife and fork together like this,' Rose said as she moved her cutlery. 'That shows that you've had enough to eat, and you say, "May I be excused?"'

Jed copied Rose's instructions without complaint and

Rose excused the children one by one. 'You need to clean your teeth for me, okay?'

Mitch grabbed a beer from the fridge. 'Can I get you one, too?' he offered.

'That sounds good,' she said.

Mitch twisted the top off before handing it to her and sitting at the table. 'So, how did it go? Did you have any problems while I was away?'

'Not at all. Your kids are delightful…'

'But…? Do I hear a but?'

'Not really.' She smiled. 'Well, maybe a little one. They may benefit from a bit more routine and structure.'

'Are they really wild?'

'Not yet, but there are a few things that could use some tweaking. Things like table manners. There's not much emphasis on that when they eat with the staff but I think it's important.'

'Is that what tonight was all about?'

'Partly. I thought it might be nice once in a while to let the kids get used to a meal where they have to use their knife and fork properly and their manners.'

'Once in a while?'

'Once a week would be good. Just you and the kids. It would do them, and you, good to have some family time.'

'I'll think about it,' he said as the children came back into the living area. Lila was carrying the book Rose had been reading to them as their bedtime story.

'Why don't we read on the couch tonight?' she said to the children. 'That way your dad can listen to the story too.'

'Do you know this story, Dad?' Lila asked as she showed Mitch the book cover.

'It's about a magic tree.'

'It has all these funny people living in it.'

'And a slippery dip on the inside that you slide down on special cushions.'

'And the tree is huge and reaches right up into the clouds and magic lands come in the clouds to visit the tree.'

The children talked over the top of each other, eager to give Mitch their summary of the story so far.

'Okay, I think your dad has got the idea. Come and sit down quietly.'

Rose smiled at Mitch as she gathered the children together and settled them on the couch. Her smile lit a fire inside him, warming him from the inside. He was glad to be home. He sat at the table and listened to her read. It was peaceful and he almost couldn't remember what it was like before Rose had come to live there. A sense of calm came over him, as if this was how things were supposed to be.

His kids lay on the couch, draped across Rose. Charlie's head was in her lap and she was stroking his hair as she read. Jed was stretched out on one side of Rose and Lila lay curled on the other. Rose had one arm around Lila and Mitch wasn't sure how she was managing to turn the pages. He wanted to lie on the couch with his head in her lap too. He'd been missing her, wondering what she was up to. That was why he'd come back early. He'd wanted to see her. Needed to see her.

Rose reached the end of the chapter and he watched as his children hugged her goodnight. He could tell they'd done this before; it looked easy and effortless. They were used to having her here too and already he could see the changes Rose's presence had brought about in them. Lila was talking more—he hadn't noticed how quiet she'd become until he'd started to hear her voice again—and she and Jed had been getting on better. There'd been fewer arguments between them, or maybe Rose had just been handling them without involving him. Whatever she was doing was working. The house seemed calmer, more peaceful and happier since she had joined them. He felt all those things too.

He'd made the right decision, bringing her here. Now they had time to explore things further. He had time to do the right thing by Rose.

'Off to bed now,' she told them. 'Your dad will come and say goodnight in a minute.' She reached up and removed the tiara from her head as the children disappeared. 'I'd better get going,' she said as she loosened her hair. It fell in soft waves over her shoulders and she scooped it up, gathering it all in one hand and twisted it, draping it over one shoulder. He loved watching her do that. He found it mesmerising.

She was wearing a white dress that made her look like an angel. The dress had thin straps and hung loosely, skimming her body. Just two little flicks would knock those straps from her shoulders and the dress would fall to the floor. He could picture her naked, her blonde hair falling forward, covering one shoulder, one breast, and leaving the other breast exposed.

He closed his eyes but the image just intensified. Rose had been sleeping in his bed while he'd been away so the kids wouldn't be in the house alone, and he could imagine her lying on his sheets, her green eyes wide, her legs spread, waiting for him. He was getting aroused, growing hard. He shifted uncomfortably in his seat, trying to readjust himself surreptitiously.

He couldn't stand up and see her out. Not now. He needed a minute to recover from his fantasies. He'd been trying to ignore her, trying to ignore the attraction, his desire, but it was becoming impossible to deny.

'Stay and finish your beer,' he said.

She shook her head. 'I really should go.'

'I could use the company.' He really wasn't ready for

her to leave. He'd come back to see her and he didn't want to sit here alone.

'Are you okay?' she asked.

No. I'm thinking about you naked. I want to tear that dress off you and make love to you. Right here. Right now. I don't think I can stand to wait any longer.

He ran his hands through his hair as he thought about how to answer her. Should he tell her what he was thinking? What he'd been thinking about for the past few days? Or should he talk to her about what he *should* have been thinking about? About all the stresses of the station that he'd been unable to concentrate on because his mind had been filled with thoughts and images of her.

'I'm okay,' he said, 'although sometimes I feel like I'm barely keeping my head above water. There's a lot going on.'

She sat beside him at the table. 'It is a lot busier than I'd imagined. I thought you'd have a lot more spare time out here. I imagined that because you didn't have to go to an office, didn't have to commute, it would give you more time.'

'It's pretty all-consuming. There's always something that needs to be done. If it's not the cattle, it's the horses, or the machinery or paperwork or maintenance or staffing issues. It's really too much for one person. Cara used to do the paperwork, organise the trucks, order supplies. I have to do all of that too now. The only break I get is when I leave the station.'

'So you'll have to make the most of next weekend, then.'

'Next weekend?'

'The camp draft. We're all going to Cunnamulla, remember?'

He'd forgotten all about the camp draft and he knew it wasn't because he was busy. It was because, whenever

Rose was nearby, he found it difficult to think of anything except her. 'I will.'

'I know it's not really any of my business but do you have a plan for the future? Perhaps you should employ someone to do the books? You can't be thinking that you can continue like this indefinitely?'

'Like what?'

'Burning the candle at both ends. It's not good for you or the children.'

'What do you mean, the children?'

'They hardly spend any time with you. They've lost their mother and their father is a shadowy figure on the periphery of their lives. I'm really happy to spend time with them, they're gorgeous kids, but they need you.'

Mitch sighed. He was trying to do his best, for everyone, but it seemed that wasn't good enough. 'There just aren't enough hours in the day. It's my job to keep this place running.'

'I understand that but you also have a responsibility to your children.'

'I'm doing the best I can. I don't know what else I can do.'

'Your kids just need some love and attention. You don't have to do anything specific. Just try to be there for them a little bit more. Spend some more time with them. I remember when my father died, my mother didn't cope very well. She was on her own with three children. I was the youngest, I was eight, so the issues were different, but I needed my mother and she wasn't really emotionally able to manage. All I wanted, all I needed, was to know that my mother was there for me. But she wasn't. Ruby went off the rails. A lack of supervision was not what she needed, and if it wasn't for Scarlett I'm not sure how I would have got through it.'

'What happened with your father?'

'He had an aortic aneurysm that burst. Completely out of the blue. My whole life changed in an instant. I *know* how your kids are feeling. They need your attention. I was the apple of my father's eye. He loved my sisters but I was special to him. I was his only child and I was also the baby.'

'Scarlett and Ruby are your half-sisters, is that right?'

Rose nodded. 'Mum has had a chequered love life. She fell pregnant with Scarlett when she was seventeen. Scarlett has never met her father. Ruby's father was a liar and a cheat. My father was the first one to give her, and my sisters, any sort of stability and normality. He adopted Scarlett and Ruby and for a while we were a perfectly normal, happy family. I was spoilt but I didn't know it at the time. I just accepted things as being the way they were because I didn't know any different.

'But when he died things changed. His life insurance was enough to pay off the mortgage on the house but Mum had to go back to work. That left Ruby with no supervision and me with no attention. I just needed someone to tuck me into bed at night and read me a story. I know how your kids feel. They just want your attention. They've lost their mother, they need you.'

Cara had been the one holding them all together but she was gone now. Rose was right, he was all the kids had now, he knew that, but that didn't mean he knew how to handle it. Sometimes it was easier just to pretend everything was okay and hope that would make it so.

'I know you're mostly around,' Rose continued. 'It's not like you disappear for twelve hours a day but you seem a little distant. You were different in the city. More present. I know you're good at the fun stuff but they need more from you. They need love and cuddles. Not just a kiss on the forehead.'

'I know they need more but it doesn't come naturally to me,' he admitted. 'And I find it especially hard with Lila because she looks so much like Cara.'

'Do you ever talk about Cara with them?'

'No.' He shook his head. 'They were so young. They barely remember her.'

'Jed does,' Rose said, surprising him. 'Lila even more so. I think she would like to hear about her mum. I know Lila was only six but she remembers.'

'I don't know if I can do this.'

'Of course you can.' Rose reached out and put her hand on his hand. Offering comfort. He turned his hand over and held onto hers, running his thumb over her palm. She watched him stroke her skin. 'I'll help you,' she said. 'Just spend some quiet time with them. Start with family dinner, just the four of you.'

'Cara used to feed the kids here at the house when they were small before they really ate Shirley's cooking,' Mitch said. Remembering Cara wasn't as painful as he'd thought. The pain had eased, softened, and he was able to look back without an ache in his heart. Did that also mean he was able to look forward? 'But after she died it was easier to eat in the kitchen quarters with everyone else. It was easier for me not to have to think about cooking for ourselves.'

'I'm not judging you. I'm trying to offer a suggestion. Mum worked night shift for seven years so that she could be home for dinner and back again in the morning before we went to school. Scarlett was there overnight but Mum must have been run ragged trying to manage everything else. I know it's not easy but you do have help. Shirley will cook for you, and you can just bring the meals back to the house like I did tonight. You can talk about your day. The kids will chat if you give them a chance. But if they always eat with the staff and sit at different tables you'll never hear about their thoughts. You won't form that bond. They need that routine. Even if it's just once a week. And read to them. Tuck them in at the end of the day. Spend some quiet time with them. Give them a chance to talk about anything. Listen to them.'

'That's the sort of thing Cara was good at.'

'You can learn. Little steps. You're good with the rough and tumble but they need some gentle affection too. You can do this.' Rose thought it would be good for Mitch too. 'It will help you all to heal. You can move forward together as a family.'

Rose fiddled with her empty beer. She really should go. Mitch needed to think. But she couldn't make her legs move. They sat at the table, looking at each other but not speaking. She'd said everything she needed to say about his family. There was only one other question that needed answering now.

She waited. Waited to see if he was going to say anything. Wanting to know if he'd come to a decision about them. But he was quiet.

She was going to bed.

She pushed her chair back from the table. 'I'll see you tomorrow,' she said as she pulled her hand from under his. Hesitating, she waited to see if he would take it back.

He didn't.

She stood and he stood too.

They were inches apart. She needed to feel him and stepped forward and wrapped her arms around him, hugging him tightly. She figured he needed some human contact just as much as his kids did and kissed him softly on the cheek. 'Goodnight,' she said before stepping back. She could still see into his eyes, which were dark and unreadable. What was he thinking? He still wasn't speaking but she could feel the pull in the air, an invisible thread, holding them together.

He reached for her hand and pulled her back to him. With his other hand he tipped her chin up and bent his head and kissed her properly.

No questions. No answers.

The kiss was the question.

His lips were warm and soft but insistent.

Her response was the answer.

She opened her mouth under his pressure. Willingly acquiescing.

His hand was on the base of her spine. The pressure was firm, holding her to him. She could feel his body heat through the thin cotton of her dress. She wanted desperately to feel his fingers on her skin but instead she felt him pulling away.

'What's the matter? Have you not made a decision?' She'd promised herself she wouldn't beg or hassle him for an answer but she had to know. She had to know why he'd stopped and what he was planning on doing next.

'It's complicated.'

'Explain it to me. I think you owe me that.'

'You're my employee.'

'You pay me to take care of your children. What I decide to do in my spare time is not on the clock. It's not your responsibility.'

'But ethically?'

'How many times have you heard of the husband and the nanny having an affair? We're both single. We're not doing anything wrong. There's no law against it. Unless it's because of Cara? Are you not ready for this?'

'That's not the problem. I'm ready. When I'm not with you you're all I think about.' He ran his fingers down her arm, sending sparks from her chest to her groin. 'When I am with you I can't think of anything else but this. But my children are asleep across the hall.'

Rose smiled. She could solve that problem. 'I have a perfectly good bed a few feet away and there are no children in my house.' She could still see him hesitating. 'I've spent the past three nights here. If Charlie wakes up all he wants is a drink. Put some water next to his bed.' She doubted very much that any of the children would wake up. 'But it's your decision. You know where to find me.'

She kissed him again just to prove her point and pressed against him, feeling his erection hard against her stomach.

She wondered what he would decide to do but it was up to him now. He had to come to her willingly, she needed to know he'd thought about things.

She let him go and walked away.

Mitch watched her go. He counted the steps as she crossed the flower bed and climbed up to her veranda. Fifteen. She was less than twenty metres away but she might as well be a thousand for all the comfort it brought him.

He went to kiss his children, who were all sleeping soundly, and then climbed into his bed. His head hit the pillow and he was assailed by Rose's scent. His linen smelt of her. If he hadn't come back early he knew she would have changed the sheets. He was glad she hadn't. Her scent was comforting.

He didn't want to be alone in his bed; he wanted her with him. He'd come back to see her, to have her. He'd opened the gate. He'd had a taste of her and, just as he'd anticipated, he wasn't going to be able to shut the gate now. He was finding her irresistible.

It scared him. So many people already relied on him, could he handle another?

He tossed and turned and knew sleep wasn't going to come easily.

Lying in his bed, he stared at the ceiling.

He didn't want to lie here alone. He wanted Rose.

He got out of bed and pulled on a pair of shorts.

He walked through the dark and silent house to the laundry, where he opened a cupboard. He pulled out a box and lifted the lid. The box contained all the things he'd packed away after he'd lost Cara and his daughter. Sheet sets for the cot, baby clothes, blankets and toys. At the time he couldn't bear to look at all those things. Each one was a reminder of what he'd lost but he hadn't been able to bring himself to give them away either.

But it had been months since he'd looked in this cupboard and now he couldn't say why he'd held onto all of this. Cara's clothes were gone. He'd kept her jewellery and her wedding dress and a few other things to pass on to the children, to Lila in particular, but he'd been able to give away the rest of his wife's things. But not these baby things.

He retrieved what he'd been looking for and shoved the rest of the things back into the box and closed the cupboard doors. He would sort this out soon. His life had changed. It had moved on. It had moved forward.

He picked up the baby monitor and the remote. He plugged the monitor into the hallway outside the children's rooms and put fresh batteries into the remote. He switched it on and then he took those first few steps.

He made his way across his veranda and over the dry and dusty flower bed and climbed the steps to Rose's house.

Moving forward.

CHAPTER NINE

A SOFT KNOCK on her door startled Rose.

She went to answer it, knowing it could only be Mitch, but that didn't lessen the surprise.

She hadn't really expected him to come over. She'd resigned herself to the fact that his resolve was stronger than his desire.

The hallway light illuminated his face but his eyes were dark, intense, and she knew he'd come for one thing and one thing only.

Her.

He lifted his hand. He was holding a baby monitor. Scarlett had the same one for Holly. Rose saw the green light shining; the unit was switched on.

She smiled and took his hand and pulled him inside before either of them could change their minds. Her heart was pounding and with a shaky hand she took the monitor from him and put it on the table in the hall.

Mitch gathered her in his arms and kissed her. His fingers were at the back of her neck, under her hair, and they felt like heaven as his touch sent tingles shooting down her spine.

Her bedroom was to their right. There was no need to go any further into the house but now it was she who hesitated.

'Have I read this wrong?' Mitch asked as she stepped back. 'Have you changed your mind?'

'No. But there's a complication.'

'What is it? I seem to have become quite good at problem solving tonight.'

She'd spent the past few days wondering what he'd decide, hoping he'd choose her, but she still hadn't figured out what to do about the thing that scared her most. Her foot.

He smiled at her as he waited for her answer and Rose knew she'd have to figure something out. She wasn't going to pass up this opportunity again.

There was no way around it. She'd have to tell him.

She took a deep breath and gathered her courage. 'I have ugly feet.'

Mitch's smile widened and she could tell he was trying not to laugh.

'It's not funny.' She pouted.

'*That's* the complication? Whoever said feet had to be beautiful? They just have to get you from A to B.'

'Well, mine don't do that too well either.'

Mitch frowned. 'What are you talking about?'

She had to tell him. This was never going to work otherwise.

'Remember how you commented on my terrible balance?'

'Yes.'

'There's a reason for that. Something I haven't told you.' Rose took another deep breath—inhale for four, exhale for eight. 'After I contracted meningococcal I had to have three toes amputated on my right foot. My foot is ugly.'

'Is that all?' Before she knew what was happening he had gathered her back into his arms. He held her close, held her tight, and she felt safe. She rested her head on his chest. 'Did you think I wouldn't find out?' he asked.

'I know it makes me sound vain and shallow but my foot is really ugly.'

'So what were you planning on doing? Making love under the covers with the lights out?' She could hear the smile in his voice. She knew he was teasing her but she also knew her declaration hadn't fazed him in the slightest.

'That would be one solution,' she replied. He might think he wasn't bothered by her foot but he hadn't seen it yet.

'Did you really think I would care? I was a doctor. I've seen plenty of things that are worse than a few missing toes and I know plenty of people who are missing bits. It doesn't change how I feel about them, it doesn't change how I treat them. It's a couple of toes.'

'I hate the way they look.'

Mitch stepped back and looked directly into her eyes. 'I'm not attracted to you because I thought you might have sexy feet. I'm attracted to you because you look like a gorgeous, golden angel. You are kind and gentle and you remind me of the good things in life. You make me smile and laugh and make me feel like I could be happy again. You are beautiful, and missing a couple of toes doesn't change any of those things about you, but if it would make you feel better why don't you get into bed, dim the lights and when you're comfortable, call for me?' He kissed her lightly on the lips. 'I'm not going anywhere. I'll wait right here.'

She had to trust him.

She nodded and did as he asked.

A short time later Mitch stepped into her room. He had removed his shirt in the passage and he dropped his shorts as he came through the doorway. He was naked and glorious and she forgot all about her foot. There was no room in her head for anything but the sight of Mitch, naked and ready and eager for her. She lifted the edge of the sheet and he joined her under the covers. His hands reached for her, pulling her to him, and under the light of the moon and to the background chorus of green tree frogs they made love in her bed and it was perfect.

He was gentle, understanding and considerate. He was all the things she'd hoped for and he made her feel whole again.

He was perfect.

She fell asleep with a smile on her lips and his voice in her ear. 'You are beautiful, Rose. Every inch of you.'

Rose spent the next week in a state of blissful delirium. Mitch was generous, attentive and thoughtful, not to mention gorgeous, and every evening he was hers, solely and totally and completely, for an hour or two.

They would share a drink on the veranda before he joined her in her bed before returning to his own.

She longed to be able to spend a whole night in his arms but she wasn't sure if that would ever happen and she was determined to make the most of the time she did get to spend with him.

If anyone noticed a change in their behaviour, nothing was said. They were all too busy getting ready for the camp draft. There was high excitement around the station as the preparations were made and that was enough to have everyone focussed on that and pay no heed to Rose and Mitch's activities.

Darren and Jimmy had taken the horse truck and gone on ahead to Cunnamulla. Mitch and Rose were taking the camper trailer and most of the staff were heading to the Outback town too. They'd earned some days off after the muster. Shirley was also going, taking advantage of having most staff off the station to have a break.

Mitch got their campsite organised before they took Lila to her X-ray and physiotherapy appointments.

'Lila is doing really well,' the physiotherapist told them. 'Her X-rays show good alignment and good bony union. She can start to take some more weight through her legs and we'll eventually be able to get rid of those crutches, but not just yet. It would be great to introduce hydrotherapy into her exercise routine now if we can organise it.'

'Hydrotherapy?' Mitch queried.

The physio nodded. 'Water-based exercises. Lila could do strengthening and mobility exercises in the water. The pool is warm and the water supports her weight. She can practise walking as well. We see some really good results but it all depends on whether it's something she can do at home. I can include Lila in our pool session tomorrow so you can see what exercises she would do. Do you have a pool?'

'No,' Mitch replied. 'But I might be able to figure something out.' Rose could see the wheels turning in his mind. 'How warm does the water need to be?'

'Thirty-four degrees is optimal.'

'I think we can manage to work something out.'

'So who wants to get in the pool with Lila?' the physio asked.

Rose blanched. 'I didn't bring my bathers.'

'You can wear shorts and a T-shirt if you have them.'

Mitch looked across at Rose. She'd gone as white as a ghost. He knew what the problem was. She wouldn't want to get into a public pool. She wouldn't want to go barefoot. He would sort the problem out but they didn't need to have this discussion in front of the physio. 'Tell us a time and we'll be there.'

He waited until they had some breathing space before raising the subject again. They were back at the showground, leaning on the fence, watching the first camp drafting event and waiting for Jimmy, who was the next competitor, to ride. 'It would make sense for us both to do the exercises with Lila, more sense for you than me as I imagine you'll be the one supervising her back home,' he said.

'I don't have my bathers and I don't have my aqua shoes. I can't get into a public pool.'

She looked terrified but he thought it was important for her to do this. She needed to take this step. They both had healing to do and he knew she needed to accept her disability and come to terms with it. 'We'll do it together.'

'But what about the boys? Someone needs to supervise them,' she said, making excuses.

'We brought half the station with us. Someone will help. I'm sure Shirley will be happy to keep an eye on them.'

Rose shook her head. 'I don't want to get in the pool. Please, don't make me.' Her voice was shaking too.

'We'll go shopping. The hardware store will have something you can wear on your feet. They have a big boating and camping section.'

'Are you sure?'

'Positive. I'll be right there with you.' It wasn't Lila who needed his support, it was Rose, and he was happy to give it. 'I promise, you won't have to get in the pool without shoes but I do need you to know what Lila needs to do,' he said just as Jimmy entered the arena.

A big cheer went up from the Emu Downs crew and Jimmy was grinning from ear to ear as he rode on the back of a beautiful, dark brown stallion. They watched as he attempted to complete the circuit around the barrels in the fastest possible time. He rode well and another cheer erupted as he finished to take the top spot in the competition so far.

'Can I ask you a question?' Mitch asked as Jimmy removed his hat and saluted the crowd.

Rose nodded.

'You know Jimmy had an accident on the station a few years ago and lost a couple of fingers, don't you?'

'Yes. He told me you saved the rest of his hand. That if you hadn't been there he would have died. Bled to death. He told me you saved his life.'

'Quite possibly.' Mitch brushed her comments aside. 'But that's not the point I'm trying to make. When did you notice that Jimmy was missing his fingers?'

'When he was saddling the horse for me.'

'So you didn't notice when you first met him?'

'No. I didn't notice the first few times he saddled the horses either, I only noticed because he was teaching me how to saddle Fudge so I was paying close attention. When he was tightening the straps, that's when I noticed.'

'And when you watch him ride, what do you see?'

'Someone who is very good at what he does and clearly loves it.'

'So watching him you wouldn't guess or even notice that he's missing two fingers of his left hand, even though you know that's the case?'

Rose shook her head.

'I know your foot is a big deal to you,' Mitch said. 'I understand that, but I guess what I'm trying to say is that most people won't even notice. People are generally not that observant. We're all too caught up in our own world, our own problems. A few missing toes doesn't change the person you are. It doesn't make you any more or any less than you were before and I hate to think of you letting it stop you from doing things. You are more than the sum of your parts. I'm not expecting you to do anything that makes you uncomfortable but I think you are giving this much more significance than it deserves. Don't think of yourself in terms of what's missing, think of yourself in terms of what you do have. You are beautiful and kind and you bring joy into my life and my kids' lives. Think about that.'

'Really?'

'Really,' he repeated as he wrapped an arm around her shoulders. 'Shall we go and get you some shoes?'

Rose was in Mitch's arms as he guided her around the dance floor. The tempo of the music had changed as the evening wore on and Rose was happy to be in his embrace. No one would think it was strange. There were plenty of other couples dancing the same way, some more closely than others.

They'd had an action-packed day. The boys had competed in their camp drafting events, they'd gone to the pool for Lila's hydrotherapy session and enjoyed the various sideshow rides and games before dinner. Rose knew she should be thinking about getting the kids into bed but she couldn't bring herself to leave Mitch. Maybe just one more dance. The kids were happy playing with their friends.

Mitch's long fingers were splayed across her back. She could feel the heat of them through her cotton shirt. She felt clumsy dancing in her riding boots, she found it difficult to change direction quickly, but dancing with Mitch was much easier than dancing alone. Mitch supported her. Physically and emotionally. In his arms she could forget about her feet. Her missing toes didn't bother him and she was beginning to think about not letting them bother her. In his arms she felt whole. In his arms she felt beautiful.

She closed her eyes but resisted the temptation to rest her head on his chest. She didn't want to encourage questions from the Emu Downs crew.

Rose stumbled as an overweight man bumped against her. Mitch arms tightened around her, holding her firmly and stopping her from falling.

'Are you okay?' Mitch asked.

As Rose nodded she noticed the man lurch and bump into a second dancer. Mitch reached out a hand to steady the man.

'Careful, mate,' he cautioned. 'Perhaps you should sit down, get a glass of water and stay off the booze.'

'He hasn't been drinking.' Rose noticed an elderly woman step up beside the man. She assumed she was the man's wife.

'At all?' Mitch queried with a frown.

The woman shook her head. 'Not a drop.' She looked worried.

Mitch looked concerned now too but Rose wasn't sure why. The man wasn't drunk, perhaps he'd just missed his step on the dance floor. But before Rose was able to ask Mitch what was bothering him the man clutched his stomach and collapsed at their feet.

Mitch dropped to his knees beside the elderly gentleman.

He had smelt alcohol on the man's breath. A sweet, slightly fruity odour that made him assume that the man had sneaked in a few drinks without his wife noticing.

The man's eyes rolled back in his head and Mitch shook him gently as his fingers probed the man's neck, searching automatically for the carotid pulse.

It was present, rapid but present.

He looked up at the man's wife, who looked ready to burst into tears.

'Are you positive he hasn't been drinking?' Mitch asked. He tried to keep his tone neutral, tried not to sound as though he was accusing her of lying. 'Could he have had a few without you noticing?'

The woman shook her head. 'We've been together all night. Stan hasn't been feeling a hundred per cent so I know he wouldn't have been drinking.'

'Stan, can you hear me?' Mitch used the man's name,

hoping for a response while not actually expecting one. He had an accelerated heart rate, he smelt of alcohol and he was unresponsive.

If it looks like a rat… But Mitch knew that wasn't always the case. There were plenty of other conditions that mimicked drunkenness and this overweight, elderly man was certainly a candidate for several of the other options. Mitch needed support and Stan needed an ambulance. He needed assessment and treatment. He needed to get to the hospital.

As Mitch thought about his options he heard Rose's voice.

'He's a doctor,' she said.

He wanted to protest. He was still licensed to practise but he chose not to. He didn't want to be in this situation. He didn't want to be the one everyone was relying on. What if he got things wrong?

He just wanted someone else to come and take over.

'Call the ambulance,' he instructed no one in particular.

The response he got was not the one he wanted. 'They're busy with a suspected heart attack on the other side of the showgrounds.'

He felt, rather than saw, Rose kneel beside him. 'What can I do?' she asked, assuming he had the situation under control. 'What do you need?'

'I need a medical kit and the local doctor.'

Rose stood up as Stan's wife leant over. 'What's wrong with him?' she wanted to know, but he ignored her question. He didn't know the answer, although he could hazard a guess, but guesses weren't helpful at a time like this. Instead, he answered her question with one of his own.

'Does he have any pre-existing health problems?' Mitch could see that Stan was overweight, flushed in the face. 'Any history of heart disease, diabetes, high blood pressure, allergies, liver damage?' The list was by no means exhaustive but it would give his wife an idea of what Mitch needed to know. He searched the man's wrists, checking for a medical ID bracelet.

Stan's wife shook her head.

'He's not diabetic?' Mitch queried. He would have put money on Stan being diabetic. This collapse looked suspiciously like a hyperglycaemic attack, which could lead to a coma if untreated.

'He's had some tests done but we haven't got the results back yet,' Stan's wife explained.

'We've called for the doctor.' Rose was back. 'What do you think is wrong with him?'

'It might be a diabetic coma. High blood sugar.'

'I can help you. Just tell me what you need me to do.'

He looked at Rose and she nodded her head. He knew she was telling him he could do this. That she trusted him. But did he trust himself?

Did he have a choice?

He knew he didn't.

'I need a testing kit,' he said as he raised his voice. 'Is anyone here diabetic? Does anyone have a kit I can use?'

A small black case was handed to him. He pulled out the kit, pricked Stan's finger and squeezed the blood onto the testing strip. He slotted it into the machine and waited for the reading: BSL thirty-five mmol/litre.

He looked up and held out the testing kit, waiting for the owner to claim it. A teenage boy stepped forward and took the kit.

'Can you run to find the ambos?' Mitch asked him. 'Tell them I need an infusion set—IV fluids, a kit and electrolytes—tell them it's for a diabetic.'

Mitch saw the boy glance at the screen before he slid the kit into the bag. 'Do I tell them it's a hyperglycaemic attack?'

'Yep, thanks, mate.'

He didn't bother stressing that he needed the ambulance officers too, they would know they were required as soon as they were able to come. Mitch wondered where the local doctor was. Perhaps he'd already been called to help the ambos.

'Is he going to be all right?' Stan's wife asked as they waited.

Mitch hoped so. 'If we can get the fluids into him.'

The kid was fast. He was back with the infusion kit and handed Mitch another bag containing electrolytes, a syringe pack and a vial of insulin.

Mitch inserted the needle before replacing it with the catheter. It was a difficult process due to Stan's dehydration but Mitch was also worried that his hands would shake and disclose his nervousness but somehow he managed to attach the catheter and run the drip. He added potassium and sodium to the saline solution before giving Stan a shot of insulin.

He'd just finished when the local doctor arrived. He pulled up in a hearse and Stan's wife turned a shade of pale green and Mitch thought she might be about to faint.

The doctor pulled a spinal board from the back of the hearse and carried it across to Mitch. 'Sorry, the hearse is our only option for transporting a prostrate patient as the ambulance is still busy.'

Mitch nodded as he brought the local doctor up to speed. 'I've done all I can here,' Mitch concluded. 'We need to get him to the hospital.'

He helped to roll Stan onto the stretcher before lifting him into the hearse and telling his wife to hop in the front.

She still looked worried. 'Is he going to be all right?' she repeated.

'He'll come around once those fluids start working and

we get his blood sugar level back to normal,' he told her as he bundled her into the front of the hearse. The hospital staff could tell her more. That was their job. He was just a cattle rancher now.

CHAPTER TEN

ROSE HANDED MITCH a cup of coffee and sank into the camping chair by his side. The kids were finally in their sleeping bags, a lot later than planned due to the drama of the evening, but at least now they had five minutes to themselves.

She could hear music from the showgrounds, drifting on the slight breeze. The band had started up again. She found it hard to believe that the party was still going. She was exhausted. The adrenalin of the evening was wearing off and she could feel fatigue setting in but she knew she wouldn't be able to switch off and go to sleep. Not yet.

Mitch had been terrific tonight in a very confronting situation. Her own heart was still racing and she could only imagine how he was feeling.

'You were brilliant,' she told him as he took the cup.

'That's very generous of you. It wasn't a difficult diagnosis.'

'I didn't see anyone else with an idea,' she replied.

'It was nothing special. I'm just a country GP.'

It was the first time she'd heard him admit that he was still a doctor. Usually he protested the description, stating that he wasn't practising any more. Despite his lack of practice, he didn't seem to have lost his skills.

'I don't think anyone is *just* a country GP. You have such amazing skills, surely a part of you must miss it?' Rose had been amazed at how decisive Mitch had been. There'd been no hesitation on his part, he'd known exactly what to do. She couldn't understand why he had so much self-doubt. 'Is there no way you can live on the station and still practise?' She was certain that if he wanted it badly enough he could make it happen.

Mitch was silent for a long time. He sipped his coffee and she wondered whether he was going to answer her, or ignore her completely, when he finally spoke.

'Cara inherited the station when her brother died. It's belonged to her family for generations. She was the brains and when I was there I was the brawn, but I did continue to practise medicine. I used to go into Broken Hill once a week; I'd work three days in a row in the medical clinic and then drive home. But it all became too hard after she died. I couldn't afford to be away from the station for days at a time. I couldn't afford to be away from the kids. I had responsibilities—running the station for one thing, the kids for another.'

'You could have sold it. Moved to town and continued to practise medicine.'

He shook his head. 'It's the kids' inheritance. I couldn't make that decision.' It was also his connection to Cara. His wife and daughter were buried on Emu Downs. He couldn't abandon them. He had failed them in life, he wouldn't do the same now they were gone.

'Would you go back to it if you could? I could look after the children if you wanted to.'

'I appreciate your offer but the children are the least of my problems. Running the station is all-consuming in time and energy. I can't do both, not even with your help, and I don't want to. It's okay.'

But he knew he was telling a white lie. It wasn't okay, he

did miss medicine but he knew he wouldn't practise again. He didn't trust himself.

And one good outcome tonight was not enough to change his mind.

He couldn't have it all and he had to be content with that.

Rose wished she could work out how to convince Mitch that he should use his medical training. She supposed his argument of being time poor was a valid one but it seemed such a waste of an obvious talent. She was almost positive that he'd taken pride in his diagnosis and treatment of Stan under difficult circumstances. When they'd checked on him the next day they'd found him in high spirits, having made a good recovery.

But every time she tried to raise the topic with Mitch he changed the subject.

She was getting nowhere and on the second Sunday in May she decided to give the argument a rest. It looked like one she wasn't going to win.

It was Mothers' Day and, although they hadn't discussed it, Rose imagined that Mitch would be finding the day tough to cope with. He was short-tempered with the children on a couple of occasions in the morning, which was unlike him, and Rose decided the best course of action would be to keep the children occupied and out of his way. She didn't want to add to his stress level if she could avoid it.

She took the kids to the kitchen and together they baked a cake for Shirley before Rose took them all to the concrete water tank that Mitch had filled with warm artesian water and converted into a hydrotherapy pool for Lila. She and the children enjoyed their day and she hoped she'd successfully given Mitch some breathing space.

Lila loved the freedom of movement that being in the

warm water gave her and Rose could see obvious improvement in her strength and mobility. Each little step forward that Lila made also helped to bolster her confidence and the one-on-one time they spent together was encouraging Lila to confide in Rose. And just as Rose could see the changes in Lila she could feel them in herself too. Station life suited her, she'd decided. She was blossoming too. She was feeling stronger and fitter from the combination of hydrotherapy and horse-riding and her night-time activities with Mitch didn't hurt either. Now she just had to figure out how to get him to ask her to stay.

'Are you okay?' she asked him later that evening when they were alone together on his veranda.

'Mmm…' His reply was very noncommittal.

'Today must be hard for you,' she persisted. 'Are you missing Cara?'

Mitch didn't answer immediately before saying, 'It's not about me. I'm just feeling sad for my children who are going to grow up without knowing their mother. It seems worse on Mothers' Day.'

'You could talk to them about her. You can keep her memory alive for them.'

'I wouldn't know what to tell them.'

'Tell them about when you first met. When you fell in love. Tell me.'

'You want me to talk about Cara?'

Rose wasn't sure that she wanted to hear that story but she knew it was important. If she wanted the chance of a future with Mitch she needed to understand his past and he needed to share his feelings with her. She nodded. She wouldn't know where she stood until she understood his relationship with Cara and what it had been like. After all, Cara was the mother of his children. Rose didn't intend to replace her; she respected the fact that the children should have some knowledge of their mother, even if they didn't have the memories.

'We met at university in Brisbane. I was living in the same university boarding house as her brother, Peter. He was doing agricultural science and I was at med school. We were two years older than Cara but she followed in Pete's footsteps. She came to the city to study agricultural science too but she had dreams of being an artist. I'd visited the station with Pete so I'd met Cara before she came to the city but we didn't start dating until she moved to town. She asked me out—I wasn't sure that it was a good idea to date a friend's sister but she had other plans,' he told her.

'When she finished her degree she stayed in the city to be with me and went to art school. We moved to Broken Hill so I could do my GP training. It was close to the station, her parents and Pete, who was running the station by then, plus it's a big arts community.

'We got married around the same time but when Pete was killed in a light plane crash nine years ago we moved here. I continued to work in Broken Hill, travelling down to work three consecutive days and then travelling back while Cara ran the station. Then her mum was diagnosed with cancer and her parents moved to the city to be closer to treatment.

'Now I'm the only one left. The station is mine. I never wanted to inherit it, it wasn't my plan. Pete should still be here but now I can't let it go. It's the children's legacy, I'm just the custodian. It's a link to their family history, a family that's gone now. It's all that's left for them.'

Rose wondered how different Mitch's life would be if Cara hadn't asked him out all those years ago. He wouldn't have experienced the heartache he'd suffered but neither would he have his children. Which meant she would probably never have met him. She didn't want him to hurt any more, he'd suffered enough. He'd lost one of his best friends, his wife and given up his career. She wished she knew how to help. 'After she died, that's when you quit medicine?'

Mitch nodded. 'I told you it was because I had too much on my plate, that I couldn't manage it all, but that's not the whole truth. I could have chosen medicine over the station. I do feel like I'm the custodian, keeping the station for the children, but there would have been no one to stop me if I'd decided to sell up, move to town and continue to practise medicine. The only person stopping me was me. I gave up medicine not because I couldn't practise but because I didn't want to continue. I hadn't been able to save Cara and I lost faith in my ability as a doctor. No one wants a doctor who can't trust his own judgement. Who can't trust himself.'

But she'd seen Mitch in action. She knew he still had the instincts of a good doctor. How could he give that up? What had happened that had made him throw that all away? She needed to know. She needed to understand.

'What happened?'

'Cara was pregnant when she died.'

'Pregnant?' Rose hadn't known that. He'd lost his wife *and* a child?

'She was twenty-one weeks. I lost them both on the same day. I'd been in Broken Hill, working at the medical clinic for my usual three days. When I got home Shirley was looking after the other children. She told me that Cara had complained of a headache, nothing serious, but she'd gone to lie down. It turned out she'd had a headache for a few days but neither she nor Shirley had given it much thought.

'Cara had an appointment in town for an antenatal check coming up but she hadn't thought a headache warranted a need to go sooner or to call for the flying doctor or even to let me know. It was just a headache and Cara didn't think it was related to the pregnancy. She'd had three other pregnancies without any issues and delivered healthy babies. She was only thirty-four and not considered high risk as her other pregnancies had all been straightforward. She didn't think there was anything seriously the matter.

'But she was wrong.

'She had gestational diabetes. Her blood pressure was skyrocketing, which was causing the headache, but it was more serious than that. She'd developed pre-eclampsia that was undetected and progressed into eclampsia and by the time I got back it was too late.

'When I went to check on her she was convulsing. Then she had a stroke. By the time the flying doctor got here she was unconscious. She was still alive but they were too late. She died on the way to the hospital.

'If I'd been here, on the station, instead of in Broken Hill, I could have saved her.'

'How? You said she had a stroke.'

'I could have diagnosed the pre-eclampsia. I would have recognised the signs. The high blood pressure, the swelling of her hands, feet and face. Once detected it can be managed. Not cured but managed.'

'What could you have possibly done?'

'I could have given her magnesium sulphate to prevent more seizures but I wasn't here. I was too late.'

'You weren't to know.'

'I know but if we didn't live out here she might have been saved. This place, it's beautiful but it's so harsh. There's no margin for error. Help is so far away. If I'd been here or if we'd lived in town she would have survived.'

'And the baby?'

Mitch shook his head. 'A little girl. I admit, even if I'd been home I might not have been able to save her. The only cure for pre-eclampsia is to deliver the baby. More than likely she would have been too premature to survive. But you never know. I lost them both that day. It was the worst day of my life and something I hope I never have to go through again.'

Mitch was restless now. He stood and paced the veranda. 'I need to go for a walk. Will you come with me? The kids will be all right.'

He reached for her and pulled her to her feet. He kept hold of her hand and they walked in silence up the hill behind the house and down the other side. There was an old stone building that she'd never noticed sitting in a stand of eucalypts. Not a building really, the roof had long since rotted and the walls were crumbling, and behind the building, among the gum trees, she could see a cluster of tombstones. How had she never noticed these before?

Mitch let go of her hand and squatted down in front of the two newest stones.

In the moonlight Rose could read the inscriptions.

One was engraved with Peter's name. The other with Cara's.

There were fresh frangipani flowers on the headstones and Rose knew Mitch had already been there once today.

She read the inscription.

Cara Louise, beloved wife and mother
10th October 1980—7th May 2015

May Louise, beloved daughter and sister
Gone with the angels
7th May 2015

The seventh of May was today's date. It was the two-year anniversary of their death.

'It's today?'

Her heart ached for Mitch. For everything he'd lost. She knew the pain of loss but nothing on this scale. To lose a wife and child at the same time, how did someone recover from that?

'You called her May.'

'She was born at twenty-one weeks so I had to register her birth,' Mitch said as he stood up. His voice was heavy in his throat. 'We hadn't chosen a name yet. I named her May after the month she was born but I didn't think about how it would make me struggle every year, every May, that came after. I didn't think about how it would continue to affect me. I didn't know.'

He sat down wearily on the crumbling stone wall of the old building.

Rose took his hand. To make matters worse, this year, the anniversary of their death coincided with Mothers' Day. She fought back tears. She hated to see him hurting but this wasn't about her feelings. She just wanted to take his pain away.

He was staring at their hands, at their entwined fingers. 'I haven't practised medicine since that day,' he said.

Rose had wondered what had really prompted Mitch to give up medicine. From what she had seen he had a natural affinity with people, an instinctive desire to help, and he hadn't lost his ability to make quick and accurate decisions. She'd wondered what had made him walk away from all that but she hadn't imagined the catalyst would have been the deaths of his wife and unborn daughter. That scale of tragedy was impossible for her to imagine. 'It wasn't your fault,' she told him.

'I'm still not sure about that. It makes it hard to forgive myself.'

'Mitch, I've seen you work. I know you would have done everything possible. There are some things you can't control in life. You taught me that. You don't need forgiveness if you're not to blame.'

She waited for him to look at her, to acknowledge her words. He had helped her to accept her past and shown her how to move forward with her life. She would give anything to be able to help him do the same. She hated to see him hurting but she wasn't sure what she could do to ease his pain.

She needed to get his mind off the past. Dwelling on those tragic events wasn't going to help anyone. She leant towards him, not sure if her overtures would be accepted or rejected, and kissed him.

He kissed her back before asking, 'What do you see in an old man like me?' as if he couldn't understand what she was doing there.

'So many things,' she said, 'but mostly you just take my breath away. You did from the moment I first saw you.'

She stood up, still holding his hand, and led him back to her house. She took him to her bed, there were no old memories for him there, and comforted him as she'd learnt how to.

She lay awake once they were spent, holding him in her arms and wondering about the future. Their future.

Mitch was a good man, a passionate, kind and considerate man. He was a good father and he'd been a loving husband and Rose knew she was in love with him.

He had given her a gift. He'd opened her up to a world where love was possible. She was able to see herself through his eyes now. She had grown and matured and she had accepted the new version of herself because he had made her believe. He had made her stronger.

In her fantasies about her future she'd always imagined that her prince charming would sweep her off her feet and take care of her but now she knew she could take care of herself and also of others. She wasn't going to be the damsel in distress, she was going to bring this family back to life. Spending time with them, loving them, had restored her soul and her self-confidence, and now she knew she was strong enough to restore him too. If he would let her.

She loved him but she didn't know if that was enough. She didn't know if that would make any difference because she didn't know if he would ever give himself permission to love again.

And she didn't know what that would mean for them. Or for her.

CHAPTER ELEVEN

Rose rolled over and hit the snooze button on her alarm. Just five more minutes. That was all she needed.

She was exhausted. Last night she'd driven back from Broken Hill, returning from a three-day sports camp with the children. She'd done all the driving as well as being wholly responsible for them while they'd been away and she was worn out. Adrenalin had kept her going on the drive home. The thought of seeing Mitch had kept her buzzing. She couldn't wait to touch him, to make love to him, and she'd barely been able to wait until the children were in bed before dragging him home with her. But after he'd left her bed, after she'd come back down to earth and after the adrenalin had left her body, she'd begun to feel unwell.

Initially she'd thought she was just worn out and all she needed was a good sleep but then she'd developed a sore throat and a headache and had become nauseous and feverish. She'd taken some pain relief during the night but hadn't been able to keep it down. God, she hoped whatever she had she hadn't passed onto Mitch. They didn't both need to feel like crap.

Hopefully he'd escaped whatever lurgy she'd contracted.

She closed her eyes. A few more minutes in bed and then she might be ready to face the day.

* * *

Mitch was at the cattle yards talking to Darren when Jed came flying around the corner. He skidded to a stop in the red dust and grabbed Mitch's hand. 'Dad, Dad, come quick.'

The hairs on the back of Mitch's neck stood up and a shiver of fear ran down his spine as he recalled the last time Jed had run towards him uttering those same words.

'Lila wants you. Rose is sick. She can't get out of bed.'

Rose. Not Lila. But his reaction was the same.

His heart turned to stone in his chest and plummeted into his stomach, making his insides churn. He fought back rising nausea. This couldn't be happening. Not again.

'I'll be back,' he said to Darren before sprinting in the direction of Rose's house, leaving Jed in his wake.

Lila was waiting on the front veranda. She looked worried and he had a brief, fleeting thought that an eight-year-old shouldn't look like that but he didn't have time to stop. He took the steps two at a time, flung open the screen door and burst into Rose's bedroom. Her room was dark but even so he could see that her cheeks were flushed and he could tell just by looking at her that she had a fever.

As he sat on the bed beside her his foot knocked against a bucket that was on the floor. She'd been vomiting. He put his hand to her forehead. Her temperature was raging; she was burning hot under his fingers.

She opened her eyes at his touch. Her eyes, which were normally the soft green of an emu egg, were dull and feverish.

'Hi.' Her lips were dry and parched and he could see the effort she went to just to speak.

He didn't take his eyes off her as he spoke to Lila, who was hovering anxiously at his shoulder. 'Lila, go to the bathroom and run a hand towel under cool water and bring it back to me,' he said. He needed to cool Rose down.

She was too sick to get out of bed and he knew that was not a good sign. If she'd been feeling just a little poorly she would've made an effort to get up. The fact that she hadn't, when she should be in the classroom with the children, spoke volumes.

He needed some light, he needed to see her clearly. 'I have to open the blinds,' he said as he stood up. He raised the blinds and saw her wince as light streamed into the room.

She was dehydrated. He could tell from looking at her lips and her tongue. He gently pinched the skin on her arm. The skin tented, not resuming its normal resting phase.

'Tell me what's wrong,' he begged. 'Tell me what hurts.'

'My head and my throat.' Her voice was hoarse.

'Have you taken anything?'

She nodded slowly. 'But I can't keep it down.'

She must have picked up an infection in Broken Hill. He could feel a sweat breaking out on his forehead and back. A cold, nervous sweat. His heart was racing, gripped by icy fingers of fear. He tried to bite it back but the heavy feeling of dread settled in his stomach.

This could not be happening again.

To him or to her.

She'd been fine last night, hadn't she?

He'd been so eager to see her, to get her into bed, had his eagerness clouded his judgement? Had he really lost all his clinical reasoning skills, all his powers of observation?

Could she have been this sick and he hadn't noticed? Was it simply a virus or something more sinister? He knew it was rare but not impossible to contract meningitis more than once. It was unlikely but he couldn't afford to ignore the possibility. He couldn't afford another mistake.

He sent the children outside and then pulled down the sheet that covered Rose. His heart was in his throat as he checked her skin for a rash. It all came back to him and he knew what to look for. He just hoped he was wrong.

He breathed out when he saw her skin was clear. He hadn't even realised he'd been holding his breath.

'Can you tuck your chin onto your chest?' he asked, relieved to see that she was able to do that without difficulty. His slid his fingers around to the back of her neck, pressing gently over the vertebrae and then moving forward over her glands. 'Is that sore?'

'Just on my throat.'

She had no rash and her neck movements were okay but he could feel a wave of panic threatening to engulf him just the same. What if he was missing something?

'I'm calling the flying doctor.'

He watched as she swallowed, it looked painful, and then he listened as she forced the words out. 'Don't be silly. I must have picked up a bug. I'll spend a day in bed and I'll be fine.'

She wasn't confused, that was another good sign, but she was exhibiting several other symptoms similar to meningitis. She had a headache, a high temperature and sensitivity to light. He knew they could also indicate all manner of other illnesses but he wasn't prepared to take that chance.

He shook his head. 'I'll start you on a course of antibiotics but I'm also calling the flying doctor.' A precautionary dose of antibiotics wouldn't do her any harm but he wasn't prepared to stop there.

'Don't you think you're overreacting a little?'

He knew he might be but he wasn't about to admit it. In his opinion it was better to be safe than sorry. He wasn't going to make the same mistake twice. Even though last time he'd acted as quickly as he could it still hadn't been enough. He wasn't going to risk waiting until it was too late.

'You're not well and you've been vomiting, which means

there's a chance you haven't kept your anti-rejection medications down either.' He sounded angry but in reality he was scared. 'You need a drip and a blood test. You need to be in hospital. We're too isolated here.'

He wasn't going to argue with her. He was making a decision. It wasn't safe to keep her here.

He kissed her on the forehead before he stood up. 'I'll make the phone call and come back with the antibiotics.'

The flying doctor had a plane available to leave immediately. He'd decided as he placed the call that if they were going to have to wait he'd get his pilot to get the Emu Downs plane ready. He would take her himself if it meant getting her there sooner. He wasn't going to regret not making a decision earlier. Not again.

Waiting for the flying doctor still meant a round trip instead of one way but their plane was faster and they would have the necessary drugs and equipment and, more importantly, Mitch knew they'd be able to make objective decisions about Rose's treatment. Their assessment wouldn't be clouded by emotions, regret or past mistakes. He knew it was better for everyone if he let the flying doctor take over, but it was difficult, immensely difficult, to sit and wait. He hated waiting.

Mitch paced restlessly at the edge of the airstrip as the plane departed, airlifting Rose to Broken Hill. He thought if he stood still he might pass out. Doc Burton had been his usual calm, unflappable self when he'd arrived to take over Rose's care but that hadn't settled Mitch's nerves. He was a dreadful patient and an even worse observer when someone he loved was suffering.

He grabbed hold of the fence post and closed his eyes, forcing back tears, as the realisation hit him.

He loved her.

He breathed deeply as he thought about what that meant.

It meant his decision to call the flying doctor had been the right one. He loved her and he had to keep her safe.

'Mitch?' He heard Shirley's voice and felt her hand on his shoulder. 'I think you should go to Broken Hill, you won't relax until you've seen her again.'

Shirley had been on the station for years. She'd been there when he'd lost Cara. 'I'll look after the children,' she offered. 'Just go.'

Mitch didn't hesitate. He made the five-hour drive in a little over four hours but he barely remembered it. He parked in one of the doctors' bays in front of the hospital and didn't stop until he had to wash his hands before entering the intensive care unit.

'Joanna,' he greeted the doctor on the unit. She was a former colleague of his.

'Mitch! What are you doing here?'

'I'm looking for Rose Anderson; she was airlifted from Emu Downs.'

'She's in here,' Joanna said, indicating an isolation bed.

Fear split Mitch's heart in two. Jo took one look at his expression and added hastily, 'It's just precautionary. She's had blood tests, I'm pretty sure it's not meningitis.'

'Pretty sure?' He could feel his hand shaking as he fought to keep his emotions in control. 'Are you going to do a lumbar puncture? You know she's had bacterial meningitis before?'

'Yes, I know. And she's had a kidney transplant, but there's nothing to suggest that she has meningitis again. If I see anything that makes me suspect otherwise, I'll order further tests. She's on a drip and IV antibiotics. We'll monitor her closely for the next few hours. You're welcome to sit with her but you have to trust me to do my job. Okay?'

Mitch nodded. He gloved and gowned and donned a face mask just in case and then sat by Rose's bed while she slept.

His guilt threatened to overwhelm him. He couldn't believe he'd put her at risk by being so isolated.

He made another decision while he sat beside her.

This time he was going to listen to his head instead of his heart.

He held her hand and put his head on her mattress. He dozed off but woke when he felt her stir.

She looked confused but her green eyes were brighter and a little bit of hope flared in his chest. 'Hi.'

'Where am I?'

'Broken Hill hospital.'

'What are you doing here?'

'I had to make sure you were okay. I had to see for myself. How are you feeling?'

'Better,' she said as he put his hand to her forehead.

Her temperature had come down, so had her blood pressure and heart rate. He knew from her observations that she should be feeling better but he was still worried. He needed to sort out what was going to happen next, before he changed his mind.

'I have good news. The doctors think it's most likely just a mild virus. A common cold you must have picked up at the sports camp.'

Rose smiled. 'I told you it was nothing.'

'It's not nothing. The station is no place for you. It might have been minor this time but what if next time it isn't? It's not safe for you to be stuck out in the middle of nowhere.'

'What do you mean, "It's not safe"?'

'This is exactly what I was afraid of. Of you getting sick and being so far from help.'

'You were also afraid of sleeping with an employee,

of what people would think, but that hasn't stopped you. Hasn't stopped us.'

'I was worried about that, not afraid. It's completely different.' But none of those things actually came close to his biggest fear, *I was afraid of losing you.* But he couldn't bring himself to say that. He was afraid that giving that fear a voice would strengthen it somehow. 'I can't risk losing anyone else.'

He'd lost Cara because of the remoteness and he wasn't about to risk the same thing happening with Rose. He couldn't guarantee her safety in the Outback but he couldn't leave the station either. He had an obligation to his children, it was their inheritance.

He had resigned himself to being alone.

'I'm tough. I survived meningitis, I'll survive this. You said it's only a cold.'

Mitch was shaking his head. 'But what if next time it's something more serious? What then? Your immune system is already suppressed, which makes you more susceptible to illness. I can't keep you safe. You need to go home.'

'*What?* You're sending me away?'

'I've already lost my wife and daughter. This is a risk I'm not prepared to take.'

'You can't do that! I love you.'

Mitch was silent. He looked like he had the weight of the world on his shoulders. If only he would listen to her, if only she could make him understand—she could *share* his worries, she didn't need to contribute to them.

He was still shaking his head. 'I'm not what you need.'

'Maybe, maybe not. But you are what I *want*. You and your children. I love you all.'

'I'm doing this for your sake, Rose. It's not safe. I'll get Shirley to pack your things and send them down to you.'

'Don't you dare!' she said as tears spilled from her eyes. It felt like a little piece of her heart had been ripped off and lodged in her throat. She struggled to talk. 'You can send me away.' She knew he could, she couldn't stay on at the station if she wasn't invited or employed to. 'But please don't make me leave without saying goodbye to the children. I love your kids. I'm not going to abandon them. They've lost too many people already without the chance to say goodbye. You can't ask me to do that.' Her fate rested completely in his hands but surely he couldn't expect her to leave without saying goodbye?

Lila and Shirley were helping Rose pack her things. Mitch had agreed to let her return to the station but he hadn't given an inch on any of his other conditions.

Steve was flying her back to Broken Hill today and she would be on the bus bound for Adelaide this evening. She wasn't going to get her happily ever after.

She stood in the middle of the school room, trying to work out what to take with her. The walls were covered with the children's artwork and she'd love to take some home as a memory of her time here, but she didn't want to strip the walls. She didn't want to lay them bare. It would feel too much like her heart.

A map of the world was taped to one wall along with the lyrics for the song about schnitzels with noodles. Rose didn't want to think about all the days she'd spent with the children and all the things she was going to miss. She picked up her laptop and zipped it into its case as she fought back tears.

'Why are you leaving?' Lila asked for what felt like the hundredth time.

'I have to get well,' Rose replied, giving her the same answer she'd given every time.

'You're coming back, though, aren't you? When you're better?'

'I...' Rose didn't have the words for that answer. It was breaking her heart to leave and to know that this was goodbye. To know she wouldn't be back.

'We'll have to wait and see,' Shirley said, jumping in to fill the silence. 'It'll be a nice surprise if Rose comes back, won't it?'

Rose bent down to kiss the children one last time. She wrapped them tightly in her arms, taking a minute to remember the feeling of their little bodies pressed against her as they hugged her back. She'd said goodbye to everyone else, Jimmy, Darren, Shirley, and asked them not to come to the airstrip. She'd told them it would make her too upset but the reality was she just wanted one last moment alone with Mitch and the children.

She'd always wanted a family of her own but now she knew she didn't have to have children of her own. That was something she'd feared might not be possible after her transplant, although she'd been told it wasn't an issue. The only problem was being unable to breastfeed because of the immunosuppressant medication but she'd figured that would be a small price to pay. Now she didn't care about having babies of her own, everything she wanted was right here in front of her and about to be taken away and there was absolutely nothing she could do. She had begged and pleaded with Mitch to see reason but he'd remained steadfast, stubborn and resolute. He didn't want her and she had to get on with her life.

She couldn't stay.

He didn't love her. He certainly hadn't told her he did but she took a small slice of satisfaction as he hugged her tightly one last time and didn't hurry to let her go. She thought she could see pain in his eyes and she hoped it was hurting him to say goodbye, just like it was hurting her.

She knew he was afraid of letting himself love again, but that didn't make it any easier to walk away.

The sunlight reflected off the little plane as it took to the sky. It was another gorgeous autumn day—sunny, bright and cheerful. It was the complete antithesis of Mitch's feelings but he'd brought this upon himself. This was all his doing, he thought as he watched the plane fade into the distance, taking Rose with it.

'What the hell are you doing, letting her go?'

Mitch turned to see Shirley standing behind him. He hadn't heard her arrive at the airstrip. She had her hands on her generous hips and she looked ready to box him around the ears.

'Are you crazy?' she added. 'Now what are you going to do?'

'Nothing.'

'Nothing!' She threw her hands in the air. 'I can't believe you. It's obvious you have feelings for each other. What's wrong with taking another chance at happiness?'

'I can't keep her safe. I can't risk losing her.'

'Looks to me like that's what just happened.'

'Leave it, Shirl.'

'Just tell me this,' she said, ignoring his pleas. 'How is letting her go any different? She's gone either way. She has a brain in her head. She can make a decision. It's not your decision to make for her.'

'It's done, Shirley. It's over.'

Didn't *anyone* understand? He couldn't ask her to stay.

He couldn't risk her health. He had to keep her safe even if it meant breaking his own heart. There was no other way.

He looked to the southern sky but the plane had disappeared from view. Rose really was gone from his life.

The significance of his decision sank in.

What had he done?

Rose had accused him of being afraid. He was afraid of falling in love again, but he was even more afraid of losing her. No matter which way you looked at it, Shirley was right—he'd lost her.

But he had no other choice.

CHAPTER TWELVE

IT HAD BEEN thirty days since she'd returned to Adelaide and every morning she woke up and told herself that she'd start making a plan for the rest of her life. Start applying for a job. If she wasn't going to get her happily ever after with Mitch she needed to look for it in other places and other ways. She would have to focus on her career instead. She loved kids, and while she didn't have her own she would put her energy into educating other people's children. It was time to get busy, time to look to her future. It might be different from the one she had hoped for but new possibilities could be exciting and it would help keep her mind off Mitch.

And today really was the day she needed to get moving. Today should have been the end of her three-month stint on Emu Downs. She'd had such dreams and plans. Pie in the sky. She'd been so certain things would work out, that she and Mitch would be able to build something together, but it seemed life, and Mitch, had other ideas.

But she couldn't mourn for ever. She needed to get over him.

She pulled out her laptop. She'd been talking to Ruby about combining her work with some travelling. It was time to get out of here. She needed to get far away. She knew of a couple of people who had studied with her and gone overseas to do some volunteer teaching in the Pacific, Fiji or Vanuatu, she thought. Perhaps that would be a good option, although she had no idea how she would fund that. But it couldn't hurt to look.

She flicked on the kettle and switched on the laptop but just as the kettle boiled there was a knock on the front door.

She opened the door and stood there in shock as thoughts raced through her head, colliding with each other. So many different thoughts she couldn't figure out which ones, if any, she should verbalise.

Mitch and the children stood there. Mitch was staring at her in silence. Was he waiting for her to speak? Expecting her to speak? What on earth did he want her to say? What on earth was he doing here?

The kids had no hesitation. They launched themselves at her, wrapping their arms around her legs.

'What are you doing here?' Rose asked as the children clung to her.

'We came to see you,' Mitch replied.

'You can't just drop in unannounced whenever you happen to be in the city.' Thank goodness her mother was at work, she thought. She didn't know how she would explain this unexpected turn of events to her. 'Not after making me leave you.' *My heart won't stand it.*

'We didn't just happen to be in the city. We came to see you,' Mitch told her.

'What? Why?'

'May we come in?'

Rose stepped aside.

'I came to apologise,' Mitch said.

Rose sent the children into the kitchen and gave them some muffins she'd baked the day before and a glass of milk each then took Mitch into the lounge where they could talk in private.

'I was wrong,' he said as he paced around the small room. 'I got so caught up in the past that I couldn't see my future. Ever since Cara died I had an ache in my heart. I'd got used to it being there, but it disappears when you're around. For some reason I couldn't see that you were what I needed until you were gone. We miss you. *I* miss you. I *need* you.'

Rose sat on the sofa. Mitch's pacing was making her nervous. Mitch *being* there was making her nervous. 'I miss you too but I can't see how we're going to resolve things. You aren't going to leave the station and you don't want me there.'

'I do want you there, but you were right. I was afraid.' Mitch sat beside her and picked up her hand. 'I was afraid of losing you but now I've lost you anyway.'

'You didn't lose me,' Rose argued, 'you sent me away.'

'I wanted to keep you safe.'

'And I just wanted you to love me.'

'I do.'

'What?'

'I do love you. I was afraid to love you but I can't help it. I love you. We all love you.'

'Do you mean that?'

'Of course. There's only one thing worse than an old man and that's a foolish old man. And that's what I am. Can you forgive me?' Mitch asked as he got off the couch and down on one knee. 'I love you, Rose, and I want you to be part of our family. I want us to be *your* family. Will you marry me?'

'Marry you?'

'Yes. I want you to come home with me as my wife.'

'Back to the station?'

'Yes.'

'Can I think about it?'

'Think about it? Why? What do you need to think about?'

'Are you going to freak out every time I get a cold?'

'Probably.' He grinned sheepishly. 'But I promise I won't call for the flying doctor every time.'

'And what about if I want to have a baby? Are you going to be okay with a pregnant wife? Are you even prepared to have more children?'

'Can we take things one step at a time?'

'I'm not sure. Are babies a deal-breaker?'

'No. As long as you agree to regular antenatal checks. We can work this out. We *will* work this out. You just have to agree to marry me, to become a family.'

'Do the children know what you're doing here?' she asked. And when Mitch nodded she said, 'Come with me.'

She went back to the kitchen and sat at the table with the children. How she'd missed them, all of them.

'Lila, Jed, Charlie,' she said. 'Your dad has asked me a very important question but it's one that concerns all of us and I want to know what you think.' She took a deep breath—inhale for four, exhale for eight—in order to gather the courage to ask the children the question, hoping they would give her the answer she so desperately wanted. 'He has asked me to marry him.'

'Did you say yes?' Lila asked, as she bounced out of her chair.

'I wanted to speak to you first,' Rose replied.

'Please, say yes, Rose,' Lila said as she threw her arms around her. 'We miss you.'

'Does that mean you'll come back and live with us?' Charlie asked.

'Yes. it does.' Rose nodded. 'What about you, Jed? What do you think?'

'I miss you too.'

Rose stood up and took Mitch's hands in hers. 'We can't

change the past and we can't predict the future. I need you to promise me that you will live in the moment with me. I don't need you to worry about me, I just need you to love me. Is that okay?'

Mitch nodded and she could see tears in his eyes. 'I promise to love you and care for you and make you happy,' he said. 'I don't want to live my life without you. You are my future. You are all I need.'

'And you are everything I want. I love you with all my heart, you and the children.'

'Are you saying yes?'

Rose nodded. 'Yes, I will marry you,' she said as she stepped into his arms.

'Ready?'

Rose looked away from her reflection in the mirror and nodded at her mother.

She straightened her dress. It was her mother's wedding dress, the one she'd worn the only time she'd been a bride, on the day she had married Rose's father. It was a simple lace column dress that had been altered, taking it in at the seams to fit Rose's thinner frame. The dress was a little shorter on Rose but in Queensland's heat that didn't matter. She slipped her feet into her new ballet flats. Lucy had adjusted them also, sewing a narrow band of skin-toned elastic across the centre to help hold them on Rose's feet.

Mitch had lost far more than she had and he was prepared to look to the future. A future with her. She'd even got him to consider returning to medicine. Small steps to begin with. There was the possibility of running a flying doctor clinic on Emu Downs six times a year, and Rose thought that would be a good start. If Mitch could look ahead after the tragedies he had suffered then she could manage without a few toes. It was a small price to pay in exchange for her life. A life she was now going to share with Mitch.

She took a deep breath—inhale for four, exhale for eight. She was ready.

She had something old, something new, something borrowed. And something blue. She put her hand over her heart. Lucy had taken an old photograph of Rose's father and had it printed on blue fabric and stitched it inside the dress, over the left breast, over Rose's heart.

She smiled. 'Ready.'

She picked up her bouquet of golden roses, the only thing Mitch had asked for, and tucked her right arm through her mother's elbow. She held her left hand out to Lila and together the three of them made their way out of the house. They paused on the wide veranda of the homestead and looked out over the garden. It was lush and green after the long-awaited rains and the lawns were filled with wedding guests.

Everything Rose needed was right there. Her sisters, their husbands, Jed, Charlie and, most importantly, Mitch. The family she'd grown up with and the family she was about to become part of all waited for her.

She followed Lila down the wide wooden stairs and across the lawn. At the bottom of the garden the river was flowing again but Rose didn't notice. She only had eyes for Mitch.

He reached out and took her hand as Lucy let go and stepped back with Lila. He winked at her as the minister began the formalities. Their vows were simple.

'I, Rose Lucinda Anderson, take you, Mitchell Paul Reynolds, to be my husband, and you, Lila…' she held her hand out for Lila and the boys to step forward, Lila on her left, Jed on Mitch's right and Charlie in the middle '… Jed and Charlie, to be my family. I promise to love you and care for you all the days of my life.'

'You may kiss your wife.'

Rose's stomach fluttered as Mitch's lips met hers and she knew it was more than excitement. She resisted the temptation to place her hand over her stomach. She was keeping that surprise to herself until she could share it with Mitch when they were alone. She was going to enjoy the day—she didn't plan on having another wedding day and she wanted to make this one special. News that they would be adding to their family could wait.

Today was the start of the rest of her life. The beginning of her future with Mitch.

Today was perfect. She had everything she had ever wanted.

'Everything okay?' Mitch asked as he lifted his lips from hers and squeezed her hands.

Rose beamed at her husband. 'Everything is perfect.'

* * * * *

THE NURSE'S BABY SECRET

BY

JANICE LYNN

Published in Great Britain 2017
By Mills & Boon, an imprint of HarperCollins*Publishers*
1 London Bridge Street, London, SE1 9GF

ISBN: 978-0-263-92640-8

Our policy is to use papers that are natural, renewable and recyclable products and made from wood grown in sustainable forests. The logging and manufacturing processes conform to the legal environmental regulations of the country of origin.

Printed and bound in Spain
by CPI, Barcelona

Dear Reader,

I instantly connected with Nurse Savannah Carter, and found myself going through many of the same emotions as she did while dealing with sexy but frustrating Dr Charlie Keele.

Charlie is a bit of a rambling man. He thinks he's no good for Savannah—or any woman—and he usually doesn't allow himself to get attached. Unfortunately he is second-guessing the career opportunity of a lifetime because of his relationship with Savannah. Which means he has to take it.

Savannah was raised to be a strong, independent woman, and she's quite proud of those traits. So when Charlie breaks things off not only is her heart broken, her pride is severely wounded. And now there's a baby on the way.

Together they have to overcome the past, deal with the present and forge a future. I hope you enjoy their story as much as I did. I love to hear from readers, so feel free to shoot me an email at janice@janicelynn.net.

Happy reading,

Janice

To Jessie & Rebecca—
may your love story be one for the ages.

Books by Janice Lynn

Mills & Boon Medical Romance

After the Christmas Party...
Flirting with the Doc of Her Dreams
New York Doc to Blushing Bride
Winter Wedding in Vegas
Sizzling Nights with Dr Off-Limits
It Started at Christmas...

Visit the Author Profile page
at millsandboon.co.uk for more titles.

Janice won The National Readers' Choice Award for her first book *The Doctor's Pregnancy Bombshell*

Praise for Janice Lynn

'Fun, witty and sexy... A heartfelt, sensual and compelling read.'

—*Goodreads* on *NYC Angels: Heiress's Baby Scandal*

CHAPTER ONE

NURSE SAVANNAH CARTER stared at her flat lower abdomen via the reflection in her bedroom mirror, imagining she saw the tiniest outline of a bulge if she stood just right.

Pregnant. Her.

How long had she dreamed of this moment?

Years. Her whole life.

She'd always wanted children. Always.

Sure, she'd thought she'd be married and have a husband who was going to be an amazing father to her precious child, but since when had things gone according to plan?

Never, really. Just as this pregnancy wasn't planned. But she couldn't complain. She had a good life. A great life. A great man in her life.

Charlie Keele was a wonderful person and doctor, and if her baby ended up with a more than generous share of Charlie's genetic code, well, her baby would be a blessed child.

Charlie was brilliant, gorgeous, athletic, a man who respected her independence and beliefs, and he'd been Lucky Savannah's boyfriend for the past year.

Lucky Savannah. She smiled at the nickname. That was what her friends had been calling her since the first time Charlie had singled her out at the hospital. They'd teased even more as she and Charlie had slid into an exclusive relationship. These days she and Charlie were inseparable.

They exercised together, ate more meals together than not, worked together, and practically lived together. She suspected they would soon. For quite some time she'd been expecting Charlie to ask her to move in with him.

Expecting him to propose.

Charlie owned a beautiful brick home with lots of room and an amazing fenced-in backyard just right for a family, in an up-and-coming neighborhood. If he hadn't mentioned living together first, when her apartment lease came up for renewing, she planned to discuss moving in with him.

She was having Charlie's baby. That might rush things a bit, which she regretted. She wanted him to ask her to live with him, to marry him, when he was ready, because he couldn't imagine spending the rest of his life without her. She had no doubt that was where their relationship was headed and she had no regrets regarding her accidental pregnancy.

She wanted Charlie and she wanted his baby.

Although she'd dated in the past, she'd never met a man like Charlie. Never felt for a man what she felt for Charlie. Never felt as cherished as Charlie made her feel. It was what her parents had had prior to her father's death when Savannah was seven years old. It was what Savannah had always known she'd hold out for. She didn't need a man, but having a good one in her life gave a shiny glow to everything.

A shiny glow she'd found with Charlie.

She pressed her hand over her belly, trying to imagine that she could feel the little life inside her. Charlie's baby.

Her and Charlie's baby.

A miniature version of them growing inside her.

Savannah's smile widened as her imagination took off. His brown hair and eyes and her fair skin? Or his strong, handsome facial features and cleft chin and her blue eyes? Or maybe her red hair and his dark features? Or…the possibilities were endless. Regardless, their baby would be beautiful. Would be loved. Would be their whole world.

A baby!

They'd not talked about children, but Charlie would be happy. He loved her. He hadn't said the words out loud, but Savannah knew. She saw it in the way he looked at her, in the way he touched her, kissed her, treated her as if she was the center of his world. Charlie Keele was in love with her and would be ecstatic at their news.

She really was a lucky woman.

She was having the most wonderful man in the world's baby. They were going to be a family and have a fabulous life.

Feeling as if she was floating, she glanced at her watch. He'd be here in a couple of hours. She'd tell him their news. He'd kiss her, twirl her around, sweep her off her feet, maybe even propose. Something grand, for sure.

Her hair and make-up were done up a little more than her usual ponytail pullback and light coating of mascara, just in case.

Maybe she should drop some hints and let him figure out her news in some creative way. Like a blue and pink cupcake or maybe she could get him to take her to a toy store under the guise of picking up a gift for her friend Chrissie's son, Joss. They could stroll through the baby section and she could ooh and aah over the tiny little outfits. Or she could fill up his car with pink and blue balloons or... A dozen reveal ideas came to her, each one putting a bigger smile on her face.

Wouldn't he be surprised when he realized?

Reality was, she'd never be able to keep the news from him for long. Already she was about to pop with excitement just waiting for him to arrive. No doubt he'd take one look at her and know.

She probably had a pregnancy glow.

Savannah laughed out loud, the happy sound echoing around her bathroom.

They were having a baby.

A baby! How amazing was that?

Needing to burn some of her energy while she waited for him, she hid the pregnancy test she'd done when her menstrual cycle had failed to make an appearance. Even if he beat her back, she wanted to see his face when he found out he was going to be a father.

When all evidence was safely tucked away, she grabbed her purse to head to the nearest department store.

There were some little pink and blue items she just had to have.

Frowning, Dr. Charlie Keele stared at the contract on his desk.

The signed and countersigned contract.

He'd done it.

He'd debated back and forth over the past month, but he'd really done it. He'd signed on to accept a job two hours away.

Taking the position was an amazing opportunity, but he had hesitated and he'd known why.

Savannah.

She'd become such an intrinsic part of his life, completely entangled in everything he did. He struggled to imagine leaving Chattanooga and the most remarkable woman he'd ever known.

But every time he'd considered turning down the offer, the past had reared its ugly head, reminding him of all the reasons why he should go.

He'd signed his name on that line for Savannah as much as for himself. More.

Savannah was an incredible woman. One unlike any he'd ever known or dated. Sure, he'd had a few long-term relationships over the years, but none that he'd ever thought twice about walking away from. Walking away had always been easy.

Nothing about leaving Chattanooga would be easy, except knowing that he was doing the right thing for Savannah by leaving before she became any more attached.

She was the most independent woman he'd ever met. He'd not expected her to get so intertwined in his life. Nor had he expected himself to become so tangled up in hers.

"Don't let a woman hold you back from your dream, son."

How many times had he heard that or something similar over the years? His father had dreamt of medical school, of working as a travel doctor with an organization such as Doctors Without Borders, of dedicating his life to medicine. Instead, he'd gotten his girlfriend pregnant, dropped out of college and gotten a coal-mining job to support his new family.

He'd resented his wife and child every day since for those stolen dreams. Charlie's mother and Charlie had never been able to replace those dreams and his father had grown more and more bitter over the years. Rupert Keele had pushed Charlie toward going into the medical profession from the time Charlie could walk and talk. Talking about medicine, about becoming a doctor and traveling the world to take care of needy people, was the one time Charlie's father liked having him around. For years Charlie had thought if he could make his father proud, that might make his father love him, might make life better for himself and his mother. He'd tried his best but, no matter how good the grade, the game performance, the above and beyond achievement, nothing had ever been good enough.

Rupert hadn't cared one iota about anything or anyone except himself.

Charlie's mother hadn't been much better, blaming Charlie for her lot in life as well.

Sometimes Charlie wondered if he'd have chosen something besides medicine if he hadn't been brainwashed from birth and so eager to try to win his mostly uninterested father's affections in the hopes it would somehow magically transform his parents into good ones. Regardless, when Charlie had been eleven, his maternal grandfather's congestive heart failure had worsened and Charlie had decided that, rather than work as a travel doctor, he wanted to do cardiology, to work on healing people's physical hearts, because he sure hadn't been able to do anything with his parents'.

Charlie had dreamed of heading up a cardiology unit his whole life and now he had the chance.

If he'd learned nothing else from his parents, he'd learned giving up one's dreams only led to misery for all concerned and that he couldn't protect anyone from that misery, not himself or the people he cared about.

Which was why he was leaving Chattanooga to set Savannah free.

To truly accomplish that, he'd have to hurt her, make her hate him.

Based on past experience, that should be no problem.

Stuffing the last of the shopping bags into her closet, Savannah closed the door just as her doorbell rang.

Charlie was there.

Finally.

He had a key but always rang the bell rather than just coming in, as she'd asked him time and again.

She turned from the closet and a pair of blue baby booties sitting on the bed caught her eye.

Oops.

She grabbed up the soft cotton booties, hugged them to her for one brief happy moment, then put them in the closet with her other purchases and reclosed the door. She'd decided she was just going to place his hand on her belly and let him figure out for himself why. She'd watch as his face lit with surprise, then excitement. She felt so giddy her insides quivered.

"You okay?" Charlie asked when she opened her apartment door, his dark eyes curious as she had taken longer than usual.

By way of an answer, she wrapped her arms around his neck and pressed her lips to his.

Immediately, his arms went around her waist and pulled her close, kissing her back. A thousand butterflies took flight in her belly that had nothing to do with the little life growing there and everything to do with the man making her heart race.

His kisses always made her heart race.

"Hmm," he mused, looking confused, when he pulled back from her mouth. "What was that for?"

"Do I have to have a reason to kiss you?" she asked, batting her lashes. She wanted to just tell him, to jump up and down and scream to the world that she was having a baby—Charlie's baby. But, seriously, she should probably let him into the apartment and close the front door before doing so.

Probably.

Frowning, he shook his head. "You have to admit, that's not the usual way you greet me."

"Well, it should be." He was right. She didn't meet him at the door and throw herself at him usually, but nothing was usual about tonight. Tonight, she was going to tell him the greatest news.

His brow lifted in question.

About to burst with excitement, she searched for the right words. Loving the strong feel of him, the spicy smell of him she wanted to breathe in until he permeated all her senses. "I have good news."

She was about bursting to tell him. But it registered that he'd yet to smile, as his face took on a tired appearance and he closed his eyes, tension tightening his body. "I have something to tell you, too."

"You do?" She stepped back and motioned for him to come into her apartment. Rather than sitting down, he paced across to the opposite side of the living room.

"Yes, and maybe I should go first." He raked his fingers through his hair, turned, gave her a troubled look.

The cloud nine Savannah had been walking on all afternoon dissipated and she felt her stomach drop. She'd been off work, but had met him that morning to run at the greenway. Then, they'd hit the gym together for about an hour. He'd been all smiles when he'd walked her to her car and kissed her goodbye. He'd kissed her so thoroughly and soundly that she'd wanted to drag him into the backseat and have her way with him.

Not that that was anything new. She always wanted to have her way with Charlie. He had *that* kind of body. One she still had difficulty believing she got to see and touch and kiss and hold and…

She shook off the sensual rabbit hole her mind was jumping down. "What's going on?"

"I didn't mean to get into this first thing." He paced over to a bookshelf, picked up a framed photo of them at Lookout Mountain, stared at the smiling image of them as if he'd never seen it before rather than being part of the couple in the picture. "But it's just as well to get it out in the open."

He was the most upfront person she knew. She'd never seen him so distracted. Was something wrong?

"Charlie?"

He set the photo down, turned and faced her. His expression was clouded, which was odd. Charlie never tried to keep his feelings from her. He'd never had to. He knew she was as crazy about him as he was about her.

Only right now, at this moment, he didn't look like a man who was crazy about her. He looked like a man who was torn by whatever he was about to say, a man who was about to deliver earth-shattering news.

Fear seized Savannah's heart and she struggled to get enough oxygen into her constricted lungs.

"Charlie?" she repeated, this time with more urgency.

"Have a seat, Savannah."

She made her way to her sofa. Slowly, she sat down and waited for him to tell her what was going on. She didn't like his odd behavior, didn't like that he hadn't greeted her with smiles the way he generally did, didn't like the way her heart worked overtime.

Where was her loving, kind, generous, open lover of the past year? The man whose entire face would light with happiness when he saw her? The man whose eyes would eat her up with possessiveness and desire and magical feel-good vibes?

The man avoiding looking directly at her looked as if he was about to deliver the news that she had a terminal illness or something just as devastating.

What if…? Her hands trembled.

Oh, God. Please don't let something be wrong with Charlie. Please, no.

Not now. Not ever.

"I'm leaving."

His two simple words echoed around the room, not registering in Savannah's mind.

"What?" Her chest muscles contracted tightly around her ribcage as she tried to process what he was saying, her brain still going to something possibly being wrong with him. "What do you mean that you're leaving?"

His expression guarded, he shrugged. "I'm leaving Chattanooga. I've taken a cardiology position at Vanderbilt Medical Center in Nashville on the heart failure team and I'm moving there as soon as I can get everything arranged. I turned my notice in at the hospital today."

Her ears roared. What he was saying didn't make sense. "You're leaving the hospital?"

He nodded. "I'm working out a two months' notice, during which time I'll be relocating to Nashville."

"But...your house." The house she'd imagined them raising their child in. The big backyard. The nice neighborhood close to good schools. The large rooms. Perfect for a family.

"I'll put it up for sale. I only bought it because I knew I could turn it for a profit. I never meant to stay there. It's way too big for my needs."

Never meant to stay. Too big for his needs. Savannah's head spun.

He'd never meant to stay.

Nothing he said made sense. Not to her way of thinking. Not to the promises she'd seen in his eyes, felt in his touch.

"You've always known you'd leave Chattanooga?"

She liked Chattanooga. The mountains. The river. The nightlife. The people. The town. She liked it. Chattanooga was home, where she wanted to be.

"I've never stayed in one place more than a few years and even once I'm in Nashville, if the opportunity comes along to further my career elsewhere, I'll move."

Her brain didn't seem to be processing anything correctly. Perhaps it was baby brain. Perhaps it was that he'd dropped the bottom out of her world.

"This is about your career?" she asked slowly, trying to make sure she understood what he was saying.

Because she didn't understand anything he was saying.

He was happy in Chattanooga. Why would he willingly leave? Why hadn't she known he planned to leave some day?

"I've taken a teaching and research position at the university and a prestigious position at the hospital. It's a great opportunity."

What he said registered. Sort of. "You're moving to Nashville?"

He nodded. "The hospital is offering a relocation package. Hopefully, I'll find something to buy or rent within the next few weeks so I can be settled in prior to starting."

"Hopefully," she mumbled a little sarcastically.

He was leaving. Not once had he said a word to her about the possibility that he might leave. Not once had he mentioned that he was looking for another job. That he'd consider another job even if it was handed to him on a silver platter.

He'd made the decision without even discussing it with her. Her mother, family, and friends were here. She didn't want to move to Nashville. Upset didn't begin to cover it.

"I don't want to live two hours away from the man I'm dating," she pointed out what she thought should be obvious. "I like that I see you every morning, that we work out together, that I get to see you from time to time at work, that I get to grab dinner with you, that you get to kiss me goodnight almost every single night." Did she sound whiny? If so, too bad. She felt whiny. And angry. How could he take a job in Nashville? "That's not going to happen if you're in Nashville and I'm in Chattanooga. Do you expect me to just sit around waiting for you to have time to come home or that I'm going to be commuting back and forth to Nashville between shifts?"

He regarded her for long moments, his expression guarded. "I don't expect you to do either."

What he was saying hit her.

A knife twisted in her heart and she instantly rejected the idea.

That couldn't be what he meant.

Of course that was what he was saying. That he'd not even mentioned he was thinking about moving, about taking a different job, that she hadn't warranted that tidbit of information, spoke volumes. *He was breaking up with her.*

"You've never mentioned that you planned to move." Her words sounded lame even to herself. So what? She was reeling.

Reeling.

Maybe he meant for her to go with him. Maybe he wasn't ending things. Maybe she'd jumped to all the wrong conclusions when he'd said he was leaving. Maybe he looked so stressed because he was worried she wouldn't go with him.

The reality was she didn't want to move to Nashville. She loved her job and coworkers at Chattanooga Memorial Hospital. She wanted to stay in her hometown, to be near her family, her friends, all the things that were familiar. She wanted to raise her baby near her home, where her child would grow up knowing her family and being surrounded by their love.

Her baby.

She was pregnant.

Charlie was leaving.

With obvious annoyance, he crossed his arms. "I never mentioned that I planned to stay, either."

Ouch. Had she seen blood oozing from her chest, she wouldn't have been surprised. His comment wounded that much.

"No," she began, wondering how she could have been so terribly wrong about his feelings.

His eyes were narrowed, his tone almost accusing. "Nor have I ever implied that I would stay."

He was right. He hadn't. She'd been the one to make assumptions. Very wrong assumptions.

Her silence must have gotten to him because he paced across the room, then turned to her with a reproving look.

"Good grief, Savannah. I've taken a job that's a wonderful opportunity. Be happy for me."

Tears burned her eyes, but she refused to let them fall. Instead of telling him what he wanted to hear, she shook her head. "No, I'm not going to say I'm happy for you. Not when this news came about the way it did. We've been involved for months. You should have told me you planned to move. I deserved a warning about something so big. For that matter, we should have discussed this before you made that decision."

His jaw worked back and forth. "I don't have to have your permission to move or take a different job, Savannah."

If she weren't sitting on the sofa, she'd likely have staggered back from his verbal blow. Truly, there must be a gaping hole in her chest because her very heart had been yanked from her body. "Agreed. You don't."

"I never meant for you to think I'd stay in Chattanooga, or that I wanted to stay."

She interpreted that as he'd never meant for her to assume he was going to stay, or want to stay, with her.

She'd been such a fool. She'd believed he loved her, had believed the light in his eyes when he looked at her was love, the real deal. She'd just seen what she'd wanted to see.

Whatever that look had been, she'd never seen or felt it with past boyfriends. Maybe she'd mistaken phenomenal sexual chemistry with love. She wouldn't be the first woman to have done so in the history of the world.

Devastation and anger competed for priority in her betrayed head.

She met his gaze and refused to look away, despite how much staring into his dark eyes hurt. They were ending. She'd thought everything had been so perfect and he'd been planning their end. "I think you should leave," she began, knowing that she wasn't going to be able to hold her grief in much longer and not wanting him to witness her emotional breakdown.

She was going to break down. Majorly.

He started to say something but, shoulders straight, chin tilted upward, she stopped him.

"That you made this decision without involving me tells me everything I need to know about our relationship, Charlie. We aren't on the same page and apparently never were. My bad. Now that I know we don't want the same things from our relationship, there is no relationship. I want you to leave. We're through."

There. She'd been the first one to say the words out loud. Sure, he'd been dancing all around the truth of it, but she'd put them out there.

Not once since she'd seen that little blue line appear had she considered that he wouldn't be happy about the news… that he wouldn't be there for their child.

That he wouldn't be there, period.

CHAPTER TWO

CHARLIE SMILED AT the petite lady he'd grown quite fond of over the past couple of years he'd been her cardiologist. "Now, now, Mrs. Evans. You'll be just fine under Dr. Flowers' care. He's an excellent cardiologist."

"But you know me," the woman explained, not happy about his announcement that he was relocating. "If it wasn't for having to cross that mountain halfway in between, I'd follow you to Nashville."

"I'm flattered that you'd even consider doing so, but you don't need a cardiologist who is two hours away. Mountain or no mountain, that's not a good plan."

"Then I guess you should change your mind and stay."

If ever there was a time he considered changing his mind about his move it would have been the night before at Savannah's apartment. The betrayed look on her face had gutted him, but he'd accomplished what he'd set out to do.

He'd set Savannah free and let her keep her pride by her being the one to say the words. He'd needed to let her out, but he hadn't wanted to break her spirit.

Things were as they should be.

He was single, free to make the decisions for his life without her or any woman's interference, and she was free of him and his baggage.

His father's dying words had been pleas to Charlie never

to be controlled by what was in his pants, and a declaration that no woman was worth giving up one's dreams.

"Marriage and kids suck the life right out of you, son," his father had told him. "You go after your dreams and you make them happen. You be the best doctor this country has ever seen and don't you let a woman stand in your way, no matter how pretty she is. In the long run, she will eat at your soul until you despise her for taking away your dreams."

Those had been the exact words from his last conversation with his father. He'd heard similar all his life, had known that was how his father felt about his mother, him.

Although he'd become way too involved with Savannah for far too long, Charlie wouldn't let any woman tie him down.

Not because of his father, but because of not wanting to relive the hell of what he'd grown up with. He'd been a burden to his parents, had ruined their lives; he'd been unable to protect his mother from his father's abuse, unable to protect her from the misery he'd caused. Charlie would never marry nor have children. Never.

He'd ruined enough lives during his lifetime already.

"You hear something different, doc?"

Charlie blinked at the elderly woman he'd been checking and instantly felt remorse at his mental slip into the past. Crazy that this move had him thinking so much about his parents, his failure of a family, his past. All things he did his best to keep buried. Maybe that had been the problem over the past year. He'd kept his past so deeply buried that he'd forgotten all the reasons why he shouldn't have gotten so involved with Savannah. No more.

"No," he told the woman with a forced smile. "Just listening to your heart sounds. Your heart is in rhythm today."

"My heart is in rhythm every day. Just some days that rhythm isn't such a good one."

He finished examining her, then saw the rest of his

morning patients. Typically, this was the time he'd go to the cardiovascular intensive care unit, see his inpatients, see if his favorite CVICU nurse could sneak away to grab a bite of lunch.

He'd gotten too attached to Savannah.

For both their sakes, he'd been right to take the job in Nashville. She might not realize it yet, but he'd done her the greatest favor of her life.

"You don't seem yourself today."

Savannah glanced up at her nurse supervisor, who also happened to be one of her dearest friends. Should she tell Chrissie the truth?

If so, how much of the truth?

The man I thought I was spending the rest of my life with told me last night that he's moving two hours away? Or, *I'm pregnant by a man I was crazy about but currently just want to strangle?*

Neither seemed the right thing to say at work, where she had to hold it together and not cry out her frustrations.

"I'm okay."

Chrissie's brow lifted. "You usually walk around as if your feet aren't affected by gravity. I've not seen you smile all day. So I'm not buying 'okay'."

Savannah gave a semblance of a smile that was mostly bared teeth.

Chrissie winced. "That bad?"

Savannah nodded. "Worse."

"You and Charlie have an argument?"

Had they argued? Not really. More like he'd told her he was moving and she'd verbalized that they were through.

"I heard he turned his notice in yesterday. I wasn't going to say anything until you did, but you've looked so miserable today that I couldn't hold it in any longer."

There it was. Confirmation that he was leaving. Everyone knew. Charlie was leaving her.

"I'm not sure what to say. My boyfriend—former boyfriend," she corrected, "is moving out of town. I was shocked by the news and haven't quite recovered."

Chrissie's expression pinched. "You didn't know?"

"You probably knew before I did."

Her friend's eyes widened. "He hadn't mentioned he was considering a move to Nashville?"

Savannah shook her head. "Not even a peep."

Chrissie looked blown away. "What was he thinking? He should have talked such a big decision over with you."

Maybe her expectations hadn't been unfounded if Chrissie thought the same thing as she had. What was she thinking? Of course he should have mentioned the possibility of a move. They'd been inseparable for months. Her anger was well founded.

"Apparently not."

"You said 'former boyfriend'," Chrissie pointed out. "You two are finished, then?"

Savannah had to fight to keep her hand from covering her lower abdomen. She and Charlie would never be finished. There would always be a tie that bound them.

A child that bound them.

Still, she didn't need him, would not allow herself to need him. Some fools never learned, but she wasn't going to fall into that category.

Toying with her stethoscope, she shrugged and told the truth. "Yeah, as a couple, we're finished."

Wincing, Charlie paused in the hallway. Neither woman had noticed him walking up behind them. Neither one knew he was overhearing their conversation.

Should he clear his throat or something?

He shouldn't feel guilty for eavesdropping. If they didn't want someone to overhear their conversation they shouldn't be having it in the middle of the CVICU hallway.

"I'm sorry to hear that," Chrissie told Savannah, giving her a quick hug. "I thought you two were perfect together."

Perfect together.

They had been perfect together, but wasn't that the way most relationships started? All happy faces and rainbows? It was what came along after the happy faces and rainbows faded that was the problem.

He was just leaving before the bright and shiny faded, before hell set in and people died.

Charlie absolutely was not going to be like his father.

If Rupert had been miserable at giving up his dream of a career in medicine, then he'd made Charlie's mother doubly so until her death in a car accident when Charlie had been fifteen. That had been after a particularly gruesome argument that Charlie had tried to stop. He'd never forgiven himself that he hadn't been able to protect her from his father. He'd tried, failed, and look what had happened, at what she'd done to escape his father—to escape him?

Guilt slammed him and he refused to let the memory take hold, instead focusing on events before that dreadful night. Why his parents had stayed together was beyond Charlie. They should have divorced.

They should never have married.

No doubt his mother would have been a hundred times better off if Rupert had walked away instead of marrying her and making her pay for her pregnancy every day for the rest of her life.

Regardless, Rupert had stayed with his wife and had instilled in Charlie the knowledge that giving up one's dreams for another person ultimately led to misery for all involved. His mother had seconded that motion, and when she'd died it had confirmed that her son was not worth living for. Charlie wasn't able to make another person happy, nor was he able to protect anyone from life's harsher realities. Those were lessons he'd learned well.

Thank goodness he was leaving before he'd sunk so far into his relationship with Savannah that he couldn't resurface.

That she couldn't resurface.

The next two months couldn't pass soon enough.

Savannah didn't have to turn to know that Charlie was behind her. Something inside always went a little haywire when he was near and, whatever that something was, it was sending out crazy signals.

"All good things must come to an end," she told her friend, not going into anything more specific, wishing she wasn't so aware of the man behind her.

With time, she wouldn't even remember who he was, she lied to herself, trying to balm the raw ache in her heart, trying to cling to her anger. Anger was easier than pain.

"You really aren't going to try to make a go of it long distance?"

She shook her head. "I don't do long distance relationships."

Perhaps, under the right circumstances, she would have, but nothing about what had happened with Charlie was right. He'd blindsided her and left her emotionally devastated.

Chrissie gave her a suspicious look. "You aren't going to leave Chattanooga on me, are you?"

She shook her head again. "Nope. Not that he offered to take me with him, but I'm not leaving Chattanooga to chase after a man or for any other reason. This is my home. If I'm not worth staying for, then good riddance."

She was pretty sure her words were aimed more at the man eavesdropping than at her friend. But what did it matter? Her words were true.

If only the truth didn't hurt so much. Didn't make her so angry. Not hurt. Angry.

"As your nurse supervisor, I'm glad to hear that. As your friend, I'm sad that you and Dr. Keele have split. You two seemed to have something very special and, quite frankly, I was more than a little envious."

Yeah, she'd thought so too.

"Appearances can be deceiving."

Very deceiving. She'd believed in him and his feelings for her. She'd been the one deceived and had no one to blame but her foolish, naïve self.

Only she blamed him, too.

Why had he acted so enamored if he wasn't? He'd treated her as if she was the candle that gave light to his world. They'd been together almost a year. A freaking year. A year of her life. A year of his life. Gone. Meaningless.

Only it wasn't.

Because there was a physical reminder of that year, of their relationship, growing inside her.

Darn him for taking the happiest day of her life and turning it into the worst.

She'd cried enough tears to sail a fleet upon, had to have used up all her tears, and yet, even now, she could spring a leak that would rival Old Faithful.

A man who would so easily walk away from her wasn't worth her heartache and tears.

"Speaking of the devil," she said, turning to let Charlie know she knew he was there. She wouldn't cry. Not in front of him. If she had her way, she'd never cry over him again. "Good afternoon, Dr. Keele."

He grimaced at her formal use of his name.

Good. He deserved a little grimacing after all she'd gone through the night before and every moment since. But, seriously, what had he expected? A smile and, *Glad to see you*?

"I imagine you're here to see Mr. Roberts. He's in Room 336 and, although he's still going in and out of atrial fibrillation, he's otherwise stable on the IV medication since his admission this morning."

All business. She could do it. She would do it.

No matter that he used to smile at her with his whole being and make her feel like the most precious person in the world.

No matter that two nights ago he'd kissed her all over and done crazily amazing things to her body and held her tightly afterwards.

No matter that his baby was nestled deep inside her body.

No matter that he'd utterly ripped her heart to shreds the night before, forever destroying her faith in him. In them.

No matter that she might just hate him for what he'd done.

He was leaving.

They were no longer a couple.

She no longer looked at him with rose-colored glasses.

He was a doctor. She was a nurse. She could play that game and keep things professional for as long as she had to.

She could hold her emotions in, keep her expression detached. He didn't deserve to see her pain.

He'd be gone in two months and then letting him see her hurt would be the least of her worries.

This was how it had to be, Charlie reminded himself as he went to check on his patient.

But to look into the eyes of the woman he'd spent the past

year of his life with and see nothing but cold disdain—that he hadn't been prepared for.

He should have been. He'd known they were going to end the moment he'd told her he was leaving. He'd expected her anger. Maybe her yelling and screaming at him would have been easier than the look of disdain. He'd lived with both, growing up. The yelling, the screaming at how worthless he was, the looks of hatred.

Yet seeing that look on Savannah's face gutted him.

He examined the unconscious man, checking the read-outs on his telemetry, making note of adjustments he'd make to his care.

Hopefully, tomorrow they'd be able to decrease his sedation and start weaning him off his respiratory ventilator.

He heard someone enter the room behind him, but knew it wasn't Savannah. She gave off a vibe that caused his insides to hum when she was near and he wasn't humming. Not even the slightest little buzz.

"Do I need to reassign your patients?"

He turned to look at the nurse supervisor, then shook his head. "I'll be here for two months and plan to take care of my patients during that time."

She arched a brow at his obvious misunderstanding. "Savannah taking care of your patients won't be a problem?"

"Not for me." He put his stethoscope back in his scrub pocket, then got a squirt of antimicrobial solution. Almost methodically, he rubbed his hands until the wet solution dissipated. He tried to appear casual when he asked, "Did she ask to be reassigned?"

Chrissie shook her head. "She'd never do that. She's way too professional, no matter what her personal feelings are."

He met the woman's gaze. "Then we shouldn't be having this conversation."

Chrissie didn't back down. If anything, his stern look

had her hiking up her chin to take advantage of every bit of her still short stature. "That's probably true, but it's my job to make sure everything goes smoothly on this unit. I don't want any unforeseen problems cropping up and I'm taking a proactive approach to this potential situation."

"As far as I'm concerned, there is no potential situation. I'll be gone in two months."

Her dark eyes narrowed but, rather than say anything negative, she surprised him by saying, "Congratulations on your new job. I hear it was a nice promotion."

"Thank you. It was."

She hesitated a moment, then looked him square in the eyes. "You're sure that's really what you want, though?"

He frowned. "Of course it is. It's a very prestigious position."

"Hard to have a conversation with a prestigious position over the dinner table."

She thought he was a fool for accepting the greatest career opportunity he'd been presented with because of Savannah. Let her think that. He didn't care what she thought—what anyone thought. He knew he'd made the right decision. That he was doing what was best for Savannah by destroying her feelings for him.

Feigning that her look of pity didn't faze him, he shrugged. "I won't be lonely."

She gave him a disappointed look. "No, I don't imagine you will. Congrats again, Dr. Keele. I hope you find whatever it is you're looking for in Nashville."

"I'm not looking for anything in Nashville," he told her retreating back. He wasn't looking for anything anywhere.

Charlie grabbed hold of the bed rail and stared down at his unconscious patient for long moments.

Taking the Nashville job had been the right thing for all involved.

What hadn't been the right thing had been getting so involved with someone. He wouldn't make that mistake again.

That might not be a problem anytime in the near future anyway. The thought of anyone other than Savannah just didn't appeal.

How was any other woman supposed to compare to the way she lit up a room just by walking into it? To the way her smile reached her eyes and he knew what she was thinking without her saying a word? How she enjoyed the same things he did, shared his love of Civil War history and taking long hikes up on Lookout Mountain on the battlefield? To running with him at dawn along the Tennessee River near her apartment?

The reality was no woman ever had measured up to Savannah and he suspected they never would. The thought of sharing his days, his nights, with anyone other than her left him cold.

She was perfect and he wanted her to stay that way.

Leaving was the best thing he could do for all involved.

CHAPTER THREE

"CODE BLUE. CODE BLUE."

Savannah rushed to the patient's room. Her patient had just flatlined.

She'd been in the bathroom when the call came over the intercom.

She hated that, but her bladder didn't hold out the way it used to. A symptom of her pregnancy, she supposed.

Chrissie was in the room performing CPR when Savannah got there with the crash cart. The man was on a ventilator so she was only performing chest compressions and the machine breathed for him, giving him oxygen.

Charlie rushed in right behind Savannah. A unit secretary was there acting as a recorder of all the events of the code.

"Give him some epi," Charlie ordered, taking charge of the code, as was his position.

Savannah did so, then prepared the defibrillator machine, attached the leads to the man's chest.

"All clear," Charlie ordered and everyone stepped away from the man.

Savannah pushed the button to activate the defibrillator.

The man's body gave a jerk and his heart did a few abnormal beats.

"Let me know the second it's recharged," Charlie ordered, having taken over the chest compressions for Chrissie.

"Now," Savannah told him.

"All clear," he warned.

As soon as everyone had stepped back, Savannah hit the button, sending another electrical shock through the man's body.

His heart did a wild beat then jumped back into a beating rhythm. Not a normal one, but one that would sustain life for the moment.

"I'm going to take him into the cardiac lab. He needs an ablation of the abnormal AV node, a pacemaker, and a permanent defibrillator put in STAT."

"Yes, sir."

By this time, other staff had entered the room and a transport guy and Savannah wheeled the patient toward the cardiac lab, Charlie beside them.

Chrissie called the lab, told them of the emergency situation and that Dr. Keele was on his way with his patient.

Savannah helped to get the patient settled in the surgical lab, then turned to go.

"Savannah?"

Slowly, she turned toward Charlie, met eyes she'd once loved looking into. Now, she just wanted him to hurry up and leave.

He searched her face for something, but she couldn't be sure what, just that his expression looked filled with regret. That she understood. She had regrets. Dozens of them. Hundreds. All centering around him.

She'd been so stupid.

"You did a great job back there," he finally said, although his words fell flat.

She swallowed back the nausea rising in her throat and wanted to scream. They were broken up. He shouldn't be being nice. And if he said, *Let's just be friends*, it might be him needing resuscitation because she might just choke him out.

Rather than answer, she gave him a squint-eyed glare, then turned to go.

When she got outside the lab, she leaned against the cold concrete wall and fought crumbling. Fought throwing up. Fought curling into a fetal position and letting loose the pain inside her.

Two months.

She could do anything for two months.

Only, really, wasn't she just fooling herself every time she thought *two months*?

Wasn't she really looking at the rest of her life because, with the baby growing inside her, she'd have a permanent connection to Charlie?

A permanent connection she'd been so happy about, but now—now she wasn't sure. How could she be happy about a baby when the father didn't want her?

Would he want their child?

When was she supposed to tell him? Before he left? After he left? Before the baby got here? After the baby got here?

Never?

He'd find out. They shared too many friends. Nashville wasn't that far away. Not telling him wasn't an option, even if she could keep the news from him. She couldn't live with that secret. On the off chance that he would want a relationship with their child, she had to tell him.

Would he think she'd purposely tried to trap him into staying? See her news as her trying to manipulate him? Would he understand that she didn't want him to stay because she was pregnant when he hadn't been willing to stay for her? That he'd destroyed the magic that had been between them forever?

She lightly banged her head against the concrete wall.

What was she going to do?

A month later, Charlie shifted the box of Savannah's belongings to where he could free up a hand to knock on her apartment door.

And stood there, frozen.

Why wasn't he knocking?

Why was he just standing outside her apartment like some kind of crazy man?

He was crazy.

She'd texted him earlier that day and asked what he wanted her to do with his things. He couldn't really recall what he had at her place, other than his running gear and ear buds and maybe a few odds and ends, some clothes. Maybe, instead of saying he'd stop by and pick up his things, he should have told her to just keep it all.

But that still left him with having to deal with her belongings. She'd had some toiletries in his bathroom and some clothes that he'd boxed up. So, tonight, he'd kill two birds with one stone. Or something like that. Because he'd stripped his place of all physical reminders of Savannah and taped them inside the box. Out of sight, out of mind.

Not really—forgetting Savannah would come with time.

As he'd been driving to her place, the night he'd told Savannah about his new job kept replaying through his mind. Over and over.

She'd been so happy when she'd met him at the door, had told him she had good news. Good news she'd never gotten to share because he'd told his news first and all hell had broken loose.

She hated him. He saw it in her eyes on the rare occasion when their eyes met at the hospital. She no longer wanted anything to do with him.

Mission accomplished.

Earlier that day he'd run into her and gotten a good look. She'd been abrupt, to the point, immediately launching into a report about one of his patients. Darkness had shadowed her eyes. Her face had been devoid of the happy sparkle that had always shone so brightly. She'd looked so completely opposite to how she'd been a month ago that her greeting him at the door, her smile, her giddiness, the warmth of her kiss and hug, had played on repeat in his head.

What had caused her such joy a month ago?

Him? Yes, they had had a good relationship, but only because he'd never had any expectations of her, had never made any promises that he'd live to break.

Hand poised at the door, he closed his eyes.

He couldn't do this. He didn't feel up to being the jerk he needed to be. He needed her to keep hating him, to move on. Instead, he just wanted to ask her what her good news had been, to see joy in her eyes.

He could never do either. He came with too much baggage, too much risk.

What if he pushed Savannah as far as he'd pushed his mother? What if the same type of thing happened?

He turned to go.

Fighting the urge to slam the apartment door she'd just opened back shut, Savannah stared at the man in the hallway with his back to her. At the sound of the door opening, he turned toward her. His eyes were full of raw emotion and she thought she should definitely slam the door and bolt it closed.

"My neighbor called and told me you were loitering in

the hallway," she said as explanation for why she'd opened the door since he hadn't knocked. "She wanted to know if she should call the police."

"What did you tell her?"

"To call them," she said, even though they both knew it wasn't true. "That I hoped they'd lock you up and throw away the key."

"I thought that might have been your answer."

She raised an eyebrow and waited. Just as he could wait if he thought she was going to invite him into her apartment. She wasn't.

She'd been nauseated most of the day, but had made the mistake of eating dinner anyway because she knew she needed to eat to keep the baby healthy. Her grilled cheese wasn't sitting well in her stomach. Charlie showing up at her apartment wasn't helping.

"You looked as if you weren't feeling well when I was at the hospital earlier," he pointed out as if this was breaking news.

"It's been a long month," she said, a mixture of adrenaline and exhaustion tugging at her body.

She was showing the patience of a saint by not screaming and yelling. She'd like to scream and yell. But, really, what good would that do? He was leaving. But, way beyond that, he'd pretty much put her in her place when she'd said he should have discussed such a big decision with her. That place hadn't been beside him or as someone who had any importance in his life.

That knowledge kept her in the middle of her doorway, staring at a man she'd once thought she'd spend her life growing old with.

"Are you just going to stand there not saying anything?" she asked, injecting as much annoyance as she could muster into her voice.

Glancing down the hallway as if he half expected the police to really show up, he shifted the box he held and raked his fingers through his dark hair. “I brought your stuff.”

Her fingers itched to smooth out the ruffled tufts of thick hair left in the wake of his frustration, but she stayed them by tucking her hands into the pockets of her nursing scrubs.

“Fine,” she huffed, not moving out of the doorway, almost afraid to move for fear of jostling where her dinner precariously sat in her belly. “Set it down there and I'll get your stuff so you can leave.”

“I was leaving. You opened the door.”

His frustration was palpable and had her shaking her head.

“You'd been in my hallway long enough that Mrs. Henry was having a conniption.”

“She always was nosy.”

“I thought you liked her.”

“I did.” He raked his fingers through his hair again. “I do.”

Savannah winced. Two little words she'd once thought she'd hear him say, but under very different circumstances.

Unable to bear looking at him a moment longer, she turned away, put her hand to her lips to stay anything that might be going to come out.

“Are you okay?” he asked from behind her.

She gritted her teeth to keep from verbally attacking him. No need to have Mrs. Henry calling the police for real.

“I'm fabulous,” she lied.

You could mend a broken heart back together, but it was never the same. She'd never be the same or look at Charlie the same.

That magic giddy bubble was popped forever.

She'd trusted in his feelings implicitly and he'd shattered that trust. He'd unilaterally made a decision that had torn apart what she'd thought had been a permanent relationship and he'd not had remorse or guilt or a sense that he should have talked with her first. Her complete misjudgment of that meant she would never allow herself to trust in her own feelings again. Not with Charlie or any other man. How could she when she'd been so completely wrong about Charlie?

Exhaustion gripped her body, making standing a challenge and all she could do. "Are you gone yet? Your stuff is by the door. Grab it and go."

She just wanted him to leave. But instead he stepped into her apartment. Maybe he'd get his stuff, then go.

"Tell me whatever your good news was."

Spinning to stare at him in disbelief, Savannah's stomach dropped. Her jaw did, too.

"Tell me whatever it was you wanted to tell me a month ago, Savannah."

For a brief moment she considered telling him. Right or wrong, she wasn't ready to share her news with him. She just didn't feel strong enough tonight to face whatever reaction he might have. Not tonight.

She squared her shoulders, lifted her chin, and tried to look as if she could successfully take on the world.

Normally, she could.

"Maybe you should have thought of that before you took a job two hours away," she tossed out.

"My taking a job two hours away has nothing to do with you," he insisted with more than a hint of annoyance.

Good. His words annoyed her, too.

And hurt. His words hurt. Deep and to the core.

"It should have," she said so softly she wasn't even sure he'd hear her.

"Says who?"

"Says me." She lifted her gaze to his and dared him to say otherwise.

His jaw worked back and forth and a visible struggle played on his face. "Why do you get to decide that it should have?"

"For the same reasons you got to decide that it didn't."

He let out a low breath. He stepped closer, stared down directly into her eyes. His gaze narrowed. "You think I should have said no to the position?"

Her stomach rumbled and she clenched the tips of her fingers into her palms. "That's not what I'm saying."

"Then what are you saying?"

"That I should have mattered enough for my opinion to have counted. I didn't."

He studied her for a few long seconds. "My career means everything to me." His tone was flat, almost cold. "I won't let anyone or anything stand in the way."

Ouch. There it was. The truth.

A truth she'd not understood because for the past year they'd obviously been on the same page. Sure, he worked hard and long hours, but so did she. Their jobs hadn't been an issue. Finding time to spend together hadn't been an issue.

She'd thought they'd been each other's priority. Obviously, in Charlie's case it was more a case of convenience than priority.

She'd been easy.

No, she hadn't. She'd not immediately fallen into bed with him. Not immediately. But too quickly. The attraction had been so strong. The sexual chemistry so magnetic.

Even now, with everything that had happened, with her body threatening to reject her evening meal, his nearness made her heart race, her breath quicken, her nipples tighten, her thighs clench. He made every sense come alive, made every nerve ending aware.

She hated it. Hated that even knowing she didn't mean what she'd thought she'd meant he had such power over her body.

He wasn't the man she'd thought he was—wasn't the man she'd fallen so hard for. That man had been an illusion. She'd fantasized and projected upon him. Maybe because of their strong sexual chemistry and her desire to believe the intensity of their lovemaking was due to something more than just physical attraction. Outdated of her, no doubt, but that had to be it.

She didn't know how she was going to handle her future, her baby's future, but at the moment one thing was very, very clear to her.

She looked Charlie straight in the eyes and felt an inner strength that surprised her. Sure, he'd probably always affect her physically. He was a good-looking, virile man who gave off an over-abundance of pheromones and her body remembered all too well the magic he wielded. But he'd destroyed the rose-colored glasses that she'd adoringly looked at him through. What she now saw wasn't worthy of what she'd been willing to give him.

"You don't belong here," she told him. "Not in my apartment. Not in my life."

Not ever again.

Savannah's words stung Charlie in places deep within his chest. Places that weren't supposed to be accessible to anyone, much less vulnerable to words that were all too reminiscent of those flung at him in the past.

He took a step back.

He wavered between wanting to beg her to forgive him

and telling himself to walk away and forget her. She was right. He didn't belong. He'd never belonged. Never would.

He'd always known that. Had never been able to forget that until Savannah. Look at what that memory lapse had caused.

Looking exhausted, Savannah closed her eyes then turned her back to him and walked over to her sofa, where she sat down. "I don't feel up to doing this again, Charlie. I'm sorry, but I just don't."

Her skin had lost its color and she had crossed her arms over her belly.

"You look pale."

She didn't comment, just proceeded to turn a few more shades toward ghastly gray. Hands over her stomach, she leaned forward and made a noise that might have been a moan, but might have been a dry heave.

Despite not being invited in, he stepped further into her living room and toward the sofa. "Are you okay?"

Without looking up, she shook her head. "No, I am not okay. Get your stuff and leave."

He was torn. She wanted him to go. She really did. He could hear it in her voice. But how did he just walk out when she looked as if she was majorly ill?

Then she was.

With a panicked glance at him, she bolted off the sofa and toward the half bath just off the living room.

Worried, Charlie followed her to the small half bath, grabbed a rolled up washcloth from the basket that sat on the vanity, and ran cold water over it, all the while keeping his eyes trained on Savannah. She knelt over the toilet, gripping the sides and heaving out the contents of her stomach.

When he'd squeezed out the excess water, he folded the washcloth. He pulled her hair back away from her face, put the washcloth across her forehead, and helped support her while she leaned over the toilet.

He didn't say a word, just held the washcloth to her forehead, kept her hair back from her face, and felt torn into a million directions as to what he should do.

He couldn't leave her like this even if he wanted to.

He couldn't.

He didn't have it in him to walk away with her ill.

When her heaving seemed to have subsided, she glanced up at him with a tear-streaked face and he felt something in his chest squeeze painfully tight.

"I hate that you saw me like this."

Kneeling, he took the washcloth and gently wiped her mouth. "I'm a doctor, Savannah. I've seen worse."

A long sigh escaped her lips. "Not from me."

She looked lost, like a child, and more than anything he wanted to ease her distress and take care of her.

"I'm going to carry you to your room, help you change out of your scrubs, wash your face and brush your teeth, then put you to bed."

She closed her eyes for a moment then shook her head. "I don't need you. I can take care of myself."

"You're sick. Let me help you."

Her expression pinched, and he expected her to argue, but instead, her skin going gray again, she lowered her gaze. "No carrying. Just...just help me get to my room."

Charlie steadied her as she stood, wrapped his arms around her waist, and walked with her to her room. He stayed close until she seemed steady on her feet in front of her en suite sink, where she washed her face, then brushed her teeth. He went to her bedroom, opened a drawer and pulled out an oversized T-shirt.

His T-shirt.

How many nights had he watched her pull on this shirt

after they'd made love? Sleepily, she'd smile at him, then curl back up in bed. He'd tuck her in with a kiss, and then head to his place feeling like a million bucks. He'd never see that love-laden smile again. Never be the one to kiss her goodnight. He squeezed the worn cotton material between his fingers, then shook off the moment of nostalgia.

She was better off without him. Just look at what had happened to his mother. He had his career. His career was what was important.

"Here." He held out the shirt through the bathroom door. "Put this on."

She glanced at his offering, then bit into her lower lip.

"I'll wait here while you change. If you feel sick again or need my help, call out. I'll be right there."

Taking the shirt, she nodded and shut the bathroom door.

The lock clicked and it echoed through his head that Savannah had forever closed off a part of herself to him.

As much as he tried to tell himself that was okay, as he sank onto the foot of her bed he wondered at his great sense of loss when going to Nashville was definitely for the best.

CHAPTER FOUR

FEELING PHYSICALLY BETTER after emptying her stomach but mortified, Savannah splashed cold water over her face.

She'd just thrown up in her bathroom with Charlie right there.

To give him credit, he'd been a champ, keeping her hair back and putting the cold cloth against her forehead. But she wasn't giving him credit. No way.

Wiping her hands on a towel, drying them, she then placed her palms over her lower abdomen.

Oh, God. What was she going to do?

How was she going to explain vomiting?

She'd known for a month now and hadn't told him.

She studied her reflection—the pale skin, the tired eyes, the tension tugging at her features.

Why hadn't she told him?

Because he didn't deserve to know?

Maybe telling him would be punishment because he didn't want children, didn't want any ties to her.

Was it fear that really held her back?

The fear that, although she loved this baby no matter what, she might be on her own raising their child? She'd be fine. Just look at what a great job Chrissie was doing with Joss. Savannah could rock the single mom thing, too.

"You okay in there?"

She closed her eyes, unable to stand the reflection staring back at her a moment longer.

"Savannah?"

"I'm fine."

That wasn't true. Not really. And they both knew it, although he had no clue as to the real reason.

Charlie moved toward the bathroom door the moment it opened, staying close to Savannah's side as she came out of the bathroom.

"Let me help you into bed."

"I don't want to go to bed," she protested.

"You look awful. You need to be in bed."

She glared at him. "Good to know. Thanks."

"You know what I mean." He fought the urge to roll his eyes.

"Fine, then—I don't want to go to bed," she reiterated, shaking off his hand as he reached for her arm.

"Do you have to argue with everything I say these days?"

"No, but there's no reason for me to go to bed."

"Other than the fact you worked a twelve-hour shift, look dead on your feet, and you just threw up?"

"Yeah, other than that." She looked ready to drop. Possibly her illness was related to exhaustion, but it was just as possible his presence had led to her sickness.

"You make me sick."

He winced at the words from his past, shook them off, and focused on the fragile-looking woman in front of him.

He let out an exasperated sigh. "At least lie down and rest a few minutes while I clean your bathroom."

"Go home. It's not going to hurt if a used washcloth sits on the countertop overnight."

"I want to help you, Savannah. Let me." He did want

to help. He wanted her smiling and happy, not miserable and sick.

Maybe he was destined to have a negative impact on anyone close to him. To make anyone unfortunate enough to get close to him miserable.

She glanced toward the doorway leading out into the hallway, then sighed. Her remaining energy hissed out like a deflating balloon and she sat down on the edge of the bed. "I feel guilty letting you clean when I'm perfectly capable."

He'd really like to hold her, to stroke her hair, whisper words of comfort and stay with her until she felt better. It wasn't his place to do any of those things. Not anymore.

"If you looked perfectly capable I wouldn't have offered. You don't, so go to bed."

Surprisingly, she nodded and laid down on top of the comforter.

"I'll straighten your guest bathroom then be back to check on you."

Asking her to get into her bed struck him as odd. How many times had he gotten into that bed with her?

Odd to think he never would again.

That he'd lost that right.

That privilege.

Once he was in Nashville, had started his new job, made new friends, his having made the right decision would be reinforced. It was only because he was still here, still confronted every day with the life he'd become used to sharing with Savannah, that he was struggling.

Savannah would be much better off once he was gone and she could move on with her life. He blamed himself for allowing their relationship to go on for so long. He should have stepped away long ago, for Savannah's sake if not his own.

Then again, that was part of the problem, wasn't it? He

should have protected her from ever getting close enough to him to feel broken-hearted.

Not that his track record for protecting those close to him was anything to brag about. Quite the opposite.

Once he'd straightened her bathroom, he went back to her bedroom and wasn't surprised to find her asleep.

She hadn't planned on going to sleep as she was still lying on top of the comforter rather than beneath it. Savannah was one of those that even if it were a hundred degrees outside she had to at least have a sheet over her. The fact she had dozed off spoke volumes as to how ill she was.

He should have asked if she needed anything.

He should have checked her temperature or something.

He was a cardiologist, not an infectious disease guy, but she probably had a stomach virus. Hopefully, it would run its course within twenty-four hours and she'd feel better soon.

He went back into the living room, grabbed a throw blanket off the sofa, and put it over her. She snuggled into the comfort of the blanket, but her breathing pattern didn't change to indicate that she'd awakened.

Charlie stood over the bed watching her for a few minutes. He'd told her she looked awful, but the truth was she was the most beautiful woman he'd ever known.

Fearing he might wake her but unable to resist, he ran his fingers over her forehead, brushing back a stray strand of long red hair and gauging her temperature at the same time. That was why he was touching her. To check her temperature. To see if she were physically ill. Not because he'd longed to touch the creamy perfection of her skin, to trace over the faint laugh lines at the corners of her eyes, the high angle of her cheekbones, the pert lines of her jaw.

To check her temperature.

No fever. That was good.

But she hadn't thrown up because she felt great. Something was definitely wrong.

Which left him in a quandary. Did he go or did he stay?

Tomorrow was Saturday and he wasn't on call this weekend. He'd planned to drive to Nashville in the morning to make a decision on living arrangements. Savannah wasn't on duty either, as he'd checked her schedule earlier that day.

No, he hadn't checked her schedule.

He'd just happened to glance at the nursing schedule and he'd just happened to note that she wasn't working that weekend.

What he wanted was to crawl up into the bed beside her, to hold her close and be there in case she needed him.

But he wouldn't. He couldn't be soft where she was concerned. Not even if she was sick.

But he wasn't leaving. That much he knew.

He eyed the empty side of the bed where he'd laid dozens of times. He had no rights where Savannah was concerned.

Which was something he suspected would haunt him a lot longer than he cared to admit.

He'd stay the night and be there if Savannah got sick again, would be there if she needed anything. Then he'd go back to being the world's biggest jerk.

Savannah woke with a start, stretched her arms above her head, then realized her living room throw was tucked around her.

Everything from the night before came rushing back. Charlie. Getting sick. His putting her to bed.

She glanced at her alarm clock. It was early. Much earlier than she'd like to be awake on a Saturday. But at least her stomach wasn't churning as it had been the night before.

At least, not yet.

So far, every day this week, she'd had mild nausea in the mornings that had escalated throughout the day and peaked in the evenings. Leave it to her to have such oddly timed "morning" sickness.

But other than the woes of her breakup with Charlie, her nausea, and some fatigue, she felt good. She had a doctor's appointment in two weeks and supposed she'd find out then how she was really doing. Until then, she'd take her prenatal vitamins and just take each day as it came.

She got out of bed, went to the bathroom, brushed her teeth, then left her room to go to the kitchen to get a glass of water and a couple of crackers in hopes of warding off nausea later in the day.

The moment she stepped into the open floor plan of her living room/dining room/kitchen, her gaze landed on the man draped across her sofa. He was too long for it and looked horribly uncomfortable.

But there was also a peace on his face as he slept.

A peace she hadn't seen over the past few weeks.

Because, despite how much he'd devastated her with his decision, Charlie wasn't walking around ecstatic either. Actually, every time she'd seen him he looked stressed, tense.

She stared at him way longer than she should have, studying his features, yet again wondering if their child would look like him.

Lord, she hoped so.

Yet did she really want a constant reminder of the man who'd broken her heart?

Their child would be a constant reminder regardless of who he or she looked like.

She'd been right about one thing. The rest of her life was going to be entangled with Charlie's. Not in the way she'd dreamed, but they would share a bond.

Because of that bond, she'd eventually have to make peace with him, would have to figure out how to just be his friend or his acquaintance or whatever it was they were destined to be.

They were going to be parents together.

Savannah got her water, went back to her room, and crawled beneath the comforter, all too aware that a month ago Charlie would have been in bed beside her and she'd have snuggled up against him. Now, she had no right to touch him, no right to snuggle next to him.

Not that she wanted him in her bed. She didn't. She was just fine by herself. Better than fine.

She didn't need him. Only…

Tears came quicker than they should have, but eventually she dozed back into sleep.

"I wasn't sure what you'd feel like eating this morning, if anything, so I made you a few choices."

Stretching in her bed, Savannah blinked at the man carrying in a tray of food. "You cooked for me?"

Not meeting her eyes, he nodded. "It's not much, but I went with what I could find."

Which was pretty limited. Eating had been a chore the past week and she'd not bothered going to the grocery store. She'd made sure to eat a small healthy meal each evening, but otherwise she'd been grabbing food from work.

"I'm surprised you found anything at all."

She eyed the scrambled eggs, toast, oatmeal that had to be made from an instant package, small glass of juice, and another that had water. "Looks good, but you shouldn't have."

Really, he shouldn't have. She needed to stay angry with him. Anger was so much better than the alternative emotions running rampant through her.

Setting the tray on the bed, he studied her. "You look better this morning. You got really pale last night. Virus?"

Now was the time to tell him the truth. He'd given her the perfect opening to tell him about their baby. Only she couldn't find the words that early in the morning to tell him. She tried. She opened her mouth but the words didn't come out, no matter how hard she tried to force them out.

"I'm not sure if anything's been going around the hospital or not," he continued, studying her as if he were gauging how she was going to react to him this morning. "Nothing on the cardiac unit, at any rate."

"Hopefully it will stay that way." Those words had come out just fine. Why hadn't the others? One simple two-word sentence was all she needed. *I'm pregnant.* She eyed the food and her stomach growled. She picked up a piece of toast, took a bite, and was grateful it settled happily into her stomach. She ate slowly, but felt better than she had all week. Hopefully that was a good sign that she wasn't going to be as nauseated.

"What are your plans for the day?"

She shrugged. "I'm not sure."

"I'm headed to Nashville to look at a couple of apartment complexes. I'm pretty sure I'm going to lease one of them, based on online reviews and a virtual tour, but wanted to take a look at a few others before committing."

Yeah, he wasn't so good at committing.

Which probably wasn't fair since he'd never given her any reason to think he would commit, other than just be in a relationship with her for a year and treat her as if she was his every desire. Which was good enough reason, right?

"Do you want to go with me?"

Her head shot up. He looked as surprised as she felt, then his face took on a remorseful appearance.

"You threw up last night and here I am trying to put you in a car for four plus hours today. I wasn't thinking."

No, he hadn't because he obviously regretted the invitation.

"I am feeling better this morning. I'm not nauseated." Not that the idea of four hours in a car appealed to her, but she did have news she needed to tell him. Maybe being trapped in a car with him would help her find the right words to tell him that she was having his baby.

Although she probably shouldn't be bragging too much about not being nauseated because this was the first morning in over a week that she'd not felt at least a little ill.

"I don't have other plans so I guess I could go with you."

He looked torn at her answer and for a moment she thought he was going to take back the invitation.

No worries, Charlie, she silently assured him. *I'm not going to beg you to change your mind about us. We are through.*

But on the way home from Nashville would be the perfect opportunity to tell him the truth. Not with the fun little baby items she'd bought the day she'd done the pregnancy test. Not with any cute little reveal ideas she'd looked at online. Just the blunt facts while he was trapped in a car with her so they could discuss the ramifications of the fact they were going to be parents.

"What do you think?" Charlie asked Savannah as she walked through the last apartment they were looking at. He couldn't believe she was there with him. The invitation had slipped out of his mouth and when she'd agreed he hadn't been able to bring himself to withdraw it.

"They're all nice." She sounded almost bored.

"But?"

"The first one we looked at seems the most practical.

With being on Twenty-First Avenue, it's close to the hospital and I like its layout the best. It doesn't have much of a yard available, but you don't really need a yard. Centennial Park isn't that far if you felt the need for grass beneath your feet."

"That's the one I liked best, too." It was part of a small apartment complex that housed ten units. She was right that there wasn't much of a yard, but that wasn't a deal-breaker.

She averted her gaze, not wanting him to see whatever he'd see in her eyes. She supposed she would visit him there at some point. They'd be sharing custody of their baby.

Not that the baby would be able to be away from her for the first year, as she intended to breastfeed. But there would come a point in time where she'd be dropping her child off to Charlie for them to spend time together.

Sadness hit her. Just the thought of being away from her child unnecessarily made her heart ache. Made her all the more angry at Charlie, at herself, that she'd put so much stock into their relationship.

"I'm going to go back there so I can sign the appropriate papers and get this checked off my to-do list."

"Is it a long list?"

"Long enough. Moving isn't easy. Haven't you ever moved, Savannah?" He sounded incredulous that she might not have.

"Sure, but only from home to college, then into my apartment after graduation."

"You always lived alone?"

"Nope. I had a roommate in the dorm and one when I first moved into the apartment. She got married and I just never replaced her." That had been right before Charlie had come into her life.

She sat in the car while he ran in to sign the forms at the apartment complex, then they grabbed a meal at a restaurant a friend had told him about. Amazingly, Savannah's stomach held out okay, but she ordered fairly bland just in case.

Their conversation ranged from awkward to relaxed when they'd forget their new status for a few minutes, then back to awkward when they remembered.

Savannah's heart ached and she had to remind herself of why she was there—not to make nice with Charlie, but so she could tell him about their baby on the drive home.

But by the time they got into the car, her head pounded and she closed her eyes. She couldn't tell him. Not like this. Not in a car, when things felt so wrong. Not until after her doctor's appointment and she knew more details.

Not until she could handle whatever reaction he might have.

"You'll understand if I don't invite you in," Savannah said, her fingers clutching the car door handle.

Charlie frowned. He hadn't planned on going in. Getting some space between him and Savannah was what he needed. Still, something in her tone irked him and he found himself saying, "You should invite me in. We could have a good last month together, Savannah."

She gave him a horrified look. "You mean sex?"

She made the word sound like it should have four letters and he pushed on. He needed to destroy whatever glimmers of feeling she still had for him.

"You can't deny it," he said with a tone so smooth it almost disgusted him. He could only imagine how dirty it made Savannah feel.

"You were more to me than sex, Charlie."

Were. As in past tense. Which was how it needed to be. She needed to find someone who could protect her and give her a fairy tale. Too bad the thought of her with someone else made his blood boil.

"I could make you feel good." He raked his gaze over her. "That hasn't changed and we both know it."

"Everything's changed."

He wanted to argue that some things would never change, but then realized what he'd be admitting if he said that. Did he believe he was going to spend the rest of his life wanting this woman? Missing this woman?

To think that was foolishness. They'd both move on—her to someone who deserved her, him to his career. She deserved so much better.

He was to blame for her misery. No surprise there. He'd been making people miserable since before his birth. So much so his own mother had preferred death to him.

Savannah hesitated on opening the handle, looking indecisive, but, without another word, she opened the door and disappeared into her apartment complex, leaving him to wonder what she'd been considering saying.

"Goodbye, Savannah," he said to his empty car and drove away without a backward glance. She was right. Everything had changed.

CHAPTER FIVE

"HER ECHOCARDIOGRAM SHOWED an ejection fraction of fifteen percent, but apparently that is an old finding and related to a myocardial infarction she suffered three years ago. She's here because the defibrillator she had put in at that time keeps going off, causing her to lose consciousness."

Charlie studied Savannah as she kept her voice professional and monotone, just as she had at every other point their paths had crossed over the past two months.

"Defibrillator malfunction?" he asked.

"The ER doctor who admitted her didn't think so. She's been in and out of ventricular tachycardia since arriving. He started her on—" she named the medication "—which has stopped the defibrillator from firing, but her shortness of breath is worse."

"That's why you called me?"

Her lips pressed into a thin line, displaying her annoyance with his question.

"Her heart rate has stayed in the low sixties and her blood pressure on the low side of normal, but when I assess her I know something is spiraling downhill."

He wasn't familiar with Iva Barton. He was taking the call for one of the other cardiologists, who'd squeezed in a vacation prior to Charlie's last day.

Which was quickly approaching.

Just one more day and he'd be in Nashville.

He and a couple of friends had moved his personal items last weekend. He was leaving most of his furniture to stage his house and had signed the real estate agreement just this week. Everything was happening fast.

Like the seconds ticking away with Savannah staring at him in question because he'd not commented on her assessment.

"I'll go check her."

"Thank you." Relief flickered across her face. Had she thought he wouldn't?

"Come with me?"

She looked hesitant, then shrugged. "Okay, Dr. Keele."

He could almost smile at the way she'd let him know she was only going with him because doing so was her duty. Fine, he was only asking in his professional capacity. He'd soon be gone. Asking her to come wasn't going to hurt a thing.

A pale woman in her early seventies lay in the hospital bed with multiple lines and telemetry wires attached to her frail body. Her gaze went to his the minute he entered the room, as if she wondered what poking and prodding he'd be doing.

"Hello, Mrs. Barton. You already know this, but Dr. Richards, your regular cardiologist, is out of town, so you're stuck with me. Your nurse has been filling me in. Sounds like you've had quite the day. How are you feeling?"

She grimaced. "Like I was kicked in the chest."

"When did that start?"

"When my defibrillator went off this morning." The white-haired woman clutched at her thin chest, rubbing across her sternum. "I haven't felt right since."

"Dr. Richards had scheduled her to see an electrophysiologist, thinking her defibrillator wasn't working correctly," a woman in her early thirties said from the chair next to the hospital bed. "Her appointment was actually scheduled for tomorrow, but then it went off this morning and she passed out. I called for an ambulance to come get her."

"You did the right thing," he assured the concerned woman, obviously the patient's daughter, then turned back to his patient. "Your heart is weak and your tests show that your defibrillator is going off because your heart keeps going out of rhythm. That's why you've been feeling funny."

"Why has my rhythm changed?"

"There are lots of things that can do it, but most likely it's due to the large chunk of damaged cardiac muscle from your heart attack a few years ago. Your body is working hard to try to compensate for that loss, but not doing so well. I've looked over what tests you've previously had at Chattanooga Memorial and the ones from the emergency room this morning. I'd like to schedule you for a viability test. I think a mechanical heart pump called a LVAD would be of benefit to ease the workload of your heart and increase your ejection fraction."

"Dr. Richards mentioned that to me at my last office visit, but said we needed to figure out this rhythm thing first." The woman glanced toward her daughter, then said, "I think my defibrillator is malfunctioning."

"From the way your rhythm looks, I'd say the defibrillator was doing exactly what it's supposed to and saving your life."

The young woman next to the bed stood, took her mother's hand. "What do we need to do?"

"We'll get the further testing done and go from there as to our next step."

When they stepped out of the ICU room, Savannah pinned him. "You think an LVAD is going to solve her problem?"

"Only one of them. I'd bet money she needs a ventricular ablation to correct that rhythm. The sooner the better."

"You want me to get the tests ordered?"

He nodded. "Once we get that and she's stable, we'll talk about transferring her to the heart failure team at Vanderbilt."

Savannah's face paled at the mention of where he would be transferring to himself. "Drumming up some business?"

"They are cutting edge when it comes to LVADs."

She didn't say anything.

"You should know that I do what's right for my patient. Always."

"Just not your girlfriend."

He frowned. She'd barely spoken to him since their Nashville trip, had gone out of her way to avoid him. The past month hadn't been easy, but he'd done it. Had even made a point to repeatedly go out with friends, knowing Savannah would catch wind of it and that it would fuel her dislike.

"Get the tests entered into Mrs. Barton's chart," he ordered as if he had no heart. "I'm going to make some calls to get everything started."

"Yes, sir." She said it so formally he had to look to make sure she hadn't saluted him. He wasn't so sure she hadn't.

What was he doing standing outside Savannah's apartment door again? Charlie wondered later that night.

Hadn't they said everything that needed to be said?

Apparently not or he wouldn't be here. With gifts.

Which seemed rather ridiculous, considering, but she'd always admired the vase. An interior decorator had chosen it, but Savannah had always been drawn to the intricate cut glass. The tickets, well, it wasn't as if he needed tickets to an upcoming Chattanooga concert. He'd bought them because she liked the band. It only seemed fitting he give them to her.

He heard her pause on the other side of the door, no doubt to glance through the peephole.

"No one's home," she called through the door.

"I have something for you."

"A going away present?" Sarcasm dripped from each word. "Isn't that supposed to be the other way around?"

"I have everything I need." He hoped his words rang with truth. He wasn't really sure, but he did know what Savannah needed. More importantly, what she didn't need. "Tomorrow's my last day at the hospital. What I have to say won't take a minute. Hurry up before Mrs. Henry calls the law."

He heard a thud. If he had to guess what had made it, he'd say she'd lightly banged her head against the door. After a few seconds, he heard the chain jingle and saw the door open.

Savannah stood there in yoga pants, an oversized T-shirt that hung from her body, and her hair pulled up in a ponytail. She didn't have a speck of make-up on, nor did she need it.

Or maybe she did because when he looked closer he noticed dark circles beneath her eyes that used to not be there.

"You look tired. If I did this to you, I'm sorry." More so than he'd ever be able to convey. The last thing he'd ever want was to hurt Savannah, but wasn't that part of the problem? He always hurt those he got close to.

"You didn't. I did it to myself."

He wasn't sure he understood what she meant, but she

stepped aside to let him enter the apartment. He didn't hesitate to enter, for fear she might change her mind.

She shut the door, but made no move to go further into the apartment, just stood near the door as if she might fling it open and tell him to leave at any moment.

"I'm leaving for Nashville tomorrow after work. I felt I should come by before I left."

"You owe me nothing." Something on her face said she didn't believe that.

Maybe he didn't either and that was why he was there.

"You and I had a good time together. I'm sorry we ended under less than ideal circumstances."

Her lower lip disappeared between her teeth.

"I brought you this." He held out the vase. "You always admired it."

"You'll understand if I refuse."

Yeah, maybe he did understand. Still, he wanted her to have it. What she did with it after he was gone was up to her, even if it was to smash it into a thousand pieces.

"Then I guess you can toss it after I leave. There are two tickets to go see that band you like stuck inside. Maybe you can take Chrissie or whomever you replace me with." He moved over to a shelf and set it down in an open spot, started to turn back toward her, then realized why the spot was open.

Because the photo of them at Lookout Mountain was gone.

He must have lingered long enough that she realized what he was staring at, because she moved from the door and came to stand next to him.

"I don't want the tickets any more than I want the vase."

"I've no use for them, Savannah." He turned to face her, was struck again by how fragile she appeared. Unable to resist, he brushed his fingers over her face, smoothing back a few stray hairs. The feel of her skin beneath his fingertips branded him with a thousand memories of touching her face, of touching her body, of holding her tight while the world ceased around them.

"I want you to have the tickets. I bought them for you."

Not meeting his eyes, she trembled beneath his fingers.

He needed to leave. He'd done what he came to do.

"I miss you, Savannah." God, he hated making that admission, sure he hadn't meant to. The words had jumped from him, unbidden but true.

Her gaze lifted to his and she put her hand over his. Warmth at her touch burned through him.

His heart squeezed in his chest so tightly he thought it might pop. Part of him longed to take her into his arms and promise her anything she wanted just so long as she'd keep touching him. There were too many reasons for him to go for him to do that.

Her eyes locked with his, she moved closer.

He swallowed. Hard. She was so close he could feel her body heat, could feel his already pitiful defenses melting away.

Her gaze darted to the movement at his throat, then her lips grazed his neck.

Groaning, he closed his eyes, knowing he was about to give in to the very real need within him. His lips covered hers and his body sighed with relief, with recognition of the woman kissing him. He had missed her. So very much.

Her taste. Her smell. The feel of her. Everything.

Over and over, long lingering kisses full of desperation.

"I want you so much, Savannah."

One last time he wanted to know what it felt to be loved by her. Selfish, but he wasn't capable of stopping of his own free will. She should stop him, should push him away, for her own sake. But she didn't say anything, just ran her palms over his shoulders and pulled his shirt free of his pants, perhaps wanting one more time herself. She slid her fingers beneath the material. His muscles contracted.

No one had ever made his body react the way Savannah had. It was as if she had his nerve endings on a puppet string and could make them dance and sing any way she pleased.

Oh, how she pleased.

Her hands, her mouth, her body. He was a goner.

Maybe he'd been a goner from the beginning.

Whatever she wanted was hers. Fortunately, she didn't ask him to make promises. She didn't say anything at all, just stripped off his shirt in a few quick moves.

Her eyes ate him up, devouring what she'd uncovered and making him hard in the process. She wanted him. It was a heady sensation to look into her eyes and see that desire burn.

Why she was touching him, kissing him, now, he wasn't going to question; he would just count his lucky stars, knowing it was probably something similar to his own reasons.

He'd needed one last time.

Savannah knew she was crazy. Certifiable.

But it didn't matter.

Nothing mattered except this moment. In this moment she was going to take what she wanted. Charlie.

She shouldn't. She knew that. But, really, what did it matter? Tomorrow night he'd be gone and she'd be alone.

Until she told him the truth.

That thought gave her a moment's pause, but he scooped her into his arms and carried her to her bedroom, all the while kissing her mouth as if he couldn't bear not to and she pushed aside her flash of hesitation.

For now she could pretend it was real, that when morning came reality wouldn't set in. It would. She acknowledged that. But, for the moment, she was going to exist in that make-believe world because in the real world, even if he said all the right things, he couldn't undo the damage from the past two months and she wanted this one last time.

Hot, covered in sweat, heart pounding, body satiated, Charlie collapsed on top of Savannah.

His weight must have been too much for her because she wiggled and pushed at him.

"Sorry," he said, rolling over onto his side.

"For?"

"Squashing you."

"Oh, that." She waved off his concern and the hand he went to hold her with. She glanced around at the tangled bed sheets. "We shouldn't have done this."

"You wanted me as much as I wanted you," he reminded her.

"I'm not denying it. You know how to make my body do miraculous things."

"You're a sensual woman."

"But not a sensible one."

Her words stung. He didn't want her to think of him as a big mistake. He'd been thought of that way, way too often during his life. He didn't want Savannah to feel that way, too. Yet wasn't that really how she should think of him?

"Let's not overanalyze what just happened. Let's just accept it for what it was."

"One last booty call?" she interrupted.

"You were never that," he corrected.

"I was never more than that."

He winced at her conviction. "How can you say that?"

"Because it's true," she insisted.

"I've told you repeatedly that I enjoyed what we shared." He sighed, knowing this wasn't an argument he could win. It wasn't even one he should try to win. "Let's not talk. I'll be gone tomorrow so just let me hold you for a few minutes now."

Her eyes closed. "Fine."

He held her, tracing his fingertips over the lines of her spine, noting how her bones protruded. "Have you lost weight?"

"I thought we weren't going to talk."

"Promise me you'll eat."

"I do eat."

Something in the way she said it made him stare at her. "You've been sick again?"

"I'm fine."

"Apparently not if you're losing weight."

"I've not lost weight and I'm not sick." She sat up and tugged on the sheet, trying to cover her body.

That was when he noticed what he had been too distracted to notice. He studied her lower abdomen. It was only the slightest change, almost imperceptible, even on close inspection. Almost. He glanced up at her, denial and a thousand questions running through his mind.

Oh, God. He knew. Charlie knew she was pregnant.

They'd just had one-last-time-before-he-left sex and he'd noticed her beginning of a pregnancy bump. Savannah hadn't thought about that when she'd thrown herself at him. All she'd been thinking was how good being in his arms had felt.

But her little three-month-along belly stuck out just enough that he'd noticed the subtle change.

"Savannah?"

She tugged the covers further over her body, realized it wasn't near enough. She got up and put on her yoga pants and T-shirt.

"Tell me I'm not seeing what I think I saw."

"You didn't see what you think you saw," she responded as emotionless as she could.

"Yes, I did." The words came out as if they'd escaped from a mangled throat.

"Then don't ask me to tell you that you didn't."

"Explain yourself."

"What do you mean, explain myself? I'd say it's pretty self-explanatory and I didn't get this way by myself so don't go giving me that big bad doctor tone."

"It's true?" He sounded incredulous, and not in a good way. More like he was about to be sick or run away.

He was about to run away.

Drive away, at any rate.

She shrugged. "It doesn't matter."

"You're pregnant? That sure as hell matters to me. How long have you known?"

Savannah winced, guilt slamming her. "A while."

"How long?"

"You remember my good news that I never got to tell you?"

His face was pale, almost ashen. "Since then? Two months and you couldn't find a moment to tell me?"

"I tried." She shrugged as if it were no big deal even though she knew better. "It never felt right. You were leaving. I was staying."

His jaw dropped, worked back and forth. "You weren't going to tell me?"

"I was going to tell you. I just hadn't figured out when."

"When our kid started school? When he hit puberty? Left for college? When?"

She flinched. "Before then. Way before then. Before he's born, but I don't know exactly when I would have told you. Not until after you were moved and settled, I think."

"He? It's a boy?"

He'd zeroed in on the pronoun, but she shrugged. "I don't know. I go for my first ultrasound tomorrow."

"How far along are you?"

"About three months."

His silence spoke volumes long before he looked up and met her gaze. "We always used protection."

She snorted. "Obviously, it wasn't foolproof."

"Obviously. Damn."

Tears stung her eyes. "No, not damn. I don't want anything from you, so don't go damning me or my baby."

"You're pregnant with my child."

Her mouth twisted. "I guess I should be grateful you assume it's yours."

Charlie frowned at Savannah's taunt. Of course he assumed her baby was his. "Who else's would your baby be?"

"I don't know." She hung her head into her hands. "I don't want to fight with you."

Despite how his mind was reeling, how all of him was reeling, remorse at how upset she looked hit him. "We aren't fighting. We are having a discussion about the fact that you are pregnant with my child, have known for two months, and failed to tell me."

"Like you failed to tell me you never planned to stay in Chattanooga? That you had accepted another job?" Although her eyes were red-rimmed, her chin jutted forward defiantly. "Would it have made a difference if I had told you I was pregnant?"

"What do you mean, would it have made a difference? You should have told me."

"What would be different if I had told you two months ago?"

He just stared at her tear-filled eyes and saw his mother. Saw the endless tears, the fights, the heartbreak. Heard the misery of what he'd caused his parents.

He wasn't his father. He'd never be his father. Never.

Only he'd gotten Savannah pregnant.

He wouldn't let Savannah be his mother. He wouldn't do that to her.

He couldn't.

"I'd like to think a lot of things would be different."

"But not you leaving?"

"No, the fact you are pregnant isn't a reason for me not to leave." If anything, her being pregnant was reason for him to leave, to set her free from the misery that was his legacy.

She nodded. "Finally something we agree on."

Her sarcasm was getting to him. "But we do have a lot of things we should've been talking about for the past two months."

"It's six months before the baby arrives. That's more than enough time for whatever we have to say."

Six months. Savannah would have a baby. He would be a father. Six months. Six months. The two words strummed through him like a jungle beat, picking up in tempo with each beat.

"I can't stay." He wasn't sure if the words were for her or as a reminder to himself. His heart pounded. His hands shook. His mind raced. Six months and Savannah's life would change forever.

Her life had already changed forever.

Just as his mother's life had changed forever when she'd gotten pregnant.

Savannah glared. "I'm not asking you to stay."

Charlie's throat swelled so thick he wasn't sure air could get inside. He'd done this. Had changed her from the happy woman she'd been into this angry, bitter woman.

Like father, like son.

No. He wouldn't be like his father. He wouldn't make Savannah pay for getting pregnant for the rest of her life. He'd do right by her financially, more than right. He'd make up to Savannah all the things he hadn't been able to make up to his mother and he'd not stick around to make her miserable the way his father had. He'd go to Nashville, pursue his career, be a silent father to his child, there if needed, but otherwise someone who was far in the background. Savannah would be a good mother. She'd had great role models. Their baby would be better off without his physical presence.

"I don't know what to say," he began after silence lingered too long between them. "I wasn't expecting this."

She gave him a look that cut to the core. "Don't you get it? You don't have to say or do anything. This is my body and I take responsibility for my baby. You can leave and never look back."

That was what he should do. Walk away and stay out of their lives completely, other than financially. "I can't do that."

He wasn't sure what he could do, but he knew he wanted to do more than just give Savannah and their baby child support.

"Why not?" she asked, her tone full of accusation. "It's what you planned to do an hour ago."

"This is now."

Her eyes narrowed defiantly. "You can't stay."

He closed his eyes, felt tortured. He'd done to Savannah what his father had done to his mother. Not to the extent that Rupert had abused his mother, but Charlie was well on his way. He should have ended things months ago, long before he and Savannah got so attached. He'd known he should have, had repeatedly planned to tell her he needed space, but he just hadn't been able to step away. Not until the job offer from Nashville came. Then he'd had to face that it was time for him to step out of the picture so both he and Savannah could move on with their lives.

For him, that meant a career bump. For her, he'd thought she'd marry someone who could give her the life she dreamed of and raise a family. She was pregnant. He'd ruined everything for her, stolen her dreams.

His life's legacy. Dream-stealer.

He swallowed, trying to clear the lump in his throat. "I'm as much to blame for your circumstances as you are. It wouldn't be right for you to face this alone."

But, even as he said the words, he acknowledged that she would be alone because he'd be in Nashville, and that was right where he needed to be.

CHAPTER SIX

CHARLIE HAD WANTED her ultrasound information, but hadn't said he'd be at the appointment. Since he'd asked for the details, Savannah kept glancing up from her magazine toward the entrance to the radiology department waiting area every few seconds, thinking he'd show.

He hadn't.

Of course he hadn't.

Today was his last day working at the hospital. There was a going away party for him this afternoon in the break room. Hadn't she purposely chosen to take today off for her ultrasound appointment so she could miss the goodbye Charlie to-do?

She'd said her own goodbye the night before. That was the only excuse she could come up with for why she'd had sex with him. That and the fact her body craved him. Apparently, immensely disliking him didn't make a hill of beans' difference to how her body responded to his.

A pity, really. Maybe goodbye would have been easier had the sex been horrible. Maybe that was what she'd hoped. If so, no such luck. If anything, he'd brought her even higher than she recalled. Must be pregnancy hormones.

The ultrasound tech poked her head out a doorway and

called Savannah's name. She set the magazine she'd been idly glancing through down in the seat next to her, then followed the woman back to the ultrasound room.

The tech gave her instructions to change into the hospital gown, then to lie back on the examination table. When Savannah had changed and was on the table, the woman came back into the room and gave a quick rundown of what to expect.

"Nothing will hurt, but the transvaginal view may be a little uncomfortable. I'll be as gentle as possible."

Savannah nodded.

"The conducing gel may be a little cold. Sorry."

Savannah didn't care. She couldn't take her eyes off the computer monitor as images began to appear. She'd seen ultrasounds during nursing school, had helped in labor and delivery during that rotation, but this was different. This was her baby. At first she wasn't able to distinguish features, but then images became recognizable.

A head. A body. Two arms. Two hands. Fingers. Legs. Toes. With the way the baby was turned she couldn't tell if the gender was a boy or a girl, but it didn't matter, just that she was looking at her baby.

"Is everything all right?" she asked as the woman marked the dimensions of the baby's head, length, and then zoomed in on a rapidly beating little heart.

Savannah's own heart beat like crazy at what she was seeing. That was her precious baby's heart. Love filled her. She'd thought her heart already overflowed with love for this baby, but seeing the image of her child made it all so much more real. She couldn't imagine how her heart was going to hold so much love when she actually got to hold her baby.

A knock sounded on the door and both Savannah and

the ultrasound tech turned as the receptionist poked her head in, clearly guarding the door.

"Dr. Keele is here and insists he's supposed to be present for this. Is it okay if I let him in?"

Relief that he'd shown flooding her, for their baby's sake, Savannah nodded and the woman said something to someone behind her.

In seconds Charlie was in the room, his gaze fixed first on her, then the monitor screen.

"Sorry I'm late. I did an ablation on Mrs. Barton this morning and got held up later than intended." He spoke to her but his eyes were on the screen, studying every detail of the image the woman had zoomed into.

"Is she okay?" Savannah asked, searching his face for some sign of what he thought of their baby.

"Considering her level of heart failure, she's doing great. I hope to get her scheduled for the LVAD next week."

"That's fabulous."

"What's fabulous is that healthy little heart," he said, studying the screen.

"Everything looks good?" she asked him rather than the tech.

"I can't say much as to anything other than the heart, but that's a beauty of a heart. Must take after his mother."

"His?" the tech asked. "Do you want to know the sex of the baby today?"

"Yes," Savannah said at the same time as Charlie said, "No."

He corrected himself. "Whatever Savannah wants is fine."

"Well, normally I wouldn't be able to tell you at twelve weeks, but you're actually closer to fourteen so I can confirm it with more certainty. I can write it down and she can look later if you don't want to know?"

"I…" He hesitated. "That would be fine."

Savannah frowned. He didn't want to know if their baby was a boy or a girl? How could he stand not knowing? How could he not be looking overjoyed at the precious image on the screen?

The ultrasound tech went through pointing out different features on the ultrasound, then printed pictures for both Savannah and a separate one for Charlie.

He held the photo loosely in his hand as if he wasn't quite sure what to do with it.

"Here—" the tech handed her a piece of paper "—I wrote the sex of your baby on this. You can look at it whenever you decide you're ready to know."

"Thank you."

"No, thank you," the tech countered. "I love my job and watching new parents see their baby for the first time."

"Thank you," Savannah told the tech again as the woman popped out the disk and handed it to her.

"This has a video clip and all the photos on it. Enjoy your baby's first pictures."

Her baby's first pictures.

Savannah glanced at the image in her hand and knew she'd never seen anything more precious.

Charlie thought he might pass out.

Which was saying a lot. He stood for hours on end doing intricate heart surgeries and had no issues. Seeing a 3D image of a three-month-old fetus should not have him shaking.

Yet he was.

Because the baby was his responsibility.

What he'd once been to his father.

Only when he glanced at the photo he couldn't find the

hatred his father had felt. Nor the resentment his mother had felt. He couldn't find anything except a deep ache inside.

He was going to be a father.

He'd gotten Savannah pregnant.

He was leaving this evening to move two hours away. Savannah and his baby would be here, in Chattanooga.

That was for the best.

He'd lived the other option and it had been hell.

But seeing his baby, seeing Savannah's excitement at every image, got to him, because that was something he didn't have, would never have.

Something he couldn't let himself have because he couldn't risk doing to her what his father had done to their family.

Maybe his father had even felt torn at the beginning, had thought he was doing the right thing when he'd married Charlie's mother. Maybe they'd been happy to begin with. Maybe.

All Charlie could recall were the fights and the tears.

The bitterness and resentment.

The agony that had been his mother's life.

The misery that had been his life, his father's life.

The tragic end to his mother's life.

His teeth clenched. He wanted no part of it.

Not for Savannah.

Not for their baby.

Not for himself.

He didn't want to be like his father, didn't want Savannah to be like his mother. He glanced at the photo he held. He wanted better for his baby than what he'd had.

The sudden need to do something overwhelmed him.

"Thank you for this," he told the tech. He nodded to Savannah without meeting her eyes, then left the room.

He heard Savannah apologize to the tech for his abrupt behavior, explaining he had to get back to work.

A memory from the past slammed into him.

A memory of his mother making excuses for his father's abrupt behavior. To him. To neighbors. To his school teachers.

Funny, he'd forgotten that during his younger days his mother would try to explain away his father's lack of affection, explain away why he was gone more than he was home. Before the end she'd quit making excuses. For his father and for herself.

Now, Savannah was pregnant and making excuses for him.

Already it had started.

He was following in his father's footsteps whether he wanted to or not.

Which was why he folded up the photo and slid it into his pocket. He couldn't look at it anymore. He couldn't be involved because that life in Savannah's belly would be a helluva lot better off without Charlie in it.

That much he knew.

He'd set up some type of trust for the baby, for Savannah, to help with financial needs, and he'd stay away.

Maybe Nashville wasn't far enough to keep him away from what he was leaving in Chattanooga.

The only thing strong enough to keep him away was the past.

"He left, knowing you were pregnant? I mean, I know he left last month," Chrissie corrected herself, waving her spoon around as she talked. "But he knew you were pregnant and he still left?" Her friend shook her head in disbelief. "How could he do that? I didn't understand before and I sure don't now that I know he knows you are pregnant."

They sat at the small four-person dining room table and kept their voices low as Joss was curled up asleep on the sofa.

Savannah shrugged. "I didn't want him to stay. Not because I'm pregnant. Not at all. Not anymore."

Savannah forced herself to take a bite of the vegetable beef stew she'd put in her crock pot that morning, prior to leaving for her twelve-hour shift. The stew might have been the best thing she'd ever stuck in her mouth. Savannah wouldn't know. Nothing had much taste these days, but at least most of her "morning" sickness had passed and she'd eat fairly healthy for a few nights on the stew. Chrissie had jumped at the chance to sit and talk with Savannah as, for the most part, Savannah had shut her friends and family out for the last month. She'd moped around long enough, and had decided it was time to get back to living life, back to feeling like herself. She was strong. She didn't need a man. She had this.

She'd invited her friend over to eat and have a girls' pow-wow. She'd told Chrissie earlier in the month that she was pregnant, had told everyone at work earlier that day. She hadn't necessarily been ready to face the knowing eyes of her coworkers, but she'd caught more than one coworker staring at her midsection as if trying to decide if she was or wasn't, despite her attempts at hiding her pregnancy beneath her scrubs. The first three months had been easy to conceal her barely-there belly. But, over the past month, her tummy had blossomed.

Other than a few expressions of, "Oh, honey!", everyone had been supportive. Even the *Oh, honey!s* had hugged her and said they'd help any way they could. She'd faked a big smile and told everyone how happy she was at the prospect of being a mother.

She shouldn't have had to fake that smile.

She was happy about being a mother. At times, she was over the moon at the thought of being a mother. At others, she wanted to crawl into the fetal position and cry.

Darn Charlie for stealing her joy.

Darn her for allowing him to steal her joy.

Darn him for leaving her.

Darn her for caring.

"We're better off without him." She rubbed her stomach, and felt the tiny movements she'd been feeling for the past few days. At first she hadn't been positive if the tiny flutters were the baby or her body. Now, there was no doubt when she felt the little movements. Her baby was growing and she should be ecstatic. Instead, the first time she'd been positive of what she'd been feeling, she'd called her mother and described the feelings, described her joy, then burst into tears that she couldn't stop. Thirty minutes later her worried mother had shown up on her doorstep and ended up staying the night. Pathetic.

Not how her mother had raised her. After her father had died, Sally had struggled to make ends meet. She'd been a stay-at-home mom, but Savannah's father hadn't planned on dying so young and hadn't had life insurance. He'd left his family rich in love, but otherwise poor. Determined that Savannah would never be caught in a similar situation, Sally had raised Savannah to think for herself, to be able to take care of herself financially, to be strong and independent.

No doubt she'd disappointed her mother.

"I don't need him." She didn't. She might have had a weak moment or two, but that didn't mean she needed Charlie. She would raise her baby and she'd do a fantastic job.

Leaning back against her dining room chair, Chrissie frowned. "What is wrong with that man? How could he just leave like that? A blind fool could see that he's crazy about you."

Spooning another bite of stew, Savannah shook her head. She'd thought the same thing, once upon a time. She'd gotten over that foolishness. "That was just sex."

Chrissie didn't look convinced. "I sure didn't think that's all it was."

"Welcome to the club." She wrapped her lips around the spoon and slowly pulled it from her mouth, then sighed.

"Now you do?"

"He's gone and I've not heard from him since he left. Of course it's what I think."

Chrissie took a drink of her soda. "I'm not sure what to tell you, except I've never seen a man more besotted than he was for you."

"Sexual attraction," she reminded.

"Then I envied you sexual attraction, because it was palpable every time he looked at you or said your name. You walked into a room and he couldn't take his eyes off you." Chrissie shook her dark head in denial. "I just can't believe he left you. Especially knowing you're pregnant."

"Believe." Any sliver of hope she'd had had been crushed when he'd walked out of the ultrasound room without a backward glance. Literally and figuratively. He'd been gone a month and she'd not heard from him. Not even a text to say, *Hi, how are you? How's pregnant life?* Nothing.

Because he was gone.

Gone and wanted her to know he was gone for good.

Fine. Let him stay gone. She had her family, her friends, and her precious baby. She'd ended up flushing the folded paper with the baby's gender written on it, deciding that she wanted to wait. The baby's sex didn't matter. Either way, Savannah was going to love this baby so much that it wouldn't matter that his or her dad wasn't there.

She did love this baby that much. More.

"Honestly, since he never planned to stay in Chattanooga, I'm glad he's gone. The longer he stayed the more difficult letting go would have been." Not that she could imagine it having hurt any more than it had, but still.

"Maybe he had to leave for some secret CIA mission or something that he wasn't allowed to tell you."

"Hah," Savannah scoffed at her friend's outlandish suggestion. "Nice try, but let's face it. Charlie was a jerk and, as far as I'm concerned, good riddance."

A knock on her apartment door had both women looking at each other and Savannah scooting back her chair in hopes the noise didn't disturb Joss.

"You expecting someone?"

"No." She wasn't. She glanced through the peephole and saw a fiftyish-looking man in a business suit carrying a large legal-sized manila envelope.

"Fancy-looking salesman," she muttered to her friend, then called, "Who is it?" through the doorway.

"Kinda late for a salesman," Chrissie muttered from where she still sat at the dining table.

"George Peterson," the man answered. "I'm here on behalf of Dr. Charlie Keele."

On behalf of? Had something happened to Charlie?

Without another thought, she undid her safety chain and flung the door open. "Is Charlie okay?"

The man looked startled at her question. "He's fine."

She sighed in relief, tension letting loose of her neck and shoulders. "Then who are you and why are you here?"

He held out the envelope. "I'm an attorney. Dr. Keele hired me to conduct some business transactions for him and to personally deliver this to you. Everything has been recorded at the court house and this is your copy."

"My copy?" She knew she probably sounded crazy, but she had no clue what he was talking about. What had been recorded at the court house?

Then it hit her.

A lawyer representing Charlie.

Legal-sized papers recorded at the court house.

Her heart squeezed so tightly it skipped a beat.

Charlie was going for custody.

She gritted her teeth together, then shook her head. "I don't want those."

The lawyer looked even more startled. "Dr. Keele has been very generous."

"I'm sure he has," she spat out, placing a protective hand over her belly. "But you can tell him to kiss my—"

"Ma'am, I think you should—"

This time she cut him off. "And I think you should go. You're not welcome. You can tell Dr. Keele he's not, either."

The lawyer looked torn a moment, then shoved the envelope toward her and left before she could toss it back.

"I'll fight him on this," she called out to the retreating man, who glanced at her over his shoulder, a confused frown on his face.

"What was all that about?" Chrissie asked, walking up next to her and staring down the hallway.

"Charlie is filing for custody."

Chrissie's mouth dropped open. "Seriously? I thought he didn't want anything to do with the baby?"

"Obviously I was wrong about that, too." She waved the envelope in front of her friend. "He can't have my baby."

Okay, so logically she knew he could, and would, have time with their baby. That was what she wanted, right? For her baby to grow up with a loving father to be there for him or her, even if he hadn't been able to be there for Savannah? She did want that, but the thought of him taking her to court… Her stew threatened to make a reappearance.

How dare he do this to her so coldly? Without even discussing it with her first? They'd been together a year. A year! Didn't she deserve an actual pick-up of the phone and, *Hey, I've decided I do want to be a part of my child's life. Let's talk about it?* How could she have thought she knew him so well, inside and out, and have been so very wrong?

She'd thought he loved her. Lust and love were two very different things. Because she'd wanted to believe she'd credited Charlie for being more than he was. He was nothing better than every other Joe Schmoe looking for a good time.

Yet even now she had a difficult time convincing herself of that. Look at what a great con job he'd pulled on her that, even after a month of not hearing from him, she still struggled to believe that he wasn't the awesome man she'd put up on a pedestal. After he'd proved that she didn't matter enough to discuss major life decisions with, such as moving two hours away or wanting legal rights over their child.

"Maybe he just wants visitation," Chrissie suggested, staring at Savannah. "If so, that's a good thing, right?"

It was. Although anxiety coursed through her, she truly did want Charlie to be a part of their baby's life. Yes, that made things a hundred times worse for her because it would mean seeing him, but their baby knowing his or her father was more important.

If Charlie wanted reasonable legal rights to their child, she wouldn't fight him despite what she'd flung at the retreating lawyer.

She threw the oversized envelope down on the dining room table next to her half-eaten bowl of stew and slowly sank onto a chair. Chrissie joined her and took her hand into hers, holding her tightly. They sat in silence for a couple of minutes before Chrissie nudged her.

"Maybe you should open the envelope to see what it says."

Savannah closed her eyes and tried to go back to the happy place where she'd existed just a few months ago when she'd thought she was the luckiest woman alive. She'd been so naïve, so trusting, so caught up in being in love that she'd just looked at Charlie through rose-colored glasses and seen what she wanted to see. Foolish. Never again would she be so easily fooled. Never again would she open up and give her heart away.

She didn't need him.

She didn't need anyone.

"Savannah? How can you not rip that open?"

Resting her head in her hands, she sighed. "I don't want to know what it says."

"Well, I do." Chrissie picked up the envelope as if to open it. "If you're not going to open this, I am."

"Give it to me." Savannah took the envelope from her friend and tore into the end. Nausea rose from the pit of her stomach. Her baby's future had been reduced to legal documents compiled by a lawyer.

She pulled out the blue-backed document and a key, stared at it in confusion, read the lawyer's letter in even further confusion.

In total shock, she lifted her gaze to her curious friend. "He's lost his mind."

Chrissie gave her an expectant look. "Well, what did he ask for? Surely not full custody. And what's up with the key?"

Words failed her so, with unsteady hands, she gave the papers to her friend and closed her shaky fingers around the key, letting the metal dig into her palm. She welcomed the discomfort, hoping it pulled her back to reality.

Chrissie's eyes widened. "Savannah! Oh, my!"

She nodded. Exactly.

"He's given you his house. Savannah, this is unbelievable. He deeded you his house!"

CHAPTER SEVEN

HE MIGHT NOT be home, Savannah told herself for the hundredth time since she'd taken off toward Nashville. It was a Thursday morning. He was probably working. Or he could be out of town. Or it could be his day off work and he could be out with someone.

That made her pause.

It had been a month. Had he moved on? Started dating someone else? When she showed up at his house, would he have another woman there?

Had deeding his house to her made him feel absolved from his obligations to her and their child?

Ha, she was going to give him a piece of her mind over his high-handedness. She didn't want his house or his money or anything material from him.

She didn't want anything from him, period. Not anymore.

She was on her way to tell him that and to throw his deed and key in his handsome face. He couldn't just do something like that. It wasn't okay and a big gift, a huge gift, didn't make it okay that he'd walked away from their child.

She was going to tell him that. And more. And…she didn't know what, exactly. Just that since the night before she'd been burning inside, had woken with that burn still present and, before she'd made a conscious decision, she'd been on her way to Nashville rather than the grocery store, as she'd originally set out to.

He would likely be at work, so she'd go there first. But, if not, she knew right where Charlie's apartment was. Sure, the weather had been better two months ago when she'd gone with him to Nashville than the cold drizzly rain that was falling today, but that was okay. The weather matched her mood.

No, if the weather matched her mood the wind would be howling and the sky would be blood-red, not a dreary gray.

She clung to her anger. Anger was better than sadness and loss. She'd experienced enough of that over the past few months. No more.

How dare he?

That was the question she asked herself over and over as she headed north on I-24 toward Nashville. Just inside the city limits, the traffic slowed to a sudden stop in all four lanes.

Savannah's heart thudded like crazy as she applied her brakes, hoping they didn't lock, hoping she'd keep from slamming into the large black vehicle in front of her.

The next few seconds drew out in slow motion, with her heartbeat doing overtime. Her sweat glands too as her skin was drenched with clammy stickiness. Despite the rain-slick road, she somehow got her sedan stopped just inches before crashing into the sports utility vehicle in front of her.

Heart pounding, she let out the breath she hadn't realized she'd been holding.

In the next second she cried out as the impact from whatever had been behind her crashed into her with great force, ramming her car into the SUV.

Her body jerked forward against her seatbelt, digging

painfully into her chest and shoulder. What breath she had remaining inside her gushed out in a hard whoosh. Her neck snapped forward, then whipped back. The sound of metal crunching into metal deafened her ears.

The second she thought it was over, another impact hit as another vehicle failed to stop in time. She jerked forward and back again, this time not as hard as the previous, but pain ripped through her body all the same.

Tensing, she prepared herself for yet another hit and another as no doubt more cars would join into the interstate pile-up, but none came. Just the sound of the rain still falling around her and nothing more.

Trying not to panic, she began to take stock of the damage. To her and to her car.

She hurt. Her neck. Her shoulder. Her belly. She took a tentative breath. Pain shock-waved through her. Not good.

She wiggled her fingers and her toes. Everything seemed to be moving as it should. Maybe. Odd, but she really wasn't sure if she'd moved at all. She tried to raise her arm, but doing so hurt too much so she quit trying. She must have bit her tongue or the inside of her cheek as the strong metallic taste of blood filled her senses. Or maybe it was her nose, she thought as a drop of blood fell from her nostril. Despite the pain, she wiped at her face, registered the red liquid on her hand. She wasn't sure why her nose was bleeding as she'd had her seatbelt on, but it definitely was.

Or maybe the blood came from somewhere else on her face? She wasn't sure. Did it even matter where the blood was coming from?

That there was warm liquid between her legs, she also registered.

No, she thought. No. No. *No*.

"Ma'am, are you all right?" a man who appeared to be in his early twenties asked from outside her shattered driver's door window. She glanced at her busted windshield, at the shattered passenger door window, at the SUV that was where the front of her car should be.

She glanced down, realized her steering wheel was against her chest, that she couldn't see the lower half of her body.

"Ma'am?"

She turned back toward the driver's window, opened her mouth to tell the young man that no, she wasn't okay, that she couldn't feel her baby moving, and to please do something, but nothing came out. She was still trying to tell him as her eyes became too heavy to stay open.

So she closed them.

Charlie made his way toward the heart failure unit at Vanderbilt University Medical Center. He'd consulted on a patient that morning prior to heading over to teach a class to second year medical students, and wanted to pop his head back in to check on the woman before seeing his scheduled afternoon patients.

His stomach rumbled as he passed a food cart.

The food didn't smell that appetizing, but his stomach was lodging its protest that he had once again forgotten to eat lunch.

Had he eaten breakfast?

He honestly couldn't remember. Every day ran into the next and they all seemed the same. They all seemed lackluster. They all seemed to be missing something.

Maybe it was him missing something.

Or, more accurately, missing someone.

Savannah.

His throat tightened just at her name consciously passing through his mind.

He'd not talked to her. Not a single time. He'd decided staying away altogether was best.

He'd thought about her, though. A lot. Almost all the time.

He also thought of their baby, despite doing his best not to think of the life he and Savannah had created. How could he think of anything else?

He was going to be a father.

He knew nothing of being a good father. Nothing.

That Savannah would be a good mother wasn't even in doubt. She would be an excellent mother, just as her mother had been. In that respect, their child had hit the parenting jackpot. Savannah would do everything she could to give their child a good life.

As would he.

After her ultrasound, he'd contacted his realtor, told her he wanted to pull the house off the market, then he'd had his lawyer take care of everything else.

Savannah and their child would have a nice home in a good neighborhood. She wouldn't have to worry about providing a roof over her and their baby's head. She wouldn't have to worry about anything financially. He'd see to that. If she wanted to stay home and raise their child, she'd be able to.

It was the least he could do since he couldn't be with her.

Guilt hit him.

Guilt he shouldn't be feeling. He was taking care of her. In a much better way than if he was physically there because he wouldn't be making her miserable, making their child miserable. He wouldn't be standing in the way of her happiness.

He was doing for her what his father should have done for his mother. He was letting her be free so she could live her life without being encumbered with a man who would eventually resent her presence and destroy who she was. Not to mention the damage he could do to a child's mental and emotional stability.

Currently, it was difficult to imagine that because he craved Savannah's presence so intensely he dreamed of her every time his eyes closed. He'd see someone with red hair and be struck with the memory of the first time he'd unclipped Savannah's hair, the way her long tresses had tumbled over her shoulders, how silky the strands had felt between his fingers as he'd kissed her throat, her neck, her creamy shoulders.

He missed her.

But his father's voice echoing through his head couldn't be silenced. Nor could the memory of his mother and her tragic death.

Savannah was better off without him.

Much better off.

No matter how much he missed her, he'd stay away.

He checked on his patient, made chart notes for one of the residents to follow up on, and left the unit. He'd gotten to the elevator and pushed the down arrow when his cell phone rang.

He glanced at the number. It wasn't one he recognized.

He started to ignore it as he'd soon be stepping into the elevator and would likely lose the signal anyway, but some inner force had him sliding his finger across the screen.

"Charlie Keele?"

Charlie didn't recognize the male voice. "Yes?"

"This is Sergeant Oliver Casteel. I'm with the Metro Police Department."

The elevator dinged and the door slid open, revealing an elderly couple and a nurse inside the car already. Brow furrowed to form a tight knot between his eyes, Charlie motioned for the elevator to go on without him and stepped away from the doors. He couldn't fathom why the police would be calling him, but he sure didn't want to step into the elevator and possibly lose the signal.

"You were listed as the emergency contact for Savannah Carter."

Listed as the emergency contact.

Charlie's knees threatened to buckle. There were very few reasons why the Police Department made phone calls.

"She's been in an accident."

"Is she..." His voice broke and he couldn't finish his question. He was used to dealing with life and death, with emergencies. Yet nothing had prepared him for this phone call and the very real fear gripping him. Savannah had been in an accident and the police were calling him.

"She's been in a multi-car accident. She's alive but seriously injured."

She was alive.

"I'm calling because she had you listed as her emergency contact," the officer continued.

His brain raced. "I'll let her mother know and head to Chattanooga immediately."

"Chattanooga?"

What the officer had said registered. "She's in Nashville?"

"She's been airlifted to Vanderbilt University Medical Center."

Airlifted. Vanderbilt. Savannah was there.

"I'm there. Here." Savannah was here. "I work there. Here." He wasn't making much sense, had no idea what else he said to the officer, knew that he responded to the man's comments about Savannah's personal belongings and her car being totaled and towed to a local garage, but all he really focused on was getting to the emergency department.

Today, the hospital seemed a hundred times larger than he knew the building to be.

He had to flash his name badge a few times but, fortunately, once in the emergency department, it didn't take long to find her. The helicopter had obviously just landed and she'd only been inside the hospital a few minutes. She was surrounded by nurses and at least two emergency room physicians. A portable X-ray machine was being rolled up to no doubt check for internal injuries.

"She's pregnant, just over four months," he said to no one in particular. At this point, he had no idea if she'd lost the baby. He just knew pregnant women didn't get X-rays unless it was an emergency.

Blood streaked Savannah's face. Wires and tubes jutted out from everywhere. She lay on the gurney quite lifeless other than the soft moaning of pain that the hustle-bustle and machines couldn't quite drown out.

This was an emergency.

Oh, God, please let her be okay.

Please let their baby be okay.

He tried to objectively assess what he could see of Savannah. Tried and failed. He had no objectivity where she was concerned.

His eyes took in her pale appearance, her blood-streaked face, her lack of movement, her legs that had been elevated as if to prevent shock. Had she lost that much blood?

"Can I help you?" one of the nurses asked, glancing up from where she punched data into an infusion pump.

"Is she...?"

What was he asking? Of course she was still alive. The monitors showed a heartbeat, sounded a reassuring beep. Then there were the painful moans. But Savannah wasn't awake. There was too much activity around her. Intravenous lines rapidly putting fluid into her body and even a pint of blood being infused as fast as her veins would take it.

"You are?" the nurse asked, eyeing him as if she was going to call Security any moment.

What could he say? He was nothing to Savannah. Not anymore.

"She's pregnant with my baby."

Was she still pregnant with their baby? Had the wreck robbed her of their child?

The emergency room doctor and nurse exchanged looks, then the nurse who'd been talking to him stepped away from Savannah, glanced closer at Charlie's name badge. "I'm sorry, Dr. Keele, but I'm going to have to ask you to step out. We've got to get her into surgery STAT. One of the doctors or myself will come find you as quickly as possible and let you know what's going on."

With that, another nurse escorted him out of the cubicle and to a waiting area, where he waited. And waited.

Charlie had no idea how much time had passed. He'd had the presence of mind to call one of the residents and have her see his scheduled afternoon patients but, other than that, he wasn't sure he'd had a rational thought for hours.

What his thoughts had been was irrational. He'd wanted to pull rank, to barge into wherever Savannah was and demand to know exactly what was going on. To do that might slow down her care, might waste vital time being spent on him rather than her.

So he sat.

He thought of breaking hospital policy and logging into Savannah's medical chart and finding out what was happening. He could be fired for doing so. Yet the thought was tempting.

Surgery? What kind of surgery? What about the baby?

Did Savannah have internal injuries? God, he wished he knew something—that he knew she was going to be okay.

If he didn't hear something soon, maybe he'd use his badge to at least get someone on the emergency room staff to tell him something because the waiting was killing him.

Savannah's mother wasn't faring much better. Other than asking if he knew anything when she'd first arrived, she'd not said much to him. Savannah's cousin had driven her mother and her aunt the two-hour trip and the three of them sat praying while he paced back and forth across the room. No doubt she hated him. No doubt she should. He'd gotten her daughter pregnant and walked away. Despite his knowing that was best for Savannah and their baby, to an outsider that made him look like the bad guy. That was okay. He knew in the long run his not being in Savannah's life would be more beneficial to her and their child than living the hell that had been his and his mother's life.

Just when he thought he couldn't stand anymore, the nurse entered the room and motioned to follow her. He motioned to Savannah's family and they went with him. Without really telling him anything, the nurse put them in a consult room.

Within a couple of minutes of being shown the room, a vascular surgeon he vaguely recognized entered the room.

A vascular surgeon.

Why had Savannah needed a vascular surgeon? He'd been expecting an orthopedic or an internist or a hospitalist or an obstetrician, but not a vascular surgeon. Maybe, with as much blood as Savannah had apparently lost, he should have.

"How is my daughter?" Savannah's mother asked. The surgeon didn't directly respond, just made brief eye contact with the older women and Savannah's cousin, then turned to Charlie.

He rose to his feet and shook the man's hand.

"Hello, Dr. Keele. I'm Dr. Trenton. I hear you've recently joined our heart failure team. My nurse says you're acquainted with Miss Carter and were her emergency contact."

Savannah's mother didn't look happy at having her question ignored, that he'd been who the police officer had called, and, honestly, Charlie didn't blame her.

He didn't recall telling the nurse much of anything about himself, other than he was Savannah's baby's father, but maybe he had said more. Or maybe she'd done some research. She'd seen his name tag. A simple Internet search would have told her that much and more. As far as being acquainted with Savannah, he wasn't sure how to label himself so he just nodded and asked Savannah's mother's question. "How is she?"

"Lucky to be alive and in recovery. Barring something unforeseen, I believe she's out of the woods now that her bleed has been repaired. She was pretty banged up. Mostly deep bruising, as far as we can tell, except her peroneal artery was lacerated in her left leg. We're not exactly sure what cut her, just that she had a significant puncture laceration. Fortunately, one of the accident witnesses was a firefighter and he got her free from the car, made a pressure bandage for her leg, and kept her legs elevated. He saved her life, but she still lost quite a bit of blood."

"But she is going to be okay?" Had Charlie asked or her mother? He didn't know. It didn't matter. All that mattered was that Savannah was going to be all right.

Dr. Trenton nodded. "I have every reason to believe she is going to be fine. The surgical repair of the artery was a success. She's off the ventilator the helicopter team put in to maintain an airway in case of internal injuries and she's breathing just fine on her own. As far as we can tell, there aren't any broken bones. I don't expect any surgical complications. We'll monitor her for a few days, just to be sure and to make sure there aren't any unforeseen internal injuries."

Charlie let that register, then asked what no one had mentioned, not even Savannah's family. "The baby?"

The man met his gaze and gave him a somber look. "She hasn't miscarried yet, but her body did sustain major trauma. Certainly, the baby is at risk."

"She's going to lose our baby?"

The surgeon sighed. "I wish I could tell you a definite no but, with the trauma to her body, a miscarriage is a real possibility. She had a few contractions earlier but they seem to have stopped now that her blood volume levels are normalized. A high risk obstetrician has been assigned to the case and will be overseeing her care once she's transferred out of recovery. No doubt she'll be able to give you much more information than what I know. What I can tell you is that Miss Carter's ultrasound has showed the placenta is intact and, best we can tell, there aren't any leaks. The baby's heartbeat has remained strong and steady, but again, Miss Carter lost a lot of blood and had to have several pints infused. The neonatal unit is aware and on standby if she or the baby gets in distress. A team of doctors will be monitoring them both closely."

Even with the hospital's excellent neonatology unit, their baby wouldn't survive at such an early stage of pregnancy. Savannah was only four months pregnant. Definitely, the hospital was equipped to handle early deliveries and had many successful cases of survival, but four months was too early. Way too early.

Charlie's eyes prickled with moisture and he sank to one of the vinyl-covered chairs in the small waiting area.

"Thank God Savannah's going to be all right," her

mother said, not commenting on the baby. “When can we see her?”

The surgeon nodded at her mother, then said, “It’ll be another fifteen or twenty minutes before she’ll be released from recovery, then she’ll be transferred to the high risk obstetric unit.” He met Charlie’s gaze. “Normally, you wouldn’t be able to see her until she was transferred onto the floor but, as a courtesy, Dr. Keele can see her before she’s transferred.”

Savannah’s mother grumbled, but didn’t say anything beyond.

Charlie closed his eyes. He would like to see Savannah.

Question was, would Savannah want him there?

If she didn’t, could he really blame her?

CHAPTER EIGHT

SAVANNAH HURT.

All over.

And inside.

She hurt there, too.

"Take a deep breath," someone told her. The voice was kind, gentle, comforting almost, and sounded so far away.

"Savannah, you need to take a deep breath."

The voice wasn't as soft this time. There was more urgency to the tone. A beeping was sounding in the background that didn't quite fit in Savannah's fuzzy mind.

A deep breath. She could do that. She pulled air into her lungs then stopped at the excruciating pain.

Maybe she couldn't do that.

Why did it hurt to breathe?

"I know it hurts," the voice empathized. "But you need to take some deep breaths and get your oxygen saturation higher. Dr. Trenton isn't going to release you to be transferred to your room until you're stable. Breathe."

Transferred to her room.

Despite how heavy her eyelids felt, Savannah pried her lids apart. Fluorescent lights shone in her eyes and she quickly closed her lids to block out the brightness.

She was in a hospital. That much registered.

"Blue," the voice that had told her to breathe said. "With

that red hair, I wondered if they would be. Your eyes, that is."

Savannah exerted great effort and ordered her eyes to open again. Slowly, they obeyed and she struggled to focus on her surroundings.

"I was hoping you'd open them on your own before I had to do your next neuro check."

A bright room with artificial lighting. So bright it made holding her eyes open even more of a challenge. Or maybe it was the fact that they felt so puffy, almost swollen shut, that made it so difficult to keep her lids pried apart. Even the slightest movement sent new shockwaves of pain through her body.

"Take another big breath to keep your oxygen saturation up," the nurse repeated. "Your baby needs you taking big breaths."

Her baby. Oh, no. Had she? No, the woman had told her to breathe deeply to get her O2 sats up for her baby. If she'd miscarried, her breathing wouldn't affect her baby.

Her baby was alive.

Still, she wanted reassurance, especially as she didn't feel any movement. Not that she always did, just that currently she felt nothing.

Nothing except pain. Great pain.

"My baby? Did I…?"

"Your baby is still holding his or her own. See." The woman gestured toward a monitor.

Savannah squinted toward the direction the woman gestured. There were a lot of monitors and medical equipment hooked to her, two of which displayed steady heartbeats, one much more rapid than the other. One hundred and forty-eight beats per minute. Her baby had a good, steady fetal heartbeat.

She was in a hospital. Her baby was alive. She was alive. Why was she in a hospital? Why did she hurt so much?

"What happened?"

"You don't remember?" the nurse asked.

She closed her eyes and strained to recall. Horror joined her pain. "I was in a wreck. My car was hit and then I hit the car in front of me and was trapped between them."

"From what I was told, that sounds right," the nurse agreed. "There was a fender bender that put traffic at a sudden stop on the interstate. Apparently, you were able to get stopped, but the driver behind you wasn't paying attention and never braked. One of the witnesses said the driver was texting while driving." The nurse gave a disgusted look. "You were slammed into by that car and that smashed you into the car in front of you. Then, another car hit the car that hit you and crushed you in between the two vehicles even more. I'm not a hundred percent that's accurate, but it's what I was told. Regardless, you are lucky to still be with us."

Savannah relived the impact followed by another impact. She remembered thinking the hits, the being jerked forward, was never going to end, that she was going to die in her car.

"Was anyone else hurt?" she asked, almost afraid of the answer. When in nursing school, she'd done a few rotations where she'd worked the emergency department, worked motor vehicle accidents. She knew how serious they could be.

The nurse winced and Savannah knew someone had been injured. By the nurse's expression, seriously injured.

"The driver who hit you, the one texting while driving, died instantly."

Savannah's heart squeezed. That impact that had jarred her very being, someone had died in that instant.

She could have died.

Her baby could have died.

Her gaze went to the fetal heart monitor, taking in the rapid little heartbeats.

She might hurt all over, but at least her baby was alive.

"Sad." Her throat felt so dry, almost swelled shut.

The nurse seemed to read her mind and offered a sip. "Just a little one to begin with, though, until we see how you do."

Savannah was grateful for something wet. The nurse held the cup to where she could take a sip through the straw. She'd barely gotten a few drops in her mouth when the nurse pulled back the cup. "Sorry. Just a little for now. I'll give you more in a few minutes if you do okay with that."

She wanted more, but her nurse's brain understood the reasons why. Not that she felt her brain was working correctly. She didn't. A fog clouded her mind, making thinking a conscious effort rather than something that came naturally.

Just how hurt was she?

Her left leg felt crazy heavy, much more so than her arms and right leg, which also seemed to be made of lead. Pain racked her body and yet pinpointing where she hurt, or even where she hurt most, seemed impossible. Quite simply, every inch of her hurt. She was sure it did.

When she hurt so completely, when the wreck had been as bad as she was realizing it was, how could her baby have survived?

"I can see my baby's heart beating, but you're sure he or she is okay? That nothing happened during the wreck?"

"You've had several tests. Your ultrasound didn't show any abnormalities. It seems your body absorbed most of the impact of the wreck and protected your baby."

Hopefully. She wanted to protect her baby, to always

keep her baby safe from harm. She'd slept through an ultrasound where she could have seen her beautiful baby? That was sad.

"Did they take pictures?"

The nurse's brows rose. "Pardon?"

"During my ultrasound, did they take pictures of my baby?"

Smiling gently, the nurse shook her head. "Not that I'm aware of, but I've no doubt you'll be having another ultrasound prior to leaving the hospital. Probably a few more. You can ask the sonographer to print you a photo at that time."

Savannah went to nod, but her head didn't cooperate.

Panic must have shown in her eyes because the nurse touched her arm.

"You're in a neck stabilization brace. You got whipped around hard. The hospitalist overseeing your care wants you left in the brace for now to keep your neck stable. Nothing's broken," she assured her. "The doctor is just being cautious."

What had the wreck done to her body? All she'd asked about was the baby.

"What is wrong with me?"

"Mostly severe bruising, multiple lacerations, a few of which required stitching, and then you had a puncture wound on your leg that tore the peroneal artery. That's why your left leg may feel really heavy. One of the vascular surgeons repaired the bleed."

An arterial bleed.

"I checked your wound before you woke up. He did a great job. Once it's healed, you'll only have a tiny scar."

At this point the size of a scar seemed such a trivial matter.

Just so long as her baby was going to be okay, everything else was trivial. The fog that clouded her mind moved in thicker, darker.

Exhausted, she closed her eyes. When she next opened them, the nurse was standing over her, telling her to breathe deeply again.

The last time she'd breathed deeply, she'd hurt. Vaguely she recalled talking to the nurse. She couldn't recall if they'd just had the conversation or if it had been hours ago.

She already hurt. She sure didn't want to do anything that made that pain worse.

But she had her baby to think about.

She took a few deep breaths and reminded herself that the intense pain was worth it if it helped the baby.

"Good job," the nurse praised.

Charlie wasn't supposed to be on this side of medicine. He just wasn't. He'd been there, done that with his grandfather. His mother had died instantly in her car wreck and his father had been ill for a while but, stubbornly, had died in his sleep at home rather than at a hospital where he could have received medical care. Only with his grandfather had Charlie sat at the hospital. He'd felt so helpless then.

He felt so helpless now.

Even more so as the nurse led him through to the recovery room where Savannah lay on the hospital bed. The scene that met him had his knees threatening to buckle.

Her face had multiple bruises and lacerations. Her left upper and lower eyelids were a purplish blue and significantly swollen. Her lower lip was swollen and busted in the middle. Her neck was in a stabilization brace. Her left leg was propped up on a pillow and covered with the white blanket that was tucked around her.

"This is Dr. Keele. He works in cardiology," the nurse

introduced him to the recovery room nurse who was hovering over Savannah.

The recovery nurse gave Charlie's escort an odd look, one that clearly asked why he was there.

"I'm a friend of your patient," he explained, realizing the woman wondered why the nurse was bringing a cardiologist to see her post-op vascular patient.

At his voice, Savannah's eyes opened, her left only partially parting beneath her swollen lids. Her eye was bloodshot where capillaries had burst and bled, trapping the blood.

She didn't speak, just touched her tongue to her lips as if to moisten them. The recovery room nurse, in tune with her patient, dabbed Savannah's lips with a moist swab.

"There. That should help."

Savannah moved slightly, as if trying to nod, then let out a soft moan.

"Don't try moving right now other than to take some big, deep breaths," the nurse instructed. "I'm going to step over here for a few minutes to give you a bit of privacy." Her gaze met Charlie's. "Make sure she keeps breathing deep."

Charlie wasn't sure he wanted to be left alone with Savannah. Then again, having the nurse observe their conversation couldn't be a good thing either. Who knew what Savannah was going to say to him? She'd probably tell him to go to hell.

The past few hours, he'd felt as if that was where he'd been.

What did it matter what she said? She was alive, could say whatever she wanted, and he'd just be thankful that she had the ability to speak.

He stepped next to the hospital bed, placed his hand over hers, grateful for the warmth he felt there, for the lifeblood still flowing through her body.

"Dr. Trenton says you're going to be okay," he said, his thumb rubbing over her hand and his voice choking up. Should he touch her? How could he not? He wanted to pull her into his arms and hold her close and protect her from the whole world.

As if he could protect her.

He couldn't. Just as he'd not been able to protect his mother. She'd died and it had been his fault.

He stood next to Savannah's hospital bed, caressing her hand and wishing he knew what to say to make everything better.

Wishing he could take away her pain.

She stared at him from between her swollen eyelids that looked as if they were getting heavier and heavier. Her oxygen saturation alarm sounded, indicating that her level had dropped and earning them a concerned glance from the nurse.

"Take a deep breath, Savannah. You've got to breathe deep to keep your sats up."

"Don't tell me what to do," she mumbled, but took several deep breaths after doing so.

"I just want you to be okay."

"How can you say that?"

His heart cracked at her question.

"How can you think otherwise?" he countered.

"You left me."

There it was. He had left her. How could he ever make her understand that he'd left for her own good, for their baby's good? She hadn't grown up in his house, hadn't heard the fights, felt the blame, the guilt. No, Savannah's parents had loved each other and her until the day her father had died. Her mother had continued to shower her with love every day since.

"Your mother is here."

Her gaze shifted, looking for her.

"Not here in Recovery, but in the waiting area."

Her cracked lips formed a semblance of an "O".

"Your cousin drove your mother and aunt up."

She stared at him but didn't say anything, just took a few more deep breaths.

"They're anxious to see you. Dr. Trenton says that once you are settled into a room he will let them visit."

"Did I lose our baby?"

Did she not know? Had no one told her? Or had she just forgotten or thought they'd lied to keep her spirits up? Was she unaware of the baby heart monitor beeping just as it should?

Then again, she'd sustained trauma and could have been told a dozen times and still not recall at this stage in her recovery.

"The fetal monitor is real, the results are real. Our baby is hanging in there."

She seemed to consider his comment a few minutes, then her worried gaze met his. "Am I going to miscarry?"

He didn't want to have this conversation with her. Not now. Not ever.

"I don't know, Savannah. I hope not."

"Why? Why would you care one way or the other? You don't want our baby."

Her words stung. Stung deep.

"I never said that."

"But you don't."

"I don't want you to miscarry, Savannah." Odd, as the best thing for her would be for her to be free of him completely. Yet he knew how much she wanted this baby. He'd seen it on her face in Chattanooga. He saw it now.

"They will do everything they can to keep you from miscarrying. If you do end up delivering, you couldn't be at a better neonatal unit than at Vanderbilt to increase our baby's chances of survival."

"Too early," she mouthed.

It was, but he wasn't going to confirm her fears.

"Babies are surviving at earlier and earlier gestation." Yes, they both knew the statistics weren't great and that the risks of complications were high.

Savannah didn't answer, just grunted, and closed her eyes.

Her alarm sounded again.

"Take a deep breath, Savannah."

"No," she countered but did so anyway, her sats immediately responding in a positive manner.

"Is there anything I can get you?" he asked, wishing there was something he could do to ease her pain and suffering. Wishing he could have somehow taken her place and be the one lying in the hospital bed instead of her.

"I don't want anything from you." It was the clearest sentence she'd said since he'd entered the recovery room area.

His gaze met hers.

"I was… I was coming to tell you…to give back your house."

What she said registered.

She was here because of him.

If he hadn't given her the house she wouldn't have driven to Nashville, wouldn't have been on I-24 when her car got struck, wouldn't by lying in this hospital bed recovering from serious injuries.

This was his fault.

He might not have been the one driving the car that slammed into Savannah, but it had been his fault she'd been in the wrong place at the wrong time.

Just as his mother's wreck had been his fault.

"I'm sorry, Savannah." He was. So very sorry.

She didn't respond to his apology, just closed her eyes.

"I'm so sorry," he repeated, this time a little louder.

"Just go," she finally said, her eyelids not budging. "Just leave me alone."

Savannah's head hurt, but as far as she could tell her brain was working. It was working, right? Because she was telling Charlie to go away.

Okay, so what she wanted to do was beg him to hold her, to let her cry over her pain, over her aches, over how scared she'd been when she'd braked, the moment of relief when she'd gotten stopped prior to ramming the car in front of her, then the sheer terror when she'd felt the impact, and then again. She wanted his comfort over the fear she might lose their baby.

She didn't want to lose their baby.

Despite how heavy her hand and arm felt, she moved her hand to cup her abdomen. Several blankets were between her palm and her belly.

She wanted to move them but didn't seem capable so maybe her brain wasn't working so well after all because she was telling her hand to move, but her arm wasn't cooperating.

"Let me." Charlie pulled back the blankets and guided her hand to her slightly rounded belly.

She expected him to immediately pull away, but he didn't. Instead, his hand stayed there with hers.

On cue, their baby moved. Just the tiniest of flutters, but one that made Savannah's heart sing. She shifted her hand, placed Charlie's over where she'd felt the movement.

His hand rested there for several long moments, but moved away before anything happened.

Disappointment filled her that he'd moved before getting to feel the magic of their baby's movements. But more than that. Disappointment filled her that he was no longer touching her, that the comfort of his touch was gone.

His touch shouldn't comfort her. She didn't want him or trust him. His touch should enrage her.

Yeah, maybe she was wrong. She'd told him to go, yet she did want him there.

Her brain wasn't working at all.

Maybe she had a concussion.

Actually, she probably did have a concussion.

She'd had a hard hit, had whiplash.

What had they told her was wrong with her?

She didn't know. Maybe they hadn't told her. Maybe she was dreaming. After all, why would Charlie be standing over her with that look in his eyes?

That look that for so long she'd believed was one of love.

He didn't love her.

Yet, when she stared into his eyes, she'd swear there were unshed tears there, that there was such raw emotion that he must care about her.

But thinking about it, trying to figure it out when she hadn't been able to understand for months why he'd left, made her brain hurt worse.

Her brain already hurt enough. Too much.

"Take a deep breath, Savannah."

Annoyed, she took another deep breath. "Why are you still here?"

"I'll be here until I know you're okay."

"I'm okay."

"God, I hope so." He sounded so sincere that she couldn't stand it anymore.

"Go away, Charlie," she moaned. "You are nothing to me anymore so just go away."

She expected him to argue, to say something. He didn't say anything for so long that Savannah opened her eyes.

Her breath caught.

He was gone.

Had she just dreamed that he was there?

At this point, reality and non-reality all seemed to swirl together.

CHAPTER NINE

"I FEEL FINE," Savannah protested for the hundredth time and was mostly telling the truth. Yes, she hurt all over still, and especially her left lower leg, but every day she felt a little stronger than the day before. "I want to go home."

Although, not really. Not until she was one hundred percent sure she wasn't going to go into early labor. If that happened, she wanted to be in the hospital, where her baby could get immediate medical attention. Five days had gone by since her wreck and although she'd had several contractions, they'd stopped on their own each time. The obstetrician had started injections as a precautionary measure to more rapidly mature the baby's lungs and every day that she didn't go into labor was critical time for her baby to continue to develop.

"Leaving the hospital is not going to happen for at least another twenty-four hours," Dr. Kimble told her.

Twenty-four hours. That both excited and scared her. She was ready to be home, back in Chattanooga, away from Nashville and wondering if she'd see Charlie that day. She hadn't since the recovery room. Which was her own doing. She couldn't remember much of their conversation, but she'd told him to leave. She hadn't wanted him there.

"Thank you. I'll let my family know so someone can be here to bring me back to Chattanooga tomorrow."

The doctor shook her head. "I don't want you that far away from the hospital for at least a week, preferably longer."

"A week?"

She nodded. "I want to check you closely until I'm sure you and the baby are stable."

"But I live in Chattanooga," she reminded her. "I can't make that drive back and forth."

She didn't even own a working car at the moment.

"You're right. You can't make that drive back and forth. You need to stay in Nashville."

She stared at the doctor. She didn't want to stay in Nashville. She wanted to go home. Driving back and forth sounded better and better.

"You don't have to drive back and forth. You can stay at my place."

Savannah hadn't seen Charlie since the recovery room. For a while, she had truly questioned if he'd been there or if she'd imagined him. But her mother had commented on how he'd kept vigil in the waiting area, how he'd called her, how he'd arranged for a room at the Loew's Plaza Hotel and paid for it.

Her mother had gone home last night, fatigue overcoming her and Savannah insisting she go home. Under protest she had, but had called to check on her several times today.

Chrissie and a couple of the nurses from the cardiology floor had driven up to visit earlier in the week, and several other coworkers had called to check on her.

But until this moment she'd not seen or heard from Charlie.

The high-risk obstetrician didn't seem taken aback by Charlie's presence, which told Savannah that he'd been communicating with the specialist. Perhaps that should upset her, but at this point she didn't care.

"That's preferable to her driving back and forth two hours each way," the obstetrician agreed. "She'll need to be confined to bed rest, of course."

"Of course," Charlie agreed.

"There are excellent specialists in Chattanooga," Savannah pointed out, annoyed that the two were making decisions about her as if she weren't right there in the room and capable of making decisions for herself. She might have been in a major automobile accident and suffered a concussion, but she hadn't lost her mind. Not yet, anyway.

"Agreed, but I'd like to keep a check on you myself and I'd prefer you not to be in a car for the two plus hours each way. You need rest, not an exhausting ride."

"Two hours isn't an exhausting ride. Not really," she argued, despite knowing she'd do whatever was best for her baby.

"Regardless, I'd rather keep you here longer than for you to travel far from the hospital."

Did they really expect her to agree to stay at Charlie's? If circumstances were different she might suspect a set-up, but Charlie had left her, not the other way around.

Why would he volunteer to let her stay? Guilt?

"I will stay in Nashville," she agreed without actually agreeing to stay at Charlie's. Yes, she'd do whatever she had to do to protect her baby, but staying at Charlie's wasn't required to do that.

Only perhaps it was.

The only way Dr. Kimble would agree to release her to leave the hospital the next day was with the understanding that she would be under Dr. Keele's care. Hello, he was a cardiologist, not an obstetrician. It wasn't as if he was trained to deliver babies or to take care of pregnant women. He wasn't. Still, they were Dr. Kimble's conditions.

Not happy with the arrangement, Savannah allowed the

nurse to wheelchair her out to Charlie's car, allowed Charlie to stow the bag of her things Chrissie had brought to her when she'd visited, allowed the nurse to assist her into Charlie's car.

It hit her again at that moment that she no longer had a vehicle. Hers was demolished. At some point she'd have to deal with her auto insurance carrier, with buying a new car, with getting behind the steering wheel and not thinking of the crash.

Her head hurt at the thought.

She'd deal with that later.

She settled back into the seat and closed her eyes.

"It's just as well I live so close. Dr. Kimble wants you to keep your legs up as much as possible."

"I don't think sitting in a car is going to cause me any problems."

"There's no reason to take any chances."

She kept her eyes squeezed shut and didn't respond. What was the point? For the next few days, maybe the next week, she was stuck as Charlie's house guest.

Charlie settled Savannah onto the sofa. With her feet propped up on one end and several pillows on the other, she lay there looking pale and much too quiet.

He'd half expected her to argue at every point, but she hadn't. She hadn't responded with anything more than one-word responses and a few thank-yous.

Not so long ago he'd felt closer to Savannah than anyone in the world. Now, in many ways, a stranger lay on his sofa.

A stranger because the withdrawn, obviously in pain woman wasn't the woman he'd known in Chattanooga. Not even close.

He'd done that to her.

Not directly.

But he was responsible for her pregnancy, for her unhappiness, for her being on that interstate.

He'd only been trying to help.

Just as his father had only been trying to help when he'd married Charlie's mother. That hadn't turned out so well.

Neither had Charlie's involvement in Savannah's life.

Perhaps he should have hired a nurse to take care of her twenty-four-seven. He sort of had.

What would she think of the fact that he had hired her friend Chrissie to care for her while he was at work?

She surely would appreciate that he hadn't hired a stranger to stay with her. Her mother had thought it a good idea and given her blessing. Plus, Chrissie had jumped at the opportunity to make what he'd offered to pay her to stay with Savannah. Fortunately, the nurse had just worked four twelve-hour shifts in a row and was off for the next four days. Charlie had hired her for three of those four days. She would be with Savannah while he was at work through Friday. He was off work and call this weekend. He'd care for Savannah himself on Saturday and Sunday, had rearranged his schedule so he could go with her to her appointments with Dr. Kimble and Dr. Trenton on Monday. They'd figure out what needed to happen from there.

Regardless, he'd make sure she was taken care of.

Always.

Which might not be his right.

It wasn't even now.

But he felt responsible for her, for their baby.

He wanted to take care of her.

And their baby.

Which was why he'd paid for a hotel room for Chrissie and her son for them to go to in the evenings after he got home. He'd take care of Savannah and their baby while he was home from work. Chrissie had agreed to return to his apartment if he had any emergencies and had to leave after hours.

He studied Savannah on the sofa. He'd given her a blanket, and she'd covered herself. She looked frail and banged up, with her black eye, bruised face and body, healing but still swollen lip, and bandaged leg.

"Can I get you anything?"

Without looking at him, she shook her head.

"Something to eat or drink?"

Again, she shook her head.

"Are you not going to talk to me?"

She opened her eyes, looked up. "What do you want me to say?"

Good question. What did he want her to say?

That she forgave him for doing this to her.

Only which *this* did he mean?

Her pregnancy or her car wreck? For being the same jerk his father had been? For not being able to give her the things she deserved?

He sank into a chair. "I'm not sure. I just don't like this awkwardness."

"You expected otherwise?"

"With us? Yes," he admitted, raking his fingers through his hair. "I guess I do. You and I should never be awkward."

"Why not?"

Another good question.

"Because of what we shared." Which really didn't make sense, even to his own ears. They were no longer a couple.

"What we shared no longer matters, Charlie. Haven't you figured that out yet?"

He understood what she was saying. She'd fancied herself in love with him. She was no longer under any false illusions, but that didn't mean they had to be enemies.

"You will always matter to me, Savannah," he admitted.

"Because of the baby?"

He thought for a moment. "The baby doesn't have anything to do with the fact that what we had was special. You were special."

Her lashes lowered as she looked away. "Not special enough."

"What's that supposed to mean?"

"I'm through with this conversation." She tugged the blanket up around her and turned her head away from him. "None of this matters anymore, Charlie. Not to me."

Frustrated, mostly with himself, Charlie sat in the chair and watched her, could tell the moment her tense body relaxed with sleep and she rolled back toward him. Still, he watched the rise and fall of the blanket, the peace that settled onto her bruised, swollen face.

A face that was more precious to him than any other.

A face that had haunted him.

He'd gotten so attached to Savannah that he'd recognized letting her go was going to be difficult. So he'd taken the decision out of his hands by doing something he'd known would upset her and make her push him away.

He'd purposely flubbed up his relationship with Savannah, making her hate him, because, deep down, he'd worried whether or not he'd be able to do right by her and walk away.

Savannah woke with a pressing need to go to the bathroom. Opening her eyes, it took her a moment to remember where she was.

Charlie's apartment.

In Charlie's living room. On Charlie's sofa. With Charlie asleep in a chair a few feet away.

The soft rise and fall of his chest mesmerized her. She struggled to tear her gaze away from his relaxed body.

Tears pricked her eyes. She'd never thought she'd see him sleeping again. Had never dreamed she'd be staying in his Nashville apartment, that he'd be taking care of her.

She still didn't fully understand why she was here, why he was shifting his life around to accommodate her.

Guilt?

Probably.

Was that why he'd deeded her the house?

Why he'd volunteered to keep her at his apartment?

Because he felt guilty that she'd loved him and he hadn't felt the same? That she was pregnant with a baby he didn't want?

Didn't he realize none of that mattered now? She no longer loved him and didn't need him to help her with the baby. She had this. Or she had before her wreck, and soon enough she'd be back on her feet and have her life back under control.

Trying to make as little noise as possible, she scooted up on the pillow, then slowly sat up, wincing in pain as she did so. Her eyes stayed on the sleeping man.

He didn't really look as if the past month had been overly good to him. He looked tired. Plus, he'd lost weight from his already lean frame, making his face look a little gaunt.

Her bladder reminded her of why she'd awakened. She'd toured the apartment with him prior to his leasing it so she knew where the guest bathroom was. She hated to wake Charlie to help her to the toilet when she'd be just fine going by herself. She preferred going by herself.

She didn't need him for that either.

Gritting her teeth to keep from groaning at the pain, she slowly stood from the sofa, made sure she wasn't tangled in the blanket, then hobbled to the bathroom.

See, she had this, and hadn't needed him at all.

* * *

Charlie woke with a start, his eyes immediately going to the sofa.

The empty sofa.

Savannah was gone.

"Savannah?" he called, leaping out of his chair. "Savannah?"

"Here," she answered, calming his racing heart as she limped into the living room. "I had to go to the bathroom."

"You should have woken me."

"Why?" she asked, settling back onto the sofa without taking the hand he offered. "I've been going to the bathroom by myself for more than two decades."

"Why can't you accept my help?"

"I am accepting your help. I'm here, aren't I? But I refuse to be treated like an invalid. I can see myself to the bathroom without you hovering over me."

"Point taken, but for the record I want to hover over you."

"Why?" she asked, staring at him pointedly. When he didn't immediately answer, she shook her head. "Never mind. Forget I asked. I don't want to know."

Which was just as well because he didn't know the answer—just that he wanted to take care of her.

"Are you hungry?"

She didn't look interested in food. Or much of anything else other than closing him out. "Not really, but I know I need to eat for the baby."

"And for you," he reminded.

She shrugged. "The baby is more important."

Charlie didn't respond because she wouldn't like his answer. "What would you like?"

"Just whatever you have is fine."

"My housekeeper grocery shopped today. I put several

items I knew you like on her list. I can make you pretty much anything."

"Make me a fairy princess," she said without looking at him and without any inflection in her voice.

"Let me clarify," he began. "I can make you anything to eat you want. If I don't have whatever it is you're hungry for, I can run down the street and pick it up at the grocery store on the corner."

"Just something light would be good. I really don't want to be a bother. Maybe some eggs and toast?"

She wasn't a bother. Far from it. He was glad she was there, that he was able to do something to help, something to stop himself feeling so helpless, something to help amend all the wrong he'd done.

"With strawberry jam?" he offered, knowing she loved the stuff.

Her face perked up. "You have strawberry jam?"

Bingo.

"I do as of this morning."

"Then, yes, I'd like jam with my toast."

Charlie had waited on her hand and foot for the past couple of evenings. Her friend Chrissie had sat with her during the daytime, which was great and gave Savannah someone to spill her heart to.

"Being here is driving me crazy," she moaned. "How am I supposed to forget the man when I'm staying at his house?"

"Doesn't matter. You weren't forgetting Charlie when you were in Chattanooga and he was here."

Savannah frowned at where her friend sat on the floor playing with her two-year-old son. She started to argue that she was, but Chrissie didn't look as if she'd believe her.

"Sure I was. But it helped when I wasn't having to look at him every night."

Chrissie's eyes widened. "He's sleeping in here?"

"Only because I'm in his bed and he hasn't set up the guest bedroom yet. I tried to get him to let me stay on the sofa, but he said he didn't want me lying on the sofa day and night." Because he was being thoughtful. *Ugh.* This would be easier if he wasn't being so nice. If he was being a jerk, like he was in Chattanooga, she could tell herself she was better off without him. She was better off without him. He'd told her point blank that she didn't matter as much as his career did. He'd left her when she'd thought things were perfect. "So," she continued, "I'm in his bed night after night. It's torture being here."

Chrissie snapped two blocks together and handed them to Joss. "Because it's where you want to be?"

Okay, so she wasn't as immune to the man as she'd like to be. This wasn't breaking news. But she didn't want to be here.

"I know his housekeeper changed the bedding before my arrival, but the room smells like him. This whole apartment smells like him. Everywhere I look, every breath I take, he's there. I'm surrounded by him," she whined. "And, even though I can't stand him, it is torture to have to be here when he's pretending to be all nice."

Helping with another two blocks, Chrissie laughed. "Keep telling yourself you can't stand him, if you must, but you still have it bad, girl."

"No, I don't. I took my heart back when he made the decision to move from Chattanooga without so much as a word to me first."

Chrissie shrugged, eyeing her son. "Since when does the heart just let us take it back when it's convenient?

The heart knows what it wants even when our brain tells us otherwise."

Savannah eyed her friend, grateful for what she heard in her voice because it distracted her from her own woes.

"You never told me about Joss's dad," she gently reminded.

"Yeah, well, that's because he isn't what my heart wants so don't go getting ideas about me," Chrissie warned. "He was just a guy I met in Atlanta at a charity fundraiser we'd both volunteered at. I never saw him again. He hasn't been at the annual fundraiser since so I don't imagine I ever will."

Interesting that her friend had obviously thought he might be. "He worked in the medical profession?"

"I think he was a nurse or a paramedic. I don't know." Chrissie shrugged. "He was working triage so I guess he could have been anything." Her friend gave a wicked little smile. "We really didn't talk much."

Interesting. It was difficult to imagine her friend hooking up with a man she didn't know. Chrissie had barely dated prior to Joss being born and almost never now that she had her son. "A wild weekend, I take it?"

Chrissie's smile faded. "A weekend where I forgot who I was and just went with the flow. Look where that got me." She gestured toward her son, who looked up at her and grinned a grin destined to break a million hearts someday. Chrissie's face lit with love.

"Right where you wouldn't trade lives with anyone," Savannah reminded her. "He's precious."

Chrissie smiled and leaned forward to kiss the top of Joss's head. "That's true. I love this little guy more than anything."

Savannah was going to feel the same way about her baby. She already did. Her and Charlie's baby. Could she fully love her child and detest the father? She sighed. "I've got to make some type of peace with him, haven't I?"

"It's not like you're at war. He wants to be a part of your life."

"No, he doesn't," she denied. "He moved to get away from me."

Chrissie's brow rose at Savannah's claim. "He moved to take a ridiculously awesome career opportunity."

Savannah frowned. "Whose side are you on?"

"I'm not picking sides."

Savannah waved her hand as if trying to get Chrissie's attention. "Hello. Best friend here. You're automatically supposed to be on my side."

"Let me point out to you that the man took care of your mother while she sat at the hospital with you, and that he kept vigil at the hospital while you recovered. And, oh, yeah, he even deeded you his house in Chattanooga. And we're not talking a shack. We're talking about a gorgeous home in a great neighborhood. Not that I'm taking sides..."

Yeah, there was all that. There was also that she'd thought they were wonderful and she'd been wrong, that he'd betrayed her trust, betrayed her heart, and that she would never trust him again. "Am I supposed to be impressed?"

"I'm impressed," Chrissie admitted.

"I'm impressed." Joss repeated his mother's words and both women smiled at the boy who was otherwise ignoring them and building a fort with his blocks.

"I'll also point out he brought you to his home so he could take care of you and, best of all, he's paying me a load of money to do something I offered to do for free."

"I wouldn't have let you do that," Savannah pointed out, considering all her friend said.

"Neither would he."

"So, he has a few redeeming qualities."

Chrissie arched a brow. "A few?"

"Need I remind you that, despite those redeeming qualities, he made the decision to move to Nashville without even mentioning the possibility to his girlfriend—me—who he'd been seriously dating for a year?"

"I haven't forgotten."

Savannah frowned. "You've decided that was okay?"

"No." Chrissie's brows rose. Joss climbed into her lap and ran his little finger along the bunched skin between her eyes. Chrissie took his hand and kissed his fingertip over and over, making him giggle and wrap his little arms around her. "What I've decided is that I'm sticking with my original thoughts. He's crazy about you, but works for the CIA and is on a secret assignment."

"You and your secret agent theory." She rolled her eyes. "He doesn't work for the CIA. He's a cardiologist. He had a great job. Yes, maybe this one is better, but he doesn't act as if he's happier here."

"Maybe he's not." She punctuated her sentence with a kiss to Joss, who still hugged her. "Maybe he realizes he made a huge mistake. Maybe, rather than shutting him out, you need to remind him of how good it was between you two."

Savannah put her hand over her belly, thinking that before long she'd be the one loving and being loved by her child. The thought made her heart sing.

"That's a lot of maybes, the biggest one being that maybe I want him back. I don't."

"You're right," Chrissie agreed. "It is a lot of maybes. It's obvious he has strong feelings for you."

Her heart squeezing a little, she asked, "How is that obvious?"

"Savannah, have you paid attention to how he looks at you? I've said it before but it bears repeating. I'd give my right arm for a man to look at me the way Charlie Keele looks at you."

"That's..." She stopped. Lust? She wasn't exactly what dreams were made of. Perhaps she never had been, but especially not now, with her black eye, bruised, swollen face, healing leg, and pregnant belly.

"That's what?" Chrissie asked, tickling Joss and causing him to twist and turn in her arms.

"I don't know. I started to say that it was just sexual attraction, but I'm about as far from sexy as a woman could be."

"Don't even think that man doesn't want you, because he does. It shows in how he watches your every move."

She wasn't sure if Chrissie's observation disappointed her or thrilled her. Maybe a little of both. She might be physically recovering from her wreck, but she wasn't dead. Her body reacted every time Charlie was near. "So you think this is still just about sex?"

"I didn't say that."

"Then what?" she asked in exasperation.

"I think you need to set aside your pride for the remainder of time you are here and remind Charlie what he lost."

"You think I should seduce him? Hello, even if I wanted to, which I don't," she quickly added, "look at me."

Chrissie ignored her protest. "Pride, or whatever it is keeping you two apart, needs to be set aside to give whatever feelings are there a chance to flourish."

"We had a year to flourish," Savannah reminded her. They had flourished. Then he'd killed them. "I don't need him, Chrissie. I'm better off without him."

"You have the rest of your life to regret not opening yourself up to the possibility that maybe Charlie was more torn about his decision than you give him credit for. Maybe his taking the job was a test to see if you'd go with him. Or maybe it was a test to see if he'd get over you. Or maybe—"

"Or maybe he did exactly what he wanted and my being pregnant threw a big ole wrench in his plans to move on with his life and he feels guilty that he knocked me up."

"Maybe." Chrissie kissed Joss's forehead, then was the recipient of a very wet smack to her lips, smushed together between his little hands.

"Again, that's a lot of maybes."

Chrissie nodded. "All I'm saying is that I think you need to set the chip on your shoulder aside and just remember this is the man you are in love with and this may be your last opportunity to show him the error of his ways."

"Apparently you aren't hearing a thing I'm saying. I'm not in love with him, and you mean I should fight for him, but why shouldn't he be the one fighting for me?"

"Maybe in his own way he is," Chrissie suggested.

"He left me." Did she sound as whiny as she felt?

Chrissie didn't look sympathetic. "You let him."

"I couldn't have stopped him."

Chrissie just gave her an expectant look that said she didn't believe her.

"I couldn't have," she repeated, knowing it was true. She hadn't mattered enough for Charlie to stay. Besides, even if she could have, Charlie had wanted to go, to pursue his dreams. "I wouldn't have."

"Because you love him," Chrissie said matter-of-factly. "When he comes home, remind yourself of that, remind him of that."

Savannah frowned. "I'm not telling him anything of the sort." She sure wasn't reminding herself of something that wasn't even true. She didn't still love him. She didn't. She couldn't. Wouldn't.

"Don't tell him," Chrissie smugly suggested. "Show him."

CHAPTER TEN

CHARLIE'S DAY HAD been busy. He liked busy days. Normally. Today, he'd just wanted to go to the apartment he called home.

Not that the place had felt much like home. It hadn't. Maybe because he'd bought the place in Chattanooga and grown so comfortable there. It had been a great house, a great yard, a great neighborhood. A place for settling down and staying forever.

Not that he'd ever meant to do that. He hadn't. He'd bought it as an investment. The place had been marked way below market value for a quick sale due to a bank foreclosure.

The house would be a home, would have love and happiness inside it. With Savannah and their son or daughter.

He closed his eyes and tried to imagine him in the house with them and couldn't. He wasn't destined for such happiness.

But Savannah was and he'd do what he could to make sure she and their child had all their physical needs met.

His child would grow up with a loving mother, with a peaceful home, with lots of love and happiness. It was the best gift he could give.

The gift he would give.

"Dr. Keele, there's a hot load coming in. You're needed

in the heart lab." The nurse filled him in on the patient's details. "Dr. Sansbury and Dr. Louwitz are both already tied up. That leaves you on call this evening."

Glancing at his watch, he nodded. "Thanks. I'll head that way and get scrubbed up."

He didn't want to go to the cath. lab or anywhere that had anything to do with his career. He wanted to go to his apartment.

He wanted to go to where Savannah was.

Home.

No. Savannah wasn't home. He couldn't do that to her. He just couldn't. Not now or ever. Having her at his apartment made him forget things he needed to remember. Savannah deserved better than someone like him and it was time he reminded her of that.

"He's not going to come home after all," Savannah mused to her friend.

"Sure he is. You said he texted that he got a call about a procedure."

He had texted that he'd gotten called into doing an emergency cath. But that had been hours and hours ago.

"It's after eight."

"He'll be home."

On cue, the apartment door rattled with Charlie's key.

Both women glanced up. Savannah lay on the sofa and Chrissie sat with a sleeping Joss against her chest. The little boy had given up about twenty minutes before and dozed off.

"Sorry I'm late," Charlie said to no one in particular as he came into the apartment.

"It's not a problem," Chrissie assured him.

Savannah didn't say anything. What could she say? She

was a guest in his home and he'd gotten tied up at work. Despite her whining to Chrissie, she had no rights here.

"He's asleep?" Charlie asked, gesturing to the little boy.

"We wore him out today playing."

"That's good."

When Chrissie went to stand, still holding her son, Charlie came over to her. "Can I help you?"

Chrissie shook her head. "Nope. I'm leaving his bag and things here for in the morning. I've got extras at the hotel."

"I hate that you are staying at a hotel. Are you sure you don't want to just stay?" Savannah offered, thinking she probably shouldn't be inviting someone to stay at an apartment that wasn't hers. Her anxiety over being alone with Charlie was enough that she did so without hesitation, though.

Charlie didn't say anything, just waited for Chrissie to respond.

"No, I'm good and like my time with this little guy. I will see you in the morning." Chrissie made a puckered lip face toward Savannah, blowing a kiss without using her hands as they were full of her son. "I will let you hand me my purse."

Charlie glanced toward where she gestured, then grabbed the pocketbook. "You're sure there's nothing else I can do?"

"Maybe get the doors for me to make it easier, but, regardless, I can do this. We single moms get good at these kinds of things."

As Charlie first opened the apartment door and then her car door so she could put the child in his car seat, it struck him that Savannah would be a single mom. She'd have to maneuver their child from one place to another without help.

Because he wouldn't be there.

He winced at the thought and reminded himself of all the reasons why he'd moved to Nashville to begin with.

Chrissie snapped Joss's seat, checked to make sure the connection was secure, then she straightened, turned to Charlie.

"Be nice to her."

Charlie frowned. "Do you think I need to be told to be nice?"

"Do you?" she asked, giving him a look that said she thought he did. "She's been through a lot and I don't just mean the wreck."

"Me?"

Still standing by Joss's open car door, Chrissie shrugged. "You hurt her pretty bad."

"That was never my intention."

She nodded. "I believe that, which is why I still like you. Just make sure you don't hurt her more."

"You think she shouldn't be here? That I shouldn't be taking care of her right now?"

"That depends."

"On?"

"On what your intentions are."

"I have no intentions." He didn't, except to make sure she didn't live the life his mother had lived.

Chrissie studied him in the dim light of the parking lot. "If you truly mean that, then you shouldn't be taking care of her. You should have stayed away. Maybe you should ask yourself why you didn't."

Charlie wanted to ask what she meant, but Chrissie just walked around the car and opened the driver's side door.

"I'll see you in the morning. Oh, and by the way, I don't believe you on the 'no intentions' comment."

With that she closed the door and drove away.

"Did she get off okay?" Savannah asked when Charlie came back into his apartment.

"She did." He sat down in the chair Chrissie had vacated minutes before and stared at the woman propped up on his sofa.

"Long day?" she asked, studying him as closely as he was studying her.

"It was." Too long. "I'm sorry I was late."

"You don't have to apologize," she advised. "You owe me nothing."

"Perhaps I do."

"What do you mean?"

He raked his fingers through his hair. "Ignore me. I'm tired and talking out of my head."

"Have you eaten? Chrissie made a casserole. It's in the kitchen if you're hungry."

He hadn't eaten. His stomach seemed to suddenly remember that and growled. "Casserole sounds fabulous. I'm starved."

"Did you eat lunch?"

He thought back and couldn't recall eating.

When he didn't answer, Savannah shook her head. "No wonder you've lost weight."

"A few pounds."

"You didn't need to lose weight. You were perfect as you were." Realizing what she'd said, she backtracked. "I mean…you know what I mean."

He gave a tired smile. "I do, and thank you. How's the pain tonight?"

She shrugged. "Bearable."

"I admire your resolve to not take anything for the baby's sake."

"It's not worth the risk."

"I hate to see you suffer."

"I'm okay." She was. Or at least she would be. Eventually. Her leg, that was. When she looked at Charlie she wasn't so sure about other areas. Perhaps when you'd loved as deeply as she'd loved Charlie you never really healed.

After he'd eaten, he asked, "You want to watch a movie?"

Surprised at his suggestion, Savannah glanced up. "A movie?"

"I could rent something online for us to watch."

"If that's what you want to do."

She'd obviously not hidden her reluctance because he asked, "You don't?"

She laughed a little lamely. "I'm just sitting here with this leg propped up following doctor's orders. Whatever you want to do is fine."

"We could do something else if you'd like," he offered; being that thoughtful guy again was making it so difficult to remember that he'd walked away from her so coldly. Walls began slamming up all around her and she shook them off. No, she wasn't going to shut him out. Tonight she'd just pretend that all the negative hadn't happened. She'd not question her motives too closely and she'd just do her best to relax and rejoice that she was alive, that her baby was alive, that she was with a man who once upon a time had made her feel like the luckiest woman in the world and that, for better or worse, she was going to have a baby with him.

She named a card game they'd played numerous times in the past, sometimes just the two of them, sometimes with friends.

He looked surprised. "You want to play cards?"

She nodded. She would rather play cards than watch a movie. Playing a game, she wouldn't have to try to think of anything to say and yet they would talk. After all, if she was going to be here for a few more days, they needed some sort of truce.

"Yes, I'd like to play cards." She smiled what was her first real smile at him for months. "I like beating you."

Surprise flitted across his face and his brow arched. "You don't beat me at cards."

Good eyebrow arched, she tsked. "I might have been the one with a concussion, but it's your memory failing. I always win when we play cards."

He studied her a moment, his eyes intense in their darkness, his expression just as deep. Then his features softened and the corner of his mouth inched upward. "Right. You do." His smile came on full force. "When you're my partner."

Savannah's breath caught in her chest and she was grateful the pulse oximeter monitor was no longer monitoring her because the alarm bell would be sounding. *Breathe, Savannah, breathe.*

"Ooh, that was sneaky," she chided, her gaze not leaving his. "And not true."

"We'll see." His smile fell. "Or we would, except I don't have any cards here."

"Good thing for you I do." She reached into the bag that Chrissie had brought her. Inside were romance novels, puzzle books, an adult coloring book and pencils, cards, a learn-to-knit kit, and several other occupy-her-time-while-recuperating items her friend had given her. She pulled out the card box and waved it in front of her. "Because I'm awesome that way."

His lips curved in a smile and he looked more relaxed while awake than she'd seen him in months. "Yeah, you are awesome that way, but you are still going to lose."

Nope. He was wrong. Whether she toppled him in cards or not, she had won. Because he was kneeling down to sit on the floor on the opposite side of the coffee table and they were smiling at each other. That definitely made her feel like the winner.

She just wasn't sure why she felt that way.

Chrissie's time was up and she wouldn't be coming back to stay with Savannah. Which was just as well. Savannah felt able to take care of herself, despite the way Charlie treated her as if she were a fragile invalid.

Yes, she still hobbled around and looked like someone had beat her with a stick, but she felt stronger each day.

Plus, it was Friday and her baby had gotten in another week without being born. Every day was so critical. Plus, with each passing day the odds of going into premature labor decreased.

"I brought Chinese," Charlie announced, entering the apartment with a plastic bag full of food. "I hope that's okay."

"I told you in my text that Chinese was fine," she reminded him. She'd be glad when he quit being so accommodating. Accommodating Charlie was too much like Pre-Leaving for Nashville Charlie, and it was too easy to forget they were no longer a couple.

"Yeah, but I thought you might have changed your mind."

"About Chinese?" She frowned. "Never."

"I'm glad your appetite is back. I wasn't the only one who'd lost weight."

"I hadn't lost weight. It was just distributed a little differently."

"Even naked I didn't immediately realize," he mused.

She gave him a *duh* look. "That's because you were naked and distracted."

"True, but I can't believe I didn't straight away notice."

"I was only three months pregnant, barely showing, and even I forgot I was pregnant," she admitted, a bit stunned that she was doing so. "I'd never have kissed you or let you take me to the bedroom if I'd been thinking clearly."

His expression tightened and she realized what she'd said and went to clarify.

"It wasn't that I didn't want you, Charlie. I did." She still did, but she'd keep that to herself. "I just wouldn't have chosen for you to find out I was pregnant that way."

His expression remained terse. "Sometimes I wonder if you wanted me to find out at all."

She understood why he felt that way. She'd known two months without telling him. Two months when she'd agonized back and forth and came to the same conclusion. How could she tell him prior to his move without him thinking that she was trying to force him to stay? So, right or wrong, she'd kept her news to herself. "I would have told you. Doing otherwise was never a real option. I just thought it best if I waited until you were settled in your new life."

He leaned back against the sofa, closed his eyes, and seemed to take in what she was saying. "I'm sorry, Savannah."

Her throat tightened. "For?"

He half shrugged. "Putting you in this situation."

"Again—" she searched for the right words "—it's not how I would have chosen and certainly wasn't intentional, but I always wanted children. Our baby is a blessing. At least, that's how I see it."

The skin pulled tight over his cheekbones and if she didn't know better she'd swear his eyes looked glassy.

"Not everyone thinks that way."

His words stung deep. No, she imagined he didn't think that way. This pregnancy was a major inconvenience to him.

She was a major inconvenience to him.

Which she hated. She just wanted to go home. If it weren't for the baby, she would beg Chrissie to come get her.

Something that should be so beautiful, so wonderful, wasn't. Not to him. She refused to let him keep stealing her joy at becoming a mother. He didn't want to be a part of her and the baby's life. Fine. "I don't expect anything from you."

She didn't want anything from him. Sure, she wanted her baby to have a father's love, but if he couldn't give that, then so be it. She'd love their baby enough for the both of them.

Charlie sucked in a deep breath. "It's the expectations I have of myself that are the problem."

Trying to calm the anger surging through her, she took a deep breath. "What are your expectations of your role with our child?"

He closed his eyes and shook his head back and forth. "Financially, I'll take care of you and the baby."

She let what he'd said sink in. "I don't want your money."

"It would be unfair on you not to give our child the advantages I can provide."

"You gave me your house, Charlie. That wasn't necessary."

"To me, it was. I don't want you to worry about where you raise our child."

Where she raised their child.

"I can give our baby everything he or she needs," she assured him, daring him to claim otherwise. Chrissie did it, and did it well. She could, too.

Charlie shook his head. "I will help you financially, but otherwise it would be best if I stay out of the picture as much as possible."

A vice gripped her heart and squeezed it dry. Money. That was what he was offering their child. Not fatherly love. Not to be there to see a first smile, hear a first word, witness a first step. Money.

Disgust filled her.

"Best for who? Our baby? How is it best for a child not to know his or her father?"

His face was ashen, his eyes hollow pits of pain that poked holes in her anger. "Not all fathers are worth knowing."

What he said sank in and she realized how little she truly knew of his childhood. He didn't talk about his parents. Never. She knew they'd both passed on but, other than that, nothing. "Was your father not a good father?"

His lips twisted wryly and he shook his head. "Not on his best day."

"I'm sorry."

His shoulders lifted, fell in a half-hearted shrug. "It's no big deal."

But obviously it was and she wanted to ask more, to know more, to understand him, but he seemed done with their too emotional conversation. He stood from the chair and picked up the empty food containers.

"You need anything?"

She shook her head and watched him disappear into the kitchen, knowing he wasn't capable of giving her what she needed.

Savannah was getting around better and better. Charlie didn't doubt that her specialists would soon release her to go back to Chattanooga. Perhaps they even would today at her appointments. Currently, they sat in Dr. Trenton's office, waiting for him to recheck her leg.

Charlie had wheeled her into the hospital in a wheelchair, but she was walking around his apartment more and more and depending on his help less and less. Mostly, she was still resting, following her obstetrician's recommendations, but otherwise Charlie felt she'd be pushing herself full force.

"Your leg is doing great," Dr. Trenton praised after he'd done pulse checks. "I'm very pleased with your progress. The repaired artery and the surrounding muscle tissue will continue to heal from the puncture wound. I'm releasing you from my care unless you have further issues."

"That's good news," Charlie immediately said, earning him a glare from Savannah. One that said she'd misunderstood what he'd meant. She thought he was ready for her to leave.

He wasn't.

Despite her injuries and his guilt over the role he'd played, the happiest he'd been in Nashville had been since she'd arrived. He had no right to feel happy about her being there, though. It was his fault she had gone through all of this.

"I can go back to Chattanooga?" Savannah asked.

"As far as I'm concerned, yes. However, I wasn't the one holding you up," he reminded her. "Dr. Kimble will have the final say on when she thinks it's safe for you to venture that far from our neonatal unit."

Savannah nodded. "As ready as I am to go home, I want to do what's best for the baby even more."

Dr. Kimble wasn't as accommodating on Savannah's leaving.

"You were in a major automobile accident, suffered a great deal of trauma, and although, with each day that passes, your risk of premature labor and complications goes down, I do think it's too early for you to travel two hours away."

Savannah sighed, but didn't argue with the obstetrician.

Her eyes ate up the monitor during her ultrasound, taking in every detail with an excited gleam in her eyes.

Charlie found it difficult to pull his gaze away from Savannah's face to actually look at the monitor, too.

Her face shone with joy. She was so in love with their child. She really did see their baby as a blessing. Her expression said so.

Had his own mother ever looked at his ultrasound with a similar expression? Somehow, Charlie didn't think so. He didn't doubt that she'd loved him in her own way. She had always seen to it that he had his basic needs met. But he wasn't so sure that she'd ever really wanted him.

Because of him she'd been trapped in a life married to a man who made her miserable, abused her verbally and, at the end, physically. Whatever dreams for her future she'd had were snatched away because of Charlie's very existence. Although his father had always been verbal about what he'd sacrificed for marriage and fatherhood, he couldn't recall his mother having mentioned what her plans had been prior to her pregnancy, just that he'd ruined her life by being born.

Now, Savannah's life was drastically changed due to a pregnancy. Because of him, yet another person would have to give up their dreams.

"Everything looks and sounds good," Dr. Kimble praised Savannah as the baby's heartbeat echoed throughout the room.

That. Was. His. Baby's. Heart.

He tried to meet Savannah's gaze, but she refused.

"Try to stay off your feet as much as possible for at least another week and see me again on Monday, sooner if there are any problems. I plan to repeat an ultrasound at that time."

"I'm game for as many ultrasounds as you want to do,"

Savannah told Dr. Kimble as she pulled one of Charlie's sweatshirts down over her belly. Sitting up, she tugged the waistband of her yoga pants up, decided it was too tight, then slid it back down to rest beneath her belly.

"I love getting to see my baby."

Dr. Kimble smiled, handing Savannah a piece of paper. "Most women do."

"Thank you," she told the woman, took her appointment slip, and headed to the checkout desk.

When they got back into his car, Charlie pulled out of the hospital parking garage, but he ached inside.

His apartment was close. He usually walked to the hospital but, with Savannah supposed to stay off her feet as much as possible, walking wasn't an option and he'd taken his car. Traffic was heavy and they sat at a red light one traffic stop up from the turn to his place.

"Please don't make me go back to your apartment," she surprised him by saying.

He glanced toward her. She stared out the window at the hustle and bustle on the street despite the cool temperature.

"You heard Dr. Kimble—"

"I don't mean at all," she clarified, turning toward him. Her eyes were red, puffy, and not just from the remains of her wreck. "I mean right now. I know I still look frightful." She touched her face over her bruised, swollen cheekbone and eye. "But I am so tired of being cooped up there. Take me somewhere. Anywhere. Just not back inside that apartment."

"You don't look frightful." He glanced at his watch, gauging how much time he had before his afternoon appointments started. He'd rescheduled his morning, but not his afternoon. He had just under three hours before his first appointment. He'd allowed plenty of time because he hadn't been sure how long her appointments would take or if she'd need any further testing.

From the passenger seat, Savannah sighed. "Now I'm the one who is saying I'm sorry. I shouldn't have said that. I know you need to get back to the hospital. Thank you for taking off this morning to bring me to my appointments."

"I wanted to be there." He had. Soon she'd be strong enough to go back to Chattanooga and then he wouldn't be there for appointments. He'd miss out on so much.

"I want to be there when you have our baby." His words surprised him almost as much as they surprised her.

They did surprise him.

Her eyes big, she stared. "If that's what you want."

"I do." Surprisingly, he meant his words. He couldn't imagine not being there when their baby made his or her appearance into the world.

Which made no sense. Not being there made even less.

"Promise you'll call when you go into labor."

Still staring at him as if he'd grown a third eye, or worse, she nodded. "Anything else?"

He thought a moment. "Are we having a boy or a girl?"

She shrugged. "I don't know."

His eyebrows rose. "But the paper the sonographer gave you…"

"I never looked."

He arched his brow. "You didn't?"

She shook her head.

"Why not?"

She'd not hesitated in saying she wanted to know the gender of their baby. Why wouldn't she have looked?

"I decided I'd wait."

But he knew.

"You wouldn't be able to keep it a secret from me," he guessed. "So you opted not to find out, too."

Her face said he was right even as she continued to try to bluff him. "I thought we had already established that I'm better at keeping secrets than you're giving me credit for."

She was referring to her pregnancy, and she was right. He hadn't even suspected.

"Once I knew about the baby, keeping the gender from me would have been more difficult."

"Why?" she pushed. "Until my wreck, we didn't talk."

He winced. She was right. They hadn't.

"If I could go back in time..." His voice trailed off, mostly because he wasn't sure what he was going to say. Had he been about to say that he'd have talked to her? Insisted she talk to him? Or had he been implying something much more profound? Something he had no right to imply because he wouldn't change having left Chattanooga.

She seemed to sense that he himself didn't know because she didn't push him to elaborate despite the curiosity shining on her face.

"Where are we going?" she asked instead as they crossed over I-440.

"The mall."

"The mall?"

"You need new clothes."

She glanced down at her yoga pants and his sweatshirt. "Sorry, my clothing selection here in Nashville is limited."

"Which is why we're headed to the mall."

"I won't be here long enough to justify clothes shopping."

"You'll be here long enough for dinner tonight."

"Dinner?"

"I figure you're tired of takeout and my limited cooking skills. Although you look great in anything, I imagine you're ready for clothes that fit your growing body properly."

"Are you saying I'm getting too fat for my clothes?" she

asked, a playful gleam in her eyes that told him she wanted to keep the peace between them as much as he did.

"You're not fat, Savannah. Far from it. But I did see you slide your waistband back down due to discomfort."

"The struggle is real." She patted her protruding belly. "But I have clothes that fit at home. Chrissie is going to bring me some on her next day off."

"No need. I'll get you whatever you need today." When she started to argue, he glanced her way, met her gaze for a brief second before refocusing on the road. "Let me do this, Savannah. I want to do this."

"I don't need you giving me things, Charlie."

He knew that, had never doubted it. "Let me anyway."

She hesitated, not wanting to say yes, but at least considering what he was saying. Finally, she sighed. "Okay. But I'm paying for anything I get. And, for the record, I'm not keeping the house."

He'd let her think that, but he planned to buy her clothes. As far as the house, they'd save that discussion for another day. He whipped his car into the Green Hills mall parking area. He wasn't much of a mall person, but surely this place had maternity clothes.

CHAPTER ELEVEN

SAVANNAH STARED AT her reflection in the mirror. Odd that Charlie had bought her first real maternity clothes for her. A pair of black pants and a pair of jeans, both with stretchy front panels, a couple of nice tops, and the long-sleeved black dress she currently wore with the black boots and maternity support hose he'd also bought her.

She'd argued, but he'd insisted. The cashier had refused to take Savannah's credit card when Charlie had shoved cash at her. She'd considered refusing the purchases, but that would be childish.

She'd styled her hair, put on make-up from what Chrissie had brought her to cover her bruised face, and looked almost like a normal person. Almost.

With time her bruises would fade, already they were much improved from her wreck. Her swelling was going down. Her lacerations healing well and barely visible beneath her make-up.

Soon she would be able to go back to her old life.

The baby moved, shifting within her belly. She wouldn't ever really be able to go back to her old life. Not really.

She didn't even want to.

Oh, she needed to get back to work as soon as possible. She'd planned to take time off after the baby's birth and having to use her paid time off days due to the wreck just wasn't good. Plus, whether she was working or not, she still had expenses such as water, electricity, rent.

She needed to get back to work.

Back in Chattanooga, reality still existed. Bills still existed. She needed to get back to reality.

She brushed the hair from her face, revealing where her sutures had been. The wound was healing well and barely noticeable, but she dropped the hair back, covering it. She wanted to look good, or at least the best she could.

Ridiculous, considering how different she looked from just a few months ago. She'd been at her best and he'd left. Nothing she could do was going to change that.

She no longer even wanted to change that.

The apartment door rattled with his key and she took one last look in the mirror at her reflection.

She didn't need him or anyone.

Charlie took one look at Savannah and let out a low wolf whistle. "You look great."

Her cheeks glowed a rosy red. "I did the best I could under the circumstances."

"Like I said, you look great." He walked to her, turned her slowly to inspect her new outfit. "A little loose, but another few weeks and you'll fill this out perfectly."

"At the rate I'm gaining weight, it may be too small in a few weeks." She laughed a little self-consciously.

"Savannah?" he said, hearing the doubt in her voice. "You know you're beautiful?"

She still wouldn't meet his eyes.

He tilted her chin upward, forcing her gaze to his. "You. Are. Beautiful."

She stared straight into his eyes, her own a little shiny. "Thank you."

Her lower lip quivered and something shifted inside his

chest. Maybe his head too, because he bent to press his lips to hers. Gently because he didn't want to hurt her. Her busted lip appeared healed, but he didn't know how sore she still was.

She stood on tiptoe, met his kiss in a sweet caress that had him wanting to take her into his arms and do a lot more than just kiss her lips.

But he kept the kiss soft, kept his hands to himself, and pulled back, smiled down into her confused face, all the while reminding himself he had no right to kiss her.

He shouldn't be kissing her.

"You always had the most amazing mouth," he said instead of the apology he should be issuing. He had no rights. He'd done enough damage to Savannah, and yet…

"My mouth always felt pretty amazing when you were kissing it," she countered, her gaze searching his. She had questions, lots of questions.

Too bad he didn't have answers. He didn't. Not for her or himself.

For tonight, he'd just enjoy being in her company. He owed it to her and to himself to not let history repeat itself, but one night of not focusing on all the things he should be doing wasn't going to change a thing.

He took her hand and gave a reassuring squeeze. "Come on. Let me take you out to dinner and show you off to the world."

Savannah bit her lower lip as she stared at the man sitting across the table from her.

The candlelit table.

What was he doing?

Buying her clothes, taking her to a fabulous restaurant, and having them put at a private, almost romantic, booth.

This wasn't a romantic meal. He wasn't wooing her.

They were two people who'd had their chance at being a couple and they'd failed. He didn't want her and she didn't want him.

Offering her a piece of bread he'd just sliced from the fresh loaf the waiter had put on the table, he smiled. Really smiled. One that reached his eyes. One that dug dimples into his cheeks. One that set off explosions in her head.

She shouldn't be here. They shouldn't be here. They weren't a couple. They shouldn't be acting like one.

"Is that what we're doing?" she asked out loud.

His forehead scrunched as he tried to figure out what she meant.

"Acting like a couple?" she clarified.

Setting the bread back on the wooden cutting board, he considered her question.

"Acting implies a pretense. I'm not pretending, Savannah. We're not a couple. Just two people who used to enjoy each other's company. I still enjoy your company."

"This feels pretend."

"Why?"

"Because it feels reminiscent of the past."

"This is the here and now."

"I don't want you to get the wrong idea."

He laughed a little ironically. "I'm not going to get the wrong idea, Savannah. I know you hate me."

Was that what he thought? That she hated him?

"I don't hate you."

"Not yet."

"I can't imagine ever hating you, Charlie."

"It'll come."

"What makes you think that?"

"It's just what happens."

His answers made no sense to her. She stared at him from across the table. "Is that how you feel about me?

That you hate me or that you're going to at some point in the future?"

He looked as if her question shocked him. "Why would you think that?"

"For the same reasons you think I'm going to hate you."

He shook his head. "You're a much better person than I am. I can't imagine anyone has hated you during your entire life."

The way he said it made her think someone had hated him. Someone who had hurt him dearly.

"Have you ever been in love, Charlie?"

"No." He stared at her as if she'd lost her mind. "Nor will I ever be. Some people aren't meant for such things."

"You're one of those people?"

He nodded.

"Why is that?" she pushed. "Are you heartless? Or just have so many walls that no woman can ever get through to you?"

"Neither. I'm just not capable."

For so long she'd believed otherwise. She'd believed he'd been in love with her. She'd have bet her life on it.

"What about you?"

She blinked at his question. "What about me about what?"

"Have you ever been in love?"

Besides him, he meant?

"No. I don't need a man, Charlie. I forgot that for a while with you, but the reality is I do just fine on my own. Always have. Always will."

"You're right. You're the strongest woman I know."

She wasn't that strong. Not really. But she'd fake it until she made it. Or something like that.

Their conversation remained light through the rest of their meal, mostly with Charlie telling her stories about his class at the university and the research he'd gotten involved with. All of which fascinated Savannah.

"How did you end up in cardiology?" she asked after the waiter had taken their dessert order.

"For as long as I can remember, I knew I was going to be a doctor. My grandfather had congestive heart failure and was in and out of the hospital with exacerbations. I remember sitting at his bedside with my mother. His cardiologist came in and I listened to him and knew at that moment that I wanted to specialize in cardiology. From that point on, I've never considered doing anything else."

"How old were you?"

"Eleven."

"You've known what you wanted to do since you were eleven years old?" she asked incredulously.

He nodded. "I've no regrets. I enjoy what I do."

A memory of the night he'd told her he was leaving for Nashville flashed through her mind. "That's right. Your career means everything to you."

Did it? Charlie wondered. If life were different, if he were different, he wasn't so sure he'd feel that way.

But life wasn't different. He wasn't different. He was a person his own parents hadn't loved. A person who had caused his own mother to take her life.

Yeah, it was much better for him to focus on his career. He could control his career.

Emotions and relationships were things that were unpredictable. You couldn't make someone love you. He'd tried his entire childhood. And even if a person thought they loved you...he'd witnessed time and again over the years as "love" had faded into fights and eventually a breakup. He didn't fool himself that he was any better than his friends and colleagues. Eventually, he and Savannah would have reached crisis point and everything would have fallen apart. She'd have realized she didn't really care about him, that he was unlovable.

He'd just sped that process up by taking the job in Nashville. Only he'd been too late. He'd already gotten her pregnant.

"Do you have names picked out?"

Her gaze lifted to his and a myriad of emotions swam across the deep blue of her eyes. "Not really. Any family names you've always considered passing along to one of your kids?"

"I never planned to have children." He raked his hand through his hair. "I guess the responsible thing would have been for me to have had a vasectomy, but I thought we were always careful."

"I'm sorry I messed up your plans."

Her words cut deep, echoing how he'd felt most of his childhood, most of his life. Never did he want Savannah to feel that way, for their child to feel that way.

"It's my fault, not yours. But no, there's nothing I'd want to pass from my family to our child. My grandfather is the only pleasant memory I have of anyone related to me."

"The one who died when you were eleven?"

He nodded. "He was the only person who ever seemed to want me around."

"That's sad."

He shook his head. "Nope. That's life."

"Not my life."

"I'm glad you had a better upbringing, Savannah."

"It wasn't always easy. My parents were crazy about each other. When my dad died, my mother was devastated and suddenly struck with the reality that she didn't know how to do anything or how to take care of herself and me."

She paused, took a sip of her water. "While my mom devoted herself to me all day long every day, my dad worked, took care of the finances, the house, everything."

"That must have been hard on her, and you, after he died."

"Looking back, I think she would have had a mental breakdown if it weren't for having to take care of me. She pulled herself together and did what she had to do. She got a job at the school where I went so her schedule would be the same as mine, and then she babysat in the evenings and on the weekends. Everything she did, she did for me."

Charlie couldn't imagine. Had his parents ever done anything for him? Maybe. He was probably being too harsh. After all, both of them had given up their lives because of him. Perhaps they'd felt they'd already sacrificed enough. Plus, he'd had glimpses of what he'd craved from time to time from his mother. She'd be having a good day and would take him to the park or read him a story. Those times had been far and few between, but they had occasionally happened.

"You were lucky."

"Did your mother work outside the home?"

He shook his head. "She might have been happier if she had."

"I can't imagine being happier having to leave your child."

"Do you plan to keep working after the baby is born?"

Her brow furrowed. "Of course I am. I have bills."

"I'll give you child support, Savannah. Enough that you wouldn't have to work if you didn't want to."

She shook her head. "That would make me completely dependent upon you. I'd never do that. I can take care of myself and this baby. I don't need you or anyone."

She was right. She could, and would, take care of herself

and their child. Her words stung, though. Not that he didn't know she didn't need him. He did know that.

Maybe he'd always known deep down. Although he and Savannah had been perfectly in tune, he'd always known he wouldn't stay and that she'd be fine. Maybe that was why he'd felt so safe letting their relationship go on as long as he had.

"I've no doubt any judge will award you a great deal of support, Savannah."

She traced her fingertip over the rim of her water glass. "I'm not going to take you to court, Charlie. All I want from you is our baby. Nothing more."

Which was just as well, because all he had to give her beyond that was money. Although she would make do and would provide just fine for their child, there was no reason for her to struggle to do so. They'd cross that bridge closer to the time for the baby to arrive. For now, he didn't want to argue with her.

"Our baby is lucky to have you, Savannah."

Glancing down at her plate, she shrugged. "Our baby will be loved, Charlie. Always."

"Like I said, our baby is lucky to have you."

Had Charlie's parents not loved him? More and more, Savannah found herself wondering about the couple who'd brought Charlie into the world.

He was such a high-functioning person that it was difficult to see beneath the super-successful layers to the inside she was beginning to think wasn't nearly as whole as she'd once thought.

Unable to resist, she reached across the table, took his hand in hers. "Our baby is lucky to have you too, Charlie."

He winced. "We both know that isn't true."

"Regardless of where our relationship is now, Charlie, there is no one I'd rather be the father of my child than you."

He pulled his hand free. "That's crazy. There are a lot more desirable genetics out there than my screwed-up ones."

She shrugged. "Possibly, but I stand by what I said. You are an amazing cardiologist who genuinely cares about people, a brilliant man who sees things more clearly than most, a beautiful man with a body most men would envy and most women would desire to have their way with." She could feel the heat burning her cheeks as she spoke, but she pushed on because he needed to hear the truth. "You're fun, witty, and make me laugh—or at least you used to," she clarified. "All those are traits I hope our child inherits."

"I think you have the wrong guy," he finally said, looking a little uncomfortable as he took a drink.

She shook her head. "No. Although I did miscalculate a few things about you that were pointed out a few months ago, you are still you. The past few days, staying here with you and you taking care of me, has reminded me of that. Thank you."

"For?"

"Taking care of me. I hate that you've had to, but I do appreciate that you have."

"It's my fault you needed taking care of."

"My wreck was a series of unfortunate events—the fender bender that caused the initial slowing down on the interstate, the driver behind me who was texting rather than paying attention to the road. You had nothing to do with my wreck."

"It's my fault you were on that road."

"I chose to be on that road. You didn't force me to drive to Nashville. I did that of my own free will."

"You're being too generous to me."

She laughed. "No, Charlie. I assure you, being too generous with you isn't what I've done over the past few months. Quite the opposite. I keep trying to dislike you but it just won't happen, no matter how much I want it to."

He winced again. "You would be better off if you hated me."

She took a deep breath. "I thought so, but I was wrong."

"How so?"

"Because you're basically a good guy. Just because you didn't want the same things from our relationship that I did doesn't make you less of a good guy. It just makes you not the guy for me."

The skin pulled tight over his cheeks and he took another drink. "You'll find the right guy. You're a wonderful woman and any man would be lucky to have you in his life."

"You're probably right," she agreed, studying the man across the table from her and wondering if she already had found the right guy for her. "But if I never do, I'll be just fine. I don't need a man to make me feel complete. I had a good life before you and I'll have a good life after you."

As she said the words out loud, she knew they were true. Not that her life was the one she'd envisioned, but she would have a good life. She wasn't so sure about the man sitting across from her.

"I hope you have a good life too, Charlie."

He frowned. "I do."

Savannah didn't believe him.

"Truce for the baby's sake?" she offered.

He nodded. "Just so long as you understand that for me nothing has changed from how I felt on the night I told you I was moving to Nashville."

"Just so long as you understand that for me everything has changed from how I felt before the night you told me you were moving to Nashville," she countered.

"Fair enough."

The waiter set down a strawberry shortcake with homemade cream sauce, whipped topping, and two spoons.

Savannah sighed in appreciation. "That looks amazing. I'm pretty sure both spoons are for me since I am eating for two," she teased, committed to the truce between them. A truce was the best thing for their baby, the best thing for both of them.

Being angry with him for being a jerk would be easier in many ways, but the reality was she couldn't stay angry at a man who was taking such great care of her when he didn't have to, other than the little fact that he hadn't loved her nor wanted to stick around for the rest of her life. Now that she didn't want him to, maybe they really could forge some type of truce that would allow them to raise their baby in peace.

CHAPTER TWELVE

"RUMMY!" SAVANNAH BURST out laughing and slapped the card Charlie had just played.

He glanced at the card, at the ones she'd already played, then rolled his eyes. "Obviously, I'm not paying close enough attention."

"Obviously not," she agreed, turning the cards over to show they were "dead". "It's not like you to make a mistake like that when it's just the two of us playing."

Savannah was right. It wasn't like him to make such a simple mistake during a card game, but his brain wasn't on the game.

It was on the woman sitting across the table from him. They were both sitting on the floor on opposite sides of the coffee table that had been cleared for their game.

Much as most nights over the past couple of weeks, they went to eat, then came home and played games. Cards, chess, checkers, it didn't matter just so long as they were busy.

If he didn't suggest something, she did.

It was as if they were afraid to have time alone that wasn't crammed full of something to do.

As if they might get into trouble with idle time on their hands.

Charlie might.

Although, if one looked closely, her bruises could still be spotted, overall the past three plus weeks had faded all but the larger ones. Her lacerations had healed nicely and even the sutured area on her face was looking good and barely noticeable at her hairline. Her lip was healed. Her leg stronger to where standing no longer hurt. No doubt, when she went to her appointment on Monday, Dr. Kimble would release her to return to Chattanooga. She was doing great, was over five months pregnant. There was no reason for her to stay in Nashville.

Except he didn't want her to leave.

The thought of his apartment without her left him cold.

And distracted.

"Charlie, you just played the wrong card again," Savannah pointed out when he dropped a card onto the one she'd just played. "Your head is not in this game. Are you okay?"

"Fine," he assured her, but wasn't positive that he was telling the truth.

Savannah would be going home in a couple of days.

He lifted his gaze and collided with her blue one.

She searched his as if seeking the secrets to his very being. No one knew his secrets. Some things were better kept locked away.

"Please tell me what you're thinking," she said, her gaze remaining locked with his.

"It doesn't matter."

"Why do I get the feeling it matters a great deal?"

"I was thinking about how much I'm going to miss you when you go home on Monday."

"Am I going home on Monday? Dr. Kimble didn't say that at my follow-up, just that we'd take it week by week, and I wasn't ready at my last office visit."

"We both know you're a lot stronger than you were at that appointment and the one before. The ultrasound showed everything looked great with the baby and you've not had any contractions since you were in the hospital."

"That's a good thing, though, right?"

"Yes," he agreed. "I want you well, the baby well."

"The baby is doing well." She laid her hand across her belly that seemed to be expanding daily. Considering she'd had very little of a belly a month ago, now she had a definitely pregnant-appearing one.

Her hand moved as her belly fluttered and she smiled. "I don't know if I will ever get used to that."

He watched her from across the table as she stared at her belly and laughed out loud after a moment. She glanced up at him and smiled. "Do you want to feel?"

Did he? She'd put his hand on her belly once before but the baby hadn't moved, not to where he could feel anything other than the warmth of Savannah through her shirt.

Which was enough to have him scooting the table out to where he could get close to her. When he was settled next to her, she took his hand and placed it over her stomach where hers had been previously.

"I never know how quickly he or she will move. Sometimes it's almost constant and sometimes he or she just stops the moment I start trying to let someone else feel."

"Who else have you let touch your belly?"

"Don't sound so jealous because we both know you're not, that I've been right here for over three weeks. It's not as if I've had an opportunity to hang out with other men and ask them to palm my belly."

"I know that." He did and yet her words did strike him with jealousy. Before he could say anything more, a little nudge bumped against his hand. Eyes wide, he glanced up at her. "That is amazing."

She nodded. "I think so every time I feel him or her move. I can't believe we'll soon get to hold our baby."

He glanced up and stared at her a bit in awe. "You really do want this baby, don't you, Savannah?"

She looked at him as if he'd asked the most ridiculous question ever. "Of course I do. How could I not?"

How could she not? How did he explain how his own parents hadn't wanted him and what a negative impact he'd had on their lives?

"Not every woman wants to have children."

"Not every man wants to have children either," she countered, arms crossing and resting on top of the little shelf her stomach made.

"Some men aren't meant to be fathers." Even as he said the words he couldn't lift his hand away from the roundness of her belly, couldn't remove his palm from feeling the miracle of life growing within her.

She placed her hand over his, tracing over his fingers. "I guess that's something we should have talked about."

"One of the many things we should have talked about."

"It's funny," she mused, staring at where his hand cradled her stomach. "I thought I knew you inside out and really I didn't know you at all."

Her words, so full of hurt and a sense of betrayal, cut him. "You did, more than you think."

She shook her head. "I didn't know the important things—that you planned to leave Chattanooga, that you didn't want children, that your career was more important than anything else. I didn't know a lot of things that I should have known."

The baby moved against his hand, just a little fluttery feel—a knee? An elbow? A foot? A hand?—rolling against his palm. His gaze lifted to Savannah's in awe.

"How do you sleep with all that going on inside you?" he asked, because he wanted to know and because he couldn't respond to her comment. She was right. She should have known those things about him. There were things he'd purposely kept hidden.

She smiled softly, stroking her fingers across her belly. "Sometimes it isn't easy. I can only imagine how it's going to be these next few months, especially if he or she has the hiccups."

His brow arched. "The hiccups? How can you tell?"

"I feel them. They're these rhythmic little movements inside me. I researched it online because I kept thinking I might be too early to feel them, but apparently babies start hiccupping in the first trimester after the central nervous system forms. I probably feel them so easily because I was so small before pregnancy."

"You're still small."

"Ha, not hardly." She patted the round curve of her belly. "Next time I feel hiccups, I'll let you know so you can feel too." Her gaze met his and he'd swear he could dive off into the deep blue of her eyes and get lost forever.

"If you want," she added, suddenly looking uncertain.

He pulled her closer to him, holding her as he wrapped his arm around her and put his hand back over her stomach. "I want."

He did want. So many things that he couldn't begin to label, or even acknowledge.

Life was better that way.

Her life. His life.

Their baby's life.

He couldn't forget that.

Savannah slid behind the steering wheel of the used car she was considering purchasing. Her pulse thundered like a wildebeest stampede across the Serengeti and breathing became so difficult you'd have thought she'd been leading the herd.

"Maybe I don't want to buy a car yet," she mused, earning a frown from the salesman and a look of concern from Charlie.

"You'll be going home soon," Charlie reminded her, his gaze coming hard her way from the passenger seat. "You need transportation."

The salesman, worried he might lose a prospective customer, reiterated, "We have other models much nicer than this one."

"There's nothing wrong with this car," she said. "I'm just not sure I'm in the market for a different vehicle."

"Well, you can't go back to driving the old one," Charlie reminded her as he motioned the salesman off and closed the passenger car door.

He was right. The insurance company had declared her old car totaled and cut her a check for the value. She'd bought the car used a few years ago so the amount hadn't been much. Oh, how she dreaded having a car payment. Especially now, when she'd want to take time off work for a while when the baby came along.

That was why she was hesitating.

It had nothing to do with fear.

Fear of driving.

Fear of being behind the wheel of a car.

Fear of another vehicle smashing into hers.

Fear of the pain that followed.

Yeah, fear had nothing to do with why she hesitated to start the ignition.

"Savannah?"

"Hmm?" she answered without looking at him.

"It's going to be okay."

That had her turning his way. "What?"

"I know you're scared, but it's like riding a bicycle. You'll be fine."

"I have some nasty scars on my knees from bicycle wrecks."

"But you still went right back on your bicycle every time."

He was right. She had. She'd been younger then, more foolish. Driving this car felt foolish.

"Driving the car is going to be the same," he gently told her, placing his hand on her knee. "It's a little scary just because the last time you drove you were in an accident, but it's going to be all right."

Hearing him give voice to her fears made them seem all the more real.

"You're sure?"

"There are no guarantees in life, but I do know you're a good driver, Savannah." His thumb stroked across her pants in a reassuring motion. "Statistically, that decreases the risk of you being in an accident."

"I was in an accident."

"Which statistically decreases the risk of you being in another accident."

She stared straight ahead, took a deep breath. "I feel as if I'm sitting in Driver's Education class and about to drive for the first time—only without the excited anticipation and a whole bunch of fear thrown in."

"Was that the first time you drove? In Driver's Education class?"

She nodded and took a deep breath. "Here goes."

She turned the key, started the car, and put it into reverse.

"You're pretty good for a beginner," he teased when she pulled the car out of the lot. "But if you think you're going to get an 'A' in this class, you might have to become the teacher's pet."

"Ha ha. You wish," she countered, wondering at how sweaty her palms were as she gripped the steering wheel for dear life. "So, when was the first time you drove?"

"I was fourteen and snuck out of the house to drive to a girl's house."

"Why doesn't that surprise me?"

He grinned. "She was sixteen to my fourteen. I had to do something to convince her I wasn't a kid."

"At fourteen, you were a kid."

"I didn't feel like a kid."

"Why's that?" She flicked her gaze his way, saw a flurry of emotions cross his face.

"I grew up a lot faster than some kids do."

As before, she found herself wondering at his childhood, wanting to know more.

"Tell me about your childhood."

He didn't say anything.

"Charlie, work with me here. I need distraction." She kept her tone light, teasing. "Tell me about your childhood so the fact I'm driving a car for the first time in four weeks will quit being foremost in my mind. I don't want to think about my wreck."

"I don't want you to think about your wreck."

"Then distract me."

"What do you want to know?"

"Where did you grow up?"

"Kentucky."

Kentucky. She hadn't known that.

"Your parents have both passed on?"

He didn't say anything, so she glanced his way to see the tail end of a nod. She had known that already, so she wasn't sure why she'd asked, maybe in hopes of getting him to talk about his parents.

"No siblings?"

"Nope."

"Sounds lonely."

Lonely? Yeah, Charlie's childhood could be thought of as lonely. Not that he hadn't had friends. He had. Lots of them. And girlfriends. He'd had a lot of those, too.

Such as the sixteen-year-old he'd snuck out to see the first time he'd driven a car, the first time he'd done several things. He'd been lucky he hadn't wrecked his mom's car and that his dad never found out what he'd done. He'd have beaten him black and blue.

But his father never had and his mother had decided if he was old enough to sneak out to see a girl he was old enough to run errands for her. Too bad he hadn't been the one driving the night she'd died.

"How did they die?"

Savannah's question brought him back to the present. Sort of. "My old man died of lung cancer, brought on by a lifelong cigarette habit that wasn't helped by working in a coal mine. My mother was killed in a car accident."

Savannah's foot tapped the brake harder than she should have as she stopped at a red light. "Your mother was killed in a car wreck?"

Unable to speak, he nodded.

"I'm glad you didn't lose me and the baby that way, too."

His gaze cut to her and he wasn't sure what to say. Savannah's wreck had been an accident, something beyond her control. His mother's wreck had been a single-car incident. The wreck had been ruled an accident, but Charlie had never believed that. His father hadn't either.

Not that his father had shown much remorse, or emotion at all. He'd just seemed to accept that his wife was gone.

Charlie never had.

"Me too." For a moment he allowed himself to consider

having lost Savannah and the baby in the wreck. Pain shot across his chest and he immediately put the thought out of his head, reminding himself that she sat next to him, living, breathing, beautiful. He squeezed her thigh and found himself never wanting to let go. "Very glad."

What would he have done had Savannah died in that wreck? What would be different?

Everything.

She pulled away from the red light and within minutes they were back at the car lot.

"You're sure you don't want something newer, more reliable?" he asked, thinking it was his job to look out for her and the baby, to protect them as much as he could. He'd buy her a new car, one with an excellent safety record, one recommended for a single mom, with all the bells and whistles to make her life easier. But she'd already shot that down.

"I researched online and this car is rated well. It's a good price and, despite your suggestion that I need a brand new car, I really don't need or want the expense of something new."

"I told you I'd help you," he reminded her, wishing she'd let him help her more.

She switched off the motor, turned and met his gaze. "And I told you that I didn't need your help. I got this."

"I think that's the last of my stuff." Savannah glanced around the living room as if she expected to see something she'd overlooked. "If you find something I've missed, maybe you could ship it to me?"

"Or I could bring it to you when you go into labor."

Labor. She hoped that would be at least three to four months from now, preferably the full four.

Months without seeing Charlie.

Her throat tightened and her eyes pricked with moisture.

Saying goodbye hadn't been easy in Chattanooga, and it wasn't now. Maybe his having just walked away from the ultrasound had been better.

She stared at him and searched for the right words, but none seemed to really convey what she wanted to let him know.

"Thank you for taking care of me these past few weeks, Charlie."

"You're welcome." He shrugged as if it were no big deal. Possibly to him it wasn't.

She moved to him and wrapped her arms around him as much as her belly would let her.

"Thank you," she repeated, knowing she was thanking him for much more than he realized, maybe even than she'd realized until that moment. She felt a peace she hadn't felt when he'd left, a peace that came from the knowledge that, although the thought of being without him hurt, she would be just fine. She and their child would be okay, no matter what he did or didn't do.

She could do this.

He hugged her back, then tilted her chin toward him. "You're sure you're ready to go?"

She was going to miss being here with him. "It's time I go home."

He stared into her eyes, so much emotion flickering in the dark depths of his.

"Savannah." Her name came out of his mouth a bit broken and a whole lot needy.

Her lips parted. He was going to kiss her. She could feel it in the quickening of his heartbeat, in the intake of his breath, in the tensing of his body against hers, in the way he was looking at her.

The way he'd always looked at her, with need and want and desire and whatever it was he felt that she used to label love. No matter what it was called, Charlie looked at her in a way no man had ever looked at her, in a way she'd never wanted any other man to look at her, and that she doubted she ever would. This was Charlie. Her Charlie.

For the past few weeks she'd wanted him, wanted him to kiss her and touch her, and although he had touched her hand, her face, her belly, her leg, he hadn't really touched her. Not sexually. Not possessively. Not like he was looking at her at this moment.

His head lowered, his breath was warm against her mouth; her body was full of excited anticipation.

"I hope that's everything because your new car is about out of room," Chrissie said, coming back into the apartment. "Thank goodness we sent part of your stuff back with your cousin."

Savannah stepped back from Charlie just as lights went off above Chrissie's head.

"Oops, sorry. I'll be down in the car when you're ready." She turned around and walked back out of the apartment.

Although Savannah had started driving again, she hadn't argued with Charlie when he'd told her he didn't want her making the two-hour drive by herself, especially since she'd have to cross the mountain. Her cousin had driven Chrissie up early that morning, then headed back to Chattanooga with a load of Savannah's stuff. Chrissie had helped her pack the remainder of the things she'd accumulated in Nashville into the sedan she'd bought with the insurance money plus a chunk of her savings.

She'd been so grateful for all Chrissie had done but at the moment she just wanted to scream at her friend's interruption, because somehow she knew that nothing would ever be the same once she left Nashville. Charlie would move on with his life. She'd move on with her and the baby's life. The closeness she felt with him at this moment would never again be.

Maybe it was just as well that Chrissie had interrupted.

Savannah smiled weakly at Charlie. "Timing has never been her strong suit, but I love her anyway."

"No, I imagine not." But he didn't take Savannah back into his arms, just stared down at her with so much emotion in his eyes that Savannah's heart hurt. He recognized, just as she did, that nothing would ever be the same between them, that they'd never have this moment back.

He took her hand and gave it a gentle squeeze. "Goodbye, Savannah. Don't forget to call when you go into labor."

She nodded. "I won't forget."

"You want me to help you down to the car?"

Giving him a wry smile, Savannah shook her head. "I got this."

She did. She would be just fine. She knew that. But *just fine* felt a little flat when she was looking at what could have been for the last time.

"Thanks again." With that, she said goodbye to Charlie.

CHAPTER THIRTEEN

SAVANNAH WENT BACK to work part-time the following week. Being out of work for over a month, the changes to her body during that time, had her worn out when she got home at night to where she crashed almost immediately. She worked a shift on, two shifts off to give her time to recover in between for the first few scheduled times back, possibly indefinitely until after the baby arrived. When she finished her fourth shift, she crashed onto her sofa and was so thankful she had the next two days off.

"Is my grandbaby moving?"

Savannah glanced at where her mother walked into the living room. Her mother had been a lifesaver over the past few weeks, checking on Savannah, making sure she ate. She'd brought over a plate of homemade goodies that night that Savannah had picked at before settling onto the sofa.

"He or she is always moving, Mom. You wanna feel?"

Her mother sat next to Savannah and placed her hand over her belly. "I can't wait until I get to hold this baby."

Savannah smiled. "You're going to be a great grandma."

"I am, aren't I?" Her mother beamed, then her smile faded. "A much better grandmother than mother."

Savannah practically gawked. "What are you talking about? You were an amazing mother. I just hope I'm half as good."

"Oh, honey, hope for much more than that," her mother urged, giving Savannah's stomach a love pat. "I was such a mess after your father died. I didn't know if I was coming or going. I've often wondered if I scarred you for life."

"You were grieving Daddy. We both were a mess."

Her mother nodded. "We were and I channeled it into making sure you were everything I wasn't."

"In what way?" Savannah asked, truly baffled.

"I wanted to make sure you knew how to take care of yourself—that you never depended on a man the way I'd depended on your dad. Which in theory doesn't sound so bad, but I think I was also trying to shield you from ever feeling the pain I felt at losing your dad."

"That's not a bad thing."

"Not being able to feel that kind of pain means never loving like I loved your father."

"Pain is overrated."

Her mother shook her head. "Love is worth any amount of pain. Until you met Charlie, you never let anyone get close enough to hurt you."

"We see how that turned out." Savannah sighed. "Not so well."

Her mother shrugged. "Maybe. Maybe not."

"What's that supposed to mean?"

"Without Charlie I wouldn't be having this grandchild." Her mother rubbed her belly and the baby moved, as if recognizing the spoiling this woman was someday going to do.

"That's true," Savannah admitted. "But if not Charlie, then I would have met someone else, someone who could have loved me and our baby."

Her mother looked thoughtful for a moment. "I don't understand a lot of the ins and outs of your relationship with Charlie, but I do recognize love when I see it."

She bit the inside of her lip. "You're wrong."

"I don't know," her mother mused. "He sure went to a lot of trouble to take care of you after your wreck."

"That was guilt-driven."

"And that's your pride talking," her mother countered.

Savannah's gaze cut to her mother in shock.

"Sometimes pride can get in the way of seeing the truth."

"My pride isn't blinding me to anything."

"Except the truth," her mother said softly.

"You speak as if I was the one who pushed Charlie away by being prideful. I didn't. He left of his own free will."

"And you can't forgive him for that."

"There's nothing to forgive. He wanted to move. He moved. I'm here and want to stay here. End of story."

"Not a very good story ending."

Savannah frowned. "For someone who really hasn't said much about my breakup with Charlie, you sure are talkative tonight."

"I've been holding my tongue because I thought you two would eventually figure out what is so obvious."

"And what's that?"

"That you love each other."

Walls went up and sirens blared. "You're wrong."

"About him or you?"

"Both."

Her mother stared at her for a few minutes, then leaned over and kissed her cheek. "Just think about the things I've said. We all make mistakes, Charlie included. Maybe it's time for you to acknowledge that you made a mistake in letting him leave."

Savannah stood, hugged her mother goodbye, then sank back onto her sofa.

Her mother was wrong.

She didn't love Charlie. That was gone.

Sure she missed him and still thought he was the sexiest man alive, but love? How could you love someone who had walked away from you of his own free will?

Her shoulders lifted at the memory of the pain she'd felt that night.

You didn't love someone who had hurt you that way.

She'd not heard from Charlie. Not a peep. She'd thought he would at least text to check on her, but he hadn't.

Then again, she'd not texted him, either. She'd thought about it multiple times, such as the evening she'd come back to Chattanooga, the night before her first shift back at the hospital, that night when she'd gotten home. She'd thought about him almost non-stop, but she didn't text and she didn't call.

What would be the point? The fact that she'd stayed with him in Nashville while recuperating had changed nothing, not really, even if their truce had clouded her mind.

Had reminded her of all the reasons she'd fallen for him to begin with. Things she'd just as soon not have remembered.

Leaning back on her sofa, her feet propped up on the coffee table, she picked up her phone and stared at it.

What would he do if she texted him?

Would he answer?

Was he at home or still at work?

She'd been gone three weeks. Did he miss her? Miss eating together and playing games together and just having her in his apartment? Did he want her back?

Then again, why would he?

He'd left Chattanooga when she'd been at her best, when they'd been at their best, and he'd gone anyway.

She didn't want him back. She'd moved on the best a pregnant woman could. They'd had something good and he'd thrown it away for reasons she still didn't fully understand.

He'd nailed home the lessons her mother had taught

her about not depending upon anyone other than herself. She shouldn't have. She wouldn't make that mistake again.

Tossing the phone onto the other side of the sofa, she closed her eyes.

That was when she felt the first one.

Charlie logged off his work computer and locked up his office at the hospital. He'd put in another long one. Which was just as well since he'd cut back so much during the time Savannah had been at his apartment. He'd sure not been there long enough to be asking residents to cover his patients and classes, yet he had following Savannah's wreck.

The weather was crisp and cut through his jacket, but part of him welcomed the cold, welcomed that he felt alive.

Something he hadn't felt so much over the past few weeks.

Because Savannah was gone.

He missed her like hell.

His apartment felt empty without her. His life felt empty without her. Yet she was better off without him. He had to remember—this wasn't about him. It was about Savannah and their baby. It was about making sure the past didn't repeat itself any more than it already had.

He had his dream job. He worked for a major trauma and research hospital where he got to live his dream, something his father, his mother, had never gotten to do.

Which should have him jumping over the moon.

Instead, he had to force himself to continue to put one foot in front of the other on the trek back to his apartment.

When he reached the complex, he glanced up at his window. No light.

Because no one was home.

Savannah wasn't there.

She'd gone back to her apartment, rather than the house

he'd given her. The lady who cleaned the house had told him no one had been there other than herself. Hopefully, Savannah would see reason and move into the house prior to the baby's arrival. Or maybe when she went home from the hospital. He wanted her to have the house, to have the security of knowing she and the baby always had a place to call their own.

If nothing else, she could sell the house and use the money to give her and the baby a good start.

Not that he wouldn't help her with anything she needed. He would. Already, he'd talked to his lawyer to have a trust set up for the baby to ensure money was there for college. He made a great living, had invested wisely, and there was no need for Savannah and their baby to ever worry about basic needs.

Not that she would. Savannah was an independent woman, used to taking care of herself. She'd do just fine with or without his help. She didn't need him. She'd move on with her life, find someone who didn't come with his baggage, and she'd be happy.

He wanted her to be happy.

He did.

But…

Charlie mentally slapped himself. What was wrong with him? He wasn't the type to feel sorry for himself. Especially when he had what he wanted.

He had his career. He hadn't let a woman interfere with his goals. He'd kept his eyes on the prize, moved to Nashville, and achieved what he'd set out to achieve all those years ago.

"Don't let a woman hold you back from your dream, son."

Anger filled Charlie as his father's words coursed

through his mind. His father was gone, no longer in his life. If only he was no longer in his head.

What would his old man say about the woman becoming the dream?

The dream that was unattainable because he couldn't take care of her, couldn't love her and let her love him.

He walked into his living room and sank onto the sofa. His gaze fell onto the deck of cards sitting on the coffee table.

She'd left them, along with a note telling him no man who was as good at cards as he was should be without a deck.

He picked them up, shuffled them back and forth.

He wasn't good at cards. He wasn't good at anything.

No, that wasn't true. He was a good cardiologist.

Savannah's words of praise replayed through his mind.

He began to slap cards down on the coffee table, one after another in neat rows.

She'd been telling him how she saw him and he tried to look at himself through her eyes. He was a fine cardiologist who had spent a lot of time honing his craft and trying to be the best he could be, pushing himself mentally. He did care about his patients. Every single one was someone's family member, possibly some little boy's only lifeline to affection.

Savannah's other words of praise soared through his mind.

He didn't know about how enviable his body was, or even how desirable, but he did enjoy pushing himself physically, too.

Taking in the stacks of cards in front of him, he began turning over the cards remaining in his hands in sets of three.

He'd made her laugh.

Thinking back over the year they'd been together, they'd laughed a lot. More than he had his entire life. More than he'd known he could laugh.

Even this past month, once they'd called their truce, he'd laughed, and so had she.

He'd been happy.

Guilt hit him. He didn't deserve to be happy.

Not when he'd been the reason his parents had been so unhappy.

A memory of Savannah talking about their baby, of her palm resting protectively over her rounded belly, of the joy in her voice when she spoke of their child hit him.

That was what a baby should give to his or her parents.

A baby was a blessing, wasn't that what Savannah had said?

Their baby was a blessing.

His parents hadn't seen him that way. He tried to imagine the resentment, almost hatred he'd felt emanating off his father, the apathy he'd felt from his mother at times, and he tried to imagine feeling that way about his and Savannah's baby.

He couldn't.

He tried to imagine if he'd been at a different point in his life, if he'd been in school still, or maybe not even in school yet, and how he would have felt if he'd had to change his dreams because of a baby, and tried to let the way his father had felt wash over him.

It wouldn't.

The stacks of alternating colored, numerically sequenced cards in front of him grew as he continued to slap them down.

He tried to imagine Savannah being so overcome by life and depression and whatever else his mother had been facing that she'd take her life.

He couldn't.

Savannah was a strong woman. She would fiercely protect their child, and she'd love their child. No matter what.

She'd never dump the emotional load on their child that his parents had dumped on him.

She would be a good mother.

He'd been right when he'd told her that their child was lucky to have her.

He flipped over an ace and started a new stack as Savannah's words dug into his mind.

Their baby was lucky to have him, too.

Not really. Look at what a great start to being a dad he'd already made. Then again, wasn't being out of the picture what he believed was the best for his child? For Savannah?

He shifted through the cards, faster and faster, building the stacks in front of him, until only two cards remained.

He'd not been able to protect his mother from his father's abuse, nor had he been able to protect her from herself. His very existence had driven her to end her life.

He couldn't protect Savannah from being like his mother and he'd rather die than drive her to that state of unhappiness, to destroy a child's self-esteem and sense of lovability, the way his parents had his.

Savannah deserved so much better.

His own parents hadn't loved him. How could he ever expect someone else to love him? To really deep down love him?

He played the last two cards and stared at the game he'd just won.

Yay for him. He'd just won at Solitaire.

Which pretty much summed up his life expectations.

His head became too heavy to hold up and he dropped his face into his hands.

He could win at being alone.

He might lose if he tried another life game. The stakes were certainly a lot higher. The possible casualties tragic.

His life goal had been a game of Solitaire.

Because he'd thought he wasn't worthy of being part of a team, not outside his career.

He and Savannah had been a team. A good one. When he'd gotten the job offer in Nashville, he'd almost said no because he hadn't wanted to leave her.

Which had scared the hell out of him and put him into defensive panic mode.

He glanced up, stared at the cards through blurry eyes.

He'd devastated Savannah, had seen the walls she'd built at his betrayal. She'd cared for him and he'd hurt her. She didn't need him and wouldn't risk letting him behind those walls again.

But he needed to be behind them.

How was he supposed to convince her to love him the way she loved their baby? That he wanted to spend the rest of his life being a team player? Being on her team and always having her back? And knowing that she'd always have his? That they'd love their baby and protect it from the harsher realities of the world together?

He scooped up the cards. Maybe he'd start with asking her to play him in a game of cards.

A game with really high stakes.

CHAPTER FOURTEEN

SAVANNAH SHOULDN'T BE doing this.

But she had made a promise.

A promise she intended to keep, no matter how difficult doing so felt. She gripped the phone as the other end of the line rang.

"Savannah?"

Charlie's voice sounded so good. Better than it should have. And worried. Very worried.

"Is everything okay?" he asked.

Squeezing the phone tighter between her suddenly clammy fingers, she cleared her throat. "I told you I'd call and so I'm calling."

"You're in labor? It's still too soon."

She shook her head, then realized that he couldn't see her. "No, I'm not in labor. The other promise I made you."

Silence came over the line, then he softly said, "Our baby has the hiccups?"

She nodded, then rolled her eyes at herself. How ridiculous that she'd called him to tell him something so trivial. He was two hours away. She'd promised to tell him so he could place his hands on her belly and feel the magic inside. He probably thought she was crazy.

"Yes," she said, feeling foolish. "The baby has the hiccups. I can feel them with my hands, so I really think you could, too."

But he didn't ask her why she was calling to tell him something so trivial, nor did he tell her she was crazy. He simply said, "I'll be right there."

She believed him. She didn't question the two-hour drive from Nashville to Chattanooga. Nor did she tell him it was doubtful the baby would still have the hiccups two hours from now. Goodness, she hoped not! Instead, she told him to be careful, which he couldn't have been because a knock sounded on her front door twenty minutes later.

When she saw Charlie on the other side of the peephole, she unlocked the door and flung it open.

"Charlie? How?" she asked, not understanding how he'd gotten there so quickly.

Looking a bit sheepish, and maybe a little uncertain as to what kind of welcome he'd receive, he reminded her, "I told you I'd be right here."

"But...how did you get here so quickly? No matter how fast you drove, you couldn't have gotten here this quick. I'm not even sure if you could have gotten here this quick by helicopter."

He shrugged. "I didn't have to drive fast to get here. I was just outside Chattanooga when you called."

She stared at him incredulously. "You were?"

He nodded.

But that meant... "Why?"

He gave a half-shrug. "I had a premonition about those hiccups. Let me in before Mrs. Henry calls the law?"

He smiled and it was the most beautiful thing she'd ever seen, making her take a step back.

He came into the apartment. She closed the door behind him, turned to look at him, not quite believing that he was really there, that he'd been on his way to Chattanooga when she'd called.

"You having any other premonitions?" she asked, not sure what to say now that he was here. She felt ridiculous for calling him, and yet he had already been on his way to Chattanooga. *Why?*

A light shining in his eyes she hadn't seen for quite some time, he grinned down at her. "A few."

"Such as?"

"That I'm going to kiss you and you're going to tell me that's okay."

Her heart grabbed hold of her ribs and rattled them around a bit. "You're sure that's your premonition?"

He nodded. "Is that okay?"

She should tell him no. She really should. But he had just driven for two hours.

"I suppose it's okay."

He kissed her. Her mouth. Her throat. Her face. He kissed her as if he were starved for her and hadn't seen her in a month of Sundays rather than just a couple of weeks ago.

He kissed her as if he'd missed her.

He kissed her until her feet floated off the ground and her insides turned to putty.

Then he kissed her more.

Dropping to his knees, he lifted the gown she wore, revealing her very round belly.

Even in the three weeks since she'd seen him, her belly had expanded. She wasn't svelte or sexy or anything that would light any fires, but she stood proudly anyway, because this was her body, their baby growing inside her.

His gaze lifted to hers and she saw the emotion there, that same one she'd seen all those months ago and thought it meant he loved her, the same one she'd questioned time and again when she'd been in Nashville. She wouldn't fool herself that love was what she saw now, but there was something. Something sweet and pure and real.

He leaned forward and kissed her belly as if it were the most precious thing ever. It was.

Her knees threatened to buckle and she grabbed hold of his shoulders to steady herself. Why was he kissing her? Why was he caressing her belly?

"I guess the hiccups are gone?"

She nodded, staring down at him with her confusion no doubt showing on her face. She couldn't have hidden it if she'd tried.

"I'll just have to stick around until the next time. Let's hope it takes a while, because I don't have any place to go and definitely don't feel up to driving back to Nashville tonight."

"You can stay here." After all, he had let her stay at his place while she recuperated. Letting him stay was the least she could do.

"That's a great idea," he said, kissing her belly again as his hands caressed her. "But we'll have to figure out some way to pass the time."

Was he suggesting…? Surely not. She'd stayed at his place for a month and he hadn't made sexual advances toward her other than when he'd kissed her. To think that within five minutes of him being back in Chattanooga he'd be propositioning her was crazy.

"Let's play cards."

"Cards?" Were her fingers digging into his shoulders? Probably, but she had to hang on because she felt off kilter.

"Yep. I have the deck you gave me in my pocket."

"Is that what that is?"

He grinned up at her. "What did you think it was?"

Still not understanding why he was there, why he was

kissing her, her belly, and not understanding him wanting to play cards with her, she took a step back.

"Fine. Let's play cards, but no whining when I beat you."

He followed her to the sofa, pulled the coffee table closer. "I'm changing up the rules a little for this game."

"Sure you are. How else do you have a chance of winning?"

"Something I've realized, Savannah, is that when I'm with you, I'm always the winner."

She wrinkled her nose at him. "Have you been drinking?"

He frowned. "You know I don't drink."

"Why are you here, Charlie, because I know it's not to play cards with me?"

"You called," he reminded her.

True, she had.

"You were already on your way here."

He nodded. "I was."

"Why?"

"To ask you to play cards with me."

"You were sitting around in Nashville, bored, and decided you'd drive two hours and ask me to play a game of cards?"

He snorted. "Would you believe that's exactly how it happened?"

Rolling her eyes, she shook her head and sat down on the sofa. "Fine. We will play cards. What are we playing and what are these new rules that are supposed to help you win?"

He pulled the deck of cards from his pocket, then dragged a chair to sit opposite the coffee table from her. "You choose which game you want to play."

"Solitaire," she flung out at him.

For the first time since he'd entered her apartment, the

sparkle in his eyes dimmed. "No Solitaire. You have to choose a game we can play together."

"How can you change the rules to a game if I'm the one who chooses the game?"

"You'll see. Just choose a game."

"Fine." She named a game.

"Good choice."

"So what are these new rules that are supposed to help you beat me?"

"I don't want to beat you."

"You drove two hours to lose?"

No, Charlie hadn't driven two hours to lose. Just being near her already made him feel like a winner.

"I've already told you, I'm always a winner when you and I play together."

"Right." Her tone was sarcastic and she rolled her eyes as she reached for the cards he held. "I'll deal first."

He handed her the cards, watched in silence as she dealt. When she set the cards onto the table, she glanced up at him, eyes full of expectation.

"Time for you to tell me these rules, unless you're planning to make them up as we go to increase your odds."

He took a deep breath and hoped this went the way he'd been rehearsing it in his head for the past two hours.

"The rules really haven't changed so much as the stakes."

"The stakes?"

"Winner takes all."

"All of what?" she asked as she arranged her cards in her hand.

"Whatever he or she wants from the other."

"But I don't want anything from you," she reminded him, frowning.

"Maybe you'll think of something while we're playing."

Maybe he'd think of something to help him win because she sure hadn't dealt him the best hand he'd ever been given.

"Then you agree that you think I'm going to win?"

With the way his cards currently looked, probably.

"It wouldn't be the first time, but, truth is, I plan to win this game." He did. Somehow. Some way. He would win.

"Because you want something from me?"

He nodded, studying his cards so intently he hoped connections that weren't there would suddenly appear.

"What?" she asked, as if unable to help herself. Good, he needed her to be interested. He needed her a lot more than that.

"You'll find out after I win."

"Ah, *that's* your strategy," she accused him, drawing a card from off the top of the deck. "Try to convince me to let you win. Better luck next time. I'm not that kind of girl."

The corners of his mouth tugged upwards. "I know. I like that about you."

She tossed a card from her hand down onto the table.

"Actually, there are a lot of things I like about you," he said, going for casual despite the fact his insides quaked.

She glanced at him from above the cards she held.

"Like how smart you are," he continued.

"Yes," she intoned. "All men like smart women. It's always their favorite quality in the opposite sex."

"I'm not all men, and I do admire that quality in you. Along with quite a few others." He drew a card off the top of the deck, then discarded one he didn't need.

When he didn't elaborate, she asked, "Such as?"

"Such as how intensely blue your eyes are when curiosity is burning inside you," he teased, buying himself a little time to try to figure out how to play his cards right. Figuratively and literally.

"That's corny and superficial."

"You're a beautiful woman, Savannah. You've always turned me on."

She glanced down at her rounded belly. "Oh, yeah, I'm the stuff dreams are made of."

He nodded his agreement. "You are. My dreams."

Her mouth pinched into a tight line. "Don't say things like that."

She picked up the card he'd discarded, placed it into her hand, then tossed one she didn't want.

"Why not? It's true."

She set her cards down on the table. "If this is your strategy to win, I don't like it. Nor is it going to work."

He arched a brow. "What would work?"

"To beat me in cards?"

He nodded.

Her gaze narrowed. "Cheating?"

He shook his head. "I won't cheat you, Savannah. Not ever again."

Her mouth fell open. "You cheated me?"

"Not like what you're thinking. This was more a case of cheating myself."

"Now I'm really confused," she admitted, picking her cards back up and gesturing for him to take his turn.

He did, liking the card he drew, and tossing one of the useless ones from his hand onto the table. "I was cheating myself of what you and I could have had, because I was scared of how I feel about you. Scared of us."

There. He'd admitted the truth to her. A big truth that left him vulnerable. But it wasn't enough and he knew it.

"When I got the job offer from Vanderbilt, I felt I couldn't say no. To do so would mean admitting that you were more important to me than my career or anything else."

She took her turn, quickly drawing and discarding. "I never wanted to stand in the way of your career."

"You didn't. But the truth is my career was only an excuse to leave."

"Why did you need an excuse to leave?"

He picked up a card, tucked it in beside another card, then discarded. "Because I didn't deserve you or the happiness I'd found with you."

"Because?" she asked as she snatched up the card he'd discarded.

Part of him questioned their sanity. Here they were, having the most important conversation of their relationship, and they were playing cards while doing so. Yet wasn't that what he'd intended to some degree?

Maybe because he'd needed something to focus on besides what he was admitting to her.

"Because I destroyed my parents' lives." The admission spilled free from his lips much easier than he'd expected. Because he was telling Savannah. Because he knew he had to tell her everything before the past could be healed. God, he hoped the past could be healed. "How could I be so happy when, because of me, they'd been so miserable? I was afraid I'd do the same thing to you as I'd done to them."

It wasn't exactly fear he saw in her eyes, but the emotions glimmering there were definitely not happy stars and rainbows.

"No, afraid is too mild a word," he corrected. "I was terrified I'd do the same thing to you."

"What did you do to your parents?" Her question came out as barely more than a whisper.

He took a deep breath and spoke the truth. A truth it had taken him too many years to accept. "Exist."

Savannah's brows rose and she lowered her cards. "What?"

"You heard me."

"But I sure didn't understand you. How did existing make your parents miserable and how does that affect me?"

Here went everything on the line. He'd lay it all out there and what she did with it was up to her.

"There's a lot I haven't told you, that I haven't told anyone. My parents married because my mother was pregnant with me. They hated each other," he continued. "I'm not sure it was that way to begin with, but definitely from the time I can remember, they detested each other."

"That's sad," she said and her sincerity echoed around them.

"Very. I always wondered why they didn't divorce." He raked his hands through his hair. "I wanted them to divorce. My dad had planned to go to medical school. He had a scholarship for his undergraduate and excelled at school. When my mom got pregnant, he married her, took a job at a local coal mine, dropped down to going to school at night. He lost his scholarship when he went from full-time to part-time. Eventually, he quit going altogether. He never forgave my mother for ruining his dream, and neither of them ever forgave me for destroying everything."

"I'm sorry," she offered simply.

"Me, too. They both lived in misery. My father was determined everyone else should be at least as miserable as he was or as close as possible. He pretty much succeeded."

"That's terrible," she empathized. "I can't imagine placing that type of emotional burden on a child."

Charlie could all too well.

"My father was determined that I wouldn't make the same mistakes he'd made. I hear his voice in my head, telling me to always put my career first, to never let anyone stand in the way, and I didn't."

Savannah winced. "This is where I come in. It's okay,

Charlie," she assured him. "I don't want to stand in your way. I've never wanted that. I'm fine, I promise."

Charlie took a deep breath, set his cards down and reached for Savannah's hand, and wondered if she'd ever be able to forgive someone with as messed-up a head as his. He wouldn't blame her if she couldn't.

Still, he had to tell her everything.

"It's not fine, Savannah. I'm not fine."

She frowned at him. "I don't understand."

"I've made so many mistakes over the past few months. I let you and I go on too long. When the job offer came, I didn't want to go. I took it because I felt I had to protect you."

"Protect me from what?"

"Me."

She blinked at him. "From you?"

"My father was not a good person, Savannah."

"You aren't your father," she reminded him.

"No, I'm not, but I am what drove him to that point. What drove my mother to that point. I wasn't able to protect her from him. I tried and it only made things worse. A lot worse."

"You were a child, Charlie. A blessing. It wasn't your job to protect your mother. That was your father's job."

"He's who she needed protecting from."

Understanding of just how bad things had been dawned and empathy showed in her eyes. "Did he abuse you?"

Charlie's jaw worked back and forth, memories of a fist crunching into the bones hard racking through him. "Only once."

Her brow lifted.

"I stopped him from hitting my mother. For years, I'd blocked out what I didn't want to deal with, pretending I didn't know. One night, when I was fifteen, I couldn't pretend anymore, and I stepped in, refused to let him hit her again."

"Oh, Charlie," Savannah empathized. "Surely that had your mother waking up that she needed to get you both out of that bad situation."

"She got out," he said, trying to keep his voice steady. "She killed herself that night, but not before telling me that it was my fault he hit her and my fault she was leaving. She died because of me."

It was the first time he'd given voice to what he knew in his heart. He'd not been able to protect his mother and she'd taken her life to escape the reality of her world. A world Charlie had helped shape into the unbearable mess it had been.

Savannah gasped, then frowned. "I thought your mother died in a car wreck."

"She did."

"Oh."

Oh. Charlie's head dropped and he wondered why he was telling Savannah all this. He'd never told anyone. Maybe some things were better left unsaid.

"I'm not sure what to say."

See, Savannah agreed.

"I don't expect you to say anything."

She pulled her hand from his and rested it protectively over her belly. The motion was very telling and he struggled to continue onward with his admission.

"Caring about another person terrifies me," he admitted. "Being responsible for another person terrifies me."

"You aren't responsible for me."

"But I am responsible for our baby."

"I've not asked you for anything," she reminded him. "You don't have to be any more responsible than you want to be."

"That's just it," he admitted. "I want to be responsible in every way. For our baby and for you, Savannah. That's what the stakes are. I want you and our baby. I want you to give me a chance to make things right."

Her blue gaze lifted to his, seeking answers to the questions he saw in her eyes.

"That isn't a game, Charlie. You can't just win those things."

He closed his eyes, then opened them, stared into hers. "No, I know I can't win those things. Not really. But playing a card game with you seemed like as good a place as any to start trying to win you back into my life."

"I wasn't the one who left," she reminded him, her chin lifting a little higher.

"Words aren't my strong suit and I'm obviously failing miserably at telling you what I'm trying to say. Let me try again." He took her hand back into his, kissed her fingertips. "Savannah, you are my dream. The only one that really matters. You and our baby. I don't want to ever hurt you or make you miserable or have you look at me with anything other than happiness in your eyes. Until tonight, I never let myself consider that it wasn't me who'd made my parents miserable, but that they'd done that to themselves."

"You were an innocent child, Charlie. Of course it wasn't your fault."

"But I didn't see that, Savannah. Not until you showed me the truth. Forgive me, Savannah," he continued. "Forgive me for not seeing what was right in front of my eyes."

Tears streaming down her cheeks, she refused to look directly at him. "It's not my forgiveness you need, Charlie."

Was she unable to give him a second chance? He'd known it was possible, but he'd hoped otherwise.

"You need to forgive yourself," she continued, her words cutting deep into his chest.

Forgive himself?

"You feel guilty that you were born, that your parents had to raise you, that you tried to protect your mother from your horrible father. Charlie, how would you feel if that was our child?"

"That's what I don't want to happen."

"It never would," she said so confidently that he stared at her in wonder. "You would never hit me, Charlie."

He grimaced at the thought of physically hurting her. He couldn't imagine any circumstance where he ever would.

"Nor would you ever mentally and emotionally abuse our child into believing he or she was to blame for your own miserable life. Your father was an ill man, Charlie. I didn't know him, but he obviously needed help."

"Probably."

"Definitely," she corrected. "As for your mother—" she let out a long breath "—I don't know why she stayed, but she was no better than he was. It was her job to protect you, Charlie—" she stressed her words "—not the other way around. She should have removed you from that situation before your dad ever had the chance to get inside your head, before you were ever put in the position of having to step in to stop her from being physically abused, and she sure shouldn't have said the things she said to you on the night she died."

He closed his eyes. "Logically, I know you're right, but how do I know I won't turn out just like them?"

"That one's easy." She took his hand and pressed a kiss to it, looked up at him with her tear-filled blue eyes. "Because you didn't."

He started to deny her claim, but stopped. She was right. He wasn't like his father. He wasn't like his mother either.

His heart surged with emotion. "I love you, you know."

Tears now spilled over onto her cheeks.

"I've never said those words out loud as an adult, not to anyone, but they're true. I love you, Savannah, and I need you in my life. Now and always. I was afraid I would do to you what my father did to my mother, what I thought I'd done to her. But I was wrong."

Leaning over to wrap her arms around him as best she could, she buried her face against his neck. "I can't believe you're really here, that you're really saying these things to me."

"I should have been here every day, telling you how I feel every day. I don't want to lose you, Savannah. Please tell me I haven't. At least agree to play me for the chance to win a second chance. I promise not to blow it this time."

She straightened, wiped at her tears, then picked her cards up again and nodded.

"Okay?" he asked, not exactly sure what she was agreeing to.

"Let's play cards, Charlie."

He picked up his cards, looked at his still sorry hand, then nodded. He might not win this game, but he was determined to spend the rest of his life trying to win the love and respect of the woman sitting across from him.

Without another word, they each took their turn, studying their cards carefully before each move.

Finally, prior to Savannah laying down her discard, she met his gaze. "So, if you win this game, you get a second chance with me?"

He nodded.

"And if I win?"

"Did you ever figure out what it was you wanted?"

She nodded, then tossed out a card.

The card she tossed fitted perfectly into Charlie's hand. One more card and he'd be able to lie down. He wasn't sure how he'd pulled his hand together, but with each round things had improved.

"Care to share what that is?" he asked as he discarded.

"If you want to know," she said as if it were no big deal as she drew then tossed another card. A card that went perfectly with the card she'd previously tossed down.

The card Charlie needed to be able to lie down and win the game.

His gaze dropped to the discard pile, then he glanced up at her. "It's not like you to toss away cards you need."

"I don't need those cards," she denied.

"No?" He arched his brow at her. "Let me see your hand, Savannah."

She frowned. "I thought you said you wouldn't cheat."

He turned his cards up on the table, revealing them, but he didn't declare himself the winner, even though he was.

And not just at the card game.

Her gaze dropped to his cards for a brief moment, then she smiled. "You win."

"Because you cheated."

Her lips twitched.

"Let me see your cards, Savannah."

She slowly flipped her cards over. Recalling the cards she'd tossed her previous few plays, he shook his head. "Cheat."

"I didn't cheat."

"You didn't win when you should have."

"Maybe I didn't want to win at cards."

"Since when?"

"Since you changed the game rules."

His heart surged with what she meant.

"I love you, Savannah."

"I think I've always known that, Charlie. Even when you left me, deep in my heart I just couldn't accept it."

"I'm sorry I left, Savannah. I thought I was doing the right thing."

"For future reference, anything involving you leaving me is never the right thing. I love you, Charlie."

"I can't believe I'm lucky enough for you to love me."

"It's easy to love you, Charlie," she assured him. "You're a very lovable man."

Something inside him cracked at her words. He was lovable. Savannah said so and he saw the sincerity in her eyes, heard the conviction in her voice. He was lovable and she loved him.

"Thank you," he told her, kissing her face. "Thank you for that." Knowing she'd just given him a great gift that she'd probably never fully understand.

At that moment, her eyes widened, and then she smiled. Taking his hand into hers, she placed his palm against her belly. After just a couple of seconds he felt the tiniest little jolt. A few seconds later, he felt another.

He grinned. Hiccups.

They sat there in silence for a few minutes, him taking in the miracle of the life they'd created.

"I don't know how to be a good parent, Savannah. I'll need your help."

"You'll be a great daddy, Charlie. You already have the most important part down pat."

"What's that?"

"Love."

That he did, because he did love this woman and their baby with all his heart and always would.

EPILOGUE

"ONE. TWO. THREE. Blow out your candles!" Savannah told the sweet three-year-old blond-haired little boy leaning over the picnic table to get to his birthday cake.

"I can't believe my baby is three," Chrissie whined from beside the table as she removed the candles once he'd extinguished all the flames.

Savannah's mother sat near her, holding the sweetest baby girl in the whole world.

Yeah, Savannah had a difficult time believing Amelia was already three months old, too. Time sure flew when one was having fun.

She was having fun.

Mainly due to the handsome man snapping pictures to capture the moment. He caught her looking at him, grinned, then snapped a picture of her.

She rolled her eyes at him, causing him to laugh out loud, and take another photo.

After cake had been served all round, Savannah took Amelia so her mother could eat. At least that was her excuse. Really she'd just been away from her precious baby too long.

"She okay?" Charlie asked, stepping up and kissing the baby's head. Although Amelia's eyes were blue as could be, she'd gotten her dad's dark hair. Savannah knew that most babies' eyes were blue but, due to the lighter than normal shade, she suspected Amelia would keep hers. If she ended up with dark eyes like her father's that would be just fine, too.

Either way, she had both her parents wrapped around her tiny fingers.

"She's perfect," Savannah assured him and meant it in every way possible.

"You want me to hold her so you can have some birthday cake?" Charlie offered, reaching for the baby.

Savannah laughed. "That was my excuse when I took her from my mom."

He grinned and stroked his finger across Amelia's head. "You're right, you know. She is perfect."

Savannah glanced down at the wiggling little bundle in her arms, who'd realized it was past time for her next feed and her mommy now held her. Although she'd struggled for the first few days with breastfeeding, she and Amelia had eventually gotten it figured out and she was thriving.

"She takes after her daddy."

"Her mommy," he corrected, his voice choked up. Charlie glanced around the backyard of the house he'd given to Savannah but that she hadn't accepted until he'd carried her over the threshold as his wife, when he'd brought her home from the hospital after she'd delivered their daughter.

She smiled at him, knowing losing that card game to him was the best decision she'd ever made. Not that she'd let him win since. She hadn't. Not that they finished most card games they started. They usually got distracted after just the first few hands.

She'd refused to marry him until after the baby had been born. They'd gotten married at the hospital with her mother and Chrissie there, along with their daughter.

They'd traveled back and forth between Chattanooga and

Nashville more than Savannah liked to consider over the past few months, but no more. Although she'd offered to move to Nashville, Charlie had refused. He'd finished his obligation to Vanderbilt last month and he was home to stay.

Home with his family.

Home where he was loved and loved her right back.

Home.

* * * * *

If you enjoyed this story, check out these other great reads from Janice Lynn

IT STARTED AT CHRISTMAS...
SIZZLING NIGHTS WITH DR OFF-LIMITS
WINTER WEDDING IN VEGAS
NEW YORK DOC TO BLUSHING BRIDE

All available now!